NOVELS BY NANCY TAYLOR ROSENBERG

THE
CHEATER

NANCY TAYLOR
ROSENBERG

TOR®

A TOM DOHERTY ASSOCIATES BOOK
NEW YORK

THE CHEATER

Copyright © 2009 by NTR Literary Inventions, Inc.

A Tor Book
Published by Tom Doherty Associates, LLC
175 Fifth Avenue
New York, NY 10010

www.tor-forge.com

Tor® is a registered trademark of Tom Doherty Associates, LLC.

ISBN 978-0-7653-5860-8

First Edition: June 2009
First Mass Market Edition: June 2010

Printed in the United States of America

0 9 8 7 6 5 4 3 2 1

To Hoyt

THE
CHEATER

ONE

❧

LOS ANGELES, CALIFORNIA

Stan Waverly looked good for a dead man.

With the unwavering stare of a predator, she watched the tall, dark-haired man in the Tommy Bahama floral print shirt and green slacks make his way through the crowd of people in baggage claim. The expressions on her victims' faces never failed to amaze her. Waverly had flown to Los Angeles to have a two-day fling with a woman he had only recently met. He was about to commit adultery, break one of the most sacred vows, and to look at him, you'd think he'd just won the lottery. She doubted if he'd been this happy on his wedding day.

Stan had always had women on the side, or so he had boasted the last time they'd had dinner at Lorenzo's, a small Italian restaurant located on lower Greenville in Dallas. Since Stan was contemplating making a run for the state senate next year, he'd been forced to curtail his extracurricular activities. Lorenzo's was seldom frequented by the rich and powerful, but Stan still considered it too risky. When she provided him with a seemingly foolproof solution, she had gone from sexy to downright irresistible.

The short blue dress she was wearing was one of her favorites, as it made her waist look small and accentuated her breasts. Her hair was a tousled mass of auburn curls, her lips a shimmering movie-star red. On her feet was a pair of matching blue heels. Wearing them in an airport was perilous, and for her, painful. Men loved heels, the higher the better. They didn't care if a woman was miserable.

Stan saw her and headed her direction, grabbing her around the waist and pulling her tight against his body. "Feel that," he said, referring to his erection. "That's Texas-size, sweetie pie."

She tilted her head to one side, causing the hair on the right side of her face to fall forward and obscure one eye. He was pumped up on something, probably Cialis, which was referred to as the "weekender" because it lasted several days. She doubted if he had a legitimate problem with erectile dysfunction, more a need to have a larger and longer-lasting erection. Obviously, he had wanted to impress her. How sweet, she thought facetiously. "How was your flight?"

"You look fantastic," Stan commented, stepping back so he could check out her body. "Better than I remembered, actually."

She wanted to tell him it was because he was sober. "You look great, too, baby." She clapped her hands lightly like a teenager. "I'm so excited, Stan. We're going to have a super time. I can't believe you're really here."

Stan noticed a middle-aged man in a brown jacket watching them. "Maybe we should get out of here," he said, placing his palm in the center of her back. "I doubt if anyone will recognize me here, but I can't take a chance. I do business all over the world, remember."

She gave him a wide-eyed girlish look. "I don't know why you want to go into politics, Stan. Being an international attorney sounds so exotic. You get to travel to all these great places. Do you go to Paris very often? I adore Paris. Rome is terrible in the summer. I visited the Tivoli Fountain in August and almost got sick. It was like a giant dust bowl full of smelly people." Men expected idiotic chatter from pretty women, so she had incorporated it into her routine.

"I don't have any clients in Paris," he said, disinterested. "I go to China and Japan frequently. All I do is work. Where did you park?"

"Across the street," she told him. As they headed toward the exit, she walked several feet behind him so no one would notice they were together. She had no intention of hurting his wife. Before making her final decision, she had met Belinda Waverly and even talked to several of her friends. Stan's wife was a beautiful, gracious woman, who seemed to do everything possible to please her husband. She ate like a squirrel, worked out every day, and was already busy organizing Stan's campaign. A good woman like that didn't deserve a man like Stan.

They were outside of the terminal, waiting for the light to change. Cabs and cars were lined up at the curb, people excitedly waiting for friends and loved ones, children jumping up and down, businessmen pacing and talking on their cell phones. Families were clustered together in colorful clothing, more than likely headed to Disneyland. Los Angeles was the best place to be in August. Even if it warmed up during the day, it always cooled down in the evenings. At present, it was midday and the temperature was in the low eighties. Compared to the triple-digit heat in Texas, Los Angeles was paradise.

"Did you check into the Hyatt like I told you?"

No one told her what to do, but he would learn that lesson later. "Hotels are so impersonal, Stan. I've arranged for us to use my uncle's cabin."

His face muscles tensed. "We're staying in a damn cabin? This is L.A., for God's sake. How far away is this place? I've been on a plane for three hours. I thought we were going to spend the next two days in the sack, not cooped up in a car."

"It's not far," she said with the same cheerful tone. The light changed and they crossed the street to the parking garage. "It's only two o'clock, Stan. We shouldn't have to worry about traffic this time of day. My uncle's cabin overlooks a lake. We can even skinny-dip if we want. There's not a soul within thirty miles." He still had an annoyed look on his face. Spoiled prick, she thought, knowing he was used to getting his way. "You'll love it, I promise. I stocked the kitchen with food and bought us two bottles of Dom. Don't worry. I didn't forget your Jack Daniel's. I bought enough to fill a bathtub." She halted among the rows of cars. "Are you sure you feel comfortable about this? If you're not, we can call it off right now."

Stan had just been presented with the biggest decision of his life. If he displayed even a flicker of hesitance, she might reconsider killing him. But she knew he wouldn't. None of them did. A man never refused a piece of ass, particularly one he'd never had before.

"Trust me," he said, smiling playfully, "I'm not going anywhere. I've been fantasizing about you for weeks." He paused, trying to remember something. "By the way, that company you turned me on to is terrific. Whoever came up with the idea is brilliant. I don't say this very often, but they could double their prices. I know guys who'd pay a fortune for what this operation offers."

Tell me something I don't know, she thought, stopping and unlocking the door to a black Hummer. "There's other people out there providing these kinds of services, Stan," she told him. "You have to be extremely cautious about who you use in a delicate situation like this. You might be an attorney, but I know you're also a businessman. There's a right and a wrong way to do things. The company I referred you to doesn't rely on other members. Their employees seem both discreet and professional." She stopped herself. For one thing, she sounded too intelligent, and for another, Stan would be dead soon, so there was no reason to pitch him. It was as foolish as throwing bait to a fish you'd already reeled in. Giggling, she said, "Gosh, they acted like they were the CIA or something. All this secret stuff turns me on."

He came up behind her and squeezed her breasts. "Forget the cabin," he said lustily. "Let's go to a damn motel."

She stepped forward and broke his grip, then hoisted herself into the driver's seat. "Don't be impatient, baby." Time for more chatter, she told herself. "Isn't this car fun? This is a baby Hummer, or at least that's what I call it. I didn't rent one of the big ones because I was afraid I'd be tempted to ram something just for the hell of it." Her fingers trailed around the steering wheel. "I've always wanted to drive one of these things. Besides, the road to the cabin isn't paved. They're not predicting rain or anything. I thought you'd feel safer in this than some cheap rental." Before she started the ignition, she reached into the backseat and retrieved two bottles of strawberry-flavored water from an ice-filled cooler, wishing she could pry open his mouth and pour it down his throat.

Stan removed the cap on his water and took a long swig, then smacked his lips. "This is delicious. I love a woman who takes care of things. My wife doesn't take care of shit. We have a full-time maid and she still complains. She doesn't even know how to put gas in the car."

"I'd rather you didn't talk about your wife." Belinda was an exceptionally attractive woman, but she didn't seem all that bright. She suspected it was one of the reasons Stan had married her. Women like that were easier to dominate. It chapped her that men never gave their wives credit for raising their children. Belinda had three young kids and scores of commitments in the community. She probably worked twice as hard as Stan, and he had an office full of employees to do his bidding.

"Why? You're always asking me about Belinda."

She reached into her purse to pay the parking attendant, handing him the ticket stub and a ten-dollar bill. If Stan had been a gentleman, he would have offered to pay for it. She'd leased the car, bought the booze, and saved him the cost of the hotel room. Many times it was the little things that showed a person's character. Stan had failed every test. The asshole hadn't even opened the car door for her. "Committing adultery might be a common practice for you, Stan," she said, "but it isn't for me."

"We're not going to get into a heavy conversation, I hope?" he said, finishing his water and tossing the bottle into the backseat. "If I wanted that, I could have stayed home." He turned sideways in his seat. "Just so you won't feel sorry for her, Belinda lives like a queen. She has a gorgeous home, a new Mercedes, jewelry fit for a queen, and an unlimited spending budget. So what if I get a little action on the side? I'm not a monogamous person. I was cheating on my first wife when I started sleeping with Belinda. It's not right for her to expect me to be faithful. She knew what she was getting into before she married me."

Stan pulled a small package out of his jacket pocket and handed it to her. "I got you a little present. Well, actually, it's the same perfume Belinda wears." He stopped speaking, his jaw dropping. "Shit, I can't believe I said that."

"Don't worry," she told him. "I don't wear perfume."

"You're not mad, are you? There are certain precautions I have to take. It's not like I'm unhappily married. I adore my wife."

She gave him a stiff smile. "I know the rules, Stan. Don't forget, I have a family, too." The Versed she had placed in his water was beginning to take hold. She dropped the tiny bottle of perfume into her purse, thinking it was probably one of those gift-with-purchase items that the cologne and cosmetic companies gave out periodically. Stan must have swiped it from Belinda. Not only was he an adulterer, he was cheap. She despised cheap men, especially if they had money, and Stan was a millionaire many times over. Of course, poor people didn't become senators. Politics was a playground for the wealthy.

One guy had gone so far as to ask her to change her hair color to match his wife's. Cheating was a game to them, and they loved every minute. Men wanted to be boys forever with secret decoder rings and tree house hideouts. Former cocaine addicts had told her how they missed using their credit cards to separate the white lines, or rolling up a hundred-dollar bill to snort it. The ritual seemed as addictive as the drug. When it came to men, the same appeared to be true of adultery.

Men didn't want to get caught, but this fear wasn't there for the right reasons. They didn't want their wives to discover they were having an affair because that would make it harder for them to get away with it the next time.

Versed was such a dynamite drug that she could say or do anything to Stan right now and he wouldn't remember it. Doctors and anesthetists used it for minor surgery, generally referring to it as conscious sedation. The person might fall asleep, depending on the dosage administered, but could be easily awakened to talk and interact with the physician conducting the procedure. The drug caused an individual to experience amnesia, so when he awoke, he had no memory whatsoever of what had occurred.

Stan might have chosen his words more carefully if she hadn't dosed his water. She'd given him just enough of the drug to relax him, make him oblivious to his surroundings. Without traffic, the trip from LAX to San Bernardino took close to two hours. If he knew, he'd pitch a fit. Once they reached the cabin, she would put enough Versed in his Jack Daniel's to render him unconscious. She couldn't do that now because she wasn't strong enough to carry him, at least not in one piece. She took the ramp for the 101 freeway south and began searching for Interstate 10.

"I can't believe how good I feel around you," Stan said, a goofy grin on his face. "It's like getting stoned without the grass. I haven't been this turned on for years, not since I banged my best friend's wife. I can't wait to get you in the sack." He pulled her hand over the center console and raised his hips so it would reach his genitals.

"Get your fucking hands off of me," she snarled, yanking her hand away. A moment later, she tempered her anger. Stan wouldn't remember the things she said later, but he would react to them now, and she wasn't in the mood to wrestle a guy while navigating the freeway. "You don't want me to crash the car, do you? Then your wife would find out and you wouldn't get to be a senator."

"Ah, don't be mean, baby."

She smiled at him, surprised he was so alert. He had a strong constitution, which she would have to compensate for later. "Traveling is such a hassle today," she said. "You look tired, Stan. Why don't you take a nap? I'll wake you as soon as we get to the cabin."

"Good idea," he said, sprawling out in the seat and closing his eyes. In no time, he was snoring. He continued that way until she turned onto a bumpy dirt road and reached over and shook his arm. "Man, I must have been exhausted. Where the hell are we?"

"We're almost there, sleepyhead." She rolled down the window and held her hand outside. "Isn't it beautiful up here? I hate cities in the summer. The smog becomes unbearable." They were in the forest now, surrounded by tall trees and lush foliage. The streaks of sunlight looked like flashlights shining down from the sky. She inhaled a heady mixture of greenery: earth, moisture, and various natural elements. "Smell the air, Stan. And the temperature is perfect. We don't even need air-conditioning."

The effects of the drug had worn off. Stan rubbed his chin, and then pulled out his cell phone. "Jesus, there's no reception. How am I going to keep in touch with my office?"

"My cell works, or at least it does from the cabin. I was up here with my uncle about three months ago. Can't you handle your business later? This was supposed to be our time."

Once they reached the cabin, Stan calmed down, although he still had that dazed, what-the-hell-happened look on his face. She got out and went to unlock the front door, asking him to bring in her suitcase from the trunk of the Hummer. Dropping the keys on the kitchen counter, she grabbed two glasses and opened the refrigerator to get some ice. She then removed a small bottle from her purse and poured a few drops of the Versed syrup into the glass she had just marked with a black Magic Marker. She then plunked an ice cube into each glass and filled them up with Jack Daniel's.

"Here we go," she said, handing him the drink as soon as he sat her suitcase by the door. "Cheers."

Stan sipped his drink as he glanced around the room. The cabin was an A-frame, so the room had a pitched ceiling, and there were two sofas with fabric displaying hunting scenes and a well-worn brown leather recliner. Next to one of the sofas was a large rattan basket filled with magazines and newspapers. The fireplace was made out of stone and reached to the ceiling. A stack of wood and kindling rested beside it. "Cozy place," he said, downing the last of the liquor. "Where's the bedroom? I think you owe me an appetizer. I've been riding around in one box or the other all day."

She left her drink untouched on the kitchen counter. The glasses were marked, but she had confused them once and passed out. The son of a bitch she'd been with had dropped her off at the emergency room and taken off. She'd thought of tracking him down to finish what she had started, but it wasn't worth the effort. She hoped he would be the only man to ever survive her. She thought of herself as a disease. You couldn't fault a disease for doing what it was created to do. If she didn't kill men like Stan, she would be defeating her purpose.

Removing her clothing as she headed toward the bedroom, she put on a short striptease for him. She threw her belt over her shoulder and kicked off her shoes. "Be a doll and bring my bag to the bathroom for me, will you?"

"Later," Stan said, seizing her arm and pushing her down on the bed. Something crinkled and he sat up, feeling the bed with his hand. "What in the hell is this? Shit, it's plastic or something. I don't want to sleep on a damn plastic sheet. Is your uncle incontinent? Why didn't you rent us a room at a Hyatt like I said? I didn't go to all this trouble to—"

"Hush," she said, placing a finger over his lips. "There's a brand-new set of sheets underneath. Sometimes a squirrel manages to get in, and my uncle doesn't want it to ruin the bedding. If you hadn't rushed me, I would have made sure everything was perfect."

Satisfied, Stan tugged at the front of her dress. He then flopped onto his back and let out a long sigh. "I'm so . . . sleepy. God . . . I . . . what's wrong with me?"

She sat beside him, flicking the ends of her fingernails until his head fell to one side. She should have insisted he take her bag to the bathroom. The bag wasn't that heavy, but she enjoyed watching her victim carrying the weapons she would use to kill him.

On the off chance that he might wake up, she went to

the bathroom and locked the door. Removing the auburn wig, she used soap and water to scrub the heavy makeup off her face. Her natural hair was blond and cut close to her head. They made wigs so good now that it was impossible to detect them. After she stepped out of the blue dress, she pulled on a Black Sabbath T-shirt and a pair of baggy jeans, along with a masculine-looking belt. The finishing touch was a key chain that she clipped to her belt. It was tacky, but effective.

The image in the mirror was now that of a slender young man. Of course, it was more than the clothing and haircut. She had learned to hold her jaw in a certain way, and had studied men's walks and gestures. Although she hadn't brought it this time, she'd even designed a prosthetic Adam's apple. Men had told her it was one of the things they looked at when they questioned a person's sexual identity. Cigarettes were repulsive, but they were good props, and just the smell of a cigarette denoted masculinity.

Inside the suitcase were two boxes of heavy-duty garbage bags, a bottle of Clorox, several packages of latex kitchen gloves, a yellow raincoat, a pair of plastic goggles, and two electric carving knives with replacement blades. She opened a rolled-up towel and removed two handsaws and a buck knife. Even though the carving knives sliced through tissue fairly well, she needed the saws for the bones and cartilage.

Picking up one of the electric knives and a box of garbage bags, she went into the other room, sweating profusely in excitement. She lined the floor with plastic bags so she could simply roll Stan off the bed once he was dead. Being prepared made the cleanup easier. Once he was chopped and bagged, she would burn his clothing, his personal belongings, and the bedding, scrub down anything he might have touched, jump in the rented Hummer, and take off.

Donning the yellow raincoat and goggles, she went to the

other room and straddled Stan like a horse, pinning his legs down with her knees. Pulling her hand back, she slapped him hard in the face until he regained consciousness. "I thought you wanted to fuck me," she said, seeing his eyelids flicker and open. His body buckled and thrashed, but it was a futile attempt. The drugs had turned his muscles into spaghetti.

"Why . . . are . . . my . . . God . . . help . . ."

She reached into her pocket and pulled out a snack-chip clip. "Pucker up, sweetheart." One of the more pleasurable moments should be listening to her victims blubbering and begging, but all it did was give her a headache. Grabbing his lips between her fingers, she snapped on the clip. "You know what you look like now, Stan? You look like Donald Duck. I bet your kids would think Daddy is really funny if they could see you now. Oh," she added, staring into his terrified eyes, "I guess no one would laugh at a sad little duck that can't even quack."

She reached down and unzipped his pants, feeling his erection. "How much Cialis did you take? You'd have to take a whole bottle to be hard at a time like this." She pressed his penis between her fingers. "You're always ready to fuck, aren't you, Stan?"

She stopped and wiped her hand on the bed. "Since we're on the subject of your children, would they still love you if they knew you came here to cheat on their mother?" She grabbed a handful of his shirt in her fist. "You had everything, but it wasn't enough. You're a greedy son of a bitch, Stan. A beautiful wife, children, success, none of it satisfied you, did it? You wanted more money, more women, more excitement, more power!"

She stopped and took a deep breath, picking the electric knife up off the bed. "You know what I want to be your last thought, Stan? That you threw it all away."

Turning on the knife, she flashed it in front of his face.

"You like that, Stan? Can you hear it? Does it remind you of Thanksgiving?" Her tongue swept across her lower lip as she watched his terror intensify. Adrenaline would course through his bloodstream now, keeping him awake until she silenced him. "Here's what's going to happen, Stan. I'm going to slice through your carotid artery, then you're going to bleed to death. While you're dying, remember what I told you. You flushed your wife and family down the toilet for a piece of ass!"

TWO

MONDAY, NOVEMBER 27
VENTURA, CALIFORNIA

Lily threw her towel over her shoulder and jumped on a treadmill at the Spectrum Health Club. She never had a problem getting a machine, as most people preferred the ones in the front that allowed them to watch television.

Tessa Prescott came walking toward her. Tessa was an elementary school teacher at Our Lady of Mount Carmel, a local parochial school, and her short dark hair was wet from perspiration, as was her black warm-up suit. Overweight by at least twenty pounds, she tried to hide it under dark-colored loose clothing. Smacking her gum, she said, "Hey, slacker."

"I'm not a slacker," Lily told her, setting up her program on the machine, then pressing the start button. "I'm here working out, aren't I?"

Tessa frowned. "Yeah, but since you became a hotshot judge, you don't have time for your friends."

Lily felt a stab of guilt. "That's not true. Bryce and I went to dinner with you and Fred just last week. And I always return your phone calls. Maybe not the minute I receive them, but as soon as I can."

"You've lost track of time. We went to dinner over a month ago." Tessa paused for effect, then laughed, a delightful throaty sound. "I'm kidding okay? I just hate you because you're tall and skinny. Look at me, I'm a toad, for Christ's sake. Thanksgiving was a disaster. I ate enough for five people." She tilted her head toward a young blonde standing beside her. "This is Anne Bradley. I hate her, too, but unlike you, she has to work at it. We've been taking the six-thirty spin class together, since you can't seem to get your butt here in time. Anne, this is Lily Forrester."

"Nice to meet you." Lily used her towel to wipe the sweat off her forehead. "I told you a dozen times that spinning hurts my back, Tessa. I sit all day, remember? You chase kids for a living."

"Excuses, excuses. Anne is an attorney. She just moved here from Manhattan."

Lily didn't mind small talk when she was on the treadmill, as it made the time pass faster. She didn't really care for health clubs and public places. The press of humanity was bad enough without a room full of sweaty bodies. But she endured, as exercise cleared her mind and alleviated stress. "Are you setting up a practice here?"

"I haven't decided yet," Anne responded in a smooth, measured voice. "Right now I'm unemployed and loving it. I'm working out so I'll look good in a bikini this summer."

"I think you're already there," Lily said, her eyes roaming over her toned, shapely body. "What kind of law do you practice?"

"I was with Wharton, Cannon, and Byerman." She got on the treadmill beside Lily as soon as an older gentleman stepped off. "They specialize in navigation law."

Lily found Tessa's new friend engaging. Her blond hair was cropped close to her head, a fresh, flattering look. Lily wasn't about to chop her hair off. Her hair was one of the last remnants of her youth. Although it was impossible to discern age these days, Anne appeared to be in her mid- to late twenties. She was certainly attractive, particularly to the opposite sex. It was obvious from the looks she was getting from the men and women in the room. No wonder Tessa wanted to hang out with her.

"See you guys tomorrow," Tessa said, about to take off. "Get here around the same time as today, Lily, and we'll wait for you. We don't have to take a spin class. Anne likes aerobics better, anyway. If you insist, we can even do the treadmill."

Once Tessa was out of earshot, Anne said, "She's a fun lady, just relentless. She managed to get me going, though, so I can't complain."

Lily looked over and smiled. "Tell me about it. She knows I work late. Last night I didn't get to bed until three. I think Tessa shows up here before five. I'm sorry, you were telling me about the firm you were with in New York."

Anne had her cell phone hooked to her gym shorts. When it rang, she grabbed it, jumped off the treadmill, and walked a few feet away. "I should have left my phone in the locker," she said when she returned. "That was one of the partners. They've been driving me crazy ever since I left. The attorney they hired to replace me isn't that familiar with navigation law." Once she was back on the treadmill, she added, "There's not a lot of competition in my field, which is surprising because it's so lucrative. Boats sink all the time, even cruise liners. Settle a few cases a year and you're pretty much set."

"Why did you move, if you don't mind me asking?"

"Manhattan is awful. I was always sick. You're stuffed together like sardines." Anne stopped speaking and sucked in a deep breath. "I've already done the spin class, so I'm a little winded."

"Maybe you should call it a day?"

"No," Anne said. "I do this every day. As for Manhattan, the whole city feels like a huge moving sidewalk, every inch crammed with people. I managed to save some money and decided to get out. Enough is enough, you know."

Lily checked her pulse. As pretty as Anne was, she didn't look healthy. She had dark circles under her eyes, and her skin had a dull finish to it. Lily wondered if she had moved due to an illness. Even if she was financially solvent, why would such a young, successful attorney not want to resume her career right away? It took years to build up a successful law practice. "Do you have family in this area?"

"A brother, but he travels most of the time. All my life I've wanted to live at the beach. Most of the areas on the water are outrageously expensive, so I had more or less given up. Then the firm sent me to represent one of our clients who had a yacht in Ventura, and I checked out real estate prices. Since housing was fairly affordable here, I decided to get out of Dodge."

"Most people complain about the price of California real estate," Lily commented. "Compared to Manhattan, I guess it's not so bad. Where do you live?"

"I'm renting an apartment until I find a house. Ventura is like Santa Barbara for a fraction of the price. Of course, the beach isn't as nice, but only God and Oprah can afford Santa Barbara."

Lily smiled, not wanting to mention she'd formerly resided in Anne's dream city. But Anne was right about Ventura. The city had grown up around the historic San Buenaventura Mission, founded in 1782. On one side were miles of sandy beaches, along with multimillion-dollar homes with boat slips. The rest of the city had sprawled upward into the foothills, where many of the residents had panoramic views of the ocean.

Unlike Santa Barbara, a similar city approximately twenty miles north, Ventura hadn't developed into a playground for the rich and famous. New shops and restaurants had slowly appeared throughout the years, but most things had stayed the same. Lily thought there was a tired feeling to Ventura, as if a dusty bubble had been placed over it, trapping it twenty or thirty years into the past. The nearby farming communities didn't help, especially with all the avocado fields.

The Spanish influence was still present, yet it hadn't been cultivated as it had in Santa Barbara, where lovely mission-style homes and buildings had been built to harmonize with meticulously renovated existing structures.

Lily's tension was beginning to ease. She turned the speed up on the treadmill so she could jog, and noticed that Anne had done the same. After fifteen minutes, they both got off and walked to the locker room together.

Once they dumped their towels in a basket, Anne told her, "I'm wiped. I think I'll shower and jump in the Jacuzzi. It was nice talking to you. I hope we'll run into each other again."

Lily glanced at her watch. She didn't have to be in Hennessey's office until nine. "Sounds good. I'll see you in there."

The steam rose from the large whirlpool, clouding the glass on the heavy door. Lily's nostrils were assaulted by the smell of chlorine. Anne was already in the water. She must have decided to rinse off in the shower inside the room. Because of her position as a judge, Lily wore a bathing suit. Anne, like most women, apparently felt comfortable going in nude.

As soon as she stepped into the water, Anne scooted closer so they could talk. They soaked awhile until the two other women who were there got out and they had the Jacuzzi to themselves. Lily submerged herself up to her neck, repositioning herself until the jets hit the right spot on her back. "It takes guts to start a new life on your own. You should make friends fast if you hang out at this place. Tessa will introduce you to everyone."

"She already has." Anne pushed herself onto the ledge and let her feet dangle in the water.

"Can I ask you what those are for?" Lily asked, pointing at her feet. She was wearing some kind of mesh slippers that went all the way up to her ankles. It seemed odd that she would go in nude and yet feel the need to wear shoes.

"Athlete's foot," she said. "I picked up a case in New York once, so I got into the habit of wearing these. I think they're made for scuba divers or something."

"Did you work out in the city?"

"Yeah," Anne said. "But I really have to work out now that I moved here. There, you walk everywhere." She fell silent for a while, then asked, "What's your take on the Lucinda Edgar case? You know, the preacher's wife who shot her husband."

"I think she got away with murder." Lily didn't normally pay much attention to crimes outside her jurisdiction. She had followed this case, though, as people in the courthouse had been talking about it. Although she averted her gaze, she couldn't help but notice Anne's youthful body, her long legs, perfect breasts, not too large or too small, and what every woman dreamed of: a flat, unmarked stomach.

"I don't know if I agree with you," Anne said, slipping back into the water. "I have a theory. First, tell me what you think."

"She shot her husband in the back while he was sleeping," Lily told her, moving away from the jet. The thought of a bullet in the back made her wince. She was already in pain and the day had just begun. A disk had herniated in her lower lumbar region, and it seemed to be getting worse every day. Her doctor had referred her to an orthopedic surgeon, but Lily didn't have time for an operation, and there was no guarantee it would work. Anne was waiting for her to continue their conversation. "There were no signs of physical abuse," she told her. "I don't recall all the particulars, but I think the woman's defense was she killed him because he made her wear a wig and provocative clothing. She even claimed she tripped on a pillow and that caused the pump to move into place on the shotgun. I've never heard of such an asinine defense. When the verdict came in, I was appalled."

"So you think the verdict was wrong?"

"Voluntary manslaughter," Lily said, scowling. "Dead wrong. I'm not that familiar with the sentencing laws in Florida, but the maximum term is probably six or eight years, like it is here. With good-time and work-time credits, she'll be out in half that time. How many men ask their wives to wear sexy clothing? The only way the jury bought it was because the majority were women. What's this theory you mentioned?"

"I think it was a lot more than the preacher asking his shy wife to dress up in sexy clothes or wear high heels," Anne told her, placing her arms on the rim and scissoring her legs in the warm water.

"Elaborate."

"Read between the lines." She paused. "Is it okay if I call you Lily?"

"Sure."

"The mattress the dead guy was sleeping on was on the floor. A minister might not earn a lot of money, but I think he can afford a bed, don't you?"

Lily glanced at the large round clock on the wall. She got out and dried off. "What does the mattress have to do with it?"

Anne climbed out as well, wrapping a fresh towel around her body. "Personally, I think they were swingers and the husband pushed her into it. Think about it. If you have sex with more than one person, even a king-size mattress might not be big enough. So you put the mattress on the floor." She saw the look on Lily's face and laughed. "I know what you're thinking. I'm not a swinger. The only reason I know about this stuff is the client I mentioned with the yacht paid for it by throwing these kind of parties. Internal Revenue seized the boat because he failed to report the income. When I went to look at it, there were mattresses all over the floor."

Lily was intrigued. A blast of cold air struck her when Anne opened the door leading out of the Jacuzzi, and she wrapped her towel around her shoulders to stay warm. The role reversal was strange. People were usually hammering her for information on various newsworthy cases. "Are you saying the preacher was throwing sex parties at his home?"

"Not exactly." Anne spun the combination lock, then pulled it down until it opened. "He could have invited another couple to their house, or even a single girl. Men love threesomes. Besides, this kind of thing is so popular today, they even have a swingers' section on MySpace. I mean, correct me if I'm wrong, but wasn't this type of activity kept under the table in the past? Maybe it was out in the open in the sixties or seventies. That was before AIDS. I was shocked things like that still went on."

The case was shifting directions in Lily's mind. "If this is true, wouldn't they be afraid someone might find out?"

Anne reached around to snap her bra, then pulled on her bikini panties. "I don't think there's a *they* in this equation.

I think it was the husband's idea. From what I've heard, it always is. When his wife protested, he kept pushing until she cratered. This guy was a Pentecostal preacher. I don't know what religion you are, but have you ever seen these guys on TV? They get poverty-stricken widows to send them their last dime, so they must possess strong powers of persuasion. He might have even quoted the Bible to her, where it says a wife must submit to her husband."

Lily took a seat on the bench in front of the lockers, looking down at her feet. Talking to Anne was like reading a tabloid magazine, just from a more intelligent perspective. "The man was a preacher. One of his parishioners might have recognized him."

"Maybe he reasoned that swingers weren't the kind of people who go to church." Anne wiggled into her jeans, then pulled a flowered T-shirt over her head. "Did you see the footage of the wife testifying?"

"No, I didn't catch it. I don't watch much TV."

"The poor woman was beet-red." Anne stepped into her tennis shoes, sat down on the bench beside Lily, and then bent over to tie the laces. "I don't know of any drug that can make a person blush on cue. This was a shy, introverted woman. She married a man she thought was a servant of God, only to have him turn into a perverted pig. There's no telling what disgusting things he made her do."

"I know you don't practice criminal law," Lily told her, "but the elements you mentioned are mitigating circumstances, not a justification for murder. And how did the shotgun get there? Don't tell me the preacher brought a shotgun to their alleged sex party." A judge had to watch her mouth, or serious repercussions could develop. Lily's rule of thumb was she never discussed cases she was involved in, and only discussed other legal matters after they had been officially resolved by the court.

Anne thought a few moments. "Since they were dealing

with strangers, he could have kept a shotgun in the closet for safety." Seeing Lily wasn't buying it, she held up her palms. "Okay, I'll concede she intentionally shot him. It's an offshoot of the battered woman defense, and I realize it could be used to distort justice. Still, I think the preacher probably got what he deserved."

"You've made your point, Counselor," Lily said. When Anne's cell phone rang again, she pushed herself to her feet and headed off to her own locker.

THREE

❧

MONDAY, NOVEMBER 27
VENTURA, CALIFORNIA

A chilly wind had blown in from the ocean, and the sky was as gray as a sailor's blanket. The temperature gauge on Lily's white Volvo read sixty-one degrees. Just three days ago, it was in the mid-seventies. Two weeks back, the Santa Ana winds had made it warm enough to jump in the ocean and take a swim.

She took the 101 freeway to the Victoria off-ramp. Her head turned when she passed the Elephant Bar, a hangout for local attorneys, and the first place she had connected with Richard Fowler, a fellow prosecutor she'd fallen in love with. Fowler was still around, but their relationship was over. It had been the type of love that had left a hole in her heart. She couldn't repair it, but she'd finally reached the point where she no longer wanted him.

Even if she wanted to, she couldn't unwind over drinks with the courthouse crowd as she had in the past. Her judicial appointment had separated her from her friends and many of the positive memories she had of Ventura.

The Ventura government center was similar to a small city. The courts, the district attorneys, and public defenders' offices, as well as the records division, were all housed on the right side of a large open space. A bubbling fountain stood in the center, surrounded by concrete benches and blooming flowers. To the left were the probation department, the sheriff's department, and the jail. The general public assumed the two structures weren't connected, yet in actuality an underground tunnel was used to transport inmates back and forth.

Lily turned down the ramp leading to the underground garage reserved for judges. She never would have agreed to take the position in Ventura if she had to park in the public lot because it could be seen through the windows of the jail. Minor detail, she thought bitterly, at least to the architects and the board of supervisors who'd approved it. For Lily, it was a horror story. It was hard to accept that both she and her daughter's lives had changed forever because of a parking lot.

The jail was actually a pretrial detention facility, and as a result of housing over one thousand inmates with a rate capacity of four hundred and twelve, the twenty-year-old facility had the infrastructure of a sixty-year-old building. About fourteen years ago, the county had erected another detention facility called the Todd Road Jail. Located in the city of Santa Paula, which was part of Ventura County, Todd Road was designed to hold over 750 sentenced male inmates. Only minor or repeat offenders served their time in jail. Serious offenders were sentenced to prison.

The overcrowding was even worse in the prisons. Approximately two hundred thousand offenders were incarcerated in facilities built for half that number. They were warehoused in gymnasiums, converted classrooms, even kitchens. Riots were an increasing problem. Some of the prisons were under federal mandates to release prisoners or close their doors.

As a judge, Lily had to factor in overcrowding whenever she imposed a sentence. She wanted to keep dangerous offenders behind bars for as long as possible, but the reality was there wasn't anywhere to put them. It wasn't as important an issue as global warming. Nonetheless, it was still a serious problem that society had chosen to ignore until it was too late to correct. Overcrowding in correctional institutions didn't concern people until it struck home. One couple hadn't finished paying the funeral home when they saw the man who'd murdered their daughter strolling down the aisles at a local supermarket.

Locking her car, Lily took the private elevator to the main floor, passed through security, then continued on to Judge Roger Hennessey's chambers. Hennessey was the presiding judge. He had been on leave recovering from a quadruple bypass when she'd received her appointment. She knew he didn't like her. She recalled the days when she'd tried cases before him, and how he had consistently ruled against her.

Hennessey hated all powerful women. He had tried to oust the first woman to ever be appointed to the Ventura County Superior Court, Elaine Sorbiet. He must be happy now. Elaine had retired recently, but not because of Hennessey. Her husband had been diagnosed with terminal cancer and she'd sacrificed what was left of her career to care for him.

A smartly dressed man with olive skin came walking out the back door of Division Twenty-one, his thick dark hair held in place by some kind of hair product that made it resemble strands of rubber. "You look terrific today, Lily," Judge Paciugo said, a mischievous grin on his face.

"I heard you're sitting both the Burkell and Stucky murders. Why do you get assigned all the major crimes while I have to deal with the boring civil cases?"

Vince Paciugo was a womanizer. He was also a competition junkie, and scoring with a married woman garnered a bigger trophy. "Even a dog could figure that out, Vince," she told him. "I was a prosecutor and you were a divorce attorney."

He placed his hand over his chest, playacting. "How can such a ravishing woman be so vicious? Have a drink with me tonight and I'll forgive you."

"No," Lily said, attempting to step past him. "I have a husband, remember? Bryce would beat the crap out of you if he knew you were hitting on me. Keep it up and I'll tell him."

Now that he'd left private practice and knew he couldn't get away with it, Judge Paciugo didn't harass female employees, which had obviously put a crunch on his sexual proclivities. But he'd decided Lily was fair game, for some reason. The man was basically a baboon. With the things hidden in *her* past, she had no choice but to tolerate him.

Paciugo pouted, making him look even more slimy and ridiculous. "All I want is to spend some time with you. Maybe I need some legal pointers and I'm too embarrassed to ask one of the other judges for fear they'll laugh at me."

She glared at him. "Read your law books instead of trying to fuck everything that moves."

"I love it when you talk dirty." He cornered her near the wall, his hot breath on her face, his pungent cologne swirling around her.

"Get out of my way, Vince. I'm on my way to a meeting with Hennessey."

"Oh," he said, stepping back. "Then I guess I'll catch

you later. I was joking, you know. Everyone is so serious. All I want is to have a little fun now and then." He clasped her arm, his brows furrowed. "You wouldn't say anything to Hennessey, would you?"

"I might," Lily tossed over her shoulder as she walked away.

The quiet hallways behind the courtrooms where the judges' chambers were located were a stark contrast to the noise and confusion of a county DA's office. A lot still went on in these corridors. For one thing, there wasn't much room to escape unless you ducked inside another judge's chambers, which was more or less taboo. Attorneys had access. It wasn't unusual to see one huddled with a judge.

As a former prosecutor, she was familiar with deadlines, but here everything was about moving the calendar. And moving the calendar was similar to pushing a jumbo jet without wheels. The city of Ventura wasn't that large, but the county's population had swelled to over a million people. They called it the Gold Coast. It consisted of ten cities and numerous unincorporated communities.

Lily had to handle mountains of arraignments, plea agreements, jury selections, opening arguments, closing arguments. And, of course, there was the continuous stream of motions and paperwork. Then there was the unpredictable factor—lawyers. She felt like a teacher trying to ride herd on a class of egotistical students who had the right to argue over every assignment.

Thrusting her shoulders back, she walked into Judge Hennessey's outer chambers and announced herself to his assistant. Esther Landau was in her late fifties and had worked for four presiding judges prior to Hennessey. A maniac when it came to her job, she'd once tackled an attorney who tried to barge into the presiding judge's chambers without an appointment. She forwarded Hennessey's calls to her personal cell phone when she went to the bathroom.

"You can go in, Judge Forrester." Esther had an unusually solemn look on her pinched face. "He's been waiting for you."

Shit, Lily thought, he's going to rip me to shreds. He'd probably been practicing snarling since early that morning. She thought about turning around and leaving, but she was stuck. Esther's firm gaze told her not to even think about it. She finally forced herself to step through the doorway. The good news was she had to be on the bench in an hour. Hennessey would never cause her to be late to court, so at least she wouldn't be in the hot seat for long.

"It's good to see you back at work, Judge Hennessey," she said, giving a lackluster smile to the seventy-two-year-old jurist. Although he'd been a judge for eons, a presiding judge only served a two-year term. He had lost a lot of time with his illness. If her calculations were right, he couldn't have more than a year left, unless some stupid law had been enacted that stopped the clock for someone in his situation.

Hennessey's eyes were small and deeply set, his skin ruddy and wrinkled. A fringe of white hair covered the lower half of his otherwise bald dome, and his dark-framed glasses looked as if they were about to slide off the end of his unimposing nose. Only a small amount of yellowish skin was visible, the rest covered by age spots and what appeared to be scars from old skin cancer lesions.

His heart attack had been massive. The emergency room physician had been ready to pronounce him dead when his heart suddenly resumed beating. The old fart should have given up golf and done more cardio workouts.

Lily had been in Hennessey's chambers in the past, but she now had a true appreciation of them. The room was twice the size of hers, with lacquered cherry bookcases, a magnificent antique desk, and a conference table that could seat twelve. Two studded burgundy leather chairs were positioned in front of his desk, and the walls were covered with certificates and framed photos. There were pictures of him holding golf trophies, standing beside several Supreme Court judges, and even one with the president. The room smelled like a combination of leather, polished wood, old books, and rotting flesh.

Hennessey stared at her, fingering a piece of paper. "I think you should know I don't approve of your appointment. Judge Reid should have waited until I recovered before making such a rash decision."

Her back stiffened. There was no response to this type of statement outside of a string of profanity. She struggled to keep herself in check. Hennessey was like a tiger who waited patiently for his prey, then pounced as soon as he was certain he had the kill. Although he looked as if his chair had swallowed him, he possessed the razor-sharp instincts of a world-class prosecutor. If she came back strong, he would demolish her. "I'm sure you're aware that I'm sitting the Stuckey homicide," she told him. "In addition, Burkell was just declared competent and I have the case on calendar for this morning. If this is the only thing you called me in here for, I have a number of motions I need to review before my ten o'clock hearing."

"I won't assign you any sexual assault cases," Hennessey said in almost a whisper, brushing his finger under his nose. "This makes my job more difficult. Judges who are biased on certain offenses don't belong on the bench."

"I am *not* biased," Lily countered, still reeling from his description of her appointment as a rash decision. He'd been absent for almost six months. His quadruple bypass had been complicated by a staph infection, leaving the assistant presiding judge, Alex Reid, to take over his responsibilities. As a prosecutor, she had a great track record and was highly respected in the legal community. She easily could have secured a judgeship in Santa Barbara. With Elaine out of the picture the calendar had quickly become backlogged. Of course, all the other judges were male; they needed another woman.

Hennessey spoke slowly and distinctly, his hands formed in the shape of a pyramid on top of his desk. "A person cannot remain unbiased after being a victim of a crime such as rape. And standing by helplessly while a filthy criminal violated your child must have been unbearable. She was twelve at the time, if I remember correctly?"

Lily felt as if a bucket of scalding water had been thrown at her. She was feverish, and a shaky hollowness took hold in the pit of her stomach. Images from that night leaped into the present with the same dreadful horror. Unable to stop herself, she exploded, "What happened to my daughter and me has nothing to do with my ability to render impartial verdicts. And only a tasteless person would bring up a personal matter of this magnitude in what by necessity has to be a brief conversation." She clamped her mouth closed, wishing she could snatch the words back out of the air. He would make her life even more miserable, particularly now that he'd confirmed her vulnerability.

Hennessey's watery eyes flickered with self-satisfaction. "From your emotional outburst, my assumption appears to be accurate. Maybe those rumors that circulated a few years back about you killing the rapist were true."

Lily forced her chin up as she tried to extract herself from the moment. She thought of Bryce, how much he loved her, and her daughter, Shana, who was doing so well at Stanford Law. Whatever had happened in the past was dead. No one could touch her. Unless Hennessey could prove she'd broken the law or violated the judicial rules of conduct, he could harass her but he couldn't unseat her. After everything she had gone through in her life, she could handle harassment.

"Forgive me," she said, deciding to kiss ass today and bust his balls whenever an opportunity presented itself. "What I said earlier was out of line. But just so you'll know, Marco Curazon, the man who raped my daughter, started stalking her after he was paroled from prison. He killed my ex-husband, but his real intent was to rape my daughter again." She stopped and sucked in a deep breath. "After her father was murdered, my daughter had a nervous breakdown and started saying things that didn't make sense." Giving him a disgusted look, she added, "Curazon is on death row, so there's no way I could have killed him. I'm surprised a man in your position is so poorly informed."

Forget ass-kissing, Lily decided. She didn't have it in her. Hennessey fiddled with a letter opener on his desk. Telling a judge of his stature that he was poorly informed was tantamount to accusing him of incompetence. The room sparked with tension.

After several minutes had clicked off, the game of wills was over. "I'm on a tight schedule," she said. "I'm sure you don't want to keep a courtroom waiting and clog up the rest of my day."

"Go," Hennessey said, flicking his gnarled hand. "We'll continue our conversation another time."

Not if I can help it, Lily thought, closing the door and walking over to his dragon lady. "I think your boss needs you, Esther. He might be having another heart attack. I couldn't make out what he was saying."

"Dear God!" she said, tripping over the trash can as she rushed toward the judge's chambers.

Lily scooped the stack of files out of Hennessey's in basket, tucking them under her arm as she left. Esther would run to Hennessey in a panic when she discovered they were missing. The judge was more than likely waiting for the cases to arrive so he could begin processing them. She would drop them on one of the records clerks' desks after the morning session. It was childish, but it made her feel better.

Lily had stopped living by the rules the night Marco Curazon had invaded her home. The most serious rules, not only of man but of God, she had already broken. All she wanted to do now was exist, perhaps do something meaningful. When she died, she knew exactly where she was going.

FOUR

∾

MONDAY, NOVEMBER 27
VENTURA, CALIFORNIA

Lily collided with Judge Christopher Rendell a few doors down from Hennessey's office, causing the files to spill out onto the gray carpet. By the time she bent down to retrieve them, they were in his hands. "How did you do that so fast?"

He smiled, handing the files back to her. "I used to be a great rebounder when I played basketball."

Lily said, "Walk with me, Chris." When she pushed an errant strand of hair off her forehead, she discovered it was wet. She hadn't realized she was perspiring, even though she was certain Hennessey had. "I'm sorry, I wasn't paying attention."

"The devil has that kind of effect. You look fresh from an audience with our illustrious chief."

Lily scowled. "Have you talked to him since he's been back? He's always been tough. Now he's bordering on sadistic. Maybe he just has it in for me."

"You're not the first person I've heard that from, Lily. When a person looks death in the face and comes back mean, you have to wonder what's living inside them."

"Really?" she said, pondering his statement. "I think Hennessey was born mean. He probably chewed through his own umbilical cord."

To qualify for a judgeship, a person had to be an attorney for ten years. Chris was the wunderkind of the judicial system, having been appointed to the bench at thirty-four. Now in his mid-forties, he'd graduated at the top of his class at Harvard Law at the age of nineteen. Why he chose to become a judge in Ventura was a mystery. The man was a certifiable genius, yet you would never know it by speaking to him. He had once told her a true intellect related to each person on their own level. Not only was he a perfect gentleman, he was a six-foot-five blond Adonis. Also a devout Mormon, he never discussed his personal life. A few individuals speculated that he might be gay, but no one dared to ask. Lily didn't care. She always felt relaxed and positive when she was around him. Other people had experienced the same phenomenon. She was convinced a person could be ready to jump off the nearest bridge, spend time with Rendell, and walk away with a smile on his face.

Lily wondered how he managed to combine the fuzzy perimeters of religion with the certainty of science. In addition to his law degree, he held a degree in physics from

Caltech. His plan was to spend five more years as a judge, then return to college and ultimately achieve his goal of becoming a scientist. How could any woman not desire a squeaky clean, handsome, brilliant man with a plan? If nothing else, simply to shake him up and see what happened. No one should be that perfect.

Although she hated to admit it, Lily possessed some of the same qualities as Vince Paciugo. She didn't have any intentions on following through and having an affair like he did, but she liked to flirt now and then. It was one of her means of coping, getting her mind off things and reminding herself that she was still a woman. She gave him a coy smile. "I'm a little devilish myself on occasion."

Rendell threw his head back and laughed. "I find that hard to believe, Lily. You're a practicing Catholic, aren't you?"

"A cradle Catholic. That means I had no choice. Being a Catholic is similar to being a Jew. If your parents are Jewish, then you live your life as a Jew. You might stop going to temple, but you'll always be a Jew." She curled a finger around her chin. "Do Mormons believe Jesus will come back one day and clean up this mess? Well, obviously you do, since Mormons are Christians. I guess what I was referring to is the rapture."

"That's a complicated question, Lily. Do you believe in the rapture?"

"I'm not sure," Lily said, shrugging. "Some Catholics do, I assume, but the church doesn't sanction it because they don't believe it's theologically sound. That is, except for the 'one person taken and the other left behind' passage." She let forth a nervous chuckle. "I don't know why that would matter, because Catholics don't study the Bible that much."

He looked concerned. "Is something wrong, Lily?"

She had been enjoying their conversation, talking about something she knew would maintain his attention. She should have known better than to bring up the subject of religion. When you did, people thought you were experiencing some kind of crisis. Well, she was, but like always, she was doing her best to deny it. "I guess I'm at that stage in life when a person starts rethinking things. Who knows, maybe it's time I checked out another religion."

He took her arm and pulled her aside, speaking to her in hushed tones. "If you and your husband want to come to my house for dinner one night, I'll do my best to answer any questions you have about my church. Tell me what night would be good for you."

God, Lily thought, he's going to try to convert me. At least as a Catholic, she had confession and absolution. Who knows, she might not have to stay in hell for all eternity. After ten thousand years, perhaps she could wrangle her way into purgatory.

"I don't usually do this," he said anxiously, looking around to make certain no one was listening. "It's just that you asked, and . . ."

Judge Rendell was naïve in some areas, a trait Lily found inherently charming. Women flirted with him all the time; beautiful young women that most men would jump through hoops of fire for. He never seemed to notice.

The only way out of this, Lily decided, was to blame it on her husband. Since he'd come home drunk two nights in a row this past weekend, he wasn't in the best standing with her. "Thanks for the invitation, Chris. Unfortunately, Bryce is about as interested in religion as he is in a dead cat on the freeway. He's a good man, so don't take me wrong. What can I say? I married an atheist." It wasn't really bad being married to an atheist. Bryce believed you died and rotted, that there was no such thing as an afterlife. She wouldn't mind believing that herself. Unfortunately, she knew her husband was wrong. She had visited hell, so she knew it existed.

Changing the subject, Rendell asked, "What's happening with the Burkell case? I hear he's back from Vacaville. Are they trying to establish an insanity defense?"

"Possibly." Lily gazed into his clear blue eyes. Why were Mormons so good-looking and healthy? Interbreeding, she speculated. Either that or old-fashioned clean living. "Even stark-raving lunatics know the difference between right and wrong, Chris. If a person knows the difference between right and wrong, as you know, the law says he's sane. Besides, Burkell was working up until a few hours before the crime. His public defender is Judith McBride. There's no telling what she has up her sleeve."

Although Judge Rendell was a prince of a guy, he wasn't without ambition. The Burkell case didn't carry the weight of the one she was hearing that afternoon. Instead of asking her about Elizabeth and Ronald Stucky, which could be a precedent-setting case, he'd brought up Burkell, thinking it might open up the door to Stucky. She glanced at her watch, relieved that she had fifteen minutes left before she had to be on the bench. She'd lied to Hennessey about having motions to review. She jumped on everything as soon as it hit her desk. What she couldn't finish during the day, she took home with her. She was one of the few judges who actually ended up with time on her hands. There was a price to pay, though, for taking her work home. She suspected it might be the reason her husband had gone overboard on the drinking.

Esther darted into the corridor in the direction of the records division. Walking around Rendell so his body would block her, Lily wondered if Hennessey had figured out she'd taken the files. Only an imbecile would do something that stupid. By tomorrow her career might be over, and all because of a childish prank.

"Would you like to go in my chambers and talk, Lily? You seem anxious."

She ignored his question. At the moment, she didn't want to move. "Did you know the police found over a hundred pills in Burkell's house and not one was prescribed for him? He had Vicodin, Percodan, and morphine."

"This is the latest plague," Judge Rendell said, becoming animated. "Remember how cocaine worked its way from the street to middle-class America? Well, prescription drug abuse is doing the same thing. I know of three teenagers who overdosed in the past month. The sheriff's office can't figure out who's selling them the pills. Whoever it is, they aren't standing around on street corners."

"I know where some of it's coming from." Lily recalled the day she'd found a stash of tranquilizers in her daughter's underwear drawer. Shana had claimed she'd bought them from a friend's grandfather. The more common scenario would be that she'd stolen them, but her story had turned out to be true. "People with legitimate medical problems have become drug peddlers. And you know what's ironic? The government is paying for it."

"How's that?"

"Medicare."

"Are you saying senior citizens are selling their medications?"

"Yeah," Lily answered. "Who can live on Social Security, especially in southern California? You need at least two hundred grand to buy a shack these days, and that's in a bad neighborhood. And rents are outrageous." She thought of her conversation with Anne that morning. The cost of living was high in California, but nowhere near as high as Manhattan.

"Sad," he said, frowning. "I'd like to talk more, but I have to be on the bench in a few minutes."

"Don't we all," Lily said, trailing along beside him until they reached the door to his chambers. She held on to the doorframe and leaned in. "Tell Jesus to hurry, will you? My patience is wearing thin."

"I'll make certain to do that."

As she continued to the end of the corridor where her chambers were located, she wondered where Mormons stood on the death penalty. Chris was assigned to the municipal court where only misdemeanors were tried, so it wasn't really an issue in his work. She made a mental note to ask him one day. Maybe she would even take him up on his dinner offer. Bryce would go if she insisted, although he'd probably be tanked by the time they arrived. It was funny how you never really knew a man until you married him. Her lovable, jolly husband was not only an atheist, he was on the fast track to becoming an alcoholic.

"Any phone calls?" Lily asked her assistant, Jeannie Milford, a petite young brunette who was training at night to be a court reporter.

"Judith McBride called and said she was running late."

"As if I expected anything else."

"And Judge Forrester," she said, jumping to her feet as Lily began walking away, "you've got three more messages. Your husband called, as well as Martin Goodwin and James Kidwell. Should I remind you during the noon recess?"

"The attorneys can say whatever they have to say at the hearing this afternoon." Some judges practically tried cases in their chambers, a habit Lily didn't practice. They did it for fear they would make a mistake and their rulings would be overturned on appeal. She had reviewed cases for the appellate court for several years, so she knew what would fly and what wouldn't.

She handed Jeannie the files she'd taken from Hennessey's office, deciding she needed to return them posthaste. "These were delivered to me by mistake. They look like they were meant for Judge Hennessey. Take them to records and let them sort it out. Just don't say anything about where you got them. Hennessey doesn't like people to see things before he does."

She entered her chambers and closed the door. Since she was the most recent appointment, she had the worst office. It was half the size of Hennessey's. A janitor had told her it had once been a supply room. Before she was appointed, it was used by pro tems, private attorneys who served as a judge on a temporary basis. There was a weatherworn desk, room enough for two moderate-sized chairs, and a TV was mounted on the wall. She still hadn't gotten around to unpacking her things, mainly because she had nowhere to put them. Alex had promised to give her Elaine's chambers, but he'd been too busy to do anything. In addition, he probably gave consideration to the fact that Elaine's husband might die and she'd want her job back. Right now Lily wouldn't mind stepping down. When she'd taken the job, she was under the impression that Hennessey's reign of terror was over. She looked around her and sighed. Being the new kid on the block was an exercise in humility.

Her black robe was on a hanger behind her door. She caressed it with her fingers, then slipped it on and returned to her desk to wait until her clerk called to tell her they were ready. She felt like an actress waiting offstage for a director. Most of life was an illusion, she thought, and illusions were clever deceptions. She'd mastered the art of deception long ago, but she was in need of a better imagination.

FIVE

∽

The phone rang, and Special Agent Mary Stevens shot to attention. The person calling her was John Adams, her SAC, or special agent in charge. "Agent Stevens," she said in her most professional voice.

"I'd like to see you in my office in thirty minutes."

"Of course, sir," Mary said, hoping he was ready to let her do more than open mail and sit in on meetings with the team. The Behavioral Analysis Unit where she was assigned was housed in the basement of the FBI Academy in Quantico, Virginia. A former homicide detective, she had been recruited by the Bureau when she'd attended the National Academy program, a tough, twelve-week residential training course for upper level law enforcement officers from around the world. After a year at the Bureau's headquarters in Washington, she was hired by John Adams. Adams had been a close friend of her deceased father's, and was chief of the elite profiling unit.

Mary's present assignment was to sort through all the unidentified mail. They could tell it was from outside the Bureau, as it came addressed to the Behavioral Science Unit, which still existed as part of the Academy program but no longer consulted with police agencies in the apprehension and profiling of serial criminals. The name was changed to the Behavioral Analysis Unit, or BAU.

She scratched a spot on her eyebrow, giving thought to tossing the pile of mail into the trash can. But no, FBI agents never shirked their duty. Right, she thought, peering up at Mark Conrad as he walked past her desk in his blue Brooks Brothers suit, paisley tie, and starched white shirt.

Mary had previously been employed by the Ventura police department. They had routinely cracked jokes to break the tension. The overall atmosphere at the Bureau was what she imagined it must be inside the Vatican. People talked in whispers, everything was secret, and everyone wore the same conservative clothes.

At fifty-eight, Adams was a large man with prominent features, a furrowed brow, and a serious demeanor befitting a man of his tenure and responsibilities. He suffered from what Mary called a double whammy. His once-dark hair was both graying and thinning. Since his door was open, she walked in.

"Have a seat, Stevens."

The Investigative Support Unit was housed in a subbasement sixty feet below the Academy gun vault. At one time, it had been a bomb shelter for high-ranking U.S. government officials in the event of a nuclear war. It was depressing not having any windows, particularly considering the nature of the work. Mary was accustomed to warm weather, sunny skies, and sandy beaches.

Adams's walls were covered with crime scene photos from a case he was profiling for the NYPD. The victims were all women in their late seventies to early eighties, and looking at their defiled and brutalized bodies seemed obscene. Although Mary had seen the images on several occasions, she still had an urge to walk over and rip them off the wall. The women looked fragile, even the ones who were physically large. Looking at them reminded her of her mother. She'd walked in on her not long ago while she was undressing, and had been saddened by the sight of her age-ravaged body. She folded her hands in her lap, waiting for Adams to begin speaking.

"I've been asked to have a word with you about the way you dress," he said, glancing down at her stylish heels. "What if you got in a foot pursuit in those shoes?"

"I broke the state record in the four-forty when I was in college," Mary said, giving him a confident smile. "No disrespect, sir, but I could outrun anyone in this unit regardless of what kind of shoes I'm wearing."

"That may be true," Adams said, giving her a stern look. "The problem isn't just your shoes. Those knit sweaters you wear are too provocative, and the colors are too bold. They don't fit the image the Bureau wants to project. You knew that when you signed on."

"I'm wearing a black suit, sir," Mary countered, swinging a shapely leg. "You want me to wear a black shirt, too? Someone might run over me in the parking lot."

He winced, then blurted out, "Why can't you wear a regular white shirt, for God's sake? You're exposing your cleavage."

"Don't you have anything better to do than worry about what I wear? You've got me sorting mail, so it's not like anyone's going to see me. I promise I'll wear old-lady shoes as long as you don't bitch at me about my sweaters. Jim Hunt wore a pink shirt last week and you didn't say anything to him."

"It was beige, not pink."

"It wasn't beige," Mary argued, refusing to back down. "I know pink when I see it. At least a few people around here have kept up with the times. I don't see why we have to dress like undertakers to do our jobs. In case you don't know, they have color TV sets now."

Adams looked exhausted. Mary was a relentless woman, which had served her well as a homicide detective, but made her difficult to supervise. When his phone rang, he grabbed it. "Wear anything you want. I have to take this call."

"But when will you assign me . . . ?"

Adams didn't answer. He either didn't hear her, or he thought she was being disrespectful. Her spirits sank. She returned to her desk and plunked down in her chair.

Most of the letters were from mental cases, or just well-intentioned people who didn't know their ass from a hole in the ground. One lady wrote that her neighbors were terrorists because she'd heard them speaking a foreign language. They also had "dark skin" and looked "shifty." For all Mary knew, Mrs. Early's neighbors had been speaking Spanish. But she had strict orders to forward anything even slightly suspicious to the NSB, the National Security Branch. The NSB had been formed in 1995 under a presidential directive. She tossed the lady from Idaho's letter into the outgoing bin and picked up a manila envelope.

Mary felt something inside the package. She couldn't be certain, but she thought it was a cassette tape. The envelope didn't have a return address on it, which made it somewhat interesting. She knew it didn't contain anthrax or explosives because it had already been opened and screened in the main mailroom. The unit got a good deal of mail from mental patients, containing all sorts of odd objects—fingernail clippings, pictures torn out of magazines, maps, keys, clothing, even pubic hair.

Jim Hunt stuck his head in the door to her office. At forty-five, he was an attractive man with rust-colored hair and freckled skin. "How long are you going to be assigned to this duty? Seems like a waste of talent."

"From your ears to God's," Mary said, fingering the cassette tape. "This came in today's mail. Do you know anyone who has a tape player?"

"Pete has one, I think. If he isn't there, look in the bottom drawer of his credenza. That's the last place I saw it. Those things are almost obsolete. They don't even put them in cars anymore."

"I hear you," Mary said, getting up and heading down the narrow hallway to Pete Cook's office.

Cook was out, so she checked the credenza and found a dust-covered cassette player. Before she left, she grabbed a sticky note and wrote to Cook that Jim Hunt said it was okay to borrow his tape recorder. All this effort, she thought, and the tape probably contained nothing more than meaningless drivel. That is, if there was anything on it at all. Adams had promised to give her a case to profile by the end of the week. She'd been on board a month, and he'd allowed her to sit in on team meetings, but she needed to sink her teeth into something meaty.

During her first year with the Bureau, Mary had worked out of the FBI's headquarters in Washington. She had made a name for herself by cracking a drug counterfeiting ring, which had been generating over a hundred million per year. They began by producing phony Viagra pills and then moved on to medications to treat high blood pressure, cholesterol, and heart disease. The majority of the counterfeit drugs were sold over the Internet, yet some of them managed to make their way into legitimate pharmacies, particularly the independently owned stores who had to compete with the chains.

Mary had tracked down a group of individuals in China who had copied the size, color, markings, and packaging of mainstream drugs such as Viagra, Lipitor, Valium, and dozens of others. They were also producing a counterfeit version of Tamiflu.

When she'd taken the job at the Bureau, she had relocated her mother, a retired high school principal, to Washington. Thelma Stevens hadn't wanted to leave Ventura, but she was seventy-three now and needed to be near her only living child. Mary's brother had died in a car accident years ago, and the only people her mother had left in

L.A. were her friends from church, most of them as old as, if not older than, her mother.

When she jumped at the chance to transfer to BAU so she could work with Adams and his team, she tried to talk her mother into relocating to Quantico. The woman had staunchly refused. Now Mary had to fight the traffic into D.C. on a regular basis. It was fine now, but when she got busy, it could develop into a major problem.

The only good thing about the year she'd spent in Washington was Lowell Redstone, a criminal attorney she had been dating. Her mother despised Lowell, claiming he was a pompous opportunist, which wasn't that far from the truth. Mary had no intention of getting married, so she didn't understand what all the fuss was about. Anyway, her affair with Lowell was going south. She wasn't any good at long-distance relationships. If a man wasn't in her bed, he wasn't her man.

Before she left Cook's office, Mary studied the crime scene photos tacked up on the wall. They had a serial killer at work in Wisconsin. The UNSUB, FBI lingo for an unidentified subject, had kidnapped five prepubescent boys from shopping malls throughout the state. They'd been taken to remote locations, where they were raped, sodomized, and strangled. Their lifeless bodies had been discarded on the side of the road like rubbish.

As twisted as it sounded, Mary found death intriguing. When she'd started working homicide, she could go through crime scene photos and autopsy reports as if she were flipping through magazines in a dental office. If the victims were children, however, her stomach ended up in her throat. The maniacs who killed children were abominations. If given the chance, she'd take one out in a minute. By working in the BAU, she hoped to learn what made them tick. The better she knew them, the quicker she could get the bastards off the streets.

SIX

❦

"All rise," the bailiff announced. "Division Forty-seven of the Ventura County Superior Court is now in session, Judge Lillian Forrester presiding."

After climbing the steps to the bench, Lily saw the defendant standing next to his public defender at the counsel table. An African-American in his mid-forties, Floyd Burkell owned a shoe repair shop on the west side of Ventura. His son had been thirteen at the time his father stabbed him to death. Burkell had slaughtered his wife as well. Together, the stab wounds came to a total of twenty-three.

Floyd Burkell had a gentle, almost sweet look to his face. He didn't look disturbed or mentally ill. He seemed at peace with himself. The customers who had frequented his shop were shocked when they learned the terrible crimes he had committed. They described the defendant as kind, honest, hardworking, and a pillar of the community. Murderers seldom looked or acted the part, Lily knew, something more people should realize.

Burkell had built a nice life for himself. He owned his own business, employed a number of people, had a son on the honor roll, and resided in a three-hundred-thousand-dollar home in a middle-class neighborhood. Having moved to California from the slums of Detroit, he was the personification of the American dream. How could he knock it all down in a frenzied burst of incomprehensible violence?

It happened, though. Ordinary, normally civilized individuals suddenly exploded and turned into killing machines. After she and Shana were raped, Lily had experienced her own murderous rage.

Too many things had fallen into place that night, almost as if the events that followed had been ordained by a higher power. She was the supervisor over the sex crimes division at the time, and the court had just released a man who'd assaulted a prostitute because the woman had failed to appear at the preliminary hearing. Without a victim, the state had no case. The man's file had been in her briefcase, and her father's shotgun was in the garage. She had motive, opportunity, and a weapon. She wouldn't have followed through if only one of these ingredients had been missing.

Lily flew backward in time and was holding her twelve-year-old daughter, stroking her hair and softly whispering in her ear.

The man who had raped Lily and her daughter was gone. She tried to lock his image in her mind, the glimpse she'd got of him in the light from the bathroom just before he had fled—the red sweatshirt, the gold chain with a crucifix, which had struck her several times in the face.

"It's over, baby," Lily told Shana. "He's gone. He'll never hurt you again." The shrill of the siren was fading from earshot. No one had called the police. Their agonized screams had gone unnoticed.

Time stood still as she rocked Shana in her arms and listened to her pitiful, wracking sobs. A million things raced through her mind. Two or three times she tried to pull away so she could call the police. Shana was holding her so tightly, though, that she stopped. He was long gone by now, lost in the night. Every sordid detail replayed itself in her mind. A hard ball of rage had formed in the pit of her stomach and was spilling bile into her mouth.

"Shana, darling, I'm going to get up now, but I'll be right here. I'm going to get a wash rag from the bathroom, and then I'm going to call the police and your father." Lily inched away and pulled on her robe, tying the sash loosely around her waist. The rage was somehow calming her, moving her around like a machine with a great churning engine.

"No," Shana shouted in a voice Lily had never heard before. "You can't tell Dad what he did to me." She reached out and grabbed the edge of her mother's robe as she tried to get up, causing it to open and expose her nakedness. Lily quickly retied it again. "You can't tell anyone!"

The face was a child's, but the eyes were a woman's. She would never be a child again, never see the world as a safe place without fear. Lily cupped her hand over her mouth, biting her knuckle as she stifled a scream that welled up inside of her. "We must call the police. We must call Daddy."

"No!" Shana screamed again. "I think I'm going to be sick." She ran to the bathroom, regurgitating the contents of her stomach on the tile floor before she got to the commode.

Lily dropped to the floor with her and wiped her face with cold towels. She reached up and opened the door to the medicine cabinet, pulling out a bottle of Valium a doctor had recently prescribed due to the stress of her pending divorce. Her hands were shaking as she poured out two pills, one for herself and one for Shana. "Take this," she said, handing her the pill with a paper cup of water. "It will relax you."

Shana swallowed the pill and watched with round eyes as her mother tossed one into her own mouth. She let Lily help her back to bed. Once again, she cradled her in her arms.

"We're going to call Daddy and we're going to go home, leave this house. I won't call the police, but we're going to tell Daddy. We have no choice, Shana."

Lily knew exactly what she would be subjecting her daughter to if she reported the crime. The police would stay for hours, forcing them to relive the nightmare, sealing every detail forever in their memory. Then there was the hospital and medical exam. They would probe Shana's ravaged body and comb her public hairs. They would swab their mouths. If they apprehended him, months of court appearances and testimony would consume their lives. Shana would have to sit on the witness stand and repeat every sordid moment of this night in lurid detail to a room full of strangers. She would have to rehearse her testimony with the prosecutor like lines in a play. In that room, breathing the same air, he would also sit. Then the ordeal would become known. A kid at Shana's school might learn what had happened and spread it around.

The most despicable thought of all, a fact Lily alone was far too aware of, was that after all they had suffered, would suffer, while the nightmares were still the sweating, waking, screaming kind, before they could even begin to resume a normal life, he would be free. The term for aggravated rape was only eight years, out in four. He would even receive credit for time served before and after the crime. No, she thought, he would receive a consecutive term for the oral copulation, amounting to a few more years. It was not enough. And she felt certain he had committed other vicious crimes, maybe even murder. She recalled the taste of dried old blood on the knife. This crime was a murder: the annihilation of innocence.

She also had to consider her career, her life's work, her dream of becoming a superior court judge. A door *was closing in her face. Thought by thought, she was moving further away from reporting the rape to the authorities.*

His face kept appearing before her, and somewhere in the far reaches of her mind, Lily knew she had seen him before. Her memory of the attack clouded the past and she was no longer able to distinguish reality from imagination.

She called Shana's father, then hung up and looked at the clock. A mere two hours to destroy their lives. What would this do to John? Shana was his life, his shining star, his sheltered baby girl. When Shana was born, John had shoved Lily away and centered all his attention on their child: holding her, kissing her, when he no longer kissed his wife. Starting to tremble, Lily hugged herself. She had to be strong.

It seemed like only minutes before John arrived. Time had been standing still, hanging over them like a powerful storm, its unleashed fury contained and waiting. He appeared in the doorway to the bedroom. "What in the hell is going on here? The front door is wide open." His tone was accusing, demanding, and it was vented at the woman who had left him.

Shana's muscles had begun to relax in Lily's arms. Her breathing was shallow, her body too still. "Daddy," she said, hearing his voice and crying out. "Oh, Daddy." He ran to her side of the bed and Lily released her. As John engulfed her in his large arms, she pressed her body to his chest, sobbing, "Oh, Daddy."

He looked at Lily, his dark eyes full of anger, but in their depths, fear was rising. "What happened? What did you do to her? Tell me what went on here right now, damn it."

"Shana, Daddy and I are going in the other room and talk," Lily said gently. "You'll hear us talking and know

we are here. We'll only be a few feet away." She got up and motioned for John to follow.

The Valium had calmed her somewhat and Lily told John about the attack. It was an emotionless recitation of facts. If she allowed one tear to fall, the floodgates would open. They were sitting on her newly purchased sofa with the amber light from a Tiffany lamp creating an almost surreal atmosphere. He leaned up close and touched the small cuts at the side of her mouth, but it wasn't a gesture of concern or affection. It was more like a reflex, confirmation of the reality of what she was saying. His eyes clearly said she was responsible, no matter what reason predicated. She should have found the strength to stop him. That's the way he saw her, Lily thought: invincible.

Then he sobbed, his masculine body wracked with pain, that unfamiliar and awful sound that signified a grown man crying like a child. He didn't scream or yell or threaten revenge. He was quite simply heartbroken.

"Well, do you want me to call the police? You're her father and I can't make this decision without you." Lily felt as if her blood had turned to iron. She had been raped as well. "It's not irreversible. We can always file a report later if we change our minds."

"No, I agree with you. It would only make things worse for her," he finally replied. Tears were still streaming down his face, and he wiped them with the back of his hand. "Would they catch the bastard if we reported it?"

"How do I know, John? No one knows. We don't have a vehicle description." She cursed herself for not running after him, for staying with Shana. "Maybe we're doing the wrong thing. I just don't know. I don't know." Her mind was too muddled, full of barely suppressed rage. Something inside her was diving, twisting. She had to stop it. She had to rewind the tape and erase it. John's voice sounded distant. She stared at him and tried to focus.

"I want to take Shana home, away from this place." His voice was a choked whisper. "I don't care about anything else, understand? I just want to take care of my child."

"I know," she shouted, and then lowered her voice so Shana wouldn't hear. "And she's our child, not yours. Don't you think I want to take care of her? I don't want her to suffer. I couldn't stop this." She paused, then said, "I—I gave her a sedative. Let's just bundle her up and take her home. I'll pack a bag and follow you."

He stood and then stopped, staring at her. A look of utter horror shot from his ravaged eyes. He hadn't combed his hair over his bald spot, and a long strand dangled over by his temple. He looked so old, so haggard. "Could she get pregnant? My baby, my little baby."

Lily started to say something but found herself disgusted by his weakness. This was why she had lost respect for him over the years. As she had forced herself to confront the violence of the world they lived in, he had lived in a world that didn't exist. The strong, loving man she had married had started to disappear around the time Lily passed the bar. John had cut back his hours at work, content to let her carry the financial burden of the family. But in time, he'd begun to despise her, jealous of her success. Why couldn't he make the decisions that had to be made just once? Her love affair with Richard Fowler passed through her mind, and she wished he was there instead of John. For the first time she had reached for happiness, touched the soft edge of pleasure. Pleasure, she thought. The rapist had found pleasure in her terror, in Shana's terror.

"He didn't ejaculate," Lily told him. "The sirens scared him away. We can take her to the doctor tomorrow, and they'll check her for possible diseases. There's a slim chance she could get pregnant from pre-emission sperm. We'll just have to pray."

"Will she ever get over this, Lily? Will our little girl ever be the same?"

"With you and me beside her and all the love and help we can give her, I know she will. I pray to God she will." As she said the stock, comforting words she had said to dozens of victims, their worthlessness struck home. Shana was strong. Lily had made her strong, refusing to baby and shelter her as John did. And if they didn't drag it on with the authorities, perhaps it would someday become like a bad dream. The only alternative was to become an emotional cripple, and no child of hers would fall into this abyss. She would not allow it.

After they wrapped Shana in a comforter, John led her to the door. She turned and looked at Lily, and their eye contact locked and lingered. Lily had wanted to be her friend and confidante, to guide her without her father's intervention. Instead they had witnessed hell together, forming a bond, but one forged in terror.

"You go home and go to sleep. Daddy will sleep on the floor next to you." Lily embraced her. "I'll be there in the morning when you wake up."

"Will he come back, Mom?"

The words sliced through Lily's heart. "No, Shana, he'll never come back. I'll move out of this house tomorrow. We'll never come back here again. Soon we'll both forget this night ever happened." She knew this was a lie.

Once they had gone, Lily hurriedly started throwing things in a small duffel bag. The house was dead quiet again, that ominous stillness like before, and she was shaking. The memory of the attacker's face when he had passed through the light coming from the bathroom kept flashing in her mind, and each time, she dropped what she was doing and stood there, frozen in thought, trying to put her finger on what it was she associated with his face.

Suddenly the face appeared, but not as she remembered it. It appeared in a mug shot photo.

She ran to the living room, tripping and falling on the edge of her robe, soggy and reeking of Shana's vomit. From her position on the floor, she saw her briefcase and crawled the rest of the way on her hands and knees. Her fingers trembled as she dialed the combination lock. On the third try it clicked open. She threw all the files out and frantically searched for the one she knew contained the photo. Papers went flying across the carpet.

Suddenly it was in her hands. He was the same man who had assaulted the prostitute, Clinton Silverstein's case that had been dismissed today. He was even wearing the same red sweatshirt. He had been arrested and photographed in it, photographed with that smug smile. They must have released him about the time she'd left the courthouse, giving him back his original clothes with the rest of his property. Someone either picked him up or dropped off his car. He must have followed her from the complex.

There was no doubt in her mind as she studied the hated image. No doubt at all. It was him.

Her breath was coming faster now, catching and rattling in her throat. Whatever effects the Valium had were gone. Adrenaline was pumping through her veins. She rapidly sorted through the pages of the file to the police report. His home was listed as 24 South 155th Street. Lily tore off the section with his address on it and placed it in the pocket of her robe. She went to the bedroom and threw on a pair of jeans and a sweater, transferring the address to the jeans. Digging in the back of the closet, she found her fur-lined winter hiking boots. John had insisted that she remove every single item that belonged to her when they'd separated, as if he wanted to erase her from his life.

In the same box was a blue knit ski cap. She placed it on her head and stuffed her hair inside it.

She headed for the garage. Back in the corner, behind three or four boxes, was her father's shotgun, one of the curious items her mother had given her after his death.

In the stillness of the garage, as her hands touched the barrel of the gun, Lily felt his presence beside her. Her father had wanted a son and made his daughter spend Saturday afternoons shooting tin cans. She no longer dreamed of frilly dresses and bows for her hair. She adored her father and would do anything to please him.

Spotting the small box containing the green shells containing slugs, she loaded them into the chamber and crammed several more into the tight pocket of her jeans. She didn't falter for a moment, her father's voice guiding her, pushing her on.

As she left the garage, shotgun muzzle down in her arms, her footsteps echoed even when she'd left the concrete floor and was walking on carpet. She felt heavy, rooted to the ground with resolve, no longer alone in her body. The phone rang like a shrill bell, invasive, unwelcome, but a signal, a signal to begin. It was John.

"Shana's asleep. I'm worried about you. Are you coming over?"

"I'll be there in a few hours. Don't worry. I can't sleep now anyway. I want to calm down and take a bath. He's not coming back here tonight. Just take care of Shana." Do what you do best, she thought without contempt, accepting her role, and I'll do what has to be done.

She crouched at the rear of her car and began marking the license plate. The plate read FPO322. With a black marker, she altered it to read EBO822. She threw the shotgun in the backseat, thought of covering it, and then decided it didn't matter. The rage was an unseen inferno, burning all around her, blinding her, engulfing her. She kept seeing him over Shana, his body heaving on top of her precious child.

She rolled down the window in her car and let the night air blow in her face. As she passed the farming area on the outskirts of Ventura, the smell of fertilizer reminded her of his rancid odor. She tasted his vile penis in her mouth and spat out the window.

Slowly she drove the dark streets, passing from one streetlight to another, going past one stop sign then through a traffic signal changing from red to green to yellow. In her mind they were runway lights, illuminating her descent into hell.

She was trying to formulate a plan. It didn't take her long to find the house. It was one in a row of tiny stucco residences. Across the street was a vacant lot. The yard was overgrown with weeds. On the front porch was an old refrigerator with a heavy link chain and padlock. He had probably been cited by the police before purchasing the lock. In the assault on the prostitute, he had driven a van and there was no van, just a dusty black older-model Chevy. The van could have been stolen and subsequently abandoned. The screen on the front door hung haphazardly on its hinges. One window was boarded up with glass.

Like a burglar, she cased the area, noting the nearest streetlight was a block away on the corner. She knew she couldn't enter his house to shoot him. That would be suicide. And she had no way of confirming he was inside. There was only one way: wait for him to come out. What if it was daylight and dozens of people were milling about on the street? Some of these houses had two or three families living together. She glanced at the cars parked on the streets she prowled.

Turning back toward a field she had passed earlier, she steered the car onto a dirt road. The car had been washed only a few days before. The exterior was absorbing the dust she was churning up with her tires. She parked by the road. Taking the shotgun from the backseat, she pointed it into the field and fired. The blast shattered the stillness of the night, and the butt of the gun slammed into her shoulder. Her father had been dead for ten years. She wanted to make certain her weapon of death performed. Placing it in the front seat, she spun out and headed back onto the main road.

She had to go to the bathroom but refused to stop. She willed the urge to go away and it did. As she pulled up to a stoplight and glanced in the rearview mirror, she caught sight of her image. Her face was ashen, her eyes bloodshot. She looked old and tired in the blue knit cap pulled low on her forehead. As she realized the stench of him still clung to her body and had now grotesquely blended with her own developing body order, a wave of nausea assaulted her. She bit down on the inside of her mouth, tasting her own salty blood.

As she turned down his street again, she saw a dark green van parked at the curb, its rear doors open. Her eyes turned to the shotgun propped up on the seat beside her, while her pulse raced and her stomach churned. When a dog barked somewhere, she jumped and took her foot off the brake. The car jerked forward. Pulling to the curb five houses away from his, hands locked and sweating on the cool steering wheel, she let go long enough to wipe her hands on her denim-clad thighs.

Dawn burst through the darkness.

After staring so hard at the house that her vision had blurred, she saw a distinct flash of red. She floored the car and covered the distance between the houses in seconds, until she was directly across from him. Slamming both feet on the brake, she threw the gearshift into park without thinking and grabbed the shotgun, getting out and racking the slide. He was exiting the house, halfway down the curb, headed toward the van. He saw her and stopped abruptly, planting both his feet firmly on the ground. On his face was a look of shock and confusion.

Inside that second, reason flickered behind the eyes she lowered to the sight, coursed inside the finger on the trigger, a pinpoint of light before blindness. Her body moved back inches, but the light was gone, the sight a framed portrait of red fabric pulsating with the beat of his heart. Her nostrils burned with his disgusting odor. Shana's cries echoed inside her head.

She fired.

The impact knocked him off his feet. His hands and legs flew into the air. The green shell ejected onto the street. The explosion reverberated inside her head. A gaping hole appeared in the center of the red sweatshirt, spewing forth blood: Shana's blood, virginal blood, sacrificial blood. Her throat constricted, mucus dripped from her nose, and once again the alien, detached finger squeezed the trigger. The bullet hit near his shoulder, severing his arm.

Her knees buckled beneath her. The shotgun fell butt-first to the ground. The muzzle came to rest on the soft area beneath her chin, stopping her. Moving her head, she vomited chunks of chicken onto the black asphalt, seeing pieces of flesh boiling. She pulled herself through the open door of the car, her arms locked around the shotgun. Everything was moving, shaking, bleeding, screaming. She saw objects flying through the air, trapping her inside the core of horror.

Move, she ordered her body, still frozen. Move. She grabbed the steering wheel, releasing the shotgun. Don't look. Drive. Her foot responded and the car surged forward. The intersection was there in a second. Turn.

Breathe. Turn. Drive. She had not killed a human being. Turn. Drive. Turn. The sun was shining, but all she saw was a dark tunnel in front of her. She knew she was in hell and there was no way out. "Please, God," she prayed. "In the name of the Father, the Son, and the Holy Ghost, show me the way out."

SEVEN

**MONDAY, NOVEMBER 27
VENTURA, CALIFORNIA**

"Judge Forrester," the clerk said, tapping Lily on the shoulder. "Are you okay? Can I get you something?"

Lily surfaced from the past, feeling light-headed and confused, memories from that awful day still whirling around her. "Coffee," she said, clearing her throat. "Where were we?"

"We're just beginning," Susie Martin whispered, handing her Burkell's file.

Lily tried to read, but all she saw was a blur. She felt as if she were attempting to adjust the lens on a microscope. She'd already read the contents of the file the night before. Both of the attorneys were scanning through their paperwork. When the clerk returned with her coffee, she took a sip and then looked up, turning on her microphone and moving it closer to her mouth. Only a few minutes had passed, but a few minutes in hell were an eternity. "I'm pleased that you could make it, Ms. McBride. If you're late one more time, rest assured there will be a price to pay. Am I making myself clear?"

"Perfectly, Your Honor," she answered, making no attempt to explain.

"Are we ready to go on record, Counselors?"

Clinton Silverstein pushed himself to a half-standing position. "The people are ready."

"We're ready, Your Honor," Judith McBride said.

Lily began speaking. "This is case number A345982, *State of California versus Floyd Burkell,* two counts of murder as per section 187 of the California Penal Code."

Her sojourn to the past had no doubt been initiated by her meeting with Hennessey, but seeing Clinton Silverstein had also been to blame. She had been Silverstein's supervisor in the sex crimes unit at the DA's office when she and Shana had been assaulted. Silverstein was a competent prosecutor, but his views on victims were occasionally distorted. In the attempted rape of the prostitute, Silverstein had not wanted to prosecute. Lily had reminded him that even prostitutes could be raped. The victim had also weighed over two hundred pounds, a fact Silverstein and some of the other male district attorneys had laughed about. As it turned out, the prostitute had failed to appear in court because she had been murdered.

But all that was before, back in the days when life was normal. The place she was at now was so strange and intense, she sometimes had to feel her pulse to make certain she was breathing. Focus, she told herself. Hold on to the present. She tried to relax her jaw until words finally came out of her mouth. "Have you had a chance to review the psychological evaluation on the defendant, Mr. Silverstein?"

He ran his hands through his bushy permed hair. "Yes, I have, Your Honor. The defendant has been deemed competent to stand trial, so all we need is to set a trial date." He turned to his computer, already open on the table. "December fourteenth works for me."

The public defender checked her calendar. "Not possible," she said in a snippy voice. "I'm scheduled to appear on three different matters that day."

While the two attorneys tried to work it out, Lily stared at a spectator in the otherwise empty courtroom. A proceeding of this nature wasn't known to interest the media, and the defendant had either killed or alienated whatever relatives he possessed. The person was sitting far in the back, and it was hard to tell if it was a woman or a man. The hair was brown and short. She looked for earrings, but didn't see any. The distance was too great to make out something as small as earrings. The only other identifying factor was a short-sleeved polo-style shirt, which appeared to be red-and-white-striped. Lily had an eerie feeling, wondering if it might be a criminal she had put in prison during her days as a district attorney.

Judith McBride was speaking. "We'd like to arrange a private psychiatric evaluation of Mr. Burkell. From the reports, Dr. . . . Hold on, I forgot his name." She stopped speaking and rummaged through the mess of papers she'd dumped on top of the counsel table. "Here it is . . . Dr. Julian Ackerman. He only spent an hour with the defendant, Your Honor, and he seemed more interested in eliminating an insanity defense than determining if Mr. Burkell was fit to stand trial. We never claimed he was insane. He didn't talk much, so how could I determine if he was able to cooperate with his defense? We do know the police removed a large quantity of medications from his home, some of them antidepressants and other substances used to treat mental illness."

McBride had a habit of stalling as long as possible, hoping the case would magically go away or she could pressure the DA into negotiating a settlement. Getting Lily to agree to ship Burkell to Vacaville for a ninety-day diagnostic was a coup. Lily wished she'd never allowed it. In arguments, McBride wore her down. When she had worked with her as a prosecutor, she had gone home every night with a blinding headache. The attorney's voice fell somewhere between a whine and a barking Doberman. It didn't help that she looked like a witch. Her black hair, obviously dyed, was stringy, and she favored black suits or dresses, probably because they didn't show stains. And she wondered why the defendant wouldn't talk to her.

Lily saw Silverstein out of the corner of her eye. He'd been getting his damn hair permed, and it looked like straw. Light a match, and the man would go up in flames. Silverstein claimed he didn't have time to mess with his hair, and having a perm made it easier. To be fair, the same probably held true with Judith McBride. The criminal justice system was so hopelessly bogged down, the people who held all the pieces together had become slaves instead of public servants.

Lily heard a noise in the rear of the room and saw the person in the red-and-white-striped shirt heading for the exit. It had to be a guy. The dress and walk were too masculine. She shoved the microphone aside and gestured for the bailiff, leaning to one side and whispering, "See if you can find out who that man was that just left."

"What man?" Leonard Davis said, his eyes roaming around the courtroom.

"It might have been a woman."

A tall, stick-thin man in his late twenties, Davis had relocated to California from Wyoming, where he claimed he'd been a champion bull rider. He could barely sit in the chair, let alone on a bull. He either had his thumbs tucked into the belt loops of his pants, or his hand resting on the butt of his gun.

The bailiff rocked back on his heels. "No one here, Judge, just attorneys and one bad guy. I mean, except for you, me, Susie, and the court reporter."

"Aren't you supposed to keep track of what goes on in

this courtroom? Forget it." Idiot, Lily thought, returning her attention to the matter at hand. Not only had she drawn the worst office, they'd assigned her a comic book character for a bailiff. "Your motion to have the defendant reevaluated is denied, Ms. McBride. If you will recall, you're the one who advised this court that you believed there was a competency issue, or this case would have already been resolved. I won't allow you to delay these proceedings any longer. The defendant has a right to due process, and he's already been in custody for ninety days. Have you agreed upon—"

"Ninety days and they did nothing," the public defender blurted out, crossing her arms over her chest.

Lily leveled a finger at her, her temper flaring. "You're close to being thrown out of this courtroom, Counselor."

She cackled. "I'd never be that lucky."

"If you ever interrupt me again, I'll remand you to jail." Lily waited so the public defender would know she was serious, then continued, "Now, as I was saying, have both parties agreed on a trial date?"

The two attorneys finally coughed up the date and Lily asked Susie to see if it would fit into her calendar. If it didn't, they would have to shop for a mutually agreeable date again. When Susie nodded at her, she said, "Jury selection will begin on December twenty-sixth at nine o'clock in the morning."

Judith McBride scowled, then spat out, "I'd like to petition the court to consider bail, Your Honor. My client is a local businessman, owns his own home, and has strong ties to the community. He has no prior criminal record, so it's unlikely he would flee."

"I don't agree," Lily said, incredulous. "The police captured him two blocks from the scene covered in the blood of the victims. I consider that a demonstrated attempt to flee."

"We acknowledge that," McBride went on without faltering. "The defendant was in shock. He'd just walked in and found both his wife and son murdered. How did he know the killer wasn't still in the area? Any man would flee under the circumstances."

"The people strongly object," Silverstein said, fiddling with a button on his jacket. "A bail review was already considered and denied when Mr. Burkell was arraigned on these heinous crimes. The defendant is a dangerous, violent offender who poses a grave risk to the community."

"Bail is denied." Lily scribbled her ruling in the file and handed it back to the clerk. "There were no incident reports from Vacaville, Ms. McBride. The defendant's conduct appears to have been exemplary. To address your concerns, however, I've ordered that the defendant be sent to the infirmary. The jail physician will determine if Mr. Burkell requires medication."

Burkell's expression changed. Had Judith promised she could get him off? He looked so tragic, a disturbing thought passed through Lily's mind. Was it possible he was innocent? Maybe he *had* come home that day and found his wife and son butchered. The evidence was overwhelming, though, and it would be up to the jury to decide. Lily's greatest impact would occur at the sentencing hearing. She reached for her gavel, then quickly pulled her hand back. Unless all hell broke out, only rookie judges and actors used their gavels. The two attorneys were already packing their briefcases and the bailiff was escorting Burkell back to the holding cell. Lily merely left the courtroom and headed down the back corridor to her chambers. Being a judge was beginning to lose its luster.

QUANTICO, VIRGINIA

One of the reasons John Adams had brought Mary on board was her excellent track record in solving homicides, as well as her easygoing manner, which he felt would help her stay emotionally afloat while dealing with the world's most evil and prolific criminals.

Adams had also hoped Mary had inherited her father's intuition. The two men had served together in Vietnam, and remained friends until her father's death nine years ago. Harold Stevens had risen to deputy chief at the LAPD before he'd been gunned down by an armed robber at a Quick Mart. Her breath still caught in her throat when she thought about it. All he'd done was stop to buy a bottle of wine for her mother. According to Adams and the other vets who'd served in the same platoon as her father, Stevens had a sixth sense and could spot friend or foe only seconds after making visual contact.

Mary removed the earphones from her iPod and plugged them into the tape recorder, then inserted the cassette and pushed play. A male voice began speaking. No, she thought, it appeared to be a female. She hit stop and replaced the batteries, hoping that would fix the problem. When the eerie voice began again, she held her breath as she tried to identify the unsettling nuances in the person's speech.

"I find it insulting that the FBI doesn't know about me. I've killed so many over such a long period of time."

The hair pricked on the back of Mary's neck. She sat at rapt attention.

"I've sent this recording for two reasons. First, many of the victims' loved ones are waiting in limbo, and second, to save you the effort of profiling me. I'm sure there are others more worthy of your talents, like the monsters who abuse and kill children. Everyone I kill deserves to die. I do not kill innocent people."

She hit the stop button, then rubbed the goose bumps on her arms. The tape was more than likely a prank. A lot of people were upset that Adams had selected her over agents with more time at the Bureau. She saw the looks they gave her. For all she knew, someone inside the agency could have made the tape to make her run to Adams and look ridiculous.

She played it again and realized why the voice sounded so strange. It appeared to be a myriad of voices. She recalled the days when she'd taught Sunday school at Trinity Baptist Church in Los Angeles before she'd become jaded, and the passage in Mark where Jesus met a man possessed of demons. The quote seemed to apply: "My name is legend and we are many."

Mary believed in evil. No one could work this job and deny such a thing existed. The FBI's Behavioral Analysis Unit exposed her to far more than her previous position as a homicide detective in Ventura, as every awful crime in the world was brought to their doorstep.

The more she thought of it, the tape reminded her of ransom notes where the kidnapper used words clipped from newspapers and magazines. The only difference here was the killer was using audio clips. How could this be a prank? Then again, what were the chances of her getting a tape from an unknown serial killer?

EIGHT

❧

MONDAY, NOVEMBER 27
VENTURA, CALIFORNIA

Lily met her husband that evening for dinner at Mario's, their favorite Italian restaurant. Mario's was small, but it had outside dining. After being cramped up all day in the courthouse, fresh air was a delicacy. Knowing the temperature would drop as the evening went on, she had worn her jacket. How could she complain about weather when most of the world was already experiencing cold temperatures?

Bryce was waiting at the table. He stood and rushed around to pull out her chair. He didn't reek of booze, so she gave him a quick peck on the lips. "Awfully suave tonight, aren't we? You must have landed a big account."

"How was your day?"

"Oh, you know," she said, making a wavy motion with her hand. She certainly didn't want to linger on that topic. After her afternoon session, she'd gone to the bathroom and vomited. Knowing her husband liked to talk, she said, "Isn't it strange how few restaurants there are with outside dining around here?"

He rubbed his thumb and his forefinger together. "You're talking money, honey. A person might need some clout as well. Look where you're sitting. On the sidewalk, sweetie. They don't hand out those kind of permits to just anyone. Did you get to the gym today?"

"Yes," Lily said offhandedly, her conversation with Anne almost forgotten. A crisp breeze caressed her face. Maybe if she sat there long enough, she wouldn't feel so panicked. She watched Bryce flip his tie over his shoulder as he began soaking the fresh-baked garlic bread in peppered olive oil. By the time the meal arrived, he would have emptied several bread baskets.

Just when she was beginning to feel better, her afternoon session crept back into her mind. The parents of a nine-year-old boy were charged with intentionally overdosing him with psychotropic medication, ultimately causing his death. The greater issue at stake was whether or not a child that young could be definitively diagnosed with a mental illness. The victim, Brian Stucky, had been labeled manic-depressive by a child psychiatrist.

"You're handling the Stucky murder," Bryce commented, a trickle of olive oil running down his chin. "I read in the paper this morning that the trial was starting today. It would have been nice if you'd said something to me. A lot of people are following that case."

"You know I don't like to talk about my work."

"Every medical professional and teacher who came in contact with that kid should be prosecuted," he told her, unfurling his white cloth napkin and wiping his mouth and chin. "If you ask me, the shrink should be on trial. I hate psychiatrists. Half of the people in nuthouses don't belong there. Shit, the real nutcases are sleeping on the streets. My cousin, Ben, had a mental problem and they gave him that kind of medicine. That's serious stuff. How could anyone give that to a little kid?" He peered through the glass to the interior of the restaurant. "When is the waiter going to bring our wine? That's the problem when you eat on the patio at this place. They forget about you."

Lily glanced over her shoulder, hoping the waiter would arrive before Bryce insisted they leave. He must be making an attempt to bring his drinking under control. She had never seen him drink wine except after three or four gin and tonics. She decided to break her rules and discuss the case in an attempt to distract him. "The boy's teacher testified today. She admitted that he seemed out of it for several weeks, but she didn't think it was important enough to notify the parents or the school authorities. Of course, notifying the parents would have accomplished nothing." She paused and rested her head on her fist. "It's terrible when the people who are supposed to love you decide to dispose of you."

"If these assholes are convicted, they'll get the death penalty, right?"

"No," Lily answered, pausing as the waiter filled their

wine glasses. Bryce knew next to nothing about the criminal justice system, and she had no desire to educate him. She suspected it was one of the reasons she'd agreed to marry him. That and the fact that he was an atheist, which meant she didn't have to go to church and be reminded of her eternal damnation. "Did you call me today?"

"Yes, I did, Lily," he said. "And you never called me back. I guess you were too busy."

Bryce was an advertising executive at Dunlap and Walker. She could listen to him recount the various machinations in the world of advertising without thinking, relaxing her overtaxed mind as he chattered away. "How's that big account you've been trying to steal? Wasn't it a hot dog company?"

"Veggie burgers. No one eats hot dogs these days except kids and fat guys like me."

Bryce stood six-one and weighed two hundred and forty pounds. His round face was tan from the golf course, and his stomach spilled over his slacks from too many lunches with clients. At forty-nine, he had already been told he had coronary artery disease, but he refused to adjust his diet. He was a man's man, the type who believed you lived life to the fullest regardless of the consequences. "Don't try to change the subject, Lily. Why won't these people fry for killing their kid?"

Hmm, Lily thought, he's actually interested in this case. She wondered if it was because the victim was a child, or due to the extensive media coverage it was receiving. She knew he told his clients she was a judge, and he'd obviously let it be known that she was sitting the Elizabeth and Ronald Stucky murder trial. A person in high-level sales would use anything he could to impress a client and close a deal.

Bryce was already on his third glass of wine, and she'd only finished half of hers. She wished he'd go to AA, but she knew he'd blow up if she so much as brought up the subject. If she couldn't get him to stop eating steaks and mounds of butter to keep him from dropping dead of a heart attack, she certainly couldn't get him to stop drinking.

"Bryce, the Stuckys can't get the death penalty because they're not being charged with first-degree murder. Proving premeditation would be too difficult in this case."

"I don't see why," he argued. "The people intended to murder their kid or he wouldn't be dead. If a person puts poison in someone's food day after day until he dies, that's premeditation. I admit I don't have a big legal brain like yours, but it seems pretty clear to me."

"This isn't poison," Lily told him, buttoning up her jacket. "The boy was killed by legally prescribed medication. The Stuckys' attorney claims they mistook the dosage, then simply kept on giving him the same amount. Another thing that will muddy the waters is the fact that the parents say they switched off giving the boy his medication. A jury may believe only one of them is responsible and, not knowing which, may render a not-guilty verdict on both. Their attorney should have insisted they be tried separately."

Bryce had already lost interest. His eyes were feasting on the platter of food on the way to their table.

"I have a lot of reading to do tonight," Lily said, deciding to tell him while he was still salivating over his linguini. "How about you, honey? Do you have any work you need to catch up on?"

"I thought we were going to spend time together tonight. Whether you realize it or not, we haven't had sex in over a month."

Lily sighed, watching the evening sunlight reflect off the cars on the street in front of the restaurant. She was thankful Monday was slow and there was no one within earshot. Did she really have to work tonight, or was she purposely avoiding him? There was a wall between her and Bryce, a wall she had purposely erected. He would never understand her because she had never told him that she and Shana were raped, let alone that she had killed a man under the belief that he was the rapist. She knew it was wrong to conceal such a monumental event in her life, but she refused to live with a man who perceived her as a victim.

"Did you hear what I said, Lily?"

"I'm sorry, Bryce." Because he didn't know about the rape, they had managed to have a fairly normal sex life. She didn't realize so much time had passed since they'd been together. "I should be finished by eleven."

He had an annoyed look on his face as he shoveled food into his mouth. Reaching for the wine bottle, he poured the remaining drops into his glass and sucked them down. "Eleven is too late."

"You're not a child," Lily told him, rolling her pasta on her fork. "You can stay up until midnight now and then. Friday and Saturday, you didn't come home until three in the morning. If you can stay up drinking with your golf buddies, why can't you stay up tonight?"

"I have to get up at four-thirty during the week so I can get a workout in. Then I have to fight the 405 traffic to L.A. If we moved closer to my job, I could get up at a reasonable hour. I know you wanted to keep my dad's place and all, but my job sucks the life out of me." He reached up and loosened his tie, his face flushed now. "You don't know what it's like, Lily. I kiss ass for a living, okay, not the same as sitting on a podium and having people do whatever you ask. Every day I have to engage customers in lively conversation, tell jokes like a comedian, and bust my butt to convince them that their sales will go through the roof because of my brilliant, dazzling ideas. Advertising guys like me are dirt to these people, just someone to entertain them and pick up the check. You're a judge now, though. You took the job without even asking me." He paused and stared out over the room, more sad than angry. "Sometimes I wonder."

Lily dropped her fork back on the plate. She hated emotional confrontations. She had back-to-back trials, and couldn't afford to deplete herself with Bryce's alcohol-induced ramblings. "What do you wonder?"

He blinked several times, hesitating. "If we really have a marriage. You seem to be married to your work. I feel like I'm nothing more than a convenience to you."

She made certain the tables behind her were still empty before speaking. "I waited all my life to become a judge," she said, leaning forward over the table. "I'm a complicated woman, Bryce. I told you that when we got married. I refuse to represent criminals. I'm not a domestic attorney, nor do I have any experience in personal injury. Besides, there's an overabundance of attorneys right now and they're fighting for every penny. Establishing a private practice takes years." She stopped and took a breath. She knew she was marching straight into a fight, but she couldn't stop herself. "You swore you wanted me to be happy, that living in Ventura wasn't a problem. I left the DA's office in Santa Barbara so we could be together. Ventura was our compromise. Are you going back on your word now?"

He saw how agitated she was becoming. "Give me your hand," he said, reaching across the table. "I'm sorry, honey. I shouldn't have said anything. I'm just not used to being . . . well, for lack of a better word, so unimportant."

She extended her hand until she touched his fingertips. "That's not true, Bryce. I adore you. Outside of Shana, you're the most important person in my life. I'm just overwhelmed right now. We'll spend our time together tonight like I promised. I can catch up on my reading after you go to sleep. How does that sound?"

"You sure?" he said, his face softening. "I didn't mean to cause an argument. I know your job is stressful, too."

"Maybe you can alleviate some of my stress," Lily said, smiling seductively. "Since your plate looks pretty clean, let's stop wasting time and get out of here. I'm not really that hungry."

Bryce stood, stuffing his hand in his pocket and tossing some bills down on the table, not waiting for their server to bring him the check. He started to leave, then grabbed her face and kissed her. "See you at the house."

They had arrived in separate cars and Lily was parked in the back lot, whereas Bryce had found a parking spot on the street. She ducked into the restroom, used the facilities, and then stared at her image in the mirror. Her past and her problems were beginning to show up on her face. She would wake up in the morning with a crease, and think it had something to do with the way she had slept, only to discover that it was permanent. What made it worse was the huge number of women routinely undergoing plastic surgery. Women in their seventies now looked as young as she did.

But it was more than her face. She complained Bryce didn't take care of his health when she seldom gave any thought to her own. Being slender didn't mean anything. She hadn't been to a doctor for a checkup in five years. She might have breast cancer, for all she knew, or some other dreadful disease. Stress itself killed people. The blood in her veins was probably as hard as concrete. She had pains in her chest all the time. She simply ignored them, chalking them up to heartburn.

Exiting through the back door of the restaurant, she unlocked her car and slid behind the wheel. Before he'd started drinking, Bryce had been a fun-loving, adorable teddy bear, who always had a smile on his face and constantly told how much he loved her. She wasn't sure if his present insecurities were a result of his progressing from a social drinker to an alcoholic, or if they had developed due to her appointment to the bench. It was only a job, but some people acted like she'd been made queen, complete with her own kingdom.

Bryce wouldn't be insecure if he knew how desperately she needed him. She couldn't be alone. When her daughter had lived with her, it had been easier to keep her emotions on an even keel. After John's murder, Shana had got her undergraduate degree from UCLA, then decided to attend law school at Stanford, which was located near San Francisco. Their relationship had been reduced to phone calls and occasional weekend visits. Bryce was even jealous of the time she spent on the phone with Shana. She had tried to talk her daughter into spending more time with her, but Ventura held too many bad memories. She never should have let Bryce talk her into leaving Santa Barbara.

Turning the key in the ignition, Lily took the side streets to their home in the foothills. She wasn't paying attention and almost drove through a red light. Slamming on the brakes, she reminded herself why she had married Bryce. She'd just ended her relationship with Richard Fowler, after he'd broken her heart for the umpteenth time. Since his first wife had left him for another woman, it was understandable that he feared commitment. But he had constantly told her he loved her, and made promises he evidently had no intentions of keeping. No matter how shattered she'd been, there were other reasons their relationship would have never worked. Unlike her husband, Richard knew everything. How could a man spend the rest of his life with a woman he knew had gotten away with murder? On the other hand, how could a woman trust a man who could destroy her?

Shana was a strong woman like her mother, her well-spring of strength forged from adversity. Even before the rape, she'd demanded Lily's complete attention. The rare occasions when she visited usually started well, yet always seemed to end in a shouting match. Shana would say something rude to Bryce and he would retaliate. One time she'd called him a blubber belly, and he had accused her of being anorexic. He thought Shana was a spoiled, arrogant young woman. In a way, he was right. John had indulged her every whim. After the rape, Lily had done everything humanly possible to give the girl a normal life. But Shana had eventually run back to her father.

Ironically, her marriage to Bryce was showing some of the same strains she'd experienced with John: his jealousy, Bryce's belief that she overshadowed him professionally, his inability to accept the demands of her work. She began to drift into the past again, to the night her marriage to Shana's father had ended.

Lily parked and jumped out of her car, her heels sinking in dirt as she hurried to the baseball field where Shana's team was playing. She linked her fingers through the wire fence as she watched, hoping she wasn't too late to see her pitch. The short brunette at bat swung and connected; the parents in the stands screamed as she raced the short distance to first base. The next batter hit the ball as well, but was tagged at first base. The game was over and Shana's team had won.

The girls moved to the dugout, the majority getting as close to Shana as possible. Postgame activity had changed since the year before. Instead of going for the cookies and sodas the team mother provided, a number of girls were taking out brushes and lipsticks from their purses.

John infiltrated the group of girls, putting both hands

around Shana's waist and lifting her into the air. "I'm so proud of you." They both saw Lily a few feet away and smiled. They weren't smiling at her. Lily knew they were flaunting their closeness, showing her that this was their private moment, one they didn't care to share. Placing Shana back on the ground, John stared straight at Lily and draped his arm over his daughter's shoulder, walking with her the short distance to the dugout. He glanced back to see if Lily was still watching, the other girls crowding around John now as well as Shana. Lily winced, locking her fingers on the wire fence. They both looked away.

A few minutes later, John headed her direction, stooping to pick up a few bats on the way. The baseball cap made thick crevices appear on his forehead. At forty-seven, he was eleven years older than his wife. Even though his hair was thinning to the point where more scalp showed than hair, he was still an attractive man, with a robust laugh and a bright smile, displaying rows of even white teeth in his tan and masculine face. His expression was not pleasant, though, nor was it the adoring look reserved for his daughter.

"Made it, huh?" he said flatly, tipping his baseball cap back on his head. "Managed to pry yourself away to catch the last five minutes of the game. You sure you're not missing something at the office? I mean, you don't want your family to get in the way of your big ambitions to be a judge."

"Stop it," Lily said. "I'll take Shana home in my car." She turned and plodded through the dirt in the direction of the dugout.

Shana's face was flushed with excitement. She stood almost a head above most of the other girls. Her long red hair had more gold tones in it than Lily's, and she wore it in a ponytail pulled through the back of her baseball cap.

Her wide-set eyes were such a deep shade of sapphire that they almost matched the navy blue lettering on her uniform. High, pronounced cheekbones gave her face an ethereal, elegant quality far beyond her years. With the right makeup, clothes, and photographer, Shana's face could be on the cover of next month's Vogue *or* Cosmopolitan.

One girl followed as she broke away and headed for the car. "Call me in thirty minutes," Shana told her. Once they were home, the phone in her room would ring for the next hour, each girl calling at whatever time Shana had specified.

"Oh, this is my mom. Mom, this is Sally."

Sally stood there with her mouth gaping. "You look so much alike. I can't believe it."

Shana got into the car and slammed the door, her eyes cutting to her mother with resentment. Lily was hurt when she acted like this; Shana had always been so proud that they looked alike. She used to tell Lily how all her friends thought her mother was so pretty. Lily remembered how she'd gaze up at her and ask if she'd be as tall when she grew up. Last week, Shana had screamed at her that she was a giraffe, the tallest girl in school, and ended the tirade by saying it was Lily's fault.

She tried to start a conversation. "That was a great job of pitching out there. Sorry I didn't get to see more of the game. I rushed, but the traffic was awful." Shana stared straight ahead, refusing to respond. Lily swallowed hard. "How was school?"

"Fine."

"Do you have much homework?"

"Done."

"Want to go roller-skating with me Sunday?"

"I practice softball every day and have gym class. I don't need any more exercise."

"How about the mall?"

"I thought I was grounded." She shot Lily another look full of animosity. "Can Charlotte and Sally go?"

"No, I want to spend time with you alone. I don't want to spend time with Charlotte and Sally. Besides, where is my top you loaned Charlotte without my permission?"

"Don't worry, you'll get your precious top back. I just forgot. Chill out, Mom, you're driving me crazy." With this last statement her voice went high and shrill. Then something appeared to come to mind and she turned to her mother with a sweet smile and a sugarcoated tone. "I need a new outfit. There's a dance in the gym next week."

Here we go, Lily thought, feeling the burning in her chest again. In desperation she had found herself recently doing something she despised. She'd started buying Shana things in the past year or so just to get that one little smile. As a parent, she was on an emotional seesaw. One minute she tried to uphold her long-standing rules and restrictions, then everything fell away. To compete with John, who had convinced Shana that her mother was an uncaring and absentee parent, she had to play a new game, his game. His game was to constantly shower Shana with praise and give in to her every demand, even when she did something wrong. He didn't care that Shana took her mother's things without asking and had other girls clean her room and do her homework. Would he also look away if she later began using drugs and having sex with boys?

"I just bought you all those things two weeks ago, Shana. Can't you wear one of those to the dance?"

"MOM . . . I've already worn them to school. I can't wear them to the dance."

"We'll see," Lily said, pacifying.

Shana stared out the passenger window.

"So, what else is going on? Any gossip?"

"I started my period today."

Lily was excited and it showed. Shana rolled her eyes around in disbelief at her excitement. This was something strictly feminine, something they could share. They could go home and lock themselves in the bedroom and talk the way they'd used to years ago. "I knew you'd start any day now. Didn't I tell you that I started at your age? That's why you've been so moody. I was, too. It's normal. You're a real woman now. Do you have cramps? How do you feel? We'll stop at the drugstore. What are you wearing now?" Lily knew she was rattling on, but she didn't care. This could be a new beginning for them.

"Dad already got me some pads today."

Lily's knuckles turned white on the steering wheel. She took her foot off the gas, and the car came to an abrupt stop in the suburban traffic. Cars honked and then drove around her. She turned to Shana. "You could have called me at work and told me. Why didn't you? Why are you shutting me out of your life?" She had to hear the words; like a masochist, she sought the pain.

"Dad said you were too busy and that you'd be mad if I bothered you."

The words "Dad already got me some pads today" were ringing in her ears; now they were joined by "Dad said you were too busy." In the act of not sharing that one historically female moment, the rite of passage, and the fact that Shana could go to her father without embarrassment, her daughter had destroyed her.

They drove home in silence.

John arrived home shortly after Lily and Shana. Located in what once had been the farming community of Camarillo, twenty minutes from Ventura, the house was a spacious twenty-year-old ranch with paned windows. John went and made a bowl of ice cream for himself and Shana, then carried her dish to her bedroom. Shana was inside with the door shut. John walked in, handed the bowl to her, and started to walk out. Shana reached up without looking and tugged lightly on his shirt, chatting away on the phone. When he bent down near her face, she kissed him on the mouth and immediately returned to her conversation. He smiled and left, returning to the family room to eat his ice cream in front of the television. Lily was standing in the hall. She stepped back, glaring at him. Then she went to take a shower. They did this after every game, and John had never once asked Lily if she wanted a bowl of ice cream.

Standing in the bathroom fully clothed, Lily stared at her reflection in the mirror. She was an unwanted intruder—an outcast in her own home. Without her salary, they couldn't even afford this house. Without all the late nights and hard work and the stress that had put years on her face. John just wanted to punch a time clock, collect his check, coach softball, watch television, and hang out with their daughter. When they did talk, which was rare, he wanted to talk about aliens and life after death, things that delineated the world he lived in from the stark reality of Lily's world.

She walked into the den and looked at him on the sofa. "Can we turn the television off? I want to talk."

John jumped up. "I just remembered. Shana has the cramps, poor baby, and I told her I'd bring her some Tylenol." He headed to the kitchen cabinet.

Lily grabbed the two pills out of his hand and snapped, "I'll take her the Tylenol, then I'll meet you in the backyard. I want to talk." In the backyard, Shana wouldn't be able to hear them. At least on one issue they agreed: not arguing in front of their daughter.

Lily opened Shana's door. She was still on the phone, sitting on the floor in a corner, so much junk on her bed there was nowhere else to sit. "Please get off the phone now and go to bed. You'll never get up in the morning."

The phone was left on its side as Shana strode over to her mother. "I'll get off in just a minute."

"I brought you a few Tylenol for the cramps."

"Did you bring me any water?"

"The bathroom is just two feet away, Shana. Look. See, it's still there."

"Dad, bring me a glass of water on your way," she yelled.

John entered the room as Lily was leaving. She stood with her back to the hall wall and listened to the two of them talking, discussing the game, her father bragging about how well she'd pitched. She could tell Shana was standing on her toes and hugging him around the neck as she did every night, kissing him tenderly on the cheek. He walked out the door and saw Lily standing there, her hands crossed over her chest. He waited for her to pass and followed her into the backyard.

John took a seat in the lounger. Lily sat in a nylon chair across from him. The only light was from the neighboring house, the only noise their television heard through an open window. The amber end of his cigarette reminded her of the fireflies she used to chase as a child, sometimes capturing one in a jar.

"Where were you last night?" he said.

"I told Shana to tell you, but I guess you never woke up." Lily was thankful for the darkness, that he couldn't see her face. She'd always been a poor liar. He had once told her that whenever she lied, her nostrils flared.

"I saw you," he said, his voice a mixture of anger and sadness.

Lily rubbed her arms in the damp night air, his words playing in her mind. She laughed nervously. Surely he didn't mean what she thought he meant. "Oh, really," she said, "and what exactly did you see?"

He was silent, then he repeated himself. "I saw you."

"Look, John, don't play games with me. What are you talking about?"

"I want you to move out." He stood and the voice now was all bitterness, the voice of a man to be reckoned with. "Did you hear me? I want you out of this house by tomorrow."

He was standing over Lily and she looked up in the dark, her eyes following the glowing end of his cigarette as he flicked it into the flower bed. She waited for it to explode like a firecracker, counting the seconds. She thought of spontaneous combustion, her body erupting into flames, burning from the inside out. His arm was flying toward her, a night bird, a bat, the sound of his shirt wings flapping, the slap across her face the dreaded collision. "Move in with your boyfriend, the guy you were making out with last night in the parking lot!"

Lily caught his arm in an iron grip. In front of her she saw an enormous stack of white dishes crashing to the ground, the shattered pieces flying through the air. "You want me to move out?" she screamed. "You disgusting piece of shit. You think I want to spend the rest of my life with you, working my ass off while you lounge around in front of the television and turn my own daughter against me?"

He yanked his arm away. "I never turned Shana against you. You're just too busy with your cases and your career to pay attention to your child." He was spitting the words out between clenched teeth, his chest heaving.

"What do you suggest? That I quit my job? That we go on welfare so we can both be here every minute in case Shana needs a glass of water? You've spoiled her rotten, John. She was a beautiful girl and now she's a disrespectful, demanding brat." She stopped, regretting her last

statement. "Now you're probably going to run in there and tell Shana what I said. Don't you realize that you hurt her, too, when you do this, repeat things I say to you in private? Go ahead. Tell her. I don't give a shit anymore."

Lily stepped back and collided with one of the nylon lawn chairs. With one hand she seized the chair and threw it onto the dirt side of the yard. "Look at the yard, John. You don't even see that one side is dirt. It doesn't bother you at all that you were too lazy to finish it. You only see what you want to see."

"You're a slut, a whore. You let that man use you like a prostitute."

Her voice lowered to a controlled level. "Like a receptacle, John? Is that what you meant to say? That I let him use me like a receptacle?" He didn't answer. "Maybe if you were a man and treated me like a woman, a wife, then I wouldn't have needed another man." She stepped closer, inches from his face. "You know, John, people have sex, married people, and for more reasons than just making babies." Her voice rose again and she yelled. "They have it because it feels good, because it's normal."

He was shaking, moving back away from her. "You're sick, Lily. You're not fit to be a mother." He turned and started walking toward the back door.

"I want a husband, John, not a wife."

He slammed the door and left her there in the yard. The neighbor's dog was barking at the commotion. Her breath was coming slower now. The tempest was over. She felt a lightness in her body, a floating sensation. She was finally going to be free. The only problem was Shana.

Walking down the hall, she saw the light under the girl's door. She opened it and saw Shana cramming pa-

pers from the top of her bed back into a spiral notebook.
"Can I come in for a few minutes?"

She saw the expression on her mother's face and said,
"Sure. Have you and Dad been fighting? I thought I heard
yelling out there."

"Yes." Lily turned her head, hoping Shana wouldn't
see the red handprint on her cheek. *"Can we turn the*
light out and get in bed the way we used to when you were
little?"

"Yeah, sure." Shana flicked off the light and climbed
into bed on the side nearest the wall. *"What's going on?"*

"Your father and I are going to get a divorce, honey,"
Lily said, sniffing in the darkness and feeling the wet tears
run down her face. She had felt so good in the yard; it was
what she wanted, but now she was terrified. *"Things have*
been bad for a long time. You know that."

"Will we be poor now? Sally's parents got divorced
and she says they're poor."

"I guarantee you won't be poor, Shana, even if I have to
work a second job. I love you, sweetheart. I'll always pro-
vide for you, and I'll always be here for you."

Shana sat up in the bed, her voice thin and cracking.
"Where will we live if you and Dad get divorced? We
won't be a family anymore."

Lily sat up, too, and reached for her, but she pulled
away. *"We'll always be a family, Shana. I'll always be*
your mother, and Dad will always be your father. We both
love you very much."

"I can't believe this is happening to me. I can't believe
you're doing this to me." She began sobbing. *"Today.*
You're doing this today."

The fact that she'd started her period for the first time
surfaced in Lily's mind. She fell back onto the small bed.
Shana would remember this day for the rest of her life.

"Please, honey, try to understand. I know it's hard. I just can't live with your father anymore. I wanted to wait until you were out of high school, but—"

Shana cut her off. *"Then why don't you?"*

"Because I can't take it anymore. Because I'm too old to wait that long. If we do it now, we both have a chance to find something else in our life."

Shana leaned back next to Lily, still sniffling. *"You mean another man? Find another man?"*

"Possibly, or your dad might find another woman who'll make him happy."

Shana was silent, thinking. Lily continued, *"One of us has to move out. Too many bad things were said tonight. Dad wants me to move out. I have a right to stay here, Shana, and things might be different if it was just the two of us. You know, sometimes when I go to my room or stay late at the office, it's because I don't want to be around your father. I mean, you stay in your room all the time and he sleeps on the couch. Try to see my side just once."*

"I want to stay here with Dad."

Lily felt her heart sink. She should have known it would be this way. She got up and turned the light on, sat on the edge of the bed, and wiped a tear off her cheek. *"Why? What is it I've done wrong, Shana? What haven't I done? Tell me."*

Shana reached for a tissue off the nightstand, blowing her nose. *"Dad loves me more than you do."*

Resentment rose in Lily's throat. *"That isn't true. No matter what your father has told you, it simply isn't true. You know what it is, it's because he gives in to you more, waits on you more, never demands anything from you or disciplines you. Isn't it?"*

Shana's blue eyes drifted around the room before coming back to rest on her mother. *"Maybe."*

What could Lily say? The girl had answered honestly.

She stood and was leaving when Shana spoke up. "You can sleep with me, Mom. Turn out the light."

Back in bed, Shana moved close and put her head on Lily's shoulder. "I do love you, Mom. I just want to live with Dad. You know?"

"I know," Lily said. "I know."

NINE

∼

MONDAY, NOVEMBER 27
VENTURA, CALIFORNIA

Lily surfaced from the past. Judge Hennessey's remarks had made her furious, but overall, he had spoken the truth. She could never show lenience to a violent sex offender. More importantly, she had stepped outside the boundaries of the law and taken a life. When she'd finally returned home the morning after the rape, two police cars had been parked in front. Without knowledge of the jeopardy he was putting her in, John had changed his mind and decided to report the rape.

Lily's height, at five-ten, and her makeshift disguise, coupled with the altered license plate, had kept the police from apprehending her. Bruce Cunningham, an Oxnard homicide detective, had finally closed in on her. But in the end, his disgust with the system, and his compassion for what Lily and Shana had been through, had led the detective to the decision that justice would not be served by sending Lily to prison. He would be robbing a child of her mother at a time when she needed her the most, something Cunningham could not bring himself to do.

Bobby Hernandez, the man Lily had killed, had been one of the five men who'd committed the most heinous crime in the history of Ventura, the meaningless slaughter of a young high school couple. Nothing could justify a person taking the law into her own hands, and the awful fact that Lily had to live with was Hernandez had not been the rapist! She could have just as easily killed an innocent person.

Lily turned into her driveway, then parked and stared out the window. Shana was doing remarkably well, considering the horrors she'd been forced to endure. At the age of twelve, just days after she'd reached puberty, the most sensitive time in a girl's life, Marco Curazon had brutally raped her alongside her mother. But as Lily had feared all along, one of the reasons she'd decided to track down the rapist and kill him, was Shana's nightmare had not ended with Curazon's capture and imprisonment.

John had made a very poor decision, refusing to pay for an unlisted number. He hadn't known Shana was going to move back in with him again, though, nor could he fathom that the rapist might come for Shana when he was paroled from prison. Normal people had short memories. Imprisoned sex offenders did not, and were known to return and reenact their crimes with the same victims, sometimes on more than one occasion. Fortunately for Shana, she was not there the day Curazon found his way to her home. Instead, he had run into John in the garage and killed him.

Now that Marco Curazon was on death row, Shana could finally make an attempt to put the past behind her. But getting to this point had not been easy, and Lily had struggled alongside her daughter.

Although it might be no more than a figment of her imagination, Lily wanted to believe that she was exactly where she was supposed to be—in a position to punish the individuals who committed acts of violence and wreaked havoc on society. Should she be a judge? Obviously not, but who was better equipped to understand both criminals and victims?

Lily's stance on crime was simple—show lenience toward individuals who committed crimes against property: the thieves, burglars, addicts, prostitutes, and drug offenders. She had no choice, as there wasn't enough room to warehouse them in the prison system. Criminals who murdered, raped, and physically abused children should be shown no mercy.

And if any crime was serious enough to warrant the death penalty, Lily would do everything in her power to make certain it was imposed. Sentencing a man to death was a lot easier than tracking him down with a shotgun.

She parked the Volvo in the garage and entered the house. Bryce and Lily resided in an older three-story home in the foothills of Ventura. The property had been constructed on the edge of a cliff to take advantage of the ocean views. The problem was they were directly above the 101 freeway, and commercial buildings had been erected that eliminated their view of the ocean from every room except the library. Surrounded by lush foliage, the lot was two-tiered, and Bryce wanted to put in a swimming pool on the lower level. Lily had finally knocked some sense into him. The area had flooded several years back, and a number of nearby homes had slid off the cliff, one of them with the occupants still inside.

The house had previously belonged to Bryce's father, an orthopedic surgeon. Dr. Collin Donnelly had used it as a weekend retreat from his primary home in Brentwood. Bryce's mother had died when Bryce was a boy, and his father had never remarried. His father passed away six months before they met, and Lily regretted not being able to meet him.

Since Bryce was an only child, he was the sole heir to

his father's estate. He had intended to sell the Ventura property, as he had Dr. Donnelly's other real estate holdings. When Lily saw the house, she knew it was where she wanted to live.

She had met Bryce at the Sea Shell, a casual seafood restaurant located on the pier in Santa Barbara. She was rebounding from her toxic affair with Richard Fowler, and Bryce claimed he fell in love with her the second he saw her, which she seriously doubted. Since Bryce was living in a condo in Century City and Lily was a prosecutor in Santa Barbara, it was amazing that their relationship had gotten off the ground. But Bryce had gone to extremes to win her over. Every chance he got, he would make the long drive from Los Angeles to Santa Barbara. When he was pressed for time, he'd jump on a commuter plane out of LAX and Lily would pick him up at the Santa Barbara airport.

Those were happy times. Bryce would be jumping out of his skin to be with Lily, and she was excited as well. They would drive straight to her house, where they'd make mad love until all hours of the night. He was gregarious, and Lily loved him for it. Bryce had given her back something she'd lost, the desire to live life to the fullest. He joyfully consumed everything: food, laughter, sex, booze, people, and money. They had occasionally gone on wild shopping sprees, buying thousands of dollars' worth in a few short hours. But the seriousness of Lily's new position as a judge had curbed their childlike behavior.

Bryce had married right out of college and divorced a year later. He claimed he had enjoyed his bachelor status, dating whomever he wanted for as long as they held his interest. He kept his relationships short and ended them at any hint of trouble. Only one woman had ever left him, his first wife. Bryce didn't like rejection.

When Lily finally agreed to marry him and they settled

on Ventura as a compromise between Santa Barbara and Los Angeles, she wasn't working and spent her days renovating their new home. The ceiling in the living room and library had been elevated, the kitchens and baths modernized, and a beautiful winding staircase now led to the third floor. Instead of the four small bedrooms, they had built a spacious master suite and a new bathroom with a Jacuzzi tub. She had insisted on keeping most of his father's furniture, and had lovingly refinished it herself.

Hennessey's heart attack had occurred at the most propitious time. The house was finished and Lily was eager to go back to work. She would have accepted the position regardless. All her life she had dreamed of becoming a judge.

She headed to the bathroom, removing her clothes and depositing them in the laundry bin. She then leaned back against the counter, seeing Bryce watching her from the doorway. "Can I take a shower first? I showered at the club, but Hennessey had me sweating today."

"I'll get in there with you."

As the warm water cascaded over their bodies, Bryce picked up a bottle of honey-scented body wash, squirting some in his hand and washing Lily's back with it. He then slipped his soapy fingers between her legs, gently stroking her while he whispered in her ear, "I've never loved a woman the way I love you. I want every inch of your body to be touched by my lips at some point tonight."

Bryce was a gentle and considerate lover. He thought Lily was merely shy when it came to sex. Women who had never been sexually assaulted assumed that everything related to sex would be repugnant. This wasn't true, at least not for Lily. Only the specific actions and body positioning exhibited by the rapist disturbed her. The man could never be on top, or in any way restrict her movements, nor could he use foul or demeaning language. The reason Bryce didn't want to make love to her late at night was it usually took a long time for Lily to become aroused. Bryce, like the majority of men, was visually stimulated, but Lily needed the room to be completely dark. She could panic at the glimpse of something as innocuous as a chair with a pair of pants draped over it.

She surprised him when she turned and threw her arms around his neck, kissing him passionately on the lips. She could feel his erection pressing against her body. Pulling back, she said, "I've been so distant lately. Forgive me, Bryce. The job—"

Bryce put a finger over her lips. "Don't talk. Let me help you forget reality for a while," he said as he dropped to his knees.

When they got out of the shower, he dried himself, then grabbed another towel and dropped back to his knees on the fluffy white bath mat to continue what he'd started. First he dried her, then he let the towel go and burrowed his head between her legs. She tried to squirm away, at least to turn the light off, but he wouldn't let her. "Let's go to the bedroom," she said, her voice strained.

Bryce looked up for a moment. "Not tonight."

Lily could see their reflection in the mirror and moved her head to one side. Her body suddenly sprang to life, barring her mind from interfering. The events of the day drifted away as a warm, delightful sensation grew stronger inside of her. She slumped against the wall, her mouth open and panting. "Don't stop," she begged him. "Please don't stop. God, it feels so good. I forgot how good it feels."

He didn't until she was writhing with pleasure. Then he stood and took her hand, leading her to the bedroom. He stretched out on his back and Lily started at his feet, sucking his toes, then licking his thighs, and then taking him into her mouth.

Bryce finally pulled her on top. She rode him hard, the

way he liked it, leaning down to kiss him and then bending backward until the ends of her hair grazed his thighs. She had another orgasm almost at the same time he did, this one more powerful than the first.

They lay stretched out on their backs, breathless and satiated. "That was wonderful," Lily said, curling up against his side. "I was so tense. Thanks for reminding me that I have a body."

"Oh, you have a body, all right." Bryce placed his arm around her neck, pulling her head into the curve of his own. "And I love to get my hands on it. But Christ, woman, you make me work for it. I thought you were going to bite my head off at the restaurant. What's the use of being married if you never have sex with your wife? When I was single, I could get laid seven nights a week if I wanted. A nice meal, a few cocktails, tell the chick how pretty she was, and I was in. I didn't have to listen to her problems, no one nagged me. I didn't have to put up with mangy cats or snippy dogs. What can I say? Being single wasn't bad."

"Stop it," Lily said, rolling over onto her stomach. "I hate it when you talk like that. If you liked being single so much, why did you marry me?"

"I'm just playing with you, babe," Bryce said, smacking her on the bottom. "Just because you're a judge now doesn't mean you can't take a joke. I love to get a rise out of you. You're always so damn serious."

"Why *did* you marry me?"

"I fell in love with you, Lily. I bet men fall in love with you every day. You've got something. Hell, I don't know exactly what, but you've got it. You're a lousy cook, you don't clean for shit, and you can be a royal pain in the ass."

She chewed on a cuticle. He had made her feel good, only to diminish it with a barrage of nonsensical chatter. But that was just Bryce. He talked for a living. "Things will be different once I settle into the new job. I spent two months refinishing furniture, remember? Now I've got all this responsibility." She sucked in a breath. "Roger Hennessey, the presiding judge, came back today."

He yawned. "Didn't he croak?"

"Nope," Lily told him, anxiously scratching her wrist. "He told me he didn't approve of my appointment."

Bryce got out of bed, pulling on his jockey shorts. "So that's why you were so bent out of shape tonight. If you get canned, I've got three storage bins of Dad's stuff I still haven't unloaded. He should have started liquidating his estate years ago. Instead, he dumped everything on me."

"Your father left you a great deal of money," Lily said, thinking he was being disrespectful. "You should be grateful. He could have spent it all on himself."

"Dad was ninety-four, Lily. You can't take it with you, no matter how much you like it." He bent over and pecked her on the cheek. "I'm going downstairs. Want me to get you something?"

Lily braced herself on her elbows. "Make sure Gabby goes out." Gabby was her Italian greyhound. Before they married, she'd slept in her bed. Like Shana, the little dog hadn't taken a shine to her master's new housemate. After she took a bite out of Bryce while they were having sex one night, he insisted the dog sleep downstairs.

"Oh," Bryce said, pausing in the doorway, "I've got to hit the ground running tomorrow. Big deal on the table. I'm flying out in the morning and I won't be back until Thursday. You can work yourself silly while I'm gone. I'll leave my itinerary on the kitchen table."

When he returned to bed, Lily snuggled up to his back. She remained that way until his chest began rising and falling in the quiet rhythm of sleep.

As a child, she had learned to compartmentalize her life. Here, with Bryce, within the confines of their bedroom, she was safe. Only when she felt safe could she sleep. But she couldn't sleep yet. Down the hall were stacks of files and documents, representing the atrocities human beings committed against each other. In an eerie sense, they called to her, just like they did every night. Not the murderers, rapists, robbers, or child abusers, but the victims, particularly those who no longer had a voice to speak.

Hidden between the lines of a police report, or an unnoticed spot on an autopsy photo, there might be something they wanted her to see. Sometimes when the night disappeared and the sun filtered through the stained-glass windows in the library, Lily imagined them gathered around her desk, pleading with her to turn one more page, read one more paragraph, stare at one more gruesome picture.

She quietly got up, slipped on her bathrobe, and padded barefoot down the hall. Later she would sleep.

TEN

❧

TUESDAY, NOVEMBER 28
QUANTICO, VIRGINIA

As soon as Mary Stevens arrived at work the following morning, she pulled out the duplicate tape the crime lab had made for her, then leaned back in her chair to listen to it again.

The odd voice began speaking. "I was primed for the life I now lead at the age of six. I walked in on my father while he was having sex with a woman who lived down the street. My mother was at work at the time. Although I was too young to realize it, my father was an alcoholic who lived off my mother's income. He drove me across the state line, shoved me out of the car in the freezing temperatures, and told me to hold on to a metal fence until he came back to get me."

Mary was both horrified and spellbound. Even with the constantly changing voices and the stops and starts, she was convinced she was listening to the truth. She saw a group of agents walking toward her and spun her chair toward the wall rather than be distracted.

"By the time the police found me, I was near death from hypothermia. I spent the next eleven months in a coma. The police were certain my parents would read the newspaper articles and come for me. They never did. When I finally came out of the coma, a police officer drove me around until I found the town and the house I had lived in, but my mother and father had moved away and left no forwarding address. I'll never know what lies he told my mother to convince her to leave without me. Maybe he told her I'd been kidnapped and murdered. Years later, I learned that my mother died of ovarian cancer, so she took the truth to her grave.

"I eventually found out where my father was living. I spent days watching him. I hid in the bushes outside his apartment, following him to work each day at the hardware store. I went without food and slept in a cardboard box, saving what money I could scrounge up so I could buy a gun or a knife, anything that I could use to kill him. A nice lady finally gave me money for food. I knew I could never save enough for a gun, so I went inside the hardware store and purchased a large knife from one of the salesclerks. I told him I needed it to skin fish. My father saw me as I stood in front of the register, purchasing the weapon I later used to slit his throat. He didn't recognize his own daughter.

"As much as I hated him, my father and I may be somewhat alike, even though the thought repulses me. There's a coldness inside of me. It had to be inside him, too. How else could he leave his child to freeze to death, alone and terrified?

"The faces of people I've killed over the years are buried somewhere deep in my subconscious. Once the killer emerges, it becomes a separate entity. It looks like me, talks like me, yet it is not me. I lead a normal social life, pay my bills, and even go to church on occasion."

Sure, Mary thought facetiously. Everything was just peachy.

The voice continued, "My criteria is the following: male, as men are deceitful, perverted, and violent; and specifically men who commit adultery. I execute them with unemotional precision.

"Do not think that by sending you this message I have an underlying desire to be captured. You will never catch me. Why? Because while you have been studying people like me, I have been studying you. I know you consider me a predator. Don't forget that predators serve a useful purpose in nature. My goal is to kill as many men as I can before I die. The world will be a better place without them."

Instead of removing the tape, Mary picked up the recorder and headed down the hall to John Adams's office. He was on the phone, so she remained outside his door, walking around in circles until he hung up and gestured for her to come in. "That was Detective Berger with the NYPD. I gave them a profile last month on an UNSUB who was targeting elderly women. They caught the guy two days ago, and Berger called to thank me. I don't know why. I was only on target on three points." He took a sip of coffee from a mug with the FBI logo on it, then gave her his full attention. "What's going on, Stevens?"

Mary had been unable to sleep the night before, debating

whether she should take the tape to Adams or first run it by one of the other agents. There was no way to know if the Bureau had jurisdiction, let alone that a crime had been committed. Adams had told her Friday morning that she would soon be ready to take on the full responsibilities of her new position. This might be the test of whether or not he'd been serious. "A cassette tape came in yesterday's mail," she said, dropping down in the chair in front of his desk. "I think it's something you should hear. Would you like me to play it for you?"

Adams put his hands behind his neck and leaned back in his chair. "Run it by me first."

After Mary summarized what she'd heard on the tape, her supervisor sat upright and placed his palms on top of the desk. "Why haven't we heard about a series of men being murdered? If these men were having affairs, they would more than likely be in their late thirties or forties, don't you think? A pattern like that would have caught someone's attention. The tape is nothing, Mary. We get stuff like this all the time. It was probably sent from a mental institution. Did it have a return address?"

"No, please," she said, practically begging. "Let me explain why I think we should take this seriously. Whoever made this tape went to extremes to make certain we wouldn't be able to get a voice print. My guess is he recorded words from TV, or from another audio source, and then used them to construct his message. Once you listen to the tape, you'll see what I mean."

Adams remained stone-faced. "You didn't answer me. Was there a return address? Do we know where this tape came from?"

"No return address. The postmark was from Los Angeles."

"L.A. is a smorgasbord of nutcases. Every other person is mentally ill." His face twisted into a scowl. "Most of us are running on empty right now, Stevens. We can't afford to gear up for something that may amount to nothing. I'm well aware that you're bored with your present assignment. Are you certain you're not overreacting?"

Mary bristled. "Just because I've known you all my life doesn't mean you have to treat me like an overzealous rookie. I worked homicide in Ventura for six years. I wouldn't bother you if I didn't think this was real. Jesus, you're the one who called me on the carpet for wearing heels. If that wasn't a waste of time, I don't know what is." She stopped speaking and massaged her forehead. "I apologize. I don't mean to be disrespectful. I believe we've been contacted by a serial killer, a serial killer who's pissed off that we haven't noticed him. That's what led to the capture of BTK." Dennis Rader had murdered ten people around Wichita, Kansas, and had even suggested the police and media refer to him as BTK, which stands for "Bind, Torture, and Kill." Mary added, "In one of his letters, didn't he say, 'How many people do I have to kill before you people notice me?' "

Adams pointed his finger at her. "Point well taken, Stevens. I'll get as many members of the team assembled as I can. Get a better tape player. That thing looks like it's on its last leg. You touched the cassette, I presume."

"I wear gloves when I open the mail," Mary said, wondering when he would start treating her with the respect she deserved. If she kept arguing with him, though, she would end up back in Washington, or even worse, Ventura. Living in D. C. might have worked out well for her mother and Lowell, but Mary wanted to make a difference, and BAU was the place to do it. "Conference room?" she asked on her way out the door.

"Yeah," Adams said, reaching for the phone and then stopping. "Oh, and Mary . . ." He waited for her to turn around. "I'm sorry if I've been riding you. Your father saved my life when we were in 'Nam. I know it sounds crazy, but it's hard for me to accept that you're an adult, let alone one of my agents. And . . . well, maybe in some areas, I'm overprotective."

Mary shrugged. "You recruited me, sir."

"Even if you can't get your hands on a better recorder," Adams said, shifting back to the matter at hand, "make a duplicate of that tape and have it in the conference room in two hours."

Six special agents, including Mary Stevens and John Adams, assembled around the long table in the conference room. Central supply had provided Mary with a high-quality cassette player, made several dupes of the original tape, and the group had now listened to the recording twice.

George "Bulldog" McIntyre, whose forehead was wider than Mary's entire head, spoke up in his husky voice. "The tape is chilling, that's for sure."

"I agree," Genna Weir said, the only other female in the unit. At five-seven, Weir was in peak condition, but her face looked older than her forty-one years. A steely-eyed brunette with superb reasoning abilities, Weir was highly respected within the unit and the Bureau. "And I'm not saying that just because it took time and patience to orchestrate the tape. We might not be able to hear the voice inflections, but the content certainly fits that of a murderer. Is the person a serial killer? I'm not certain. The UNSUB might be your garden-variety killer who hasn't been apprehended and craves attention."

Adams's deep voice rang out, "That's not going to happen. Even an iota of info gets leaked to the press, and every person in this room will be held responsible." He was seated at the head of the table. The room wasn't that large, and due to his six-foot-five frame, he generally sat sideways to give himself more leg room. "Male or female?"

"I'd say male," Mark Conrad offered, doodling on a yellow pad. "He kills men, but his reason has nothing to do with sex. The men he's killing are obviously a stereotype of his father."

Pete Cook, the unit's psychologist, didn't agree. "It has everything to do with sex, Mark. He saw his father with another woman. The tape talks about perverts and adulterers. I walked in on my parents having sex one time and it freaked me out. Think of how deep a wound the father left on his poor kid. He associates sex with abandonment, terror, maybe even death."

"I wasn't referring to the actual sex act," Mark replied, tugging on his earlobe. "If the UNSUB is what he says he is, which is up in the air right now, he or she is claiming the targets are specifically men who commit adultery. Those are the only men he admits to killing, so hypothetically, this could be a man or a woman. Since female serial criminals are rare, I think we should go with the premise that it's a man."

While the agents mulled over what they'd heard, Adams asked Mary to take a stab at profiling their possible killer. A muscle in her eyelid began twitching. If she'd known he was going to expect her to actually participate, she would have organized her thoughts better. "My gut tells me we're dealing with a woman. I think she wants attention for the reason Mark just mentioned, the fact that there are so few female serial killers. Mentioning church seems like something a woman might say."

"The BTK killer was president of his church," Pete Cook interjected. "Or maybe the UNSUB just wants us to mistakenly believe he's a woman."

"I've already considered that," Mary said, swallowing hard. "As to BTK, I don't believe Dennis Rader made any reference to his church in the correspondence he had with the authorities or the media."

Adams shut his eyes and then opened them. "How old do you think this woman is, Stevens?"

"Late twenties to mid-thirties."

"Why?"

Mary continued, "Because the extensive planning, which are necessary for these type of crimes, go hand in hand with maturity. A younger or older woman might not be able to pull off a series of murders, especially since the victims are allegedly men." She paused and cleared her throat. "I also believe the UNSUB is physically fit, that she works out regularly at home or in a gym. It takes muscle to dispose of an adult male body." Mary waited to see if anyone else spoke. When they just stared at her, she realized they were waiting for her to continue. "I think she's meticulous, patient, and possesses great self-control. She probably lives alone in a spotless apartment."

Adams asked, "Why spotless?"

"Because she's used to cleaning up crime scenes. If not, she would have been apprehended. Besides, why leave evidence around if she has to vacate and move to another location at the spur of the moment?" When she saw Adams nodding, her confidence kicked in. "More than likely she rents because it gives her more mobility. There's a chance that she's been treated for schizophrenia or some other mental disorder, since she perceives the killer side of her personality as a separate entity. She's attractive, and uses her looks to lure her prey, another reason I believe we're dealing with a female."

"Vehicle?"

"Some kind of van or SUV," Mary said. "The problem here is I don't believe she kills in the city where she lives, one of the reasons she's eluded the authorities." She thought a few moments, then added, "She wouldn't want to drive a vehicle which had been used to transport a body. I suspect she rents a van or SUV somewhere near the kill site. If so, this might be how we can catch her."

"Is she Caucasian, Hispanic, African-American?" Genna Weir asked, taking a sip of her coffee.

"I'm almost positive she's white," Mary told them, her eyes roaming around the room. They were testing her. Her throat was parched. She glanced at the water bottles on the side table, but knew they would know how nervous she was if she walked over and got one.

"What makes you think that?"

"Because the recorded voices she used on the tape sound white," Mary explained. "There's also the fact that minority women endure some of the worst childhood abuse imaginable, yet they seldom go on killing rampages when they become adults."

"And white women do?" Peter Cook said, a look on his face that said he wasn't buying it. "You know how many African-American women are in prison for murder?"

"Serial killers?" Mary raised her voice. "Whatever happened to our UNSUB occurred twenty or thirty years ago. I don't believe a black or Hispanic woman would kill a series of men, compile a tape like this one, and mail it to the FBI."

"Why not?"

"Because it's stupid."

The questions seemed to be coming at her from everywhere. "What about an American Indian?"

Mary had reached the end of her rope. "What percentage of the population are female American Indians? I mean, cut me some slack. Maybe the suspect, ah, UNSUB . . ." FBI lingo amounted to acronyms on top of acronyms. Most police departments had done away with the ten-code system, deciding it was safer and easier to speak plain English. Now she had to learn federal laws versus state, as well as an entire new vocabulary. "Why don't I just listen?"

Stifled chuckles made their way around the table. Adams said, "That's it, guys. Everyone get back to work." When Mary stood to leave, he said, "Not you. I'll speak to you in my office."

Several of the agents came up and shook Mary's hand. Weir and McIntyre told her she'd done a good job. Adams was already out the doorway, and Mary had to hustle to catch up with him. He was probably going to tell her she had her head up her ass. When she reached his office, she sat the tape recorder with the duplicate cassette still inside on the floor beside the chair, then placed her yellow pad on her lap.

"Check VICAP," Adams said, referring to the Violent Criminal Apprehension Program. "Search for unsolved homicides, primarily married men between the ages of thirty and fifty, as well as any missing persons who fall into that category. Missing adults don't carry a lot of weight, you realize. The type of men the UNSUB claims to be killing are obviously womanizers, so the wives and girlfriends may have assumed they simply ran off with another woman and failed to report it."

Mary said, "I realize that, sir."

He draped his jacket over the back of his chair before sitting down. "I agree with you about the age and sex, by the way, as well as the race. Your profile was good under the circumstances. I more or less sandbagged you in there. I did it because I wanted to let the team know that you're competent. You'll still have to earn their respect."

"I'm aware of that."

"Why don't you start by trying to find out if a six-year-old child was abandoned on a highway during the winter months twenty or thirty years ago?"

Mary was ecstatic. He not only approved her profile, he

appeared to be assigning the case to her. Of course, there were no witnesses, corpses, crime scenes, forensic evidence, or even a specific part of the country where the crime might have occurred. "I'm not sure that part of her story is true," she said, tapping her pen against her teeth. "She could have fabricated the abandoned child thing to send us on a wild goose chase."

"We can't do anything until we officially know a crime has been committed and that a federal law has been broken. You understand that, don't you?"

"But the killer sent this to us," Mary protested, "not a local PD or another law enforcement body. This person invited us to work the case. How can we not work it?"

"We don't know other agencies didn't receive the same tape," Adams pointed out. "Besides, criminals don't determine jurisdiction. Check with all local and national law enforcements agencies. If it was sent to the Atlanta PD, the crimes probably occurred in Atlanta."

"But sir," Mary said, her voice sparking with intensity, "it has to involve breaking federal statutes. If these men were all killed in one area, we would have heard about it. Our killer is kidnapping her victims and transporting them across state lines."

Adams moved ahead. "Send the tape to the lab. Let them try to track down the sources of the recorded voices and do voice prints. One of them might be the UNSUB's."

"Oh," she said, "who will I report to?"

"Yourself," Adams said, smiling. A moment later he fell serious again. "This is your first bone to chew on, Stevens. You may be chewing on it the rest of your career. Don't come to me unless you're certain you have a solid lead. If you need advice, go to McIntyre or Weir."

Mary stood, experiencing something she hadn't felt in a long time—the adrenaline rush that came when she tracked a killer.

ELEVEN

~

Even executioners occasionally got bored.

Courting a friendship with a judge was exhilarating. Anne remembered something she'd read one time. If a person had all the money in the world, what would they buy? The answer was if they had all the money in the world, they would already own it. After getting away with murder, there wasn't much she could do to top it.

Then a fool appeared.

If she kept her mouth shut and listened, Anne had discovered, a drunk would tell her his life story. Fifteen minutes after he'd asked Anne to go to a motel with him, Bryce Donnelly told her he was married to a Ventura county judge. The possibilities this presented her with were limitless.

Anne slapped open the doors to the courtroom, taking a seat in the second-to-last row. She had slipped in for a few minutes yesterday. When she wasn't dressed as a sex object, it was easy to move under the radar. She hated push-up bras, and wearing high heels was agony.

Anne had met Bryce five weeks ago at the Indigo Lounge, an upscale bar and grill just outside the back gate of the Thousand Oaks Country Club. In most instances, it took time and considerable finesse to get a man to talk about his wife. Bryce had humiliated and exposed his wife to a stranger and never given it a second thought. How did he know she wasn't a reporter, an attorney, or even a criminal seeking revenge?

Lily's husband claimed he worshipped her, then admitted that he'd started cheating on her a few months after they were married. He said Lily was emotionally distant, that she ignored him, that making love to her wasn't much better than masturbating. He said he had to have other women, that if he didn't he'd go crazy.

Anne would show him crazy.

Lily had blown her away from the very first moment she had laid eyes on her. She had never dreamed she could get this close to her. Why had she hooked up with a piece of shit like Bryce in the first place? Even if he hadn't bragged about his conquests, it was obvious he was a player. How could such a smart woman be so stupid?

Her pulse quickened as she waited for the courtroom to come to life. Lily was an incredible woman, and not just in intellect and accomplishments. Her curly red hair was obviously natural. Her skin was parchment-white and her nose and cheeks were sprinkled with freckles. Anne wasn't attracted to Lily in a physical sense. If she had to classify herself, she would say she was asexual. She felt as if that portion of her body had never existed.

Anne had no desire to have sex with a man, even a good one, if such existed. She hated the way their bodies stank, the hair on their chest and genitals, and the way they looked and acted when they became physically aroused.

"Is this the Abernathy trial?" a scratchy voice echoed in the empty courtroom.

Anne startled, seeing an older man wearing red suspenders hovering close to her face. "No," she said, glancing down at the schedule in her lap. "Try Division Fourteen."

She had dropped her voice several decibels, not that it mattered. She had listened to thousands of voices and

arrived at the conclusion that there wasn't a big difference
between a woman's voice and a man's. Some men had
high-pitched voices, and then there were women whose
voices were so deep, they sounded more masculine than
most men. Voice prints were something else.

"It's too cold in here," the man said disappearing out
the back of the empty courtroom.

Good riddance, Anne thought, not wanting him to block
her view of Lily. The old geezer had been right when he
said it was too cold. Things probably heated up when the
court was in session, but at the moment she felt as if she
were in a freezer. Reaching into her backpack, she pulled
out a ragged brown sweater. Dressing like a street person
was another trick she used to keep from being scrutinized.
People tended to look right through you if they thought you
were going to hit them up for money.

Anne's flight took off in two hours, but she'd been disappointed when Lily hadn't shown up at the gym that
morning, and had impulsively stopped in at the courthouse
on her way to the airport. With the big cases Lily was jug-
gling, it was understandable that she might have to skip a
few workouts.

Testimony in the Stucky murder was scheduled to resume at nine and it was only a few minutes past eight. The
schedule she had picked up at the information desk listed a
hearing on another matter at eight-thirty, a discovery motion on a pending robbery. The two male attorneys walked
past Anne on their way to the counsel table, chatting between themselves. The court reporter also appeared, along
with the clerk, who sat within arm's reach of the judge.

Anne had a system for keeping her identity straight. She
used the first half of the alphabet for her female names,
and the last when she wanted to pass herself off as a man.
To make certain she didn't get confused, she wrote the
name of the moment on her mirror in lipstick every night

before she went to bed, then wiped it off the next morning. Memory was all about repetition.

Not only was she freezing, her stomach was grumbling. She lived in a constant state of starvation. If she didn't diet, she would turn into a cow. She had ballooned up once and swore it would never happen again. People treated you differently when you were overweight. You became a third-class citizen. More importantly, married men didn't risk fortune and family for a fling with a fat girl. Women didn't want to hear it, but it was true. It didn't matter if *they* were overweight. A guy could have a spare tire as big as a beer keg, and still end up marrying the prom queen. Even in this area, men had an unfair advantage.

Anne had been watching Lily for the past month. She began by following her to familiarize herself with her routines and haunts. The judge was both lithesome and shapely, one of those lean, tall women whose skeletal structure concealed the size of her breasts. Lily was ditzy, though. A lot of bright people acted as if they couldn't find their way out of a paper bag. She had watched Lily trip, walk into walls, and wander around as if she were a five-year-old separated from her mother. She seemed to live so deep inside her mind that she didn't pay attention to her surroundings. Not paying attention to your surroundings was dangerous. She would have to caution her about that one day. Not now, of course, but later.

As for herself, she was hyper-vigilant. She drank a minimum of ten cups of coffee per day, and used stimulants to suppress her appetite. Most nights she slept no more than three to four hours. She didn't really need the coffee and diet pills to stay awake. Since childhood, she had suffered from chronic insomnia. Going several nights without sleep didn't bother her. The longer she stayed awake, the better she felt. Lack of sleep dimmed her emotions, and kept the beast inside of her from surfacing.

Once Lily took her place on the bench, Anne slouched down low in her seat, her legs stretched out under the chair in front of her. She wondered what it would be like to have such an important position, where people stood in awe of you and couldn't so much as speak unless they had your approval. Unlike Lily, she'd never had the chance to make anything of herself, at least nothing in the professional realm. Well, she thought, that wasn't entirely correct. Killing was a profession. How many women could lure a man to his death, carve him up like a turkey, and dispose of the remains where no one could find them?

Some of the stuff Anne used in alter egos came from her clients, while other things she picked up on the Internet. She was convinced the authorities would never apprehend her. That is, unless she let them. She had made a step in that direction, but it wasn't a sincere effort to turn herself in and seek redemption. She was fucked for all eternity, so all she really hoped to gain by contacting the FBI was to up the stakes and make the game more challenging.

She was a fairly proficient programmer. Computers were great because they couldn't hurt you unless you dropped one on your foot. She'd never dreamed she could make this kind of money. It was scary, thinking she was only a few steps away from being legit. She reported her income and paid her taxes. God, she thought, only in America.

Her work was clearly on point with her interests, yet on the other hand, it enraged her and gave her access to a cornucopia of victims. She never realized how many men cheated on their wives and girlfriends, and most of them were a long way from being lowlifes, at least not by contemporary socioeconomic standards. They were CEOs, college professors, preachers. rabbis, dentists, surgeons, attorneys, even men with political aspirations such as the recently deceased Stan Waverly. Regardless of the fact that no one was aware they were adulterers, their actions defined them. In her eyes, they were scum.

Anne moved through life like a ghost, drifting from one city to the other, constantly changing her appearance, her occupation, her Social Security Number, and other identifying documents. She'd taken the driving test now in fourteen states, always passing on the first try. Why were people shocked over the events of September 11 when it was so easy to hide in plain sight in the United States? When she had traveled to Europe and Asia several years back, the hotels would collect her passport and keep it until she checked out. Foreigners here were allowed far too much freedom.

As the attorneys droned on about who gave what to whom, Anne had trouble keeping her eyes open. She hadn't slept at all the night before, and she hadn't had a chance to go to the drugstore this morning for more diet pills.

A few moments later, she began to lose control. She tried to force the memories back, but they refused to be denied.

She sloshed through the melting snow to her house, her arms locked around her chest to keep out the cold. Because all she had was a lightweight coat, she hadn't been allowed to go outside for recess today. She'd wanted to tell her teacher that she was used to the cold, but Daddy would whip her if she told anyone at her school that she walked home alone. The school bus dropped her off about six blocks from where she lived. The other kids' mothers picked them up. She didn't understand why her daddy didn't come and get her, since he was usually at home. He told her he had something called a warrant, so he couldn't be out running around. She asked her mother what it was, but she never told her.

In her hands was a brown paper sack. Other kids had

cute lunch boxes and pretty clothes. Inside the sack was a picture she had colored for her momma. She wanted a new pair of shoes for Christmas, but her daddy told her Santa Claus got stuck in a chimney and died. Last year, they didn't have any presents or even a tree.

Her toes were crunched and some days her feet hurt so bad, she cried all the way to school. She never cried when she was home. If she did, her daddy would whip her with his black belt. Reaching her house, she opened the creaky gate and continued to the porch. Her daddy's black truck with the dent in the side was parked in the driveway. Her momma was always screaming at him to "get off your butt and get a job." Daddy yelled back that he couldn't get a job because of the warrant.

Her momma worked as a waitress at Good Eats Café. Every night she came home with a bag full of coins. Anne liked to watch her counting at the kitchen table, and sometimes Momma let her stack the coins. Each coin had a different stack. There was a stack for pennies, nickels, and one for quarters. Every now and then Momma brought home some dollars, which she hid where no one could find them. Daddy said she spent that money on her medicine. Anne didn't know why, because Momma didn't look sick. Some nights she would make lots of phone calls, then go out in the car late at night. When she came back, she ran into the bathroom and closed the door. Once she had seen Daddy sticking a big needle into her momma's arm. He got really mad at Anne and made her swear she wouldn't tell anyone about her mother's medicine. She prayed to Jesus every night that He would make her momma well.

Her daddy watched TV all the time and drank Budweiser. He drank one can after another. When he ran out, he would call her and make her bring him another "cold Bud." If she didn't get it to him fast enough, he would grab her by the shoulders and shake her. She didn't know why he liked beer so much. She had sipped one once when they were out of milk and it tasted so bad, she'd spit it out of her mouth.

The kids in the neighborhood made fun of her house. A lot of the shingles had fallen off, and their yard was full of junk. When her daddy took out the trash, there were so many Bud cans, they would fall out of the top. Daddy just left them scattered all over the yard. The rest of the stuff her momma said belonged inside of cars. She said her daddy was trying to sell it to make money. But no one ever came to look at the car stuff.

They'd moved here when she was in kindergarten and her daddy had stopped working. She liked the house they'd lived in before much better. On Saturdays when it wasn't too cold, she tried to pick up some of the Bud cans and put them back in the stinky trash cans. The stuff that belonged inside cars was too heavy for her to carry.

She heard a woman's voice and thought her momma had come home early. Her teacher had put three gold stars on her picture, and told her to be certain she showed it to her parents. She had colored a beautiful blue house with a green yard and pretty white flowers.

She burst through the door to her parents' bedroom, wanting to show her daddy the picture. She stopped breathing when she saw the naked woman in the bed with her daddy. Both her daddy and the woman sat up, pulling the sheet over them. What was Mrs. Murphy from down the street doing in the bed with her daddy, and why had she taken off her clothes? She turned and ran as fast as she could. Her daddy had been doing something nasty to Mrs. Murphy. She'd seen Momma and Daddy doing nasty things before and her daddy had whipped her for coming in their room when the door was closed.

She made it to the living room, then tripped and fell on the floor. Her daddy caught her by the heels and held her

*upside down. She cried so hard she was afraid she was
going to throw up, then her daddy might make her lick it
up with her tongue like he had one time when she'd puked
while he was whipping her. He threw her onto her back
and slapped her in the face.*

*"You fucking little brat," he shouted, spit flying out of
his mouth. "If you say anything to your momma about what
you saw, I'll fucking kill you. Now get to your damn room
where you belong."*

*She raced to her room and hid in the closet, clutching
the torn picture. Finally it got dark and she stopped crying, thinking it wouldn't be long until her momma came
home. Looking at the pieces of her picture, she hoped she
could paste them back together.*

*She fell asleep, then woke up and crept into the living
room. Her daddy was on the sofa drinking a Bud, but the
TV wasn't on, and Bud cans were all over the floor. She
wondered why he wasn't watching TV like he always did.
He was just sitting there smoking a cigarette. He wasn't
even listening to the radio or reading the newspaper.*

*She guessed Mrs. Murphy had gone home. Mr. Murphy
probably wouldn't like it if he knew she was doing nasty
things with her daddy. "Where's Momma?" she said from
the doorway.*

"She pulled a second shift."

*He stared at her for a long time, a look on his face that
she'd never seen before, not even after he drank all the
Buds in the refrigerator. "We're going for a ride."*

His eyes scared her. "Are we going to get Momma?"

*"You know what would happen if you told her what you
saw today, you little bitch? She'd toss my ass out on the
street. Where would I go, huh? I ain't got no money and
it's too cold to live in my truck. I've got warrants, understand? If the police find me, they'll slam me in jail."*

"I won't tell, Daddy," she said, whimpering. "Please, cross my heart and hope to die."

"You'd like it if I was gone, wouldn't you? I know about snot-nosed kids like you. You'll tell your mother the minute she walks in the door. You run crying to her all the time."

She didn't say anything because he was right. She loved her momma. Her momma never hit her or called her dirty names. Her momma cooked her meals and tucked her in bed at night. If Daddy was gone, it wouldn't be so bad. She hoped he took all the car parts with him, then maybe the grass would grow in the spring and she and her momma could plant pretty flowers. "Want me to get you a cold Bud, Daddy?"

"No," he said, crunching the beer can in his fist. "Get your damn coat."

"I'll wait for Momma here."

He came over and got on his knees in front of her. "Do you remember where we used to live, pumpkin?"

"Sort of," she said. "We lived in a brown house. And there were lacy white curtains on my windows. The old lady next door had a bunch of cats."

"What was the name of the city we lived in?' "

"I don't remember."

"Do you remember the state?"

She wasn't scared now. Daddy was playing a game with her. "I know it was far away. I got carsick. We just kept driving and driving. Then we had to sleep in the car at night."

"Is that all you remember?" He stroked a hair out of her face. "This is very important, sweetheart, so don't lie."

"I was just a little girl. I don't remember."

His face changed. His skin was twisted, the way it got when he hit her momma. She started walking backward

*when he caught her, tucking her under his arm like a sack
of potatoes. She kicked and screamed but he wouldn't put
her down. When they got to his truck, he went to the back
and returned with a rope, tying her to the seat.*

*"Why are you doing this, Daddy? I'll be a good girl, I
promise. I'll never come in when the door is closed and
I'll bring you cold Buds really fast. The rope is hurting
me. Please, please, aren't we going to get Momma?"*

*"It's too late," he mumbled under his breath, balling up
his fist and slugging her.*

TWELVE

❧

TUESDAY, NOVEMBER 28
VENTURA, CALIFORNIA

"Your husband called, Judge Forrester," Lily's assistant
said when she entered her chambers a few minutes past
noon. "He said he was going in to a meeting, but would
try to get back to you later this evening."

"Thanks, Jeannie." Lily hoped Bryce had closed the deal.
She enjoyed seeing him happy. Sometimes she didn't give
him enough credit. Any type of sales was difficult. She was
about to send Jeannie to the cafeteria to get her a sandwich
when Chris Rendell appeared in the open doorway.

"I'm not interrupting you, I hope."

"Not at all."

"Hungry?"

"Starving." Exercise made most people hungry, but it
worked the opposite with Lily. She had more of an appetite when she didn't work out. With Bryce out of town for

the remainder of the week, she hoped to be able to spend more time at the gym. He'd been anxious that morning, which was unusual, so she knew it must be an important trip for him. Bryce had taken so much time getting ready, she'd had to drive him to the airport.

"I felt bad that we had to cut our conversation short the other day," Rendell told her. "I thought we could go to Murray's. You know, my treat."

Murray's was a local steakhouse. Lily had never gone there, as she didn't eat red meat. Every restaurant had chicken these days, though, and she could make this her big meal of the day. When Bryce was away, she typically snacked. She never went to a restaurant alone, and it wasn't worth the effort to cook for one person. "How could I pass up an offer like that?" she told him, darting into her office and removing her robe and picking up her handbag. When she returned, she asked, "Should we go in separate cars?"

"Not unless you have to be back right away."

They rode the elevator down to the parking garage. Lily noticed Judge Paciugo's new black Mercedes, as well as another judge's BMW. She was somewhat surprised when Rendell walked over to an older-model Volkswagen Bug and opened the door for her. Once Lily was inside, she peered out the driver's window, eager to see how he could squeeze his tall frame into such a small space. He had it down to a science. He compressed his body at the waist, then effortlessly slid inside. To accommodate his long legs, the seats were pushed back all the way and touched the seats in the rear.

"I've never been into cars," Rendell said, turning the key in the ignition. "I bought this about fifteen years ago when I was living in Salt Lake City. As long as it keeps running, I intend to keep driving it. The gas mileage is terrific."

Lily was truly within his space now, and she didn't experience the pleasant feeling she generally did when around him. Instead, the interior of the car had a strange, almost frightening atmosphere. The only comparisons she could think of were being locked inside a closet or at a crime scene. When he wasn't looking, she glanced in the backseat. Unopened mail was scattered around, and there were several crumpled fast-food sacks, one with the distinctive McDonald's logo. She couldn't imagine Rendell going to McDonald's, but then again, Bryce was still hooked on Big Macs. When he got sick of upscale restaurant food, he headed to the golden arches. She checked Rendell's waistline and didn't notice a bulge. He was several inches taller than Bryce, which helped. They parked and walked toward the front door of the restaurant.

The interior was dark, as was common in many steakhouses, but there was a distinctive Old World charm. Instead of candles, each table had its own small lamp, which gave it an intimate, romantic feel. A waiter in a white coat with Italian features saw them and rushed over. "Follow me, Judge Rendell," he said. "Your table is ready."

"Thanks, Roman." He flashed a smile. Once they were both seated, he asked, "Would you like a cocktail or a glass of wine, Lily?"

"A Coke will be fine," she answered, placing her napkin in her lap.

He ordered a glass of merlot. "How's the Stucky trial going?"

"Tedious and sad. Ronald Abrams did the autopsy. He testified today. He was amazed the boy lasted as long as he did with the amount of drugs they were pumping into him." She picked up the menu, then dropped it back on the table. "God, I wish I could strangle these people and be done with it. Do you ever feel like you're going to lose it right there in the courtroom?"

"All the time."

Although felony crimes weren't tried in the misdemeanor court where Chris was assigned, all preliminary hearings were. A preliminary hearing was similar to a mini-trial. The purpose was to determine if there was reasonable doubt a crime had been committed and the defendant had committed it. If such was found, the defendant would be held to answer in superior court. Lily said, "How do you handle it?"

"I go home and cry." He looked embarrassed and quickly changed the subject. "I'm concerned about you, Lily. Is everything okay in your marriage?"

"Wait a minute," she answered, leveling her gaze at him. "You're asking me about my marriage when you refuse to divulge anything about your personal life other than the fact that you're a Mormon. Are you married? Do you have a family? Are you gay? Honestly, some of us are so curious, we've given thought to swiping your personnel file."

He let out a long sigh. "I never realized anyone was interested."

Lily locked her arms over her chest. "Don't tell me you're blind to the way women fawn over you, Chris. If you announced that you were single, there'd be a line all the way around the courthouse."

"Ah," he said, a tentative smile on his face. "So . . . what do you think?"

"My guess is you have a gorgeous wife and a houseful of picture-perfect blond, blue-eyed kids." She paused, rethinking her statement. "You don't keep any pictures of them in your office, but in our line of work, perhaps you're afraid someone might try to hurt them."

His eyes drifted downward. A cloak of silence fell over the table. When he spoke, his voice cracked with emotion. "My wife and daughter were . . ." He stopped speaking and took a drink of his wine. "The three-year anniversary of their death is tomorrow. A semi truck hit them head-on. Sherry, my wife, was taking Emily to see her grandparents in Sacramento. Emily's birthday is next week. She would have been seven." He stared at a spot on the wall. "I guess that wasn't the answer you were looking for."

"God, I'm so sorry, Chris," Lily said, leaning forward. "I shouldn't have said anything. I feel terrible. Forgive me, I'm a foolish woman."

"No, no," he said, swallowing hard. "I can't keep this bottled up inside me forever. I need to talk about it. It's just that nothing bad had ever happened to me before. I guess you could say I lived a charmed life. I did great in school. I married a wonderful woman, and she gave me a wonderful daughter. Emily seemed to be following in my footsteps. The teachers suggested we put her in a school for gifted children. Sherry and I were active in the church. I was convinced God would protect us from anything evil and ugly." He gritted his teeth. "When the accident happened, I completely changed. Nothing anyone said could console me. I became furious with God. Honestly, I went insane. I even gave thought to killing the driver of the truck."

"Was he under the influence?"

"No," he told her. "That's the hardest part to accept, you know. It was an accident, just a lousy traffic accident. Sherry and Emily weren't killed by a murderer, or an act of God like a hurricane or an earthquake. The truck driver was tired, the roads were wet, and the tires didn't have enough tread. How can I explain this to someone who's never gone through it?"

Lily didn't know what to say, so she didn't say anything. She could tell he was uncomfortable talking in a public place, but the restaurant was crowded and people seemed to be absorbed in their own conversations. When the waiter brought their food, Rendell just stared at it, the same tortured look on his face. She took a few bites of her roasted chicken, then placed her fork on the edge of her plate. "I'm sorry I didn't mention it earlier. The smell of red meat sometimes makes me nauseous." She forced a smile. "Maybe I'll pick the restaurant next time. Can you have them box up your food?"

He gestured for the waiter, looking relieved. When the man came over, he handed him his credit card.

Their eyes linked and lingered. Lily felt connected to him, as if he'd peered deep inside her and seen the terrible things that had happened in her life. Once he signed the bill, they both stood to leave. As they made their way out of the restaurant, Rendell placed his palm in the center of her back to guide her through the narrow walkways between the tables. The warmth of his hand penetrated her blouse. She caught a scent of his aftershave, something with a hint of lime. The odor made her think of gin and tonic, her favorite drink.

Once they were inside his Volkswagen, he just sat there, as if he were too exhausted to drive. The he turned and stared at her, a strange expression on his face. When he leaned closer, Lily was certain he was going to kiss her, but after a few moments, he pulled away.

As they were driving back to the courthouse, he said, "I'm probably wrong to say this, but I think I subconsciously asked you to lunch today with the hope that you'd tell me you and your husband were breaking up. That isn't true, is it?"

"No," Lily said, folding her hands in her lap. She started to tell him that she was attracted to him, too, but no good would come of it. Her affair with Richard Fowler had ended her marriage to Shana's father. For all she knew, it had been a rock thrown into the wheels of the universe, setting in motion the awful events that followed. The last thing Chris Rendell needed was a woman like herself, who had done what he chastised himself for merely thinking. "I haven't suffered the kind of loss you have, but I've been through some major, life-changing events."

"You and your daughter were raped," he said, glancing over at her.

All the blood drained out of Lily's face. If she had stayed in Santa Barbara, she wouldn't be confronting this on a daily basis.

"Someone in the DA's office told me," Rendell said. "I can't imagine going through something like that with your child."

"And I can't imagine losing one." Had he also heard about Shana walking into the DA's office and telling them she was the one who had killed the rapist? Lily pressed her shoulders back against the seat. "That happened a long time ago, Chris. You never get over it, of course, but in time you come to accept it, understand that there was nothing you could have done to prevent it."

"How's your daughter?"

"She's doing good," Lily told him, reminding herself to call Shana while Bryce was away. "This is her first year at Stanford Law. She plans to become a prosecutor. Personally, I wish she would go into another field."

Rendell looked puzzled. "Why?"

"I was in charge of the sex crimes division when it happened. If left up to me, I wouldn't have reported it. Not reporting a double rape went against everything I'd worked for as a prosecutor. When push came to shove, I didn't believe in the system."

Lily rolled the window down and removed her sunglasses, hoping the sun and fresh air would keep the memories from engulfing her again. As she gazed out at the passing cars, her mind propelled her back in time. She was in her Honda, a short time after she'd shot Bobby Hernandez.

*   *   *

Her body was like ice, but she was dripping with sweat. The sign read ALAMEDA STREET. The sun was blazing, the streets teeming with activity. Seeing the stop sign, she braked, waiting while three schoolchildren crossed. She had been driving aimlessly for at least an hour. The shotgun, now on the floorboard, had slid to a resting place against her feet. She kicked it back and continued.

She felt as if she could see herself from a position outside of her body. The houses were larger and the yards well tended. She was no longer in Colonia, the area in Oxnard where Hernandez resided.

She visualized the crime scene: the police cars with their lights flashing, the ambulance and paramedics, the crowd of onlookers being held back by the police. If he had survived, he would have been transported to the nearest hospital, and the emergency room staff would be trying to stop the bleeding, assess the damage. So much time had passed, he might even be in surgery, a dedicated physician trying to save his life. What she willed herself to see was his disgusting, inhuman body beneath a coarse dark blanket, lifeless.

Finding a major cross street, she made her way to the freeway and headed home. To Shana, she thought, she had to get to Shana. "He'll never hurt you again, baby. He'll never hurt anyone again."

She plucked the knit ski cap off her head and tossed it out the open window as she entered the on-ramp to Camarillo. She felt remarkably calm and controlled, both full and empty, horrified but at peace. The rage had been released, allowed to take its own shape and propelled toward its target. The evil had returned to the person who had unleashed it.

Instead of turning left in the direction of her house, she turned right. Her destination was an old church whose property included a steep slope planted heavily with avocado trees. The parking lot was deserted. Mature trees blocked anyone from seeing it from nearby streets. Exiting the Honda with the shotgun, she wiped it with the tail of her shirt and held it in the fabric until she tossed it down the embankment. As her eyes tracked it, she said, "I killed a mad dog today, Dad. You would have been proud."

When she turned onto her street, her eyes scanned the gauges on the dash. The little needle on the gas gauge was not even a fraction above, it was locked on E. A second later she saw the patrol car parked in front of her house.

Lily knew she had no option but to enter the house and confront the police. She hit the garage door opener and pulled the Honda alongside John's white Jeep Cherokee. As she let her head fall against the steering wheel, the engine still running, the garage door closed, her thoughts turned to asphyxiation. Her mind struggled toward lucidity, a capsized boat trying to right itself. She reached for the strength of rage and her earlier conviction and knew it was gone. She was naked and exposed, fully aware of what she had done, face to face with the horror. Perhaps there was just enough gas left, lingering lethally in the tank, and some slim chance that whoever was inside wouldn't hear the engine running before she turned blue and it was over.

She quickly turned the ignition key to off. Killing herself would only inflict more agony on Shana.

How had they found her, linked her to the crime in such a short time. There was no possibility of tracking the plate through the Department of Motor Vehicles, for she had altered it. Even if he had lived, he could have never identified her in her blue knit cap. Maybe he had seen the Honda. That's it. He had followed her from the court-

house. He might not know her name but he knew where she lived. Here again, it didn't play. The house where it had occurred was a rental and would take more time to track, and she truly doubted that he—in what had to be a dying statement—remembered the street and number.

Her life was over. She would be imprisoned and disbarred. There was no defense for the crime she had committed. No matter what he had done to her and Shana, she had not shot him in self-defense; she had tracked him down and executed him. She thought of defenses: diminished capacity, temporary insanity. Did she know her actions were wrong at the time? Was she cognizant of their wrongfulness? The answer was a clear and precise yes.

Reaching for the car door handle took all the strength and courage Lily had. She almost fell to the garage floor when the door swung open, as her fingers were locked on the handle.

John opened the door just as she reached the first of the four steps leading to the house. "Where in God's name have you been? I was panicked. I kept calling the house. Then I dozed off until six. You still weren't there, so I called the police." He paused, rubbing one hand across his brow. "I guess you saw the police car. I told them everything. They're talking to Shana in the den."

Lily's hand flew instinctively to her neck. The noose she had been hanging from had been cut, but only for the moment. "What did you tell them? You mean, about the rape? You decided we should report it?"

"Yeah," he said. "They said we should have reported it last night. They might have caught him in the area, somewhere near your house. With you being a DA and everything, they found it hard to understand why you didn't call the police."

Lily's mind was racing, tracking at lightning speed.

*They would need access to the crime scene to collect
evidence and take photos. Mentally starting at the front
door, she recalled the file scattered there and felt the
noose tighten again around her neck. Clinton Silverstein
knew she had taken the file, and whatever Oxnard detective assigned to investigate the murder might call Clinton
and request the file. She had to get it back, leave it in the
same state as when it had left Clinton's hands. That
meant copying the torn page where his address had been
and replacing it. She had to eradicate anything that could
link her to the crime, for that would leave her wide open
as a suspect.*

A suspect with motive and no alibi.

"Lily," a voice said. "Are you all right?"

"What?" she answered, looking over and expecting to
see John. But John was dead, and Chris Rendell was staring at her. The car was no longer moving, and they were in
the underground parking garage at the courthouse.

"You're perspiring," he said, handing her some tissues.
"Are you certain you're not ill? I didn't realize I would
upset you this much. If I had, I would have never brought
up the rape."

"We're both batting zero today," Lily told him, using
the tissues to blot her face. "You're right about not telling
anyone. I didn't have that option. After Shana confessed
to killing the rapist, the DA's office filed charges against
her." Law enforcement never linked Lily to the murder of
Bobby Hernandez, but Shana had put the pieces together
and knew her mother had killed someone, presumably the
rapist. "A homicide detective had arrested the rapist, and
the charges were dropped. By then, everyone knew. You
know what they say. An accusation is the same as a conviction in the court of public opinion."

"Why would your daughter do something like that?"

"She was trying to protect me," Lily explained. "The police were about to arrest me for the murders of my former husband and the rapist. Judge Hennessey told me the other morning that he didn't approve of my appointment. He also refused to assign me any sexual offenses because he claimed I was biased."

Rendell's face twisted into a grimace. "Everyone is biased when it comes to those crimes. Forget Hennessey. He's a fucking bastard. He has no right to talk to you like that."

"I thought Mormons weren't allowed to use foul language."

"I don't know how it got out that I was a Mormon," he told her, perturbed. "The church elders tried to tell me how to live my life. They wanted me to remarry right away and have more kids. I finally walked away. I'm still a Christian. I'm just not active in the Mormon church anymore."

"I thought you were going to convert me the other day."

He looked embarrassed. "I just wanted to spend time with you, Lily."

"Oh," she said, wondering why, out of all the available women, he'd picked her. "I have to be on the bench by two. It's one forty-five, so I have to run." She reached for the door handle, then stopped. "I'm glad we talked, Chris."

Lily wondered if anyone had seen them. All she needed were rumors circulating that she was having an affair with Christopher Rendell. The pathos surrounding him made him even more appealing. He was like a wounded bird, and she experienced an overwhelming desire to comfort and protect him.

Things were never as they appeared. The man she thought had all the answers was a sad and lonely person. He could lure her into something that could cause her life to spin off track again. What she felt for Bryce was enough. They didn't have a great love, but it kept her grounded. For now, it was all she could handle.

THIRTEEN

❧

Anne disembarked from her Southwest Airlines flight and disappeared among the throngs of people as they made their way to the baggage claim. The Las Vegas airport, just like the city, was a complete abomination. The constant ringing of bells from the slot machines gave her an excruciating headache. Overall, though, it was the dull eyes and expressionless faces of the gamblers. They kept feeding money into the machines like bloodless robots. When they won, it meant nothing. They just kept inserting coins, dollar bills, anything they had, until their pockets or the machine itself told them they had no more money.

The only game she could fathom people playing was craps. The odds were decent and it was somewhat social. That is, unless you were the only person at the table. She had money to burn, but she would rather hand it over to a reeking skid row bum than to let a croupier sweep it into the overflowing coffers of a casino.

Darting into the women's restroom, she entered a stall at the very back. Since she was disguised as a man, she couldn't enter the men's restroom and walk out as a woman. She didn't look that masculine, anyway. She didn't do facial hair. It took too much time and the glue broke her face out.

She kicked off her slip-on black Vans, dropped her baggy jeans, and pulled her sweatshirt over her head. After rolling her clothing tightly to conserve space, she stuffed them into the side pockets of her pink Valentino tote. She had plopped down two grand for the tote. Both men and women noticed handbags. When you carried an expensive bag, people respected you. And it had to be a designer who was difficult to knock off. She touched the soft leather and watched how it gracefully fell into folds. The color was exquisite, a pale shimmering pink.

Her instruments of murder had been shipped overnight via FedEx in separate parcels. She now owned three residences, all of them kill sites. They were located in remote or secluded locations such as the cabin in San Bernardino where she'd taken Stan Waverly. The Vegas property had been a steal, a nine-hundred-square-foot house in the middle of nowhere. She had made some rudimentary repairs to the interior and put in a new air conditioner. Her biggest investment had been trees and lighting. As long as it didn't freak the guy out when she pulled up, it was fine. Unlike women, men would screw anywhere. Once their dicks started throbbing, their reason and sensibilities disappeared.

She placed the lid down on the toilet and took out her compact, preferring to put her makeup on inside the stall because it was private. She'd had a lot of diversified jobs over the years, but none that had challenged her. Although she'd worked for numerous computer companies, once she'd tasted the thrill of killing, she needed something that didn't restrict her to a desk or a building. Brokering insurance and acting as a real estate agent had given her more freedom. Her best job had been in a hospital pharmacy. That's when she learned about various chemicals and how they worked inside the body. After three months, she walked away with every drug imaginable, switched to another identity, and moved to another state.

For positions that required a degree, she had no trouble fabricating one. The same applied to certificates. Companies often checked references and verified that you were

certified by Microsoft, but in the past, no one went to the
effort to confirm her degree, especially if she brought a
copy and transcript of her grades to the interview. All that
had changed, however. Employers now outsourced background checks to India. She didn't need a job anymore,
but it made it difficult for uneducated people to get work.

She kept one clean ID. In case that identity was also
compromised, she could easily find people on the Internet
who would cover for her.

That's how she came up with the perfect business.

The original name was the Alibi Connection. When
she'd first created the Web site and posted it, she'd been
shocked at the number of responses. Her customers were
primarily men, although women occasionally used her
services. Several newspaper and television shows did features on alibi clubs, and dozens of copycats had popped
up. At first she'd been angry that someone had stolen her
idea. She finally figured out that ideas were tossed out like
acorns and more than one person could catch them. The
presence of the other clubs also hid her among many.

Most of the competition disappeared due to the notori-
ety, but by then she had over three thousand members.
After a few months, and numerous members' concerns,
she removed the site from all the search engines so a person could only reach it if he had the URL. She not only
welcomed referrals, she paid the referring member a hefty
fee. Two years later, she branched off into an entirely new
area, even more exciting than the first.

When things got slow or she felt like recruiting new
members, she went on MySpace and sent teaser messages
to men who were obviously looking for women to have sex
with. Most of the services she provided were carried out
over cell phones. Unlike other companies that had eventually gone out of business, there was no charge to join. The
first thing she advised a new member was to purchase a

pay-as-you-go cell phone. That way, he could toss it in the trash if he were in danger of being discovered, and he didn't have to worry about the bill. If his significant other asked why he had the phone, he could explain that he'd been receiving too many telemarketing calls, and needed the phone in case an emergency came up at his work. After he purchased what she referred to as his "fun phone," she would give him a toll-free number to call if he needed an alibi.

Men loved it.

Finally they could do anything they wanted and get away with it. She charged a hundred dollars for simple alibis, and up to thousands if the client wanted to be gone for longer than an afternoon. If the monster inside her got out and she killed a client, she made certain all the charges on his credit card were reversed.

The credit card issue had been one of her biggest challenges. Anne resolved the problem by developing a list of merchants to whom she paid a modest sum to run the clients' credit card charges through on their accounts. Some of her clients used PayPal, but others didn't like it, as the service sometimes sent out e-mails to update information, and their spouses had access to their computers and e-mail. The companies she solicited to run the credit cards through on their account were independently owned car washes, gas stations, dry cleaners, small markets, or liquor stores. She even had several health food stores. Nothing related to the Alibi Connection would ever show up on a client's credit card and the expenditures wouldn't appear even slightly suspicious. Women were the worst when it came to running up credit card charges. They were so worried about covering a spending spree, they wouldn't dare ask their husband about charging what appeared to be necessities.

In the beginning, potential customers had been worried

about blackmail. She had assuaged their fears by telling them that the club was operated strictly by members who had just as much to lose. This wasn't true, of course. She doubted if she would turn a profit if she placed her business in the hands of liars and adulterous men. She had a number of employees, most of them working out of their homes. This was the best way, as she never had to meet them.

Each member went under a pseudonym, and she told them she kept no master client list. In most instances, a statement like that would be preposterous. Leaving a lot of paper floating around was too risky, though, since some of her clients ended up as her victims. She did have all the other clients' names and credit card numbers stored in an online computer database. How could she run a business without keeping some kind of records? Men believed what they wanted to believe.

The services her company provided were extensive. One that was very popular was the "rescue" alibi. Say a man was having dinner with his in-laws when his favorite football team was playing. Either that or he wanted to sneak away for a few hours to have sex with his mistress. A call would come in wherever he was stuck at the time, saying they urgently needed him at work. She recommended the client make certain the wife or whoever he was trying to fool answered the phone. Her employees used a VoIP (voice-over-Internet protocol) system and she had designed a program that would display the name of the company where the client was employed.

Another alibi that had been a great success was the two- or three-day business conference or training seminar. The Alibi Connection would provide the client with a detailed itinerary of his trip, a certificate of completion, hotel and rental car receipts, basically anything he needed to establish definitive proof of his whereabouts during the time in question.

She considered it immoral to take money from her victims. Then she would be killing for personal gain. She knew if she was ever captured—and she didn't fool herself, it would happen eventually—no one would care if she'd stolen or not. Regardless, she had to live up to her own standards. All she was doing was cleaning house, taking out the garbage that people left lying around in their yards.

Why didn't she kill criminals? She let the police take care of them, and judges like Lily Forrester. Vile criminals such as gang members blew each other away. Dope dealers were scum, but Anne didn't have a mind to kill them.

When Anne stepped out of the stall, she was wearing her shoulder-length brunette wig and a sheer sleeveless white cotton dress. Most women didn't realize how turned on a man got by a woman wearing a dress. Underneath she was wearing a push-up bra and a pair of T-back panties that were already riding up into the crack of her ass. Now that she'd seen Lily up close, she had gone light on the makeup. Bryce had seen her on three occasions, all of them inside a bar. Some men could only get turned on if she looked and acted like a whore. Thinking of her that way lightened their guilt somehow, as if it weren't cheating if the woman was a prostitute. Bryce was different. He fucked other women because he knew Lily was too good for him. In that respect, he was right.

Anne walked straight to the curb and hailed a cab, jumping in and pulling out her cell phone. Her rental car was waiting for her at the Venetian Hotel. Bryce would have no trouble deciding whether or not he should answer the call, since he'd purchased his "fun phone" as instructed by the Alibi Connection. "Bryce?"

"Anne?"

Bryce knew her as Anne Hall. She liked the Anne Bradley identity too much to use it with men she might end up killing. Also, Lily knew her by that name. "My flight was delayed," she lied. "Are we still meeting at the Aladdin?"

"Yeah," he said, sounding disappointed. "When will you be here?"

"I should be there in an hour, depending on the traffic. Can't wait to see you, baby. We're going to have a great time. Just think, three whole days to play."

She ended the call and leaned back in the seat, her heart pounding in excitement. Lily would be much better off without this jackass. And who would she rely on when her husband never returned from his business trip? Lily's friends all had jobs, but *she* had all the time in the world to console her. If she could finally connect with another human being who didn't want to abuse her, abandon her, or have sex with her, the urge to kill might finally leave her.

QUANTICO, VIRGINIA

As soon as she placed the cassette tape in an evidence envelope, marked it urgent, and shipped it off to the lab, Mary began working at her computer.

Her degree was in biology, one of the fields the Bureau had been eager to recruit from. She'd been able to use some of her knowledge on the counterfeit drug matter, as well as in building a case against a company that continued to manufacture and distribute faulty delivery systems used to implant stents in cardiac patients.

Mary had caught the tail end of the last case, which the Bureau had been investigating for approximately six years. Despite rumors of complications and deaths, the company continued to ship the defective product. In conjunction with the U.S. Attorney's Office, the Bureau's investigation covered thousands of technical documents and witnesses in three countries.

Another reason the FBI was aggressively recruiting agents with scientific backgrounds was the fear that a foreign entity might one day employ the use of chemical or biological weapons on U.S. soil.

Before her father's death, she had pulled down big bucks working for a pharmaceutical company in Los Angeles. Although she'd worshipped her father, and was willing to follow him into law enforcement, Harold Stevens wouldn't hear of it. She was too smart, her father used to say, and he refused to have his daughter risk her life in such a dangerous and underpaid occupation.

When the LAPD failed to capture her father's killer, Mary had quit her job and tracked him down herself, all without leaving her apartment. Her technical and computer skills were exceptional. If a person knew enough to be able to manipulate the Internet, she could find just about anyone.

Her first step now was to search for a newspaper article about a child being left on a highway. She didn't find anything, although she was appalled at the number of children who went missing every year, many of them never found. Deciding to focus on the unsolved homicides, she found two cases that interested her. A man's dismembered body had been discovered in a shallow grave outside of Las Vegas. The Las Vegas PD took six months to make a positive ID, as the head and hands had been severed from the body.

She started to move on to the next case, since it was extremely rare for a female killer to dismember her victim. She placed her head in her hands as Adams's statement that she might spend the rest of her career on this case began to sink in. In a fairly small area like Ventura, catching a killer wasn't that difficult, unless the killer skipped town or killed a complete stranger. One of the reasons serial killers were so hard to apprehend was they generally had no ties to their victims. Of course, the other possibility was human error.

Bulldog McIntyre walked into her office, a smirk on his chiseled face. "You can't be frustrated already. It's only been a few hours. Wait until you spend ten years trying to crack a case."

"I know, I know," Mary told him, leaning back in her chair and spinning it around. Stopping it abruptly with the old-lady black pumps she'd worn to appease the higher-ups in the Bureau, she placed her palms on top of her desk. "My profile may be wrong. The UNSUB could be a man."

"No shit."

"You know," she responded, pissed, "if you guys would stop riding me, I might be able to accomplish something here."

"Hang in there, ace," he said before leaving.

She tapped her mouse and scrolled through more particulars about the Vegas case. The victim, Howard Goldstein, had been married, with two young children. He owned a chain of successful restaurants in San Francisco. Goldstein's wife told police her husband had traveled to San Diego to check out the possibility of opening a restaurant there. She spoke to him on his cell phone several times and he never mentioned going to Las Vegas. He'd allegedly been staying at the Hyatt Hotel in La Jolla, a city near San Diego. Mrs. Goldstein had called and left a message for him on the phone in his room. When he didn't return on the scheduled date and stopped answering his cell phone, the wife filed a report with the San Diego PD.

Mary dialed the number on the police report. After being transferred numerous times, she was connected with a detective. "You're playing in the wrong field," Patrick Cummings told her, smacking what sounded like a wad of gum. "All we did was file a missing person report. Vegas found the body. Call them."

Sensing he was about to hang up, she blurted out, "This may be part of a larger picture."

"Really? Got yourself a serial killer, huh? Are you one of Adams's people?"

Christ, Mary thought, her heart thumping in her chest. She took a deep breath, then said calmly, "It's nothing like that. We're investigating a string of robberies."

"You guys think Goldstein's a robber? Shit, he was a millionaire several times over. Not only that, he was like fifty-something and too fat to make a getaway. Guess he ate too many pastrami sandwiches."

"I didn't say anything about him being a suspect," Mary said, a tinge of annoyance making its way into her voice. "Your report indicates Goldstein told his wife he would be staying at the Hyatt in La Jolla. When your officer checked, the Hyatt said no one of that name had been registered during the times in question."

"Look," Cummings said. "Goldstein told the old lady he was going on a business trip. Shopping around for a spot to open another restaurant or something. Not only were there no records of him staying at the Hyatt in La Jolla, we checked every hotel and motel within a fifty-mile radius and didn't find anything. They found the body in Vegas, so it's obvious he lied to his wife and went there to gamble. This is a pretty common scenario, if you know what I mean."

"I appreciate your cooperation, Detective Cummings," Mary said, thinking the call had been a waste of time.

"Hey," he said. "I don't know if this has any connection to your robberies, but I remember one thing that was odd.

Goldstein's wife insisted that she'd spoken to the hotel operator and was transferred to her husband's room at the Hyatt. Hold on." He began speaking aside to someone. "Track down that damn witness. His name is Frankie something." He returned to their conversation. "Sorry about that, Stevens. It's a madhouse around here. Okay, where was I?"

"Goldstein's wife."

"After Vegas contacted us for DNA, thinking the un-identified torso they had on ice might be Goldstein, I went out myself and spoke to the wife. Laura Goldstein's a knockout, by the way. Only a rich guy could get a piece of ass this sweet. Anyway, she pulls out her husband's travel itinerary, advising that she used the phone numbers listed there to call him. When I dialed the number for the Hyatt, some woman answered, claiming she'd had the number for over a year. To get the wife off our back, we verified it with the phone company. Must have been a typo."

"Who did she call, then?"

"Shit, how do I know? Maybe she misplaced his itinerary and got the number for the Hyatt from information."

"But you just told me he wasn't registered at the Hyatt."

"True," he said as if he'd just put it together. "The Vegas PD didn't find a room registered to him in their city, either. They decided Goldstein must have stayed with friends or flown in and out on the same day."

"What about the airlines?"

"I have to execute a search warrant in ten minutes," he shot out. "Get in touch with the Vegas authorities."

Before Mary could say anything more, the phone went dead.

FOURTEEN

❦

Bryce was perched on top of a barstool at the Aladdin Hotel, gulping Maker's Mark bourbon as if it were water. He didn't really care if he fucked Anne or not. All he wanted was someone around to call an ambulance if he drank himself into a coma.

Lily had been all over him lately. Didn't she realize that the more she pushed him, the more he rebelled? In the same way she ruled in the courtroom, his wife had come out of nowhere and declared that he was an alcoholic. He'd been drinking since high school and had never had a problem. Every day he got up and went to work, handled his accounts, and battled the 405 freeway during rush hour. What gave her the right to tell him how he should live his life?

Lying to Lily had been difficult, though, even if the alibi club Anne had turned him on to made it highly unlikely that she would find out the truth. He generally indulged his appetite for other women during the day while Lily was at work. He had scores of established accounts, which he milked year after year. There was an abundance of young talent to solicit new business, and in the digital world, creating new advertising campaigns was a snap.

Since Bryce was buddies with the VP of the company, he could pretty much do whatever he wanted. Business had been slow the past month, so he had covered the trip by saying he was going to fly to a few cities and entertain some of his major clients. He'd already checked with his secretary an hour ago and the office was dead. To make certain someone from one from his major accounts didn't call looking for him while he was in Las Vegas, he'd made cursory calls to them earlier in the week.

Everyone knew how it worked. Perks were perks. If the business was too far away for him to wine and dine his major accounts on a regular basis, he would simply cut them a check from his expense account.

Spending three days with another woman was a big step. "Hit me again," he said to the bartender, sliding his empty glass forward.

A bleached blonde, obviously a prostitute, was eyeing him from the other side of the bar. Getting blotto in the middle of the day made him look like he'd dropped his wad at the tables. Being with a pro was short and sweet, but it didn't ring any bells for him. He liked the game and the anticipation. Once he got it, the excitement was gone.

To be fair to Lily, he never should have gotten married.

He would have been perfectly content with his bachelor life if his father hadn't constantly harped on him to get married and have a family. Several times, he'd even accused him of being gay. That was a laugh, he thought. But a guy who'd been chained to a woman's memory his entire life couldn't appreciate what it was like to be single. He missed his old apartment, right down the street from his office and within walking distance of all the best restaurants and clubs. Now he spent the majority of his day cooped up in a damn car. Sure Lily didn't understand. She could get to work in fifteen minutes, then she sat on her ass all day while everyone bowed down and worshipped her.

He guzzled down the new drink, dropping a twenty for the bartender. When was this chick going to show up? If she didn't get here fast, he'd be under the table. Maybe the three-day fling wasn't that bad. If he was too tanked to nail her one day, he could catch her the next. Every guy had an erection in the morning, even boozers like himself.

Why had he insisted that Lily have sex with him last night? Then he remembered. A pal had told him a woman's suspicions were dulled for a few days after the hubby or boyfriend banged her. Having sex with their husbands was a chore, something they could cross off their "to do" list. Romance flew out the window once a guy realized his wife considered having sex with him in the same light as cleaning out the refrigerator or rearranging her closet.

He liked Anne because she was as horny and uninhibited as most men. She'd bucked and moaned in the back of his car the other night after he'd told her he had booked his ticket to Vegas. She didn't mind him taking care of her, but she refused to fuck him or even give him a blow job. Of course, he wouldn't be here today if she had. Once he got a piece, he wouldn't go to a lot of trouble to get it again. That is, unless the chick was fantastic.

Anne refused to do the deed in a motel room, claiming she might get a disease. Actually, he'd picked up a case of crabs fifteen years ago from ravishing a wild redhead on top of a motel bedspread. But Vegas was the dirtiest place possible. In Vegas you either gambled, went to shows, shopped, or fucked. The lower class might not be able to fork over two bills for a show or drop a bundle at the tables, but anyone could have sex with their old lady or girlfriend. When a guy asked a girl to go to Vegas with him, he had only one thing on his mind.

Where the hell was Anne?

He was about to ask for another drink when he saw her out of the corner of his eye. As he spun his stool around, his tongue swept over his lower lip, and his dick stood at attention. He could see the outline of her body through her flimsy white dress. Christ, she was younger and prettier than he remembered. She was a fucking knockout. And she didn't have goop caked all over her face like some of the other women he'd played around with.

What was a girl like this doing with a middle-aged slob like himself?

"Hi, baby," she cooed, sliding up to him and giving him a peck on the cheek. "Let's go, okay?"

"What's the hurry?" he told her, glancing over at the bartender. "What are you drinking today? Want a vodka tonic or a margarita?"

"The valet is holding my car out front." She coughed, then waved her hand in front of her face. "Sweetie, don't you remember me telling you that I can't be around cigarette smoke? I have asthma. Listen, my bar is stocked. We can even take a swim if you want. I called ahead and had the pool cleaned."

Bryce had no idea what she was talking about. Then he recalled her mentioning something about owning a house here. "How far away is this place?"

"About fifteen minutes," she told him. "I told you I was involved with someone else, Bryce. I can't hang out at the bar with another man."

He was already itching for another drink. The traffic in Vegas was a bitch. The drive down the strip could take up to an hour, depending on the traffic. And except for high-rise apartments and condos that cost a bundle, there weren't any houses that close to town. "You didn't mind hanging out at the bar with me in Ventura."

Her face froze into hard lines. "That was different. Smoking is banned in California. I spend most of my time in San Francisco. I was just visiting my sister in Thousand Oaks. She works nights, so I got bored. I don't make it a habit to hang out in bars."

"Oh, yeah," he said, gesturing for the bartender. When he saw him talking to the blonde he'd seen earlier, he shouted, "Hey, you! Get your butt over here and get me a damn drink before I report your skinny ass to the management. Paying customers come before whores."

"Sorry, sir," he said, rushing to pour Bryce another Maker's Mark. He then asked Anne if he could get her something.

"All I need is a plastic cup," she said, resisting the urge to kick Bryce in the balls. She hated people who thought they were better than everyone else, that just because a man held a service-oriented job, they could treat him like trash. These were the people that kept things going. They drove the ambulances, arrested the criminals, put out the fires, and served bastards like Bryce his alcohol so he could drink himself into a stupor. They deserved respect.

Bryce turned to her. "Where does this guy you're dating live? I don't want some bozo kicking the door down and shooting me."

"He doesn't live in Vegas, but he comes here frequently to gamble. And no, he's never been to my house. I inherited it from my mother last year. I've never even told him about it. That way, if we split up, I don't have to worry about him coming around and bothering me." She snatched his drink off the table and poured it into the plastic cup, then shoved it back into his hand. "Pay your tab so we can leave."

The bar had become busy. Fed up, Anne seized him by the arm. "Forget paying them. All you have to do is hang out by a blackjack table and they'll give you drinks for free."

Bryce reluctantly followed her. "Is there a liquor store close to your house?"

"Within walking distance," she told him, steering him toward the front of the casino. "I've got enough Maker's Mark to fill a bathtub. Is that enough for you? I even have a fifth on ice in the car."

"That's my girl," Bryce said, slurring his words.

Anne elbowed her way through the throng of people in the casino, putting on her sunglasses before they exited through the wall of doors. Walking over to the valet stand, she slapped her ticket and a ten spot down on the counter. "I'm the white Escalade over there," she said, pointing. "Just give me the keys and we're done."

"Nice ride," Bryce told her, stumbling into the passenger seat and fumbling around for the seat belt. Instead of heading to the strip, she turned down a side street. Smart lady, he thought, sucking up whatever liquid was left in the plastic cup. "You really got a bottle of Maker's in this thing? Wouldn't mind another drink, if you don't mind."

"Would I lie to you?" Anne reached into the backseat and pulled a chilled bottle out of the cooler, unscrewing the top and filling up his cup. She smiled and said, "Finish your drink, baby, then try and take a little nap. You don't want to fall asleep later and miss the best fuck of your life, now, do you?"

"I'm . . . not . . . missing . . . shit." Bryce gave her a lecherous glance as he tipped the cup to his mouth. Some of it dribbled onto his chin, and he wiped it off with the back of his hand. "This tastes terrible. What the hell? . . . I'm not sure this crap is even alcohol."

Before he could put it together, his eyes rolled back in his head. She stopped at a light, and his head flopped forward, his heavy body pressing against the seat belt.

Turning into an underground parking garage for one of the older off-strip casinos, generally frequented by seniors who came on buses, Anne's cheerful expression disappeared and her jaw locked. She pushed Bryce's head back against the seat, then slapped him hard in the face. She didn't see anyone nearby, but even if she did, it wouldn't matter. Dramas like this played out all the time in Vegas.

Anne tried to get her wits about her and figure out what she should do. She couldn't risk driving around with a guy who looked as if he were going to crash through the windshield. Anytime she was on the road, whether the guy was dead or alive, she was at risk. At that very moment, there were scores of men and women in Vegas who had drunk or drugged themselves unconscious. Regardless, she couldn't afford to be stopped by the police.

She decided it was time to ditch what she referred to as the meet-and-greet rental car. She pulled up alongside a black Ford Explorer with an Avis sticker on the windshield. Avis had followed her directions and left it in the parking lot. She reached over Bryce to the glove box where the paperwork was and confirmed it was the right license plate, then removed the key from the envelope. She always rented two cars, each from a different company. She transported the victim in one car while he was alive and used the other for the disposal of the body, or specifically, the garbage bags containing the parts that had once been a human being. To prolong identification, she removed the head, hands, and teeth, burying each in separate locations. She favored Vegas because there were miles of desert roads outside of town that hardly anyone ever traveled. It was also easier to dig in sand than dirt.

The first time she'd dismembered a body, she'd become violently ill. It was amazing what a person could condition herself to. On the occasions when she performed her gruesome task, she thought of herself as an employee in a meatpacking plant. Humans might have worked their way to the top of the food chain, but they were still animals whose flesh contained nutrients. She jokingly referred to them as "the other white meat" and would have gladly eaten her bastard father if she'd had the opportunity. When she thought of the millions of people who died of starvation, as well as the overcrowding in the prison system, she thought of a way they should solve both problems. All they had to do was carve up all the pedophiles and child abusers and ship them off to third world countries.

She hadn't anticipated needing the Explorer until later that night. But things weren't shaping up the way she had planned. Enraged, she balled up her fist and slugged Bryce in the face. When he still didn't react, she put her fingers around his wrist and checked his pulse. "Fucking stupid prick," she shouted, pounding the steering wheel with her fists. "If you hadn't been such an asshole, I wouldn't have overdosed you."

She got out and circled to the back, opening the hatch on the Escalade and removing a sack containing a box cutter that she'd purchased at FedEx when she'd picked up her tools. Opening the brown cardboard container, she pulled out a rope, then returned to the front and tied it around Bryce's neck to keep his head from falling forward. His double chin almost concealed the rope, but to make certain, she removed her panty hose and wrapped them around his neck like a scarf.

She was tempted to kick him out in the parking lot, but she wanted to make herself available to Lily during the waiting process. In addition, he'd made a spectacle of himself at the bar. If his body surfaced too soon, someone might remember seeing the two of them together. Although she'd worn a brunette wig, she had not disguised her facial features with makeup the way she generally did. She vowed not to make this mistake again.

Closing the passenger door, she unlocked the Explorer, hopped inside, and positioned it as close as possible to the back of the Escalade. There were empty parking spaces everywhere, but she had to work fast, as the two vehicles were blocking the aisle.

She reclined the passenger seat in the Escalade as far as

it would go. Her intent was to roll Bryce's body from one vehicle to the other. Nothing like this had ever happened before, where the guy had died before she'd taken him to the kill site. Her hands were trembling, her breath coming in quick bursts. She suddenly saw brown smudges on one side of her dress. Her eyes darted to the dust-covered Ford in the next row. She must have brushed up against it.

A vision of the ragged, filthy clothing she'd been forced to wear as a child appeared in her mind, and she covered her ears to the children's torments. Tears spilled down her face as she remembered all the afternoons she'd squatted in the knee-high weeds, peering through the slats in the dilapidated fence as she watched the children laughing and playing. She began to rip at the dress with her fingernails, panicked to get it off. On all fours, she climbed to the back and got out the clothes she'd worn on the flight from Los Angeles. As soon as she'd changed into the jeans and T-shirt, she rolled up the white dress in a tight ball. Unable to stand having it in the car, she pitched it out the window.

Finally managing to get hold of herself, she tried to figure out how she was going to get Bryce into the Explorer. He was too fat. She couldn't roll him if she couldn't get him out of the front seat and turn him on his side. Not only that, she needed something she could use to cover him. All she had were garbage bags and she couldn't very well wrap him in them, not while he was still in one piece.

A young man came out of the back door of the casino, fiddling with his wallet. She scooted down in the seat, waiting to see where he was headed. When she saw him walking straight toward the Escalade, she turned the key in the ignition. As soon as the engine engaged, she roared out of the parking lot.

FIFTEEN

❧

Lily finished reviewing a stack of motions and stood up from behind the antique desk in the library. It was only a few minutes past eight and she'd already done everything. She had even cleaned out her briefcase, something she hadn't done in months.

Carrying her cell and the house phone with her, she set them down on the edge of the Jacuzzi and stripped off her clothes. She was amazed at the abundance of time she had without Bryce around. It might be nice if he traveled more often. He always made meals such a time-consuming ordeal. They had to decide if they were going to cook at home or go out. Then they had to agree on a restaurant, order their food, wait for it to arrive, eat, and pay the check. They seldom got home by eight, sometimes later. Before getting any work done, Lily had to spend time with Gabby, open the mail, straighten up the house, and put in a load of laundry. A cleaning crew came in once a week, but Bryce was a pig and she always had to pick up after him.

It was strange that she hadn't heard from him by now. He was probably drinking. She picked up her cell and pushed the autodial. His phone rang six or seven times, then his recoding came on and she hung up. Leaving lame messages was not her style. In reality, she would have preferred not to talk to him at all. She had seen him just that morning, so it wasn't as if they had anything important to say to each other.

Lowering herself into the swirling water, Lily thought about her emotionally wrenching lunch with Chris Rendell. Bursting the bubble of fantasy surrounding a handsome, intensely desirable man was depressing. When she was in college, she'd been attracted to the stereotypical guy—tall, dark, handsome, and mysterious. She'd later determined that a lot of these men were simply stupid, just somehow smart enough to keep their mouths shut so no one would know. Rendell, of course, wasn't in that category. He was genuinely brilliant.

The contradiction with Rendell was that he had appeared so together. She had to hand it to him. He had everyone fooled. The man was a great actor. Eventually he would get over his wife and daughter's deaths. Even though it sounded trite, time really did heal wounds. A person might have to learn to deal with bad memories, but they no longer held the power to cripple you. Although she'd revisited the past again, Lily had handled the afternoon session without a problem.

She called Tessa. "I'm sorry I didn't make it to the club this morning. Was Anne there?"

"No, neither one of you brats showed up. I knew you'd like Anne, Lily. People always get along if they have something in common. Besides, she's young and beautiful. How could anyone not like her?"

"She's interesting," Lily said, hoisting one leg onto the side of the tub. "We had a long chat the other day after you left. I don't agree with everything she says, but she has a—"

Her friend cut her off. "I guess I'm not as interesting as Anne."

Lily pulled her leg back from the edge of the Jacuzzi and sat up. "Jesus, Tessa, you always find a way to make me feel guilty. Of course Anne's more interesting right now. I just met the woman. Why are you so moody? Did something happen today?"

"Yes," Tessa told her, crying. "When no one showed up, I bought a dozen brownies from the snack bar and ate them all on the way home. I weigh a hundred and fifty-three pounds now. None of my clothes fit me."

"Did you throw up the brownies?"

"No way. I'm not bulimic. If I barfed everything up, I wouldn't be fat, would I?"

Lily got out and reached for a towel, concerned for her friend. "That's not true, honey."

"Then I'll starve myself."

"You're a teacher, Tessa. You should know these things. If you don't eat regular meals, your body will think you're starving and start to store fat cells. It's the same thing with bulimics. Why are you so obsessed with your weight? You have a good job and a husband who adores you." Lily's phone beeped and she saw Bryce's number on the caller ID. "I'll call you back. Bryce is on the other line.

"Hi, baby," she said, wrapping the towel around her and heading to the bedroom so she could get dressed. Tessa and her problems were getting tedious. When her husband didn't say anything, she heard some kind of noises in the background. "I can't hear you, Bryce. We must have a bad connection. Go somewhere else and call me back."

Lily hit the off button on her cell phone and tossed it onto the bed. Walking over to the bureau, she dressed in a pair of shorts and a tank top. She waited ten minutes and then carried the phone with her to the kitchen, where Bryce had left his itinerary. Picking it up off the counter, she flipped through the pages that listed his various airline flights until she came to his hotel information. He was staying at the Embassy Suites Hotel in Lexington, Kentucky, tonight. She chastised herself for not checking out his travel plans before he left, but then again, he hadn't given her much notice. The Embassy Suites had free cocktails at happy hour, the last thing Bryce needed.

Assuming he wasn't in his hotel room, she took the papers to the library and sat down in a green leather recliner that had belonged to Bryce's father. She loved to sit here and watch the evening sun filter through the stained-glass windows.

Lily knew she should call Tessa back and explain what had happened, but she didn't want to miss Bryce's call. There was something about the background noises that bothered her. It wasn't the sound she generally associated with a poor connection, more like some type of equipment. She called his cell phone again, but he didn't answer. This wasn't like Bryce. Even when he was drinking, he always checked in with her.

She picked up the house phone and set her cell down on the desk, so the line wouldn't be busy if Bryce called back. After thirty minutes clicked off, she dialed the number for the hotel.

"Embassy Suites Hotel," a cheerful female voice said. "How may I assist you?"

"Bryce Donnelly's room, please."

"Certainly."

When no one answered, Lily called back and the same operator answered. "I need to leave a message for Mr. Donnelly."

"I'll connect you to his voice mail."

"Wait," Lily said, standing. "Can't you just take a message?"

"I'll be happy to, but all I'm going to do is leave your name and number on Mr. Donnelly's voice mail. That's the way we do it."

"Fine." Lily began speaking as soon as she heard the beep. "Please call me, Bryce. I don't care how late it is. I won't be able to sleep until I talk to you."

She started to call Shana at school, but she would sense something was wrong, and if she told Shana something might have happened to Bryce, she would be elated. She was still upset with Lily for marrying him.

Lily knew she was being paranoid, but she couldn't help it. The knot in her stomach told her something was wrong. What if Bryce had passed out in the street and had been trying to reach her when a thug came along and robbed him? In most instances, he should be able to defend himself, as long as the attacker wasn't armed. Bryce wasn't a lightweight in any sense of the word, but even a large man was worthless when he was drunk. As she thought about it, her concerns were replaced by anger. Regardless of what she'd said in her message, she refused to stay up all night waiting for a phone call. She was in the middle of a murder trial, and owed it to the victim to be mentally alert.

"Damn you, Bryce," Lily said, snatching the phones off the desk and carrying them back to the bedroom.

Driving around with a corpse was a good way to end up in prison.

After leaving the casino parking lot in Las Vegas, Anne had made it a third of the way to her house when she saw the flashing lights in her rearview mirror. Her heart began palpitating and her hands locked on the steering wheel. What had she done to cause the police to stop her? She hadn't been speeding, nor had she made an illegal turn. Had someone seen her wrestling with Bryce's body?

Anne stared at the gas gauge. The tank was full. She could try and outrun them. An officer was already walking toward the driver's door. She didn't have a gun, and even if she did, she wouldn't kill a cop. She stuck her head out the window, hoping it would block his view of her dead passenger, then mustered up her most innocent smile. "What did I do, Officer?"

"Looks like your left front tire is low," he said, squatting down to take a look at it. He stood and returned to the window. "I didn't see a nail, but you might want to have it checked. Don't want to have a flat, do you? This isn't the safest town for a pretty girl like you to be stranded."

"Thanks," Anne said. "I'll take care of it right away."

He shone his flashlight into the car. "What's going on with your friend over there?"

This was it. If she didn't do something fast, she would end up facing a murder rap. "Actually, he's my boss," Anne lied, placing her hands in her lap so he wouldn't see how badly they were shaking. "We came here for a convention. Mr. Farnsworth had too much to drink. I got him to the car, then he passed out. I'm taking him back to his hotel."

"What hotel are you staying at?"

Her mind went blank. All she could think of was the Aladdin where she had met Bryce, the last place she wanted to mention. "Oh, forgive me, Officer. I'm a little nervous. I'm afraid Mr. Farnsworth's wife will think we're having an affair. I'm staying with a friend. He's staying at the MGM."

"You're a good ways from the strip. Are you lost?"

"No, no," Anne told him, feeling queasy. "I thought if I drove around for a while, he might sober up. I don't think that's going to happen, so I guess I'll head back."

He started to walk off, then yelled out over his shoulder, "Make sure to have that tire checked."

Anne waited for him to leave, but he was just sitting behind her in his patrol car. She drove to the light, then saw the sign that indicated it was legal to make a U-turn. She had to drive toward the strip or the officer would get suspicious. Just because he had let her go didn't mean the incident wouldn't come back to haunt her. The number of people who could place her in Vegas with Bryce had grown, and one of them was now a cop.

The inside of the car was dark, though, and she wasn't sure if the officer had been able to make out Bryce's features, especially since his profile was the only thing visible. Still shaken, she smiled and waved to the officer as she drove past.

Anne couldn't allow a police officer to follow her to her house. Regardless of how meticulously she cleaned, she knew it could still contain evidence. Once the dust had settled over Bryce's disappearance, she would rip out the cheap linoleum floors and replace them. The good thing about linoleum was blood didn't sink through. Next, she would dispose of all the furniture, paint all the walls and cabinets, and list the house for sale at a bargain price. After this fiasco, she would stop using Vegas as a kill site.

She drove a few miles, constantly checking her rearview mirror to make sure the police car wasn't behind her. Maybe this had been a sign that she should stop. Ventura would be the perfect place to settle down. If the urge to kill surfaced, she would dope herself up until it went away. She could use some of the money she'd squirreled away to buy a nice house.

Fairly certain the cop hadn't followed her, she steered the Escalade into another parking structure. She circled until she reached the top level, then saw it was empty except for two dust-covered, dilapidated cars parked a substantial distance apart. People whose cars were about to be repossessed sometimes hid them in parking structures. Others reported a car stolen and stashed it until their insurance company issued them a check. Since hotel parking garages were private property, the police seldom patrolled them, leaving it up to the casinos to tow the abandoned vehicles. Cars could sit there for months, the casino operators afraid they would tow a gambler's car and lose a customer. A lot of people didn't use their cars when they were in Vegas, especially if they were cheap and old. With a handful of cash in your pocket and some decent threads, a guy who worked for minimum wage could jump in a cab and pass himself off as a high roller.

She parked and turned off the motor, wanting to check Bryce again to make certain he was dead. The dosage of Versed she'd placed in his drink had been three times what she had used on her previous victims. Even so, she hadn't expected it to really kill him. There was no telling how much alcohol he had consumed, and mixing it with a hefty dose of Versed might have been lethal. Bryce was a big man, though, and medication needed to be adjusted in accordance with a person's body weight.

Placing her cheek next to his mouth, she didn't detect even a whisper of a breath. Then she checked his pulse again. She thought she felt something, then decided it was her own heartbeat. Maybe he'd had a heart attack. His mouth was open, and a combination of drool and vomit was caked on his lips. Her eyes filled with disgust. What had Lily ever seen in this man?

Anne decided she wouldn't be in this predicament if she had followed her own rules and not deviated from the plan. It hadn't been such a big deal that she'd been seen with Bryce in the bar. There was nothing distinctive about his appearance. He looked like the majority of men who hung out in casinos. Bloodshot eyes, blubbery stomachs, tossing down booze as if it were water. She'd been too eager to get rid of him, and not merely because he repulsed her, but because she'd wanted to rush back and comfort Lily in the days and weeks that followed.

Before she died, Anne wanted to experience love, respect, and loyalty. A man could never provide her with these things, as she wouldn't let him. How could she? She knew how selfish and shallow men were, the meaningless promises they made to their wives and girlfriends, the disgusting thoughts that occupied their minds. Lily didn't have to love her romantically, as sex held no interest for her. Everything she craved could be obtained from a friend. Just a friend, she thought, tears pooling in her eyes.

No one had ever genuinely cared about her, let alone loved her. Bounced from one foster home to the other, Anne had survived by remaining silent and detached. The fewer words she spoke, the less chance there was of provoking her foster parents' wrath. Keeping to herself, though, couldn't stop the other children from ridiculing her. Four of her toes on her right foot and three on her left had been so severely frostbitten, the doctors had been forced to amputate. Being abandoned hadn't been enough. As a result of the cruelty inflicted by her father, she'd become a freak. "Go live in a circus, freak girl," the kids would taunt, laughing and pointing at her feet. "Maybe they'll feed you some elephant pies, or let you clean up the monkey cage."

She had arrived at her first foster home with a pair of crutches. They were not replaced as she grew taller, making it increasingly more difficult for her to walk. Many times she would crawl in order to give her weary body a rest. Her foster parents, knowing she wouldn't complain, assigned her the worst chores. She cleaned toilets, scrubbed floors, washed dishes, changed dirty diapers. One time they made her cut the lawn with a pair of scissors.

At night, her feet spasmed and her back throbbed from bending over her crutches. The people she lived with continually reminded her how lucky she was to have a roof over her head. Her disability and lack of social skills made it almost impossible to find a placement for her, and those who did take her in treated her badly. She rummaged around in her foster father's pants one day while he was sleeping and stole enough money to buy a train ticket to California.

Her next foster home had been located in a gang-invested neighborhood in Oxnard, but outside of being strict, Mrs. Diaz treated her fairly well in the beginning. As soon as Anne developed breasts, an older boy in the home named Ricky began talking dirty to her. Ricky climbed into her bed one night, holding her down and trying to force his dick into her mouth. It was a good thing Mrs. Diaz had heard her screaming and pulled him off her, because Anne had been about to bite his dick off. Her foster mother never punished Ricky because he was her son.

By then, other young thugs in the area were also eyeing her. Anne was terrified of being raped, remembering seeing her father having sex with Mrs. Murphy. The next time Ricky got in her bed, she shoved her knee into his crotch, laughing as he limped off crying to his mother. Ricky swore Anne had kicked him for no reason, and of course, his mother believed him. She decided Ricky was going to eventually succeed and rape her, so she stole two hundred dollars from Mrs. Diaz's purse and fled.

Anne's days on the street had been spent trying to remain unnoticed by people who would hurt or use her, picking through trash for food, and stuffing old newspapers into her clothes in an attempt to stay warm. Lack of proper nutrition and exposure to the elements had finally caused her to become psychotic. She would hold on to the rims of trash cans for days, believing she was still clinging to the fence along the interstate.

When she was sixteen, a police officer stumbled across her, filthy and incoherent. The court committed her to a state-run mental facility for six months, then managed to locate another foster home. During the two years she lived with Mrs. Daniels, a seventy-three-year-old deaf woman, Anne became determined to educate herself. She caught up with her schoolwork and managed to graduate from high school.

After she turned eighteen, the state was no longer legally obligated to care for her. Anne secured her first job in data entry at VPA Computer Systems. Mrs. Daniels was so crippled and demented by then, she failed to realize she was no longer receiving financial aid for her ward. Anne continued to live in the tiny room at the back of her home, the first decent environment she had ever had.

When old lady Daniels died, Anne carried her frail body to the attic. The dilapidated house was paid for, but she had to find a way to cash the woman's Social Security checks so she could pay the utilities. When they disconnected the electric and gas six weeks later, Anne panicked. She remembered all the times the power had gone off when she was a child, and how terrified she was of the dark. She decided she had endured more than her share of hardship, and vowed to take charge of her life.

She became proficient in the art of disguise. She went to a costume store and rented a white wig, a pair of thick glasses, and a padded undergarment that went with a Santa Claus outfit. Using an eyebrow pencil, she etched in wrinkles around her mouth and eyes, smeared lipstick on her cheeks, and caked on a ton of powder. She then put on one of Mrs. Daniels's better dresses and headed to the bank.

The teller had counted out the money without making eye contact. Old people were invisible, Anne decided. She assumed it was because no one wanted to be bothered, or perhaps because an older person reminded them of their own elderly parents and the guilt they carried for not caring for them properly.

Along with her salary, Anne had saved whatever money

remained after she'd paid the expenses on the house, and used it to purchase prostheses for her feet. By then, technology had made it possible for her not only to walk, but to even jog for short distances. She didn't do these things without pain, but physical pain she could handle. With opaque stockings, she could almost pass for normal.

Her first break came when a middle-aged man named Doug Talley at the company where she worked took an interest in her, and decided to teach her the basics of computer programming. She learned fast, and Talley quickly became a role model and father figure. When he later invited her to his apartment and tried to coerce her into having sex with him, he reinforced Anne's belief that all men were perverted and evil.

The stench inside Mrs. Daniels's house became unbearable and the attic windows were covered with swarms of flies. She realized it was only a matter of time before the flies accumulated on the downstairs windows and someone notified the authorities. Since Mrs. Daniels had been deaf and couldn't hear the doorbell, no one stopped by to check on her, and to the best of her knowledge, she had no living relatives.

When Anne decided she could no longer remain in Mrs. Daniels's home, she rolled the woman's decomposing body into a moth-eaten rug from the attic, dragged her to the living room where she had found her and propped her up in her recliner in front of the television. She had no idea how long Mrs. Daniels remained there before her body was discovered by the authorities.

Moving to an inexpensive apartment, she began to hone her body. Because of the cheap food she'd always eaten, she was fifteen to twenty pounds overweight. She dieted and exercised rigorously.

Her goal was to become the spider to the fly.

The first person Anne murdered had not been her father, as she'd stated in the recording she sent to the FBI. She had never seen her father again, nor had she made any attempt to locate him or her mother. As she grew older, she realized her mother was partly responsible for what had happened. She had failed to protect her child and remained married to a drunk, worthless excuse for a man, who consistently abused her daughter. The woman she had worshipped had also been a drug addict. She recalled seeing her father sticking needles into her arm, and her mother smiling and telling her it was medicine, then getting a dreamy, faraway look on her face. Even if her mother was afraid of getting arrested, there was no excuse for abandoning her daughter.

Anne became convinced that most men were no different than her father, and the only way to relieve the volcano of emotional pain inside her was to kill as many of them as she could. Needing to practice on someone, she chose as her first victim a bum who called himself Blue. Not the kind of thing she wanted to brag about to the FBI, the agency that tracked the most lethal and, as she saw it, the most intelligent criminals in existence.

Anne took great pride in her work. The majority of people couldn't get away with killing one person, let alone a whole string of them. The problem was she couldn't bask in her accomplishments. Besides, the only individuals who could appreciate her skills were police officers, and even they didn't truly appreciate her. Other than the idiots of society who were fascinated with serial killers, her primary fan club was the FBI's elite unit that dealt with serial killers.

Even her first kill had been perfectly executed.

Anne knew Blue from her days on the street, and he seemed to be an excellent candidate. She didn't hate Blue. He had never done anything to hurt her, but he'd also done nothing to help her. A good beggar and an even better thief, whenever Blue scored cash, he headed straight to the liquor store. For six months, she had lived in a cardboard box only a few feet away from him. Blue had known she was a kid, and also knew about her deformities. One of the other homeless people had stolen her shoes on a particularly cold winter night, and Anne had run to Blue, sobbing hysterically as she told him of her fear that she would lose more toes to frostbite. Finding himself with a full cup at the end of the day, Blue had taken off to the Salvation Army to see if he could get her a pair of shoes. Instead, he had returned drunk, clutching an empty bottle of cheap whiskey.

Anne had witnessed a murder once when she was twelve, which she now believed had been the onset of her bloodlust. She'd been living in Mrs. Diaz's home in Oxnard at the time. She never told anyone about what she saw, even when the police came around asking questions, because she was afraid her foster parents would punish her for going outside without their permission.

The memory of that day was still clear in her mind.

Instead of doing her chores, she'd snuck outside to see the sunrise, then fallen back asleep under a tree in the side yard facing the street. The sound of the gunshot had startled her, but strangely, she'd been more curious than afraid. Crawling on her stomach in the damp grass, she'd stared through the metal fence at the face of the killer, a tall, skinny person with a long neck and pale skin. In the blink of an eye, the man next door was dead. Anne thought of all the people who had been mean to her, and fantasized what it would be like to kill them. But she didn't like the sound of the gun going off. Loud noises hurt her ears.

When she'd decided to move to Ventura, she had driven by the old house in Oxnard, reliving that morning in her mind. Although everyone believed the shooter was a man, Anne had sensed something distinctively feminine. The person's features were too delicate and the skin was fair and flawless. And where was the person's hair? The killer had been wearing a stocking cap, and no hair whatsoever was visible. This was before shaving your head became popular. When the shooter turned around to get into her car, Anne saw the hair was going up instead of down. This was one of the reasons she thought the killer was a woman; she looked as if she'd pushed all her hair up inside the knit cap. Maybe it was just her imagination, but Anne held on to it, and the lady killer became her hero. The guy she had killed had been one of the thugs making moves on Anne, and then this lady came out of nowhere and blew him to pieces.

When Anne had finally tracked down Blue to make her first kill, his skin had been yellow. She knew it wouldn't be long before his liver gave out. He was squatting on the ground, nodding off, his clothes filthy and reeking of booze. Sneaking up behind him, among the high shrubs where he'd set up his cardboard home, she placed a piece of thin wire around his neck, then kicked him hard in the center of his back, a technique she'd seen in gangster movies. The wire had sliced through his carotid artery and Blue had quickly bled to death.

The gushing blood hadn't bothered her. She knew she was in a heightened state, yet she enjoyed the warmth of it. If she ever found herself abandoned outside in a frigid place again, she would find a way to cut herself and let the blood warm her. She should have cut herself on the barbed wire fence the night her father left her and let the blood wash over her feet. Then she wouldn't have become a freak.

Anne had searched the newspapers in the weeks that followed, but there was no mention of Blue's death. Even in death, homeless people were second-class citizens.

The FBI agents were fools if they believed a murderer

would tell them the truth. She didn't know what had possessed her to send them the tape, other than the fact that she was between kills and had nothing better to do. Since she hadn't heard or read anything about it in the media, she assumed they hadn't taken it seriously. Now that she had a dead guy in the car, she hoped it was true. FBI agents were sneaky bastards. Even when they knew who you were, they didn't simply rush out and arrest you like the regular cops did. They set up surveillance, waiting until they were certain they had enough dirt on you to get a conviction. The FBI was a dog she didn't want with her scent up its nose.

When a person spoke of getting high, he was generally referring to smoking pot, drinking, or doing lines of cocaine. Killing quickly became Anne's drug of choice. She compared it to eating chocolate for the first time and knowing instantly that you would want to eat it the rest of your life. For once, Anne tasted power and was instantly addicted.

She later came to the realization that killing low-life losers like Blue or her father was an unworthy pursuit. These types of men eventually self-destructed on their own. Why waste her time killing them? It was the wealthy men, the ones who had everything, who whipped her into a murderous frenzy. They had beautiful wives, adorable children, expensive homes, and bulging bank accounts. None of it was enough to satisfy their lust and greed. Before she could kill these kinds of men, though, she first had to get close to them.

Anne educated herself via the library and the Internet. She stayed late every night working at her computer in the empty office building. Her mind became bloated with knowledge. She did exhausting research on any subject that captured her attention, amazed at how easily she could comprehend and commit things to memory. She stood outside fine restaurants, studying the women's clothes, hair, makeup, as well as how they spoke and carried themselves.

In transforming herself into bait for her prey, Anne developed other skills as well. When she assumed a role of a confident, sophisticated woman, she acted the part with chilling precision. New job opportunities opened up, allowing her to move into a nicer apartment. Although her life appeared to be taking a turn upward, nothing could eradicate the burning hatred inside of her.

Anne pulled herself out of her thoughts and turned to Bryce. The fucker still looked too much like a corpse. She had to find a way to get his head down. Driving to the first level of the parking structure, she locked Bryce's body in the Escalade, then rummaged around in the trash dumpster. She found a broken piece of plywood and carried it back to the car. Once she untied the rope around Bryce's neck, she struck him in the back with the board until his knees sank to the floorboard and his head tipped forward against the dash.

"There," Anne said, draping her T-shirt over his head. The only thing left was to carve him up and dispose of him. If everything went smoothly from this point on, she might be able to make the twelve-fifteen flight back to Los Angeles. That way, she could catch a few hours' sleep and see Lily at the club in the morning.

SIXTEEN

❧

"Another dismembered body was found in San Bernardino last month," Mary said, catching John Adams in the parking lot. "He disappeared in August. They identified the body this afternoon."

"Then what's this about you wanting to go to Dallas, Stevens?"

"The victim's name was Stanley Louis Waverly. They found him in San Bernardino, but he resided in Dallas. Waverly was a prominent man, an international attorney with political aspirations. The other man, the one found in Las Vegas, was from San Francisco."

"What connects these two cases, outside of the obvious?"

"Numerous things," Mary told him, pulling her jacket closed. The weather report said it was going to snow tonight, and she'd left her coat on the back of the chair. "Both men were disarticulated in the same manner. Head, hands, and teeth."

Adams stopped at his car, pushing the button for the alarm. The expression on his face was flat, disinterested. He carried a heavy load and it showed. He normally had perfect posture, but today his shoulders were rolled forward, and he had dark shadows under his eyes. He'd recently undergone major dental reconstruction from grinding his teeth. Mary was probably headed in the same direction. "They're also in the same age bracket, mid-forties to early fifties."

"The victim in Vegas was a closet gambler, wasn't he? My guess is he was killed over gambling debts." Adams opened the door to his Chrysler and climbed into the driver's seat. "I thought you weren't going to bother me until you had something definitive. You're not a homicide detective anymore. The United States is a big place. People are murdered every day, most of them by a family member or acquaintance."

"But these men were butchered."

"We're seeing more dismembered bodies these days. Even a housewife in Massachusetts chopped up her husband the other day. She intended to boil the bones, but the kitchen caught on fire. If we have a similar case in Oregon, it doesn't mean the two cases are related."

"I understand, sir," Mary said, standing in front of the open car door to keep him from closing it. "The most compelling thing is the victims weren't where they were supposed to be."

"How's that?"

"They both left detailed itineraries. Howard Goldstein lives in San Francisco and told his wife he was going to San Diego on business."

"Is this the body they found in Las Vegas?"

"What was left of it," Mary told him, rubbing her hands together to warm them. "The San Diego PD says he was never there, although his wife swore she called the hotel in San Diego and was transferred to his room. The Dallas PD claims Mrs. Waverly told them an almost identical story. Stan Waverly is the man they found dismembered in San Bernardino."

"Get in the car."

"Thanks, I'm about to turn into an ice cube." Mary circled around to the passenger side and got in.

Adams asked, "Have you eaten?"

"No," she said, her stomach rumbling at the thought of

food. "Are you going to feed me? If I had to apprehend someone right now, I might take a bite out of them."

Adams laughed. "Your father's sense of humor was one of the things I loved about him. I didn't think anyone could make me smile today. You win the prize, kiddo."

"I hope so," she said. "I didn't bring any money." She felt a wave of pleasure wash over her. Whenever she was alone with Adams, she could sense her father's presence. They used to drink beer together in the den and watch football games, boisterously cheering for their team. She could almost smell her mother's fried chicken crackling in the kitchen from the other room, and the sweet-smelling cigars her father smoked. Her father would be happy knowing she was working under the guidance of a man he trusted and admired.

Adams's sour mood returned. "A third child was kidnapped from a shopping center today in New Mexico. The state police have asked for our help. The first two have been missing three weeks, so the chances that they're alive are remote. It eats me up when the victims are kids."

"I know," Mary said, having handled a number of child murders herself. They were the reason why many law enforcement officers resigned or asked for a transfer out of homicide.

They drove awhile in silence, both of them lost in their thoughts. "I know analyzing crime scenes is one of the most important things we do," Mary spoke up. "But if I could speak to the wives in person, maybe interview some of the people who knew the victims, I might get a clearer perspective. If these men were cheating on their wives, someone must know. They're all middle-aged, and I think it's possible that successful men might be more prone to having affairs."

"And why is that?"

"Because low- to middle-income men don't have the

time or energy," Mary told him. "I assume romancing another woman costs money. There's hotel rooms, food, booze, gifts."

"Have you requested the documents from these two homicides from FSRTC yet? That's where you'll find your clearer perspective."

Another acronym, Mary thought sardonically. She missed the days when the crime lab was simply the lab, and suspects were either bad guys or assholes. Calling someone who had tortured and murdered children an UNSUB didn't really fill the bill for her. Regardless of how sophisticated the FBI perceived itself, it was still a cop shop.

The Forensic Science Research and Training Center, on the other hand, was internationally renowned for the development of new methodologies in forensic science and was the primary means for transferring new concepts, techniques, and procedures to forensic science and law enforcement communities. It was the starship of the Bureau. More than a million examinations were conducted every year.

"Some of it came in today," Mary said, referring to the stacks of boxes she had received late that afternoon. And that presented only a fraction of the lab's findings related to the Goldstein homicide. When she said the Las Vegas PD had identified Goldstein's body, the actual work had been done by the FSRTC. "Just listen, sir. If these cases come together, we're going to find ourselves humping other agencies for dominance. The originating police departments who filed the missing person reports want to bounce me back to the agencies who recovered the remains. Everyone is in the dark as to where these murders actually occurred. I didn't want to put too much pressure on the agencies who recovered the remains until you gave me a green light and some FBI muscle."

He glanced over at her with a fatherly look. "Where's your coat?"

Mary arched a well-formed eyebrow. "If I'd known you were going to treat me to dinner, I would've brought it." She pointed at her black shoes. "And I wouldn't have worn these ugly things, either."

"You haven't mentioned the tape or any possibility of a serial killer, have you?"

"Absolutely not."

"What do you hope to accomplish in Dallas?" Adams went on. "We can have an agent from our field office handle it."

He was driving on autopilot, his immense mind sorting through every alternative and possibility. If the tape had actually been sent from the person who'd murdered Waverly and Goldstein, the FBI would have a chance at getting inside the head of an active serial killer. This was the type of opportunity a man like Adams had wet dreams about. The FBI could not only put a violent predator behind bars, they could amass data, which in turn would be disseminated to law enforcement agencies throughout the world. The most important of all was the chance to save lives.

Mary countered, "With all due respect, don't you think there are enough fingers in the pie already?"

"That's not the way the FBI works," Adams said, cutting his eyes to her.

"But shouldn't we try to control things until we get farther along? FSRTC is still working on the tape. Their preliminary reports showed no prints, no fibers, no hairs, or any type of biological material we could use for DNA typing. Voice analysis showed the tape wasn't made by one individual, as I suspected. They believe the different voices were downloaded from a computer, maybe excerpts from podcasts, online news broadcasts, or even TV shows."

The sun was filtering in through the trees as they navigated the wooded roads leading to Woodbridge, a town approximately seven miles from Quantico. "Strange," Adams said, his gloved hands locked on the steering wheel. "Why wouldn't someone with enough computer skills to do something like that simply burn it onto a CD? No one uses tapes these days, do they?"

"Maybe whoever made the tape didn't want us to know they had computer skills," Mary postulated. "FSRTC said the tape was hard to work with. It's already been damaged while making the first dupe. The UNSUB might have used tape because CDs are fingerprint magnets."

"Here we are," Adams said, turning into the parking lot of a popular Mexican restaurant. "Let's go get us some chow."

When they got out, he removed his coat and tossed it over Mary's shoulders. "Thanks," she said, "but can I go to Dallas?"

"We'll discuss it after dinner."

She halted. "I don't want to talk about it after dinner. Another man disappeared two months ago. He fits the profile of the Goldstein and Waverly cases. Forty-nine, married, Wall Street bond trader. His wife didn't report him missing until today because the firm he worked for wanted to make certain he didn't abscond with any of their clients' money."

"You know how many people disappear from Manhattan every day?"

When lives were at stake, Mary took offense at knee-jerk reactions. "NYPD only filed an incident report. No one cares about these people until their bodies surface. The murders are going to escalate, chief. The killer isn't challenged enough. That's why he sent us the tape. He's pissed that we haven't noticed him."

Instead of snowing as the weatherman had predicted, it began sleeting. Adams walked to the front of the restaurant, thinking Mary was beside him. When he reached the door and realized she wasn't there, he turned around and saw her still standing in the middle of the parking lot. With a look of frustration, he walked back to her. "Come inside so we can eat."

Mary's teeth were chattering. "I'm not hungry, sir. I'll wait out here for you." A hint of a smile surfaced. "That is, unless you agree to allow me to go to Dallas."

"Damn it," he said, getting into her face. "You're wearing my coat. If you're going to pull a stunt like this, at least do it in your own clothes. That coat was expensive."

Mary took it off and handed it to him.

"You're a bigger headache than my wife. Even when you were a kid, you never accepted no for an answer. Take me for an ice cream, Uncle John. Buy me a toy. Play a game. Here's the deal, okay? Get me out of this dastardly weather and let me get some food in my stomach. I'll make arrangements for a helicopter to transport you to Andrews. From there, you'll fly to Dallas in a Bureau plane. Happy now?"

Mary flashed a satisfied smile. "Tonight?"

"Don't you have to pack a bag?"

"Already packed," Mary told him, linking arms with him. "It's so nice that we get to spend time together."

Adams opened the door for her. When she stepped through, he swatted her on the butt. "You know how long I've wanted to do that? If your father had disciplined you correctly, you wouldn't be such a spoiled brat."

"Now, now," Mary said, deciding to toy with him. "That's called sexual harassment, boss. I'm a big girl now."

"Oh, yeah," Adams barked. "Then shut your mouth and find us a table."

* * *

As the hours passed with no word from her husband, Lily walked the empty house. She had tricked herself into believing she enjoyed Bryce being gone. She hated to be alone, particularly at night. She picked Gabby up out of her bed and cradled the little dog in her arms.

Holding the Italian greyhound made her feel better. She decided to let Gabby sleep in the bed tonight. She missed having her warm body snuggled around her feet. Bryce didn't like to cuddle, so there was really no reason to deprive her of her pet. They'd been together four years now, and she doubted if Gabby would bite him.

"Hey, girl," she said, walking over to get her a biscuit. The dog became so excited, she almost leaped out of Lily's arms. "Are you going to keep Mommy company tonight?"

Lily opened the sliding glass door and stepped out onto the patio, setting Gabby on the grass. She remembered that Bryce might call and raced inside to get the two phones. It was hard enough to incorporate a cell phone into your life. Now people had to walk around with both their cell and their regular phone. Instead of calling Lily's home number, most people called her cell. She suspected some of them did because it made them feel important to have immediate access to a judge. Basically, though, the world had simply become mobile.

Lily's cell would frequently ring in the other room, then by the time she found her purse and retrieved it, the caller had hung up and called the house. Bryce had a habit of leaving their portable phones all over the place. Nothing frustrated her more than racing to a room to answer a call and finding the cradle empty.

She started to leave Gabby in the yard so the dog could do her business when she found herself staring at the sliding glass door. The rapist had come in through a sliding glass door. She was suddenly gripped by fear, searching the shifting shadows in the yard. Someone could be lurking out there. He could have followed her home from the courthouse. Maybe he'd been watching her and knew she was alone. She'd never had such a big yard before. There was an overabundance of mature trees and bushes, all of them perfect hiding places.

Lily looked for Gabby and didn't see her. Italian greyhounds were prissy little dogs, and would occasionally refuse to go if someone was watching them. She squinted, trying to spot the dog's white coat among the juniper trees. She started to call her, then stopped. If she went inside and came back with the phones, she might forget to lock the sliding glass doors the way she had the night she and Shana were raped. She clapped her hands, then called out, "Gabby, girl. Come to Momma."

When the dog didn't immediately appear, Lily's heart began racing. She was being irrational, paranoid. Bryce was fine, and no one was hiding in her yard. "Gabby," she hollered, this time more forcefully. The dog ran toward her and leaped into her arms. Lily darted inside the house, closed the door, and locked it.

She checked the rest of the doors. As she was about to set the alarm, she noticed the door leading to the garage wasn't locked. She walked over and turned the bolt. Jostling the seven-pound dog in one arm, she returned to the alarm panel and held down the button until it peeped and turned red.

A security system meant nothing. Lily never felt safe, even when she was at the courthouse. Evil was everywhere, floating around humans like sewage. Maybe she drew it to her somehow? Or maybe she panicked like this because she still carried a grudge against God. Where had He been when her precious daughter was brutally violated? She certainly hadn't felt God's presence when she'd blown Bobby Hernandez away.

The clock in the kitchen read a few minutes past twelve. She still hadn't heard from Bryce, and her jitters had intensified. She dialed the number to the hotel and was transferred to his room. All the operators sounded the same, she thought, wondering if the hotels trained them that way. This time she let the phone ring until she was automatically transferred to the voice mail system. "Bryce, this is Lily. If you don't call me by tomorrow morning, I'm going to notify the authorities. Damn you, I'm worried sick. All I can think about is you passed out in some filthy alley. I wouldn't have to go through this all the time if you would stop drinking. Call me!"

Lily left all the lights on except the one in the bedroom. She turned down the bed and climbed in with Gabby still nestled in her arms. "My sweet baby," she said, stroking her soft coat and kissing her on the head. The little dog disappeared under the covers.

After thrashing around for an hour, Lily decided to get up and turn the lights off in the rest of the house. If a burglar saw a house fully lit when most of the neighboring houses were dark, he might think the occupants were gone or the house was up for sale. Her fear was sparking all around her. She also wanted to make certain the sliding glass door had fully engaged.

The first thing she did was retrace her steps, turning off the light she had turned on earlier for fear someone was watching her through the windows. The existing drapes in the house had been so old and dusty, she'd removed most of them and the new ones weren't back yet from the drapery company. Since they didn't cook all that often, she and Bryce spent most of their time on the second floor, where the windows were obscured by two massive trees.

As she stood in the dark, Lily's hairs pricked on the back of her neck. She was once again in the house she had rented after she and Shana's father had separated. Since her daughter had opted to live with her father because he spoiled her, the night of the rape was Shana's first night in her mother's new home. It was also the night their lives changed forever. Lily was suddenly in the midst of it.

She glanced at the bedside clock. It was almost one o'clock in the morning. Lily started to retrieve her brief-case from the living room to go over a few cases, but she couldn't muster up the energy and instead removed her clothing and crawled under the covers, thinking that to-night sleep might come. Almost euphoric knowing her daughter was sleeping in the new four-poster bed across the hall and the evening had gone so well, she turned off the light. It then dawned on her that she had not checked the doors in the little house, a chore John had always handled when they lived together.

With her terrycloth robe wrapped loosely around her, she padded barefoot in the dark, deciding to check the kitchen door first. It was a quiet neighborhood: no cars, no barking dogs, just blissful silence.

Entering the kitchen, she saw the drapes billowing in the slight breeze, being sucked through the open sliding glass door. She chastised herself for not locking it but felt the area was so safe, it probably wasn't necessary. As she pushed the drapes aside and started pulling the door in the track, a funny feeling came over her, a sense of some-thing amiss. Holding her breath in order to hear better, she heard a squeak, like the sound a basketball player's sneakers make on the court.

It all happened at once: the noise behind her, her heart beating so fast it hurt, her robe pushed up from the floor over her face and head with lightning speed. As she strug-gled to scream and free herself, her feet slid out from un-der her, but she did not fall. She was being carried in a suffocating embrace. What felt like an arm was placed directly over her mouth. Trying to sink her teeth into him, she bit a mouthful of terrycloth instead. She was nude from the waist down, the cold night air against her lower body. Her bladder emptied, and she heard the splashing against the tile floor.

She tried to move her arms, but they were trapped across her chest inside the robe. She kicked out furiously. Her foot connected with what must be a kitchen chair, and it screeched across the floor, landing with a loud thud against the wall.

The backs of her calves and feet were burning. She knew she was being dragged down the hall—toward where her daughter slept. Shana, she thought. Oh, God, no, Shana. The only sound she emitted was a muffled, inhuman groan of sheer agony coming from her stomach through her vocal cords to her nasal passages. Her mouth would not move. Her feet struck something. The wall? No longer kicking, no longer struggling, she was praying, ". . . as I walk through the Valley of Death . . ." She couldn't remember the words. Not Shana, not her child. She had to protect her child.

"Mom." She heard Shana's voice, first questioning and childlike, and then the terror of her sickening high-pitched scream reverberated in Lily's head. She heard something heavy crash into the wall, body against body, the sound heard on a football field when the players collided. He had her. He had her daughter. He had them both.

In another moment, they were on the bed in Lily's room. When he removed his arm, the robe fell away from her face and she could see him in the light from the bathroom. Shana was next to her and he was over them both. Light reflected off the steel of the knife he held only inches from Shana's neck. Lily grabbed his arm, and with the abnormal strength of stark terror, she almost succeeded in twisting it backward, turning the knife toward him, seeing in her mind the blade entering his body where his heart beat. But he was too strong and with eyes wild with excitement, darting back and forth, his tongue protruding from his mouth, he forced the blade sideways into Lily's open mouth, the sharp edges nicking the tender sides of her lips. She bit down on the blade with her teeth, her tongue touching something crusty and vile.

His face was only inches away, his breath rancid with beer. "Taste it," he said, a look of pleasure on his face. "It's her blood. Lick it. Lick a whore's blood, a fucking whore's blood."

Removing the knife from Lily's mouth and placing it back at her throat, he moved his hand from Shana's neck and shoved her T-shirt up, exposing her budding breasts. Shana desperately tried to push the T-shirt down to cover herself, turning pleading eyes to Lily.

"No," she cried. "Stop him, Mommy. Please make him stop."

He thrust his fingers around her neck. She choked and gurgling sounds came from her throat; a trickle of saliva ran down the corner of her mouth. Her eyes were glazed.

"Be calm, Shana. Don't fight. Do what he says. Everything is going to be okay. Please, baby, listen to me." Lily's voice was forced control. "Let her go. I'll do anything you ask of me."

"That's it, Momma. You tell her. Tell her how fucking good it is. Tell her you want it." His guttural words were uttered through clenched teeth. He had one knee between Shana's legs, prying them open, and the other knee between Lily's, touching her genitals. "Unzip me," he ordered Shana.

The girl's terrified eyes again made contact with her mother's. "Do it, Shana," she said, watching while her child's thin, trembling hand reached for his crotch, unable to grab the small end of the zipper. He raised his body up somewhat, but the crusty knife remained near Lily's throat.

"Do it for her, Momma," he said, shifting the knife to his other hand and positioning it near Shana's navel. "Teach her how to take care of a man."

Lily had to distract him, somehow get him away from Shana. She had to find a way to get the knife. When he finished with them, he would kill them, kill them both. Quickly unzipping him and removing his penis, she placed it in her mouth, the ragged edges of the zipper scraping her face. She smelled urine and putrid body odor, but he was becoming erect and moaning, throwing his head back, moving the knife away from Shana's body. He grabbed a handful of her hair and jerked her head back. He fell on top of Lily, looking straight into her eyes and relishing the fear reflected there. Something struck her chest, then her chin. It was a gold cross with a crucified Christ dangling from around his neck.

Suddenly he thrust himself up. "No, I want her, Momma. I don't want a whore, a fucking old redheaded whore." He expertly tossed the knife from one hand to the other and once again placed it at Lily's throat. "Watch, Momma, watch or I'll gut her."

With one vicious yank, Shana's underpants were torn off and tossed aside. Her body bounced up on the bed and then fell under the weight of him. He forced himself inside her and Shana screamed in pain. Lily had never felt so powerless in her life. There was no God. She knew it now. No reason to pray. She wished he would just cut her throat and end it all.

"Oh, Momma. Oh, Momma," Shana gasped.

Lily found her hand and squeezed it tightly. It was cold

and clammy. "Hold on, baby. Close your eyes and make
believe you are far away. Hold on."

A loud siren wailed in the street somewhere. He jumped
and sprang from the bed. "The neighbors heard and called
the police," Lily said, hearing the sound growing nearer.
"They're going to shoot you, kill you." He was backlit by
the light emanating from the bathroom, his red shirt and
face visible as he frantically tried to snap his jeans. Lily
bolted upright in the bed and screamed in raw panic and
fury. "If they don't shoot you, I'll kill you myself."

SEVENTEEN

∽

WEDNESDAY, NOVEMBER 29
VENTURA, CALIFORNIA

Lily felt someone touch her shoulder and shrieked, her
body shaking as if she were having a seizure. She saw a
shadowy image beside her and started lashing out with
her arms.

A familiar voice said, "Shit, you hit me in the eye. It's
me, Lily, Tessa. I've been calling you for hours. What are
you doing on the floor? And why are you shaking? Did
someone hurt you? Should I call the police?"

Lily pushed herself to a standing position. She'd been
on the floor next to their new white sofa, the one Bryce
refused to allow Gabby to sit on, and where the little dog
was now snuggled comfortably among the plush pil-
lows. A dim but richly hued light was filtering in through
the sliding glass door. It took a few moments before Lily

realized it was morning. "I must have gone to sleep here last night," she said, not remembering anything after she'd gone downstairs. "I guess I was having a nightmare. Why are you here? Oh, my God, something's happened to Bryce. Is he hurt? Is he in jail?"

"Calm down, Lily," Tessa told her. "Nothing's wrong, okay? You never called me back last night. I was worried when you didn't show up at the club, so I called both numbers and got your voice mail."

Lily's back and neck were killing her, and words seemed to be coming at her like bullets. "Did you ever give thought to the fact that I might have been asleep?"

Tessa placed her hand on Lily's arm. "I even tried Bryce's cell. I don't know why, but I got this strange feeling something was wrong. There were these terrible murders in L.A. last night. The news said someone had broken in and killed a couple and their ten-year-old son."

The crimes had been on the evening news. They had occurred in Inglewood, an area plagued by gangs and violence. "This isn't L.A., Tessa. Ventura County is one of the safest and most affluent places in the United States."

"Well, things happen here, too. Aren't you trying a big homicide case right now?"

Lily didn't want to argue, but most of their violent crimes were caused by domestic abuse. Even the Stucky case fell into that category, as did the Burkell homicides.

"What's the deal with Bryce? Where is he, by the way?"

How could Tessa just walk in on her like this? Lily heard the lawn sprinklers go off. They were programmed to come on at six. Even though she felt deeply for Tessa, she didn't want the burden of her problems right now. She was a good person and a loyal friend, but she drained her. Unhappy people didn't seem satisfied until they made everyone around them miserable. But bulimia and anorexia were life-threatening problems. If Tessa had an eating disorder,

Lily would have to get her to fess up and figure out a way to help her.

"You were saying?" Tessa said, her hands on her hips. "You know, why you're worried about Bryce."

"It's nothing. He's away on a business trip. You just scared me, Tessa. I thought you were a burglar." Lily's curly hair looked as if it had been in a mixer. "You really shouldn't come in without my consent. Granted, I should have called you back last night, but—"

Her friend cut her off, one of her annoying habits. "Do you want your key back? Is that what you're trying to tell me? Fine. Whatever." She tossed her hands in the air, then let them slap back against her thighs. "I knew this would happen once you became a judge. You're just too important to hang out with a schoolteacher." Tears streamed down her face as she reached into her purse and tried to pry the key to Lily's house off her key chain.

Lily took her hand and closed it. "I love you, Tessa. Give me a minute to go to the bathroom and brush my teeth. If you want, you can put on a pot of coffee for us." She glanced at the clock. "It's not even six yet, so we have plenty of time to talk. You know where everything is, right?"

"Yeah," she answered, her face brightening.

Lily went upstairs, finding her cell and house phone on the end table by the bed. When she checked to see if her husband had called, she discovered the battery on her cell was dead. The same thing had probably happened to Bryce the night before. He'd been so disorganized the other morning, he may have forgotten his charger. She went to the bathroom and plugged her cell into the charger, then checked her messages again on both phones. There were five calls from Tessa, but nothing from her husband. Now that Tessa was here and the house was filled with sunlight, Lily's concerns were fading.

She quickly brushed her teeth and went to the toilet, then headed back downstairs before Tessa came barging into her bedroom. The nightmare was still vivid in her mind. When something or someone stirred up the past, explicitly the rape, her mind went through a process of sorting through the events like a computer search engine. After a while, the memories were returned to the archives where they belonged.

Lily did wonder if there was some meaning attached to the dream. She needed to see Shana. Talking to her on the phone wasn't good enough. She would call her at the noon break today and try to coerce her into coming for a visit.

Once Tessa left, Lily got dressed for work, then went to the library to see if she could track down Bryce. She called the Embassy Suites in Lexington, and was told Bryce had already checked out. She thumbed through his itinerary, seeing his next stop was Charleston. It was strange that he was staying at a Hilton, she thought, as he always said they were lousy hotels. She dialed the Hilton in Charleston, asking if Bryce had checked in yet.

"No," a male voice advised her. "Would you like to leave a message for him?"

"Tell him to call his wife immediately."

Lily rushed to the bedroom to get her cell, hitting the number for the autodial. She should have checked Bryce's flights first, as it appeared he wouldn't be departing for Charleston until one-thirty. Where the hell was he? The mailbox on his cell phone was full, more than likely from the messages she'd left the night before. If she hadn't heard from him by noon, she would start checking the jails and hospitals.

"Fuck you, Bryce." She had to be on the bench in forty minutes. Her back was throbbing, her eyes puffy, and she didn't have time to do anything but smear on some lipstick. If he was in jail, she would let him rot there. A reality check would do him good. She carried the weight of the world on her shoulders, and he was nothing more than an overgrown frat boy.

Because she'd left late, she hit rush-hour traffic. By the time she parked her car and took the elevator to the second floor, then passed through security, it was 8:55.

Judge Rendell caught her in the corridor. "About yesterday . . ."

"Everything's fine," she said, continuing on at a fast pace. He walked alongside her. "I don't mean to be rude, Chris. The Stucky trial starts any minute. Try to catch me at the noon break." She remembered the calls she needed to make and corrected herself. "I'm really swamped today. Can it wait until tomorrow?"

"Certainly," he said with a hangdog expression. "I'm sorry I bothered you."

God, Lily thought, as he took off in the opposite direction. She had just pierced the poor man with a psychological dagger. He'd finally opened up about his wife and daughter's death, and she'd brushed him off like an overzealous suitor.

"Did my husband call?" Lily shouted as she breezed past Jeannie, entering her chamber and putting on her robe.

"No," the woman said from the doorway. "I have a stack of calls you didn't get around to returning yesterday, though."

Lily had never once taken her cell phone into a courtroom. She pulled it out of her purse and handed it to Jeannie. "Can you please figure out how to put this thing on vibrate?"

"You're cutting it pretty close this morning, Judge Forrester," she said, smoothing Lily's robe over her shoulders. "Suzie just called and said they're ready to proceed. Is something wrong?"

"No, no," Lily lied, issuing a stiff smile. "I'm just not sure how to work this phone and I don't have time to figure it out." She waited until she had it back in her hand, then slipped it into her pocket and darted out.

"All rise," the bailiff said when Lily burst through the back door. "Division Forty-seven of the Ventura County Superior Court is now in session, Judge Lillian Forrester presiding."

She recognized several reporters, and assumed some of the other spectators were also members of the media. She saw one of the attorneys give her an odd look. She decided it must be her hair. She hadn't had time to shower, and it was a matted mess. Hair as naturally curly as hers couldn't be combed once it was dry without damaging it. She kept a clip in her pocket, and pulled it out and fastened it at the nape of her neck. Wispy tendrils dangled around her forehead and ears. "Good morning, Counselors," she said, addressing the attorneys. "Are we ready to resume where we left off yesterday?"

"Yes, Your Honor," said Martin Goodwin, a tall, distinguished-looking man in his late forties.

The prosecutor, James Kidwell, stood. "The people are ready as well."

Kidwell was one of the youngest and brightest prosecutors in the state, the type Lily knew would soon seek greener pastures, either private practice or some kind of public office. He was also a nice-looking man, with alert eyes and a studied, quiet manner that seemed to serve him well in winning over a jury.

When Lily nodded, Leonard Davis, her bailiff, walked over to escort the jurors into the jury box. A combination of odors came with them, mostly cologne, but much stronger than the day before. Then another pungent scent broke through. Juror number five, a retired construction worker, had stunk up the room yesterday, which might be the reason the ladies had doused themselves with perfume and it appeared he would do so again today. She wrote the word "deodorant" on a piece of paper and would ask Leonard to slip it to him before the end of the day.

Lily's gaze drifted to the defendants, Ronald and Elizabeth Stucky, wondering how people who looked so normal could have committed such a horrendous crime. Mr. Stucky was an average-looking man, around five-eight and a hundred and fifty pounds. His sandy blond hair was trimmed neatly, and he was dressed in a navy blue suit that looked as if it had come from a rental store. He was employed as an accountant for Prudential Insurance, and probably wore sweaters and corduroy pants to work. Outside of attorneys, few men in southern California wore suits these days. He glanced over at his wife, and Lily did the same.

In her opinion, Elizabeth Stucky had more than likely been the one responsible for her son's death. Her eyes were flat and emotionless, her face and body seemed relaxed and comfortable. It was as if she were watching a performance in a theater. In contrast, her husband seemed extremely nervous. He kept pulling a small notebook out of his jacket pocket, then putting it back a few moments later. It could be that he was a smoker and the notebook was a prop, something to occupy his hands. Many times, defendants' attorneys dictated their dress during their court appearances, wanting them to make a good impression on the jury. Sometimes it worked against them. A person seldom felt at ease in clothing he or she wouldn't normally wear.

Both the Stuckys were in their early forties, childhood sweethearts who had married straight out of college. Elizabeth Stucky was far more attractive than her husband, with straight blond hair that reached to her shoulders, high cheekbones, a perfectly shaped nose, and sensuous lips.

Her makeup was perfect, and she was wearing what appeared to be a designer dress. Lily could tell by the fabric and the way it was cut. The green material rested in neat folds, held in at the waist with a matching green leather belt. Surprisingly, she seemed to be relaxed, almost happy. She must enjoy the attention.

What did that say?

A person who was innocent and was on trial for killing her child would be indignant, even panicked, more along the lines of what Lily saw in Ronald Stucky's demeanor. This woman was confident, poised. She belonged in those clothes. This was how she dressed on a regular basis. Although she held degrees in both English and history, she had never held down a job. What bothered Lily the most was that she didn't look like the mother of an eight-year-old child. She knew women like this. They spent their days going to luncheons, having facials, shopping. And Elizabeth Stucky hadn't just had a child, she'd had a problem child. Was she relieved now that the problem no longer existed?

Lily wondered why the couple had waited so long to have a child. Perhaps they had been unable to conceive. She didn't recall reading any testimony related to this point in the preliminary hearing, but if she were the prosecutor, she would make certain that question was answered during the trial.

As to the reporters present, Lily insisted no photographs be taken while the court was in session. Judicial rules left all decisions regarding the media up to the individual judge. Lily would never allow justice to be compromised by a televised trial, as had happened in numerous sensational cases. Of course, it would have been nice if she'd been able to put on her makeup, but then again, her picture had yet to end up in the paper. The primary targets were the Stuckys. The press had probably caught them earlier, and were waiting to get a shot of today's witness when he was called to testify. As the day went on, the reporters would disappear. Testimony was tedious, even for the parties involved in the case.

She glanced at Kidwell. "You may call your witness, Counselor."

He stood. "The people call Dr. Walter Hutchins."

A short, middle-aged man in a brown plaid sports coat made his way to the witness stand. After he was sworn in, Kidwell began examining him, "When did you first see the victim, Brian Stucky?"

"April seventh of last year."

"And he was referred to you by another physician, is this correct?"

"Yes, by his pediatrician, Dr. Simon Weinberg."

"I see," Kidwell continued. "And why was he referred to you?"

"Dr. Weinberg had been treating him for ADD, attention deficit disorder. The parents said he wasn't responding to the medication."

"And what medication was he taking?"

"Ritalin."

Kidwell left the bench and walked to a space between the witness and the jury box. "Isn't it true that Ritalin is a central nervous system stimulant?"

"Yes."

"And after evaluating Brian Stucky, did you arrive at a different diagnosis?"

"Yes, I did," Dr. Hutchins said, pulling his collar away from his neck.

"And what was this diagnosis?"

"He appeared to be acutely manic. His parents also described bouts of depression, where he would refuse to speak or come out of his room. It was my belief that the child was suffering from a bipolar disorder."

"Forgive me," Kidwell said, glancing over at the jurors, "I'm not that well versed in psychiatric disorders. Is this condition similar to manic-depression?"

"New name, same illness," the doctor explained.

"And did you prescribe medication for Brian Stucky's condition?"

The psychiatrist was becoming anxious. "Yes, I placed him on lithium."

"On how many occasions did you see the victim before prescribing lithium?"

Hutchins narrowed his eyes at the prosecutor. "Once."

Kidwell went back to the counsel table and held up a piece of paper. "The American Academy of Child and Adolescent Psychiatry states, and I quote, 'The diagnosis of Bipolar Disorder in children or teens is complex and involves careful observation over an extended period of time.' Dr. Hutchins, would one visit fit that criteria?"

"Well, not as you've described it," he answered. "Seeing the Stucky boy on only one occasion doesn't mean I didn't thoroughly evaluate him. He was in my office for approximately three hours. I tried to administer a battery of tests, but the boy was in the throes of mania, which made it impossible. My professional opinion was that he should be administered lithium immediately. I suggested hospitalization, but Mr. and Mrs. Stucky adamantly refused."

"Did you advise the defendants about the adverse effects of lithium?"

"Of course I did," Hutchins said haughtily. "I'm not on trial here, Mr. Kidwell. Your tone of voice is not reflective of that fact."

Kidwell wisely ignored him. "What was the original dose of lithium you prescribed for Brian Stucky?"

"I started him on six hundred milligrams."

"When did you double this dose to twelve hundred milligrams?"

He pulled out his reading glasses and slipped them on, then looked down at his lap to review his notes. "He was raised gradually over a period of three months. After the first month, he was elevated to eight hundred milligrams, and the second month to a thousand milligrams. During the third month, he was maintained at twelve hundred milligrams."

"And you saw him on each of these occasions?"

"No," Hutchins said. "I saw him on one additional occasion. He was still exhibiting manic behavior, so I raised his lithium levels."

"And this was to eight hundred milligrams?"

Dr. Hutchins sighed. "No, at that time I raised him to a thousand milligrams."

"What happened to eight hundred milligrams?"

"Mr. Kidwell," he said, "I'm a physician. I've been a practicing psychiatrist for over twenty years. Lithium is administered on an increasing scale until the levels effectively control the symptoms of the illness."

"Did you ever consider that Brian Stucky's mania might have been caused by something other than bipolar disorder?"

"No, I did not."

"Were Mr. and Mrs. Stucky advised to stop giving Brian Ritalin?"

"Yes."

"Did you call the referring pediatrician and advise him of your diagnosis and treatment plan?"

"I'm sure I either spoke to Dr. Weinberg on the phone or sent him a report."

"You're not certain which?"

"No, I just told you I couldn't recall which manner of communication I used. I may have sent him an e-mail. My computer crashed last month, so I was unable to check."

"How convenient," Kidwell mumbled under his breath.

Lily said, "Restrict your comments, Counselor."

He kicked into high gear. "Isn't it true that there's a great deal of controversy among the psychiatric community as to the use of psychotropic medication with a child this young?"

"I suppose there is," Dr. Hutchins said, a line of perspiration popping out on his forehead. "All areas of psychiatry and pharmacology can be debated. A manic child is in danger of hurting himself or others. The safety and well-being of the patient are my first priority."

"I see," Kidwell said, scowling. "Isn't it true that excessive amounts of lithium such as you prescribed to Brian Stucky can cause vomiting, confusion, disorientation, seizures, muscles weakness, and eventually coma and death?"

"I don't consider the amount of lithium to be excessive," the psychiatrist protested. "He was a large boy, and the parents consistently told me the medication wasn't controlling his symptoms. Lithium is, by and large, a fairly safe drug. Some people, even children, are known to metabolize medications differently. Mr. and Mrs. Stucky never mentioned Brian having an adverse reaction to the drug. If they had, I would have stopped his treatment at once."

The district attorney walked along the jury rail, then spun around to face the witness. "Are you aware that the defendants continued to give their son Ritalin long after he began treatment with lithium? That they were, in fact, overdosing Brian with Ritalin prior to you ever seeing him? Perhaps Brian didn't suffer from attention deficit at all. Couldn't an overdose of Ritalin cause a normal child to appear manic?"

"There's a possibility of that, yes," Hutchins conceded, clearing his throat.

"Objection," Goodwin said, slow in reacting. "Calls for speculation on the part of the witness."

"Sustained," Lily ruled. "Rephrase your question, Counselor."

"When did it finally come to your attention that Brian Stucky's parents, the defendants in this case, were overdosing him with lithium?"

"When the coroner called me," the doctor said, averting his eyes.

"No further questions, Your Honor."

Since she had been engrossed in the testimony, Lily wasn't certain if her phone had vibrated. She slipped the phone out of her pocket and saw Tessa had called twice, but there was no word from Bryce. Worrying about her wayward husband seemed trivial in comparison to the unconscionable crime committed by Elizabeth and Ronald Stucky. Several of the boy's relatives were seated in the row behind Kidwell. The district attorney had mentioned an uncle filing a civil suit against the parents for wrongful death if they weren't convicted, and the prosecutor had now additionally set up a malpractice case against the psychiatrist.

The number of medical professionals who had facilitated the murder of Brian Stucky was appalling. Even though the district attorney would no doubt address the issue with an expert witness, Lily was under the impression that even Ritalin was to be prescribed by a psychiatrist, not a family practitioner. And the Stuckys would have gotten away with it had it not been for the million-dollar life insurance policy they took out on Brian six months before his death. This act enjoined both defendants, as Elizabeth had filled out the forms and Ronald had arranged the policy through his employer. To dispel suspicion, the couple had also insured themselves for the same amount. Scores of murder suspects throughout the years had used the same tactic, some successfully and others not.

Lily had to admit the Stuckys' defense was clever. She hoped the prosecution had enough evidence to prove their case. The problem was it was all circumstantial. Juries today wanted hard evidence such as DNA. It wasn't easy for a jury to convict a white, educated person for any crime, let alone murder. If the defendants were innocent, which Lily didn't believe was the case, it would be a terrible miscarriage of justice, especially since the Stuckys had just buried their child.

The greatest weakness in the case was the Stuckys' claim that they'd taken turns giving Brian his daily medication. Lily feared this might pave the way to reasonable doubt. In the weeks prior to his death, Brian Stucky's muscles had grown so weak that he'd had trouble walking and holding his head up. Any parent in his right mind would have sought immediate medical attention. But shockingly, everyone involved with the boy had turned a blind eye: teachers, doctors, bus drivers, neighbors. This made the parents' neglect seem less offensive.

Lily's stomach turned when she saw Elizabeth Stucky smiling and chatting with her attorney. She probably had the gall to file her own malpractice suit, although the law precluded her from collecting if she was convicted. A newspaper article had said her father was the director of the prestigious music academy in Santa Barbara, and her mother was heir to a tobacco fortune. Why would she commit such an unspeakable crime, and at the same time forever tarnish her reputation in the community?

Something didn't add up.

It wasn't the money, Lily decided. The money was like a bonus, just pocket change for Elizabeth's spending sprees. She felt certain Elizabeth could get what she wanted with or without the insurance money. Something else bothered her, something she couldn't quite put her finger on. The way Elizabeth dressed, her perfectly coiffed hair, even her manicured fingernails, struck Lily as somehow relevant.

When her husband tapped her on her shoulder, Elizabeth's expression instantly soured. Ah, Lily thought, beginning to put it together. Ronald Stucky was an embarrassment to her. Being an accountant wasn't an important enough job. He was too ordinary, and she doubted if he meshed well with his wife's sophisticated friends. But Elizabeth hadn't killed her husband. To back it up a few steps, Lily was curious as to why Elizabeth had married him to begin with. Had she been pregnant? Doubtful, as she would have simply aborted the baby. Was it love? The only person Elizabeth loved was herself.

Why have a child? Lily asked herself. Then again, a child was like a toy, something you acquired after your dream house and your new Mercedes.

One of the first things a good defense attorney would attack was motive. He would show that if the Stuckys had needed money, Elizabeth's parents would have simply given it to her.

Another theory began to gel in Lily's mind. Ronald Stucky was guilty, she believed, but only due to the fact that he did nothing to stop his wife. He was obviously "pussy-whipped," as Bryce crudely called it. Ronald could have been terrified that if he didn't go along with his wife's plan, she would do to him what she had done to their son. Either that or she would testify that he was the one behind the boy's death.

Lily decided she would invite Kidwell to her chambers when they adjourned. She might think like a prosecutor, but she was a judge now, and a judge was supposed to remain unbiased, as Hennessey had rudely reminded her the other day. But regardless of her position, she was a human being and a mother.

The district attorney had blown up a photo of Brian

Stucky on an easel. Lily had tried not to look at it, knowing it would upset her, the precise reason Kidwell had positioned it within view of the jurors. She turned to it now, seeing the face of an innocent young boy with blond hair and beautiful blue eyes. But she detected a sense of sadness in his expression, as if he had somehow foreseen his fate. *Don't worry, baby,* she thought. *I'm going to make certain they pay for what they did to you.*

Lily prayed she could live up to her promise.

EIGHTEEN

❧

WEDNESDAY, NOVEMBER 29
DALLAS, TEXAS

The FBI plane touched down at Love Field in Dallas at seven-fifteen in the morning. When Mary disembarked, she saw a distinguished-looking man in a dark pin-striped suit with FBI stamped all over him. She started to call Adams and protest, but she knew it was futile. He probably hadn't told her he was calling in someone from the Dallas Field Office because he didn't want to argue with her. She collected her garment bag, computer case, and overnight bag, then exited the plane.

The day was gorgeous, the sun out, the air brisk and refreshing. It wasn't California, Mary thought, but it was far warmer than rural Virginia this time of year.

He walked over and clasped her hand. "Special Agent Brooks East," he said. "Here, let me help you." He took the two cases from Mary, then began walking. "How was your flight?"

"Not bad." Neither was Agent Brooks, Mary thought, giving him a once-over. His hands were large but soft, his nails neatly manicured. He hadn't felt the need to assert his masculinity by crunching the bones in her hand, which was a relief. These were hallmarks of a good lover. Most women didn't consider a man's hands important until they ended up with a pair of sandpaper mitts groping their body. Looking to be in his mid-thirties, Agent East was a handsome man. "Have you been briefed on this situation, Agent East?"

"Call me Brooks," he said, smiling. "You're in Texas now. We're not that big on formalities." He fell serious. "I received an e-mail from SAC John Adams late last night. I'm curious as to why BAU is interested in the Waverly homicide. The body was found in San Bernardino, not Dallas."

"I'm aware of that," Mary said, relieved that Adams hadn't mentioned the tape or the other homicides. "Are you coming along when I speak to Mrs. Waverly?"

"Those were my orders," East said, shrugging. "Your SAC said you weren't familiar with the city. I guess that means I'm your driver."

When they reached his vehicle, he popped the trunk and put her belongings inside, then held the passenger door open for her. "I hear you're staying at the Wyndham Hotel. It's a nice place and centrally located. How long do you expect to be in town?"

"I'm not sure yet," Mary told him. "Best guess is a few days."

East ducked inside the car and cranked the ignition. "Do you like ribs?"

Mary laughed. "Absolutely."

"Dallas has some of the best rib joints around. We also have some terrific nightlife, if you're interested. Are you married?"

Straight to the point, Mary thought, loving it. "No, and you?"

"Single."

Mary crossed her legs, moving her foot in circles until one of her heels slid off her ankle. When she cleared her throat to get his attention, he glanced over at her, then quickly looked away. She wouldn't mind getting to know Agent East better. No, not a bit. When the chemistry was this intoxicating, you went with the flow or wondered about it forever. Of course, the FBI, like most law enforcement agencies, preferred their agents didn't fraternize, but it was an impossible rule to enforce. Anytime you put the opposite sexes in close proximity to one another, things happened. Her relationship with Lowell Redstone was stagnant. Her mother hated him, which meant the relationship would soon be history. Anyone who laughed at such a statement didn't know Thelma Stevens. "Maybe I'll finish up early today."

"Sounds like a plan," East said. "I'll take you to dinner at Sonny Bryan's, the best barbecue house in town. Then later, if you're game, we can hit some spots in Deep Ellum."

"I think I've heard about that place. Isn't it a historical district or something?"

"You're probably thinking of the West End? Deep Ellum is historical, as well, but for different reasons. The first building built by and for blacks in Dallas, the Grand Temple of the Black Knights of Pythias, was in Deep Ellum. It used to be the best place around for live music. Right now the main calling card is nightclubs." He pulled into a parking lot for IHOP. "I assume you haven't had breakfast yet. Hungry?"

"Always," Mary said, smiling.

Once they were seated and ordered their food, she said, "This might seem like a strange question, but I may end

up staying here over the weekend. Is there a Baptist church
in walking distance of the hotel?"

"You don't have to walk to church," he said. "I belong
to First Baptist. I'll swing by and pick you up."

Well groomed, gainfully employed, *and* a Baptist.
There was no way her mother would toss this fish back
into the pond.

"I don't have time to talk right now," Shana Forrester told
her mother. "Call me around nine tonight."

Lily was in her chambers with the door closed, waiting
for James Kidwell to arrive. He'd rushed out of the courtroom before she had a chance to tell him she wanted to
speak to him. Jeannie had caught him in his office, and he
was on his way. Lily had decided to squeeze in a call to
her daughter. "Are you in class?"

"I wouldn't answer the phone if I was in class."

Only a handful of words had passed between them, and
Lily was already annoyed. "I don't want to call you back
tonight, Shana. In fact, I want you to fly home this weekend."

"Why?"

"Because I want to see you."

"Come up here if you want to see me," Shana tossed
back. "Damn it, Mom, I'm up to my eyeballs here. The
reading alone is killing me."

"I'm in the middle of a trial, honey. You didn't even
come home for Thanksgiving."

"How could I come for Thanksgiving?" the girl said,
chuckling. "You're married to a turkey. How is he, anyway? Has he been staying away from the Twinkies?"

"That's not funny, Shana."

"Yes, it is," she said. "I hate Ventura, Mom. You should
have stayed in Santa Barbara."

"I love you, honey. Please try to understand—"

"I love you, too. I'll check my schedule, okay? Maybe Brett and I can fly down for Christmas, if you promise to keep Bryce on a leash."

"Are you serious about this boy?"

"He's not a boy, Mother, and yeah, I care about him. That doesn't mean we're going to get engaged anytime soon. He's working on his doctorate, so we don't have a lot of time to be together. If we come for Christmas, you'll have a chance to get to know him."

"Christmas seems so far away," Lily said emotionally. "I miss you."

"Yeah, well, right now Christmas is the best I can do. By the way, I need more money in my bank account. I'm down to fifty dollars."

"What happened to all the money I gave you?"

"You haven't given me any money since the first of the year. I spent most of it on books, remember? Look, I'm about to go into the law library, so I have to hang up. Call me later if you want to talk more."

After Lily disconnected, she sat there, amazed at how confident and independent Shana had become. Even as a child, she was a spitfire.

Tall and slender like Lily, Shana had also inherited Lily's curly red hair. They looked so much alike, people occasionally mistook them for sisters. But Lily was an introvert and Shana was charismatic. In school, she'd formed her own posse, girls who followed her around and worshipped her. She remembered how Shana manipulated them to clean her room, do her homework, and even let her wear their favorite outfits.

Then suddenly Shana's carefree young life had been torn apart, and the same violent criminal had come back to tarnish her first year as a college student. So much had gone wrong, Lily thought, far more than the rapes.

Lily was suddenly hurled back in time. She was inside

the house after the rapes. She had moved back a few weeks after the attacks.

"Shana," Lily yelled, having just come home from work. "Come on, we're late."

John had a pile of raw hamburger in a big bowl and was mixing it with ketchup, raw egg, and onions. He was making his second favorite dish after roast chicken: meatloaf. When she came through the door, he wiped his red-smeared hands on a paper towel, and Lily instantly thought of the blood-splattered body of Bobby Hernandez. Shana appeared in the kitchen, dressed neatly in a white blouse, a black skirt, and the low heels they had purchased for her to wear to the last school dance. Her hair was pulled back with a clip at the nape, the way Lily frequently wore her hair, and she looked more like fifteen than thirteen. Her eyes were solemn.

"Go ahead and get in the car, sweetie," Lily said. "You look so pretty. I just have to run to the bathroom."

"Isn't she gorgeous?" John said, walking over and grabbing Shana around the waist and hugging her.

Just as he started to kiss her, she pulled away and glared at him. "Stop it. I told you not to do that anymore. I'm too old for that stuff."

John stepped back, his mouth open, obviously hurt. Exchanging only detached eye contact with him when he looked at her for an explanation for Shana's behavior, Lily rushed to the master bedroom and closed the door behind her, removing a bottle from the medicine cabinet. She dropped to her knees in front of the white porcelain bowl, fearing she was about to vomit. Shana was pulling away from her father, not knowing why she felt the way she did, uncertain who to trust, isolating herself from other young people. Standing and removing a Valium from the bottle, she tossed it in her mouth and leaned down to the sink, swallowing it with tap water. There was only one pill left. She would have to get the prescription refilled tomorrow.

The Ventura Police Department was housed in a dark brown building, on a street named after a sergeant who had been killed in the line of duty: Dowell Drive. The detective met them in the lobby. Lily had known her for years.

Detective Margie Thomas was close to retirement—or beyond, for that matter, probably surpassing the twenty-year mark several years back and electing to stay on as long as she could pass the physical. There was no doubt that this was her life and adjustments following her retirement would be difficult. Her hair was tinted a shade too dark to be flattering; she was heavy in the lower section of her body, making it look like she had an old-fashioned bustle underneath her navy-blue cotton shirtwaist dress. With thick, painted-on eyebrows and eyes almost a shade of lavender, she made Lily think of Elizabeth Taylor during her boozy, blubbery days.

Margie took one of Shana's hands, sat down on the lobby sofa with her, and just looked her over. "How you doing, doll?" she asked. "Boy, are you a pretty thing. You've got your mom to thank for that hair, that's for sure."

Shana didn't smile and slipped her hand from the detective's. "I'm doing fine," she answered politely. "I'd feel a lot better if you caught him, though."

Realizing she had never discussed this possibility with Shana, Lily wondered if she thought about this often, maybe at night in her room before she went to sleep, or in the early hours when she got up before everyone else. If only Lily could assure her that he would never hurt her again, that she'd made certain of it.

"Okay, this is what we're going to do today," Margie said, her voice light and breezy, as if they were going to *do something fun. "I've prepared some pictures of men who resemble the man you and your mother described. All have backgrounds that make them possible suspects. I'm going to let you sit at my desk, Shana, and look at half the pictures. Your mom will sit in the other room and look at the other half, and then you'll exchange. If you see someone who resembles the man that attacked you, you'll write down the number by his name. You may see several faces and not be certain, but that's okay. Just be sure to write down all the numbers. She paused and looked at Shana only, aware that Lily was all too familiar with the routine. "If you do see someone, then we can try to get this man in for a real lineup so you can be absolutely certain." She stopped and stood, adding, "Any questions and I'll be right across the room. Okay?"*

Lily started thumbing through the photos, seeing a number of men she'd prosecuted who were back on the street and trying to recall the particulars of each case. One face she remembered from years back, noting how he'd aged and recalling the ten or twelve counts of indecent exposure she'd pled and plea-bargained down to two counts and ninety days in jail. They called these men "weenie waggers," and statistics proved they seldom committed more serious offenses. Shouldn't even be in the lineup, Lily thought.

After about ten minutes, she was tempted to pick up the phone on the desk of the small, glass-enclosed office and call the Oxnard PD to see if she could reach Detective Cunningham. It was too early, though, so she continued to look at the faces, no longer actually seeing them, letting her thoughts roam.

Looking at the photos the way they were presented made her think of the proofs professional studios gave you, and she realized it had been over a year since Shana's last portrait. She would have to have one done in another month or so. She glanced through the glass and saw her daughter at Margie's desk, intently staring at each face. The process was a catharsis for Shana in many ways, and Lily was glad John had called the police and reported the crime. Considering the way things were shaping up, and with the simple fact that she had done what she had done and there was no going back, Lily thought that someday she might be able to detach herself from that terrible morning in Oxnard.

If Bobby Hernandez had murdered the prostitute to keep her from testifying against him, merely fulfilling that first mission that Lily had suspected all along—to kill her—then he might have followed the same pattern with her and her daughter. Perhaps God had intervened and it was His hand that had guided her, His voice she'd heard in her mind and not the ghost of her dead father. Recalling the religious fervor of her early childhood, she vowed to take Shana to the Catholic church one Sunday.

Deep in thought, she jumped when the door to the small office opened and Margie appeared with Shana. The detective was holding something in her hands, and took a seat next to Lily. Shana was ashen and wide-eyed, her hands by her sides, an excited expression on her face. Margie opened her mouth to speak, but Shana blurted out, "I found him. I know it's him. I'm certain. Show her." She reached over and pushed Margie's shoulder. "Show her. She'll know it's him, too."

Lily felt perspiration oozing from every pore in her body, and knew she would be drenched in seconds. Waiting for the heavy pressure in her chest signaling a heart attack, she felt blood rush from her face.

Margie saw her distress. "My God, you look ill," she said, turning to Shana with a degree of urgency. "Go and get your mother some cold water from the water fountain—

right at the back of the room you were in. And bring some paper towels from the bathroom and soak them in water. Hurry, now." Shana ran from the room.

"Should I call an ambulance?" she asked Lily, seeing the moisture darkening the pale green blouse she was wearing, watching as beads of sweat dropped from her forehead, over her nose, and down her chin. "Are you having chest pains?"

Lily tried to monitor her breathing and calm herself. She felt as if there were a tight band around her chest and suddenly remembered the shingles. She was just having a panic attack, long overdue. Shana had seen a photo of someone who resembled Hernandez. She would realize it was the wrong man once she saw him in person in a lineup. "I'm okay. Just too much pressure, I guess. I also have a case of shingles."

"I had those, too, one time," Margie said sympathetically. "Boy, do they hurt. Nerves. That's what they said caused it."

Shana returned, her mouth tight with concern, carrying the wet towels and a cup of cold water. She handed them to her mother and stood back, watching as Lily wiped her face and the back of her neck and then left the soggy paper towels resting on her neck while she sipped the water. "I'm fine," Lily said, reassuring Shana. "Might even be coming down with the flu or something." She placed her hand on her forehead as if checking for a fever. "Just give me a minute and I'll look at the photo."

"Relax," Margie said. "You can even go home and come back in the morning. One more day—"

"No," Shana said, her voice louder than usual, insistent, "let her see it now. Then you can put him in jail."

The detective turned and took Shana's hand. "Just give your mom a minute, honey. This has been real hard on her, too. Even if your mom agrees that this man resembles the man who attacked you, we can't just go out and arrest him. You'll have to see him in a real lineup, and we'll have to get an order from a judge to arrest him. That's the way it works."

Shana stared impatiently at Lily, impervious to whatever was wrong with her, wanting her to confirm her selection. Lily could see her chest rise and fall with every breath. "Okay," she said. "Let's see the photo."

Asking Shana to return to the desk she had been at previously, the detective handed Lily a stack of pages with photos like the ones she had been looking at before they had entered.

"Go through each one slowly and don't respond just because Shana told you she saw someone. I told her to remain outside earlier, but she followed me in here. If you do select someone, it should be based solely on your own judgment." Seeing that Lily appeared in control, the detective said, "I'm going to step outside. Come out when you're done."

As she examined each photo, she was really looking, wanting to see the man Shana had seen, certain he resembled Hernandez but knowing half of Oxnard resembled Hernandez. She occasionally glanced out the window of the office, looking for Shana. Margie must have taken her to the vending machine for a soda or to the restroom. On about the twentieth page of photos, she saw him.

My God, a dead ringer, she thought, leaving no question as to why Shana had been so excited. Even if he was not the right man, simply seeing his face propelled her back to the fear and degradation of that night. Her pain for what her daughter had suffered was agonizing. The man had an almost identical shape to his face, his eyes, his mouth, his nose. Even the way his hair was cut was similar to Hernandez's. He looked younger, however, and

Lily knew he was not the rapist. He couldn't be. The rapist was dead.

She took her time and studied his face closely. She recalled how photographs were sometimes miles apart from the actual person. They were one-dimensional, and this man, in profile, in body conformation, could look entirely different. Removing the paper towels from her neck, she felt the crisis had passed. Just go through the motions, she told herself, and even agree that he looks somewhat like the rapist, because if I don't, it will upset Shana. So what if the guy had to be yanked in for a lineup? He'd done something at one time to place himself in this position. She certainly wasn't going to worry about some unknown man with a criminal history. Once they saw him, the whole thing would be dropped. Lily would state he wasn't the man and that would be the end of it.

She picked up the package of photos and calmly left the office. Margie and Shana were walking through the doors to the detective bureau, where six desks were lined up, three to a side. It was six-thirty and only one detective was still working, files open, phone to his ear, his feet on the desk. Shana held a Coke in her hand and appeared subdued but anxious. Lily had her finger on the page containing the photo of the man she was certain the girl had picked.

The three of them met in the center of the room. "I admit, I have one that's real close, but I'm pretty sure it's not the man," Lily said without enthusiasm. Seeing the taut look of frustration in Shana's eyes, she quickly added, "But it's real close and worthy of additional investigation."

Setting the photos down on Margie's desk, she turned to the correct page and placed a finger on his face. "Number thirty-six is the one I picked." Her look was questioning, but she didn't have to wait long for a response.

"That's him," Shana said, turning to the detective. "Told you. That's him. Number thirty-six."

"Shana, I don't feel as positive as you. I want you to know that from the start, and remember, I got a better look at him when he was leaving. You were terribly distraught."

The visual image of him standing in the light from the bathroom appeared in Lily's mind: the red sweatshirt, the profile. She even recalled the top of his head as he bent down to snap his pants. She glanced back down at the photo, but also noticed the other men on the page. Out of six, two were wearing a red T-shirt or sweatshirt. Red was a gang color. She knew that—every other Hispanic in Oxnard wore red and those silly baseball caps. She then started thumbing back through the pages and saw more red shirts. One man was wearing a gold chain with a crucifix. She turned the page and saw another man wearing a cross, only smaller. If she let her imagination go now, she might end up in a mental institution. The man she had shot was the man. It must end there and end now.

"Mom, you didn't even have your glasses on that night, and you don't have them on now," Shana snapped. "He raped me, remember, and I can see perfectly." She turned to Margie and said sarcastically, "She's supposed to wear them when she drives, too, but she never does."

"I only need them to read—just a little farsighted," Lily informed the detective. "Anyway, arguing over it right now is counterproductive. Can you pull him in for a lineup?"

"I'll get right on it and call you as soon as it can be arranged. You two go home, try to get some rest, and put this out of your mind." As Shana walked past her mother, Margie gave Lily a look with those Liz Taylor eyes and shrugged her shoulders. "Life's a bitch, isn't it?"

"*You got that right,*" *Lily replied, and started walking, trying to catch up with Shana.*

By the time Lily made it out of the building, Shana was waiting by the passenger door of the Honda. As she started the car, Lily told her, "*They'll get the lineup together and we'll take it from there, okay?*"

The girl was staring straight ahead. They rode in silence for quite some time. "*Why don't you turn on the radio?*" *Lily suggested.*

"*He's still out there. I know it now. I thought he'd run away. He didn't. He's still out there. You told me he would go far away and never come back so he wouldn't be caught.*"

Lily hesitated, torn now, not knowing exactly what to say and deciding she must call the psychologist and get Shana in to see her tomorrow. She felt that assuaging her rising fear was the right thing to do, even if she became angry. "*I still believe he's long gone, honey, and like I said back there, I don't think it's him. I can see things far away better than I can close up. That's what farsightedness means. When he was close, it was very dark, but when he was leaving, he was farther away and in the light.*" *She reached for her hand, holding it tightly.* "*I don't think the man you saw was him. He's gone. You're a smart girl. You know a lot of people look alike. Even you and I look alike, but of course I'm older. If we were the same age, people could mistake us even. See?*"

Shana reached out and turned on the radio, tuning it to a rock station. She then yelled over the noise, "*It was him, Mom. When you see him with your glasses on, then you'll know.*"

NINETEEN

❦

"This area is called Highland Park," Agent East explained as they drove past manicured, wooded lots with picture-perfect homes on them. "The houses are older here and extremely pricey, primarily due to their close proximity to downtown. The crime rate is high for the same reason, but oddly, no one seems to care. See that little house over there? We're talking two million, and the new owner would probably end up gutting it."

"Brooks is an unusual name," Mary said, flirting with him.

He laughed. "Not if you're a baseball fan. I was named after Brooks Robinson. My dad thought if it was good enough for a Hall of Fame baseball player, it was good enough for me."

"Wasn't he from Baltimore?"

"He played for the Orioles. I grew up in Baltimore."

"But you have a Texas accent?"

"We moved here when I was twelve."

He turned into a long driveway. Mary's eyes widened when they reached the sprawling red brick house. The lot had to be at least an acre, maybe more. "What kind of a price tag would you put on this house?"

"Four to five mil," East told her, parking in front and getting out. He circled around and opened the car door for her.

Mary scooted across the seat so that her skirt hiked up

a few inches, then flashed her shapely legs as she stepped out. By the time they went to dinner, she would own him.

She rang the doorbell, while East stood a few feet behind her. A uniformed maid answered, and Mary showed her ID.

"Mrs. Waverly is expecting you," a pretty Hispanic woman said. "Follow me. Can I get you some iced tea?"

"That would be great," East said, taking a seat on a floral print sofa.

Mary sat down on a matching chair adjacent to him, both of them checking out the room. The walls were covered with what looked like original oil paintings, and the furniture was opulent, almost gaudy. Several pieces, like an antique desk, were gilded in gold.

Belinda Waverly entered the room, stopping to shake hands with each of them, then dropping down in an overstuffed white chair. "Did Lucy get you something to drink?"

Just then, the housekeeper came in balancing a tray. On top was a pitcher of iced tea and three glasses. Mary couldn't stop staring at Mrs. Waverly. She tried to pour a glass of tea without looking, and almost spilled it on the white Berber carpet. Beautiful was the only word Mary could think of to describe her. Although the word was used all too frequently, truly beautiful women were a rarity. And it was obvious that Mrs. Waverly's beauty hadn't been engineered by a plastic surgeon. Each section of her face complemented the other. Her hazel eyes were large and expressive, her nose gracefully slanted, her lips perfectly shaped. Void of makeup, her face had a natural, youthful appearance. Her brown hair possessed the kind of luster and body that you generally only see on young people, and her skin was radiant. A petite woman, she was wearing an aqua warm-up suit.

The couple were clearly wealthy, but the only thing about

Belinda that struck Mary as materialistic was the enormous rock on her finger. All she could think of was why.
If her husband had been murdered by their mysterious
UNSUB, why would he even contemplate another woman?
It seemed almost obscene. Variety, maybe, or the thrill of
conquest. She was beginning to gain insight into the killer's mind.

Some men *were* reptilian pricks.

Women were superior, Mary believed. They didn't rape
or molest children. They committed violent crimes on occasion, but with nowhere near the frequency of men. The
majority of women were in prison because of drugs or alcohol. With practically every female offender, regardless
of the crime, if you went back far enough, a rotten man
would pop up. Besides, Mary thought, women gave birth.
Without women, men would still be sitting around in
caves playing with their dicks.

After she took a sip of her tea, Mary unpacked her
laptop, placed it on the coffee table, and positioned the
camera on Mrs. Waverly. "Do you mind if I record our discussion? It's hard to remember everything, and I sometimes have trouble reading my own handwriting."

"I guess it's all right," Mrs. Waverly said, tears pooling
in her eyes. "You don't think I killed Stan, I hope. Except
for a few hours at the gym, I was here with the kids and
Lucy the entire time. Well, I was for the time he was supposed to be gone. They haven't told me yet when he actually died."

Time of death wasn't their most pressing problem, so
Mary moved on. "We have no reason to believe you were
involved in your husband's death. I'm with the Investigative Support Unit based in Quantico, Virginia. Agent East
is assigned to our Dallas Field Office. ISU assists other
law enforcement agencies throughout the country."

Mrs. Waverly reached for a stack of tissues she had

stuffed inside the chair. "So you're assisting the San Bernardino Police Department?"

She not only had beauty, Mary thought, she had a brain. "The main function of the ISU unit is criminal profiling."

"Like in the movie *Silence of the Lambs*?"

Mary exchanged glances with Agent East. "More or less."

"But that was about a serial killer," she said, more tears gushing forth. "Good Lord, don't tell me Stan was murdered by a serial killer." She placed her head in her hands. "Christ, this has all been so horrible. When will it ever end?" She looked up and wiped her eyes with the tissue. "Do you have any idea what it's like to get a call from the police telling you they found your husband's body, but they don't know where his head and hands went? To be honest, I don't know how I can still cry. After a while, you get numb. You have to if you want to survive."

Agent East spoke up, "I can imagine how terrible this has all been, Mrs. Waverly, but I'm sure you want to do everything in your power to bring this killer to justice."

"Please, stop calling me Mrs. Waverly. My name is Belinda." She tossed her hands in the air. "Go ahead, ask me anything you want."

Mary started filming. "How long were you and your husband married?"

"Fifteen years."

"Do you have children?"

"Three. Lindsey is nine, Craig eight, and Mike is three."

"And Stan was an attorney, am I right?"

"Yes," Mrs. Waverly said, letting out a long sigh. "He has clients all over the world, mostly international corporations. He specializes in mergers and acquisitions. Obviously, it's very lucrative. It's hard on the children, though. You know, the traveling. Last year, Stan decided he wanted to be a senator. We're already planning his campaigning. . . ." She stopped and stared off into space.

Mary always found it sad to hear a victim's loved one refer to him in the present tense. Letting go was a lengthy process, and various bits and pieces lingered. It had taken her years to get over her father's death. If she hadn't quit her job to track down his killer, she would still be grieving. "Did Stan have any enemies?"

"God, no," Belinda said. "Everyone loved him."

"He told you he was going to New York on business. Did he go to New York often?"

"At least once a month. When the kids were little, we used to go as a family." She had a faraway look in her eyes. "I love New York in the fall. We went to Broadway shows, shopped, took buggy rides through Central Park."

Mary had to keep her on track. She'd traveled too far to listen to her reminisce. "When you called the Park Lane Hotel, where Stan was supposed to be staying, are you certain you used the number listed on his itinerary? Could you have mislaid these documents and called the operator for the number, or maybe looked it up in the phone book?"

"Absolutely not," Mrs. Waverly said. "For one thing, I don't even have a copy of the yellow pages. They take up too much space. We don't call the operator because they rip you off. I think they charge almost two dollars now. Anyway, Stan and I use the Internet."

"Perhaps that's how you got the phone number, then."

"My computer had a virus, so I turned it off until I could get someone over to look at it." She adjusted her position in the chair. "I used the number my husband left for me. I've told the police this ten times. I was transferred to his room, but he wasn't there. I left a message for him, and Stan called me back right away. He said he'd been in the shower when I called."

"And what day was this?"

"The same day he left," Belinda told her. "There's an hour's difference, so I think it was around nine at night in New York. Everything was fine. It was the next day that I couldn't reach him, the day Craig fell off his skateboard and broke his arm. When he didn't answer his cell or at the hotel, I checked his itinerary and saw that he had a meeting scheduled at World Manufacturing. I called the number listed and spoke to a woman. I don't recall her name. She said the meeting had just begun, but she would ask Stan to call me as soon as it ended. Of course, you wouldn't be here if he'd called."

"Did the police check to see if this call went through?"

"They got someone's cell phone, just like they did with the number listed for the hotel. It's the most bizarre thing I've ever experienced. How could a number belong to a hotel one day, and the next day be someone's cell phone?"

"And the same thing happened with World Manufacturing?"

"Exactly," she said, pulling her cell phone out of her pocket and pushing a key. "Listen."

A young voice began speaking: "This is Ashley. Leave a message, or I'll never talk to you again."

She tossed the phone to Mary. "Listen to it again. I've listened to it a hundred times. The girl's mother called and told me to stop harassing her daughter."

"How long had the girl had the number?"

"The police said the number was assigned to her a month before I called. It was the same thing with all the numbers on Stan's itinerary. The police thought Stan just made up the numbers on the itinerary, thinking I wouldn't know the difference." Her face twisted with anguish. "I know my husband. Stan would never do something like that, especially to me."

"Who do you think typed the itinerary?"

"I don't know," Belinda said, wrapping her arms around her chest. "Stan's assistant didn't type it, nor did anyone else at his office. I guess Stan could have typed it himself. If he did, he must have typed it on his laptop, because the police didn't find anything in the computer here at the house."

East excused himself and stepped outside for some air. Mary continued, "Whoever typed it may not have stored it on the hard drive."

"I can't imagine Stan typing anything. He charged by the hour, and trust me, his fees were exorbitant. I mean, you could hire three attorneys for what my husband charged." Belinda stood up and walked over to one of the oil paintings. "All I'm trying to say is he placed a high value on his time. I guess I shouldn't be talking about money right now. Most of the artwork is going to Sotheby's next week to be auctioned off. I might be able to keep the house if I go back to work selling real estate. The kids are so young, though."

Mary poured herself another glass of iced tea. Most of the ice cubes had melted, but she needed the caffeine. "Didn't your husband have life insurance?"

"No," she said, turning back around. "Stan didn't believe in life insurance. There's a considerable age difference, twenty years to be precise. His first wife took him to the cleaners. When we first got married, I think he was afraid if he insured himself for a large amount of money, I'd put a pillow over his head when he got old and sick." She smiled. "We used to joke about it."

Although the next question was cruel, Mary had no way to get around it. She also assumed the police had addressed the same issue. "Was your husband having an affair, Belinda?"

"Most certainly not," she said, dropping back down in

the chair. "Stan and I had a great marriage. Everything was perfect. He told me he loved me every day." She linked eyes with Mary. "I know what you're thinking, that most women would say the same thing under the circumstances. Stan was in love with me, Agent—"

"Please, call me Mary."

Belinda became agitated. "Stan would have died for me, understand? Even actresses didn't interest him."

Mary heard a commotion, and a few minutes later a towheaded little boy burst into the room, running straight to his mother. Belinda pulled the three-year-old into her lap and kissed him on the cheek, then sat him back down on the floor. "Go in the other room with Lucy, baby. Mommy has company." When the boy started to fret, she shouted for the housekeeper, and the woman rushed in and carried the child away.

Mary stood, deciding it was time to wind things up. "We'd like to have contact information for Stan's closest friends and coworkers, if it's not too much trouble."

"Not at all," she said. "Give me a few minutes and I'll print out our address book for you. I already did this for the police, so you'll see a star next to the people we saw on a regular basis."

Mary walked into the foyer to stretch her legs. Something kept dogging her, but she couldn't figure out what it was. Although she had an excellent memory, it was hard to juggle all the information she had amassed over the years. She saw a large framed picture of Belinda on the wall that she hadn't noticed earlier. She wasn't surprised when she read the plaque at the bottom: MISS AMERICA, 1990.

"That was a long time ago," Belinda said when she returned, a weary look on her face. "Another lifetime, as they say."

"You're still beautiful."

"Look," she said, ignoring the detective's comment, "finding the killer isn't going to bring my husband back, but I don't want someone else to suffer like this. Let me know if I can help in any way."

"Hang in there," Mary said, staring at her a few moments before she opened the door and left.

TWENTY

❧

WEDNESDAY, NOVEMBER 29
VENTURA, CALIFORNIA

After her phone call to Shana concluded, Lily's thoughts returned to Bryce. She'd stopped calling his cell phone because his voice mail was full. Even that was cause for concern. Every businessman checked his messages. Then she realized the world communicated by e-mail. She turned to her computer and typed Bryce a message, marking it urgent and requesting notification when the message was read. There wasn't much else she could do now but wait. The hotel in Charleston told her Bryce had checked in, but he had not returned her call. After she talked to Kidwell, she'd call his office and see if anyone there had heard from him. If she didn't count the day he had left, Stan had been out of touch with her for less than twenty-four hours. It was too early to begin checking the hospitals.

"Send Kidwell in, Jeannie," she said over the intercom.

"I'm sorry I couldn't come straight from court," the young prosecutor told her. "There was a problem with the Douglas shooting. What's on your mind?"

"Sit," Lily said, leaning back in her chair. "Have you

talked to the pediatrician who delivered the Stucky boy?"

"No, it didn't seem relevant."

"I disagree," she said, a crisp tone to her voice. "You subpoenaed his school records, didn't you?"

"We've already established that Brian's teacher, Mrs. Gonzales, didn't make any notations in his file about his weakness and confusion. All we have is her testimony." Kidwell looked frustrated, as if he thought she was unhappy with the way he was trying the case. "Where are we going with this, Judge Forrester?"

"Do you have all of Brian's school records, specifically those from kindergarten and the first grade?"

"I'm not sure if they go that far back," he said, running his hands through his hair. "They transferred the boy to public school from a private school in the first grade. He didn't seem to have a problem until later, so I didn't request those records. He wasn't diagnosed with ADD until the third grade. That's when the doctor started him on Ritalin."

"How did he perform then?"

"Poorly," Kidwell said. "The school wanted to put him in special ed classes. They agreed not to if the parents got him professional treatment."

Lily sat forward in her seat. "Your motive is weak, Counselor. Elizabeth Stucky's parents are wealthy, influential people. She didn't need her son's life insurance money."

Kidwell's shoulders rolled forward. "I know," he said. "We haven't been able to come up with another motive. We just found out who Mrs. Stucky's parents were last week. I guess they're going to testify."

"And what do you think they're going to say?"

"That they would give Elizabeth money if she needed it, which might not be true. We're working around the clock to dig up something on her. You know, drugs, gambling, anything that could have caused her parents to cut her off financially. As of today, we've come up empty-handed. Other than being a clotheshorse, she's squeaky clean. The same goes for the husband."

Lily asked, "Did the father need money? Could he have embezzled money from his work? He's an accountant, so that gives him access."

"He has a huge pension, as well as a significant stock portfolio. Their house and cars are paid for, so Ronald's salary more than covers their expenses. These people are impenetrable, Judge Forrester. I don't want to lose this case. They killed this kid, and I'm having nightmares that they're going to get away with it. If you have any ideas to keep that from happening, I'm more than willing to listen."

Lily looked at her watch, realizing she would have to forgo lunch. "Okay," she said. "There may be a possibility that Brian Stucky was retarded. I doubt if he was brain-injured, but it bears checking out. He could have been oxygen-deprived at birth. Having a retarded child would have been an embarrassment to Elizabeth Stucky. Are you following me?"

"Yes, go on."

"Her husband is already an embarrassment."

"Jesus, you're right." The prosecutor became animated, scooting to the edge of his seat. "I've seen the way Elizabeth looks at him. Every time he opens his mouth, she looks like she wants to strangle him. I thought it was a ploy. You know, he did it and she despises him, but she can't force herself to tell anyone the truth because she still loves him."

"I'm only sharing my take on this as a former prosecutor," Lily said. "I could easily be wrong, understand?"

Things seemed to be taking shape in Kidwell's mind. "Rich girl falls in love and marries a run-of-the-mill guy.

As she gets older, she realizes he doesn't fit in, and that her socialite friends look down on her for marrying below her status. Her friends are married now and have kids. When they get together, they brag about their children's accomplishments. Elizabeth can't bring herself to admit she has a defective child, so she tells her friends and family Brian has a mild case of ADD, which is common enough that some of her friends' kids may have the same thing. As Brian's schoolwork gets harder, she gives him higher doses of Ritalin until the poor kid completely freaks out. Then, when he still can't perform in school, she gets a psychiatrist to give him more medicine. This only compounds the problem, so Elizabeth gets fed up and decides to get rid of him. If he dies, people will feel sorry for her, and she'll get the attention she craves." He looked up at Lily. "Are we on the same page here?"

"Precisely, Counselor."

"This is great," he said, standing. "We'll get right on it. I can't thank you enough, Judge Forrester. We might win this case after all." He headed toward the door, his head down in thought. "Oh," he said, turning around. "It may take some time to track down the pediatrician and get our hands on the other school records. I also want to interview Elizabeth's friends again to see if one of them has a kid with ADD. If we can't get this together in time, will you grant us a continuance?"

The Burkell case was pending trial. Lily also had a 245 on the docket, an assault with a deadly weapon. The DA's office was thinking of pleading it out, but if the defense rejected their offer, the case could go to trial. Then if Stucky ran over, she would be backlogged. "I suggest you and your coworkers work as fast as you can, Counselor. My calendar is stacked."

Kidwell wasn't happy, but he knew this wasn't the time to argue. She had just handed him his case.

Lily placed her hands on the desk, a stern expression on her face. "This conversation never took place. Are we clear?"

"Perfectly," he said, disappearing through the doorway.

Anne awoke starving and furious. It was almost midnight and the next plane out of Las Vegas didn't leave until six in the morning. "Damn, fuck, shit," she said, pitching around inside the car. With her right leg, she gave Bryce a vicious kick.

Something wet was on her chin. Looking into the vanity mirror, she realized it was drool. How could she have been so negligent? She never slept during the day. Part of the problem was the dark parking structure, and the fact that she had forgotten to take her diet pills. She cranked the ignition and roared off, the smell of burning rubber drifting in through the open window.

As she drove, she kept her eyes peeled for cops. The police were everywhere. A cop car was parked in front of the Shop-Quick Mart. A few blocks down, she saw another police car turning down a side street. "You're an idiot," she said, pounding the steering wheel. "You're fucked, literally, royally fucked."

The police were tailing her, waiting to see what she would do next. Pulling to the curb, she got out and checked her front tire. It looked fine, the same as all the others. Either the cop had been trying to hit on her, or he was working with the FBI. How had they tracked her from the stupid tape?

Getting back in the car, Anne eased the Escalade into traffic. She'd spent months creating the tape and making certain the FBI's forensic lab wouldn't be able to extract even a microbe of identifying evidence. The challenge was what made it worth doing. There was no DNA: no skin, no hairs, no eyelashes, and no saliva. Every time she'd touched the tape, she had worn gloves and stuffed her hair inside a plastic cap. She'd even bought a white lab coat and paper booties. How could the FBI possibly know who she was? Even she didn't know who she was.

She was alive when she should be dead.

Anne's entire life came down to that. All of the doctors had been shocked she'd survived, even labeling her the miracle girl. Some miracle, she thought. They should have peeled her off that fence and buried her, even if there was a spark of life still left inside her. No one recovered from such a horrific experience, let alone the awful years that followed.

Two worthless excuses for human beings had procreated, spawning a child born to suffer. A mistake that couldn't be corrected, her life should have ended that night on the interstate. To psychologically recover would minimize the extreme cruelty her father had inflicted. In her mind, the crimes she had committed stood as testament to that cruelty.

When Anne saw parents yank their children's arm in a public place or slap them, she could imagine the abuse they must inflict in private. If she went up to those parents and told them they were creating a monster, they would curse at her and drag the poor kid away. People didn't just wake one morning and stop beating their children. This was the real world. Shit like that didn't happen.

And as far as she was concerned, the best thing that an abused kid could do was toughen up and take it until she was old enough to move out. Foster parents could be just as brutal. She'd read stories about all these dedicated people who took in unwanted children and did wonderful things for them. Some of those kids were slaves; others were stuffed away like wool sweaters in August. The majority of them were maintained. Not starved, just hungry. Beaten, but not to the point of bruising. Degradation and verbal abuse had no limits.

Anne was at the end of the strip now. The taillights ahead of her were blinding. She blinked her eyes, desperately trying to maintain her focus. When she passed the same landmark for the third time, she knew she was lost. She didn't know her way around the city that well. Since signing the escrow papers, she'd only stayed in the Las Vegas house a handful of days. She'd fly in to meet a guy, kill him, chop him, dispose of him, and head to the airport to jump on a plane.

It was the same with all her kill sites. The less time she spent in these places, the less evidence she had to worry about leaving behind. Until Vegas ran out of water, the price of real estate would continue to climb. She'd sold one of her kill sites recently and pocketed two hundred grand.

Her throat was so parched, she had trouble swallowing, and her stomach was raging with hunger. When did she eat last? She couldn't remember. Seeing a neon sign for Wendy's, she impulsively turned into the drive-through and ordered a large Diet Coke, two cheeseburgers, and a large order of fries.

"That will be six fifty-three at the next window," a Hispanic voice said over the speaker.

She deserved to junk out. It wasn't like she did it every day. Without her diet pills, her appetite took over. All she could do now was feed it. She rummaged around inside her Valentino tote, pulling out a ten-dollar bill and placing it on top of the center console. While she was waiting, she checked the messages on her business phone. Christ, she thought, seeing over fifty. The moron she'd hired to handle this particular line must have skipped out on her. She hated depending on people.

Chuck had been her biggest mistake. He'd worked for

her for two years, and handled the solicitation of vendors to process credit card charges for the company, so he knew more than her other employees. Then one day his parole officer finally tracked him down and shipped him back to prison.

As far as Anne knew, the asshole had at least kept his mouth shut. It wasn't as if he could roll over on her, use his knowledge of her business affairs to cut a deal and reduce his prison sentence. He could have, of course, if he'd known she was killing people.

A Hispanic girl with a bad case of acne was manning the second window at Wendy's. She took Anne's money and was handing her the change when her eyes widened and she started pointing and shrieking. The other employees thought she was being robbed and rushed over.

Anne's reflexes were so dull, it took her a while before she figured out what all the fuss was about. Bryce had regained consciousness and yanked the T-shirt off his head. His face was covered in blood from where she'd beaten him with the piece of plywood. He was trying to cry for help, but nothing came out but a pathetic whimper. She burst into laughter. At least the police couldn't arrest her for murder. She could open the door and kick him out right now. What was he going to do? Tell the cops he was drunk as a skunk and fucking around on his wife in a city he wasn't supposed to be in? Besides, the last thing he would remember was leaving the Aladdin. As soon as she gave him the Versed, the clock stopped ticking.

Anne turned a cold eye to the employees gathered around the window. "Give me my food," she shouted, hearing them talking to each other in Spanish. "I paid for it, damn it. Give me my fucking food."

A man appeared. His tag noted that he was the manager. "Call the police," he said, placing his arm in front of the others to hold them back. "Hurry, dial 911."

"Don't move," Anne barked. "I'm an undercover cop and this man's my prisoner. Now give me my damn food so I can get the hell out of here."

The stunned man shoved the sack through the window.

"Thanks, amigo," she said, plucking out a fry and tossing it into her mouth. "Now tell your people to go back to work. You didn't see anything, understand? I'm taking this asshole to jail. Keep your mouths shut or you'll end up in the same place."

TWENTY-ONE

THURSDAY, NOVEMBER 30
QUANTICO, VIRGINIA

Mary had intended to stay another day to interview Stan Waverly's friends and associates, but Adams called and ordered her to return to Virginia. She tried to find out why, but he refused to tell her over the phone.

When she showed up at work that morning, she was jet-lagged and had a terrible hangover. She'd had to hitch a ride on a military transport, and they'd landed at three different bases, making it impossible for her to sleep. She dropped her purse on the floor next to her desk and reported to Adams's office. "What's going on, chief?"

He looked annoyed. "Don't you check your e-mail when you're on the road?"

"I checked it yesterday around noon," she said, taking a seat in one of the chairs. "I was so tired last night, I must have forgot." She felt guilty for shirking her responsibili-

ties. She'd spent the evening eating ribs and drinking beer
with Agent East, who had later ended up in her bed. Lowell was out, and Brooks was in. Their relationship might
be geographically undesirable, but they both worked for
the same agency. If things got serious, one of them could
transfer. Of course, that person would have to be East.
Mary couldn't leave her mother.

She gave Adams her full attention. "You said the case
was exploding. What happened?"

"Five agencies responded to the queries you placed on
LEO," he told her, referring to the Law Enforcement Online interactive computer system, or intranet, which linked
all levels of law enforcement in the Unites States. "One of
them was a homicide detective with the Seattle PD. They're
sitting on an unsolved murder from three years ago, where
the male victim was dismembered and deposited in an
abandoned boat."

"Jesus, were his head and hands missing like the other
victims?"

"Yes," Adams told her. "The victim owned a dress manufacturing company in Denver. His name was Russell Madison. Caucasian male, forty-three, married eleven years,
four children. The last time his wife, Kimberly, saw him,
he was leaving on a business trip to Los Angeles. Like the
Waverly and Goldstein cases, Madison left his wife a
neatly typed itinerary. She contacted him successfully on
two occasions, using the numbers he provided. The Denver Police Department handled the missing person report
when he failed to return home. The number Kimberly
Madison called, believing it to be the Ramada Inn in L.A.,
has since been disconnected. LAPD discovered the phone
line had been established using a fictitious ID, probably
snatched over the Internet."

"That's our UNSUB," Mary exclaimed. "This is the same

exact story I heard from Belinda Waverly. She can't figure out who typed her husband's itinerary, although she swears he never would have typed it himself."

Adams placed his arms behind his neck. "A clear pattern has developed, Stevens. These victims were doing something they didn't want anyone to know about. From what we've learned about them, it's unlikely they were CIA. They could have all been involved in some type of illegal activity, maybe narcotics, smuggling, or arms dealing. Are we absolutely certain these men didn't know each other?"

"Since they're dead," Mary said, rubbing a spot near her eyebrow, "it's difficult to ascertain. I contacted some of Waverly's associates, and they had only good things to say about him. His wife is a former Miss America, and everyone thought they had the perfect marriage. The most reasonable assumption as to Waverly, along with the other victims, is they were cheating on their wives. The real question is, who's covering for them? Someone's answering the phone at the numbers that are supposed to be hotels, businesses, et cetera."

"I'm convinced the victims' stories are cleverly concocted alibis."

Bulldog McIntyre stuck his head in the door. "Sorry for interrupting, chief," he said. "Don't want you to think I'm eavesdropping. I was walking by when I heard you say something about those alibi clubs."

Both Adams and Mary looked befuddled. A moment later, it clicked in Mary's mind and she bolted to her feet. "Thank you, Jesus," she said dramatically. "Something kept rolling around in my mind. Now I remember. This is it, don't you see?"

"No, I don't see," Adams said gruffly. "What in the hell is an alibi club?"

"It was in all the papers a few years ago," Mary said,

giving him a quick rundown of how alibi clubs operated. "I never heard anything else about them, so I decided it was some type of publicity scam. What about you, Bulldog?"

Bulldog McIntyre rode Harleys and hung out with people the FBI would classify as undesirable. A former undercover cop from Miami, his connections had helped to solve an untold number of crimes. He was also a human bloodhound. People joked that Bulldog could predict what a killer would do before the killer decided to do it. "I haven't heard anything about them recently," he said. "Guys still kid around about it. I'm single, so I don't need an alibi club, but some of my friends thought it was the best thing since chicken soup."

Adams fixed his gaze on Mary. "You're the computer wizard. Go jump on the Web and see what you can find out. If the victims were all using the same service, this could be our first major break."

Mary couldn't curb her excitement. "On the tape, the killer said she only killed adulterous men. I kept asking myself how she could find them. I mean, being unfaithful isn't something you talk about, even with your closest friends. Our UNSUB may work for an alibi club, even own one."

"I'm going national with this," Adams said, placing his palms on his desk. "What are you standing around for, Stevens?"

Mary hurried back to her office. When she typed "alibi clubs" into her browser, all she came up with were articles about the clubs from several years back. She read an interesting piece about an alibi club in D.C. established in 1884, whose members were political powerhouses. After several hours, she reported back to Adams.

"Alibi clubs have gone underground." Mary parked her pen in her hair, which was sleeked back in a knot. "I found

one in South Africa, but the Web site hasn't been updated
since 2004. There are tons of newspaper articles about alibi clubs, but nothing recent. The majority were published
between '04 and '05. I'd like to finish talking to Waverly's
associates, then I'll see if I can find anything on alibi clubs
in the chat rooms."

"I thought you said these clubs were a big deal," Adams
said, glaring at her. "Now you tell me they're history."

"I didn't say they don't exist anymore. I said they've
probably gone underground."

"You mean they don't use the Internet anymore?"

"Maybe, maybe not," she said. "Even in the past, club
members reached each other via cell phones, mainly using SMS, or text messaging. Someone who needed a person to provide an alibi would send out an e-mail or text
message that was then forwarded to all the members of
the club. Those willing to help would reply, and it would
go from there. There are a number of pitfalls to something like this, which must be why the companies disappeared."

"What kind of pitfalls are we talking about?"

"Blackmail, for example. In one of the articles, guys
said they were afraid of giving their wives' or girlfriends'
numbers out to strangers, thinking the persons might use
them in a sinister way."

"The clubs are out of business, then."

Everything was black and white with Adams. He wanted
instant answers. There was a bomb ticking somewhere,
though, and she understood why he was abrupt with her. "I
don't think they're out of business, sir. They're just more
sophisticated. You saw how Bulldog's ears pricked when
he thought we were talking about an alibi club. All business is supply and demand. Let me ask you something.
You know call girls exist, right?"

"Of course, but what does that have to do—"

"Just listen. So you know call girls exist, but do you know how to hire one?"

"This is ridiculous."

"You don't know how to hire a call girl because the people that manage them rely strictly on referrals. Referrals have probably kept the alibi clubs alive as well." She paused to allow him time to think, then added, "Another way to take them underground is to not maintain a public domain on the Internet. All the members are given is a URL. Without it, they can't find the site."

"Say they do exist," Adams said, rubbing his chin, "how do you propose we find these organizations?"

"The easiest way is to start shopping for an alibi," Mary told him. "I'll devise a phony ID and pose as a married man. You're going to have to be patient, though. This may take some time."

"Who's working on the phone records?"

"The various investigating agencies, I presume."

"That's too disjointed," Adams said. "I'm going to put Genna Weir on it. Once we get the case files from Seattle, I'll call a meeting of the team and we'll see if we can get a better handle on this thing. Has the lab identified where the voices on the tape came from?"

"Not yet," Mary told him. "I'll call them."

When she got back to her office, she checked the rest of her e-mails. One was from Andy Cutler, a deputy sheriff in Lincoln, Nebraska, who recalled a fellow deputy finding a young girl abandoned along the Interstate during a particularly brutal winter approximately twenty years ago. The child was unconscious, and had no identification on her. One of the local papers, which had since gone out of business, ran the story for several weeks, hoping to get a response from the girl's family. Other than that, Cutler didn't know what happened to the girl, and the deputy who'd found her was now deceased.

Mary called Adams and told him the news. "This may confirm that the event the UNSUB referred to on the tape actually occurred."

"I'm not impressed with the alibi clubs," he said. "Follow up on this first."

Although Mary was grateful for the information Officer Cutler had provided, she knew it wouldn't lead them to the killer's doorstep, as the person who had sent the tape had said her father drove her across the state line. Nebraska bordered on Iowa, South Dakota, Wyoming, Colorado, and Kansas, and she didn't even have the girl's name. None of the hospitals in Lincoln had records of an unidentified child suffering from hypothermia. During the past twenty years, the hospitals had computerized their records, and much was lost during the transition.

Mary called social services in Lincoln, but they had no record of an abandoned child during the time span in question. She wondered if a nurse or someone else at the hospital felt sorry for the girl and took her in. The most important thing now was to find out where the killer's base of operation was today, and she felt fairly certain she'd left Nebraska, as none of the murders had taken place in that part of the country.

She went to Genna Weir's office to bring her up to date. Bulldog was present as well, slouched in one of her chairs. "Did you find any alibi clubs?" he said, laughing. "If you do, I've got a buddy who wants their numbers."

Weir snapped at him, "You're incorrigible. How could you laugh about something like this?"

"Because I love to get a rise out of you," Bulldog answered. "Every guy I've talked to about the alibi clubs thinks it's fabulous. What are you bitching about, Weir? I bet there are some ladies out there that wouldn't mind slipping out on their husbands now and then?"

"This is a male thing," insisted Weir, a feisty brunette

who had a tendency to come across like a drill sergeant. "Men cheat far more than women. And even if a woman wanted to have an affair, she wouldn't use some stupid service. You guys are lucky someone gives a shit. If my husband deceived me like that, I'd say good riddance."

Mary entered the conversation. "Bulldog, did you or any of your friends keep any information about the alibi clubs?"

"Are you kidding? When I told my ex about it, she went ballistic. No guy in his right mind would keep that kind of stuff around." He paused a moment, thinking. "Shit, I know why I remembered the alibi clubs now. I was goofing off on the 'Net the other day and came across a similar site. This one is a dating service for married people interested in having affairs. I think it's called Personal Affairs. For fun, I posted an ad to see if anyone answered."

"You're a moron," Weir barked. "We're trying to catch a serial killer, not get you laid. If you don't knock it off, I'm going to tell Madeline and she'll slice your balls off while you're sleeping."

"No, wait," Mary said. "Type it in your search engine. I can't find the alibi clubs. Maybe this is a spin-off."

"Jesus Christ," Weir exclaimed, staring at her computer screen a few moments later. "Listen to this. 'Married and looking? Seeking an extramarital affair? Welcome to Personal Affairs, a service designed for persons seeking an extramarital relationship. Why you are here is our main concern. Our mission is to help you sort out your thoughts, provide a safe, secure outlet and direction for your extramarital dating. We are not a sex or personals site for cheating housewives that provide empty promises. Our clientele are well educated and informed before they become members. All our members are married or permanently attached, but looking for something extra. We are honest, forthright and caring, three things we value in our extramarital web relations. We've been satisfying married people since 1996.'" She turned to Mary. "This looks more like the main event than a spin-off."

"You're right," Mary said. "I'll see what I can find out. Bulldog, if someone answers this ad you placed, string them along. But whatever you do, don't meet them. If you do, you may end up in a body bag."

TWENTY-TWO

❧

THURSDAY, NOVEMBER 30
VENTURA, CALIFORNIA

The sound of her windshield wipers clicking was somehow reassuring. Although it was a miserable rainy day, Lily was eager to get to the courthouse. The empty house had turned into a nightmare, where she ran into her past in every room.

Bryce should have called by now, regardless of the circumstances. She had stayed up half the night checking with hospitals and jails in the Lexington and Charleston area. He was scheduled to return today at noon. Knowing she wouldn't be able to pick him up, he had told her he would take a shuttle. If she wasn't in trial, she would drive to the airport herself and give the bastard a piece of her mind.

She kept asking herself if Bryce was mad because she nagged him all the time about his drinking. If he was, he had a strange way of showing it. They'd made love the night before he had left.

When she arrived at work, Chris Rendell appeared beside her in the corridor. "Can you talk?"

"I'm sorry I haven't been able to get back to you," Lily told him. "You don't have to apologize for the other day, if that's what you're concerned about. I pried into your personal life, so you had every right to ask me about mine."

"I shouldn't have brought up what happened to you and your daughter. I wasn't thinking. Will . . . will you see me again?"

"I'm seeing you now."

"I don't mean right now," Chris told her, flustered. "Can I take you to lunch again? I wanted you to have a nice time, then I ruined everything."

"Sure, Chris, but not today. Check back with me next week. This week has been a disaster."

"The Stucky trial?"

"That and other things." She turned and placed her palm in the center of his chest, feeling the warmth of his body. "I'll call you one day next week, I promise."

She speculated what would happen if Bryce never came home. Maybe he had decided he wanted a divorce, and had left rather than confront her in person. An unbroken chain of nights stretched before her. She couldn't live alone. The demons she'd been battling wouldn't stay in the shadows much longer. And someone like Tessa couldn't make her feel safe. Being with another woman reminded her of that terrible night with Shana.

Even though her daughter had been a child at the time, Lily perceived all females as inherently vulnerable. Men didn't get raped. That is, if you discounted the men in prison. Rendell was tall, strong, and sympathetic. "Do I have your home number? You know, in case I want to call you the night before to arrange our lunch date?"

"Here," he said, scribbling the number on the back of a business card.

"Thanks, I'll be in touch."

That morning in court, James Kidwell asked for a continuance. Lily told him, "Approach the bench, Counselor."

When Kidwell stepped up, she pushed the microphone aside and covered it with her hand. "We talked about this yesterday, didn't we? I told you my calendar was too tight to grant a continuance."

"I know," he said, a string of perspiration popping out on his forehead. "But I still haven't heard back from the pediatrician. And since Brian went to a private school, I have to subpoena the records. If what you suspect is true and the boy was retarded, we'll have to reorganize our entire case."

"You have until Monday," Lily said abruptly. "And need I remind you I'm putting extra pressure on myself and this court to allow you this time? I expect results, understand?"

"Of course."

Lily continued the case and adjourned for the remainder of the day. She should call Hennessey and inform him of the status, but she would rather try to deal with the situation on her own.

She returned to her chambers and checked her calendar. Jury selection in the Burkell homicide began on December 26. The prosecution was far from putting on their case in the Stucky homicide, and then there was the defense, which could last for weeks. After that were closing arguments. Even without the continuance, the schedule had been tight. They might have to resort to night sessions.

Glancing at the clock, Lily saw that it was almost eleven. If she left now, she might be able to reach the airport in time to pick up Bryce. Just as she was about to leave, Jeannie buzzed her on the intercom. "I have a Detective Carl Smith with the Las Vegas PD on the line. Do you want me to put him through?"

"What does he want?"

"He wouldn't say."

"Tell him I'm in court and ask him to call back." Lily

picked up her purse and her umbrella. A moment later, Jeannie called again. "Your husband's on the phone, Judge Forrester."

She punched into the line and immediately started shouting, "Where the hell are you? Why didn't you call me, for God's sake? I've been worried sick."

"I'm in jail, Lily," Bryce said weakly.

She flopped back down in her chair, relieved but furious. "I was afraid that's where you were. I told you this was going to happen if you didn't stop drinking. What were you arrested for? DWI?"

"No," Bryce said. "The police have charged me with attempted rape. Please don't scream at me, okay? You have no idea what I've gone through."

She remembered the call from the detective in Las Vegas. She hadn't taken it because she had assumed the call had been misdirected. There was no case on her calendar that involved the Las Vegas authorities. "You're not in Las Vegas, are you?"

"How did you know? God, how can I explain this to you? I know I told you I was going on a business trip. I lied, okay? I came here to meet a woman."

Lily's mouth fell open in shock. She tried to speak, but the words were stuck in her throat.

"I made a mistake, honey," Bryce went on. "I love you. I swear, I never wanted to hurt you. I tried to make it so you wouldn't find out. I just wanted . . . I don't know how to explain it. There's no excuse for what I did, but I didn't rape anyone. This woman is insane. I swear, I never laid a hand on her. I need you to line me up a good attorney. You can sign on my bank account. There's fifty grand in there. Give them whatever they want. I have to get out of this place. My life is at risk."

"Your life," Lily hissed at him. "What about me? Who is this woman? Where did you meet her?"

"I—I've been seeing her for a month or so," Bryce stammered. "She's no one, Lily. I met her in a bar over by the country club. She enticed me to meet her in Vegas. I was a fool."

"How did she entice you?"

"She refused to sleep with me unless I went away with her. I had a few drinks while I was waiting for her at the Aladdin, maybe more than a few. I must have passed out in her car. All I know is when I woke up, blood was dripping into my eyes. She told the police she hit me in self-defense. The bitch is a sadist or something."

Lily took several deep breaths. She wanted to kick him in the balls, claw his eyes out. He was an animal, a lying, perverted bastard. "You tried to rape her, didn't you?"

"No, I swear," Bryce pleaded. "God, you have to believe me. I could go to prison. Please don't let them do this to me."

She wanted to stop, hang up, but she couldn't. She needed to hear every sordid detail. "Where did the crime occur?"

"There was no crime, Lily."

"Stop bullshitting me, Bryce," she snapped. "I need to know what happened. How can I help you if you don't tell me the truth?"

"I must have passed out on the floor in a parking garage at the Sands. The hotel is closed. They're about to knock it down and build something else. When I woke up, the cops were there. They cuffed me and put me in the back of the police car. She was just standing there, looking pathetic, like I'd done something awful to her. Maybe I made a move on her. I don't remember. How could she possibly say I tried to rape her? She came here to have sex with me, for Christ's sake. I was too drunk to do anything. I was blasted, man. I've never been that wasted in my life. I've been trying so hard to please you and stop drinking. I needed to let loose and have some fun for a change."

"Don't you understand what attempted rape is?" Lily

said, her words crackling with venom. "The moment a woman says no. If a man continues to force himself on her after that point, he's committing a crime, and one that carries considerable penalties. I'm not sure you have a defense, Bryce. Being drunk isn't a defense against attempted rape."

Lily could see her career skidding off track. Her marriage was obviously over. How could she remain married to a man who would sexually assault a woman? "I can't talk to you anymore, Bryce. You make me sick."

"Please, I know you're angry. I'd be furious if you'd done something like this to me. Get me an attorney, Lily. That's all I'm asking. Once I make bail, I'll come home and we'll work through this. I'll find a way to make it up to you somehow."

"Get your own damn attorney," Lily said, slamming the receiver down.

She stood and walked around the room, her hands clenched into fists at her side. That he'd tried to rape someone was bad enough. What made her blood boil was his belief that he could worm his way out of it. While she'd been frantically worrying about him, he'd been trying to get his dick into another woman. Who was this hideous man? Had her entire marriage been a sham?

Thirty minutes passed and she finally cooled off enough to buzz Jeannie and ask her for Detective Smith's phone number. She would never get the truth out of Bryce, and at the moment she had no intention of helping him.

"Detective Carl Smith," a deep voice said.

"Ah, Detective Smith, I'm sorry I couldn't take your call earlier. I spoke to my husband, Bryce Donnelly, and he explained the situation. Since you called me, I assume you know I'm a judge. I'd appreciate it if you told me precisely what occurred?"

"Well, central dispatch got a call from a woman named

Anne Bradley at one-fifteen this morning. She said Mr. Donnelly—"

"Anne Bradley!" Lily was flabbergasted. Could it be the same person? "What does this woman look like?"

"Nice-looking blonde, short hair, pretty face. As I was saying, Ms. Bradley called in from her cell phone, saying your husband tried to rape her. The patrol unit responded to the garage at the Sands Hotel. Damn place is closed and they still haven't blocked off the parking facility. The Sands is scheduled to be demolished next week, in case you don't know. We're losing a lot of these old hotels. Kind of sad, if you ask me."

"Was the victim injured?"

"Yeah, he roughed her up. She's got some scrapes on her knees where he pushed her down on the concrete, and her clothes were torn. She's also got skin under her finger-nails. Won't know if it's Mr. Donnelly's until the lab processes it, but he's got scratches on him."

Anne was a fairly small woman. Lily felt her stomach turn at the thought of her trying to fend off a man the size of Bryce, and how frightened she must have been. "My husband says he was beaten."

"Oh, that, well, the little lady fought back. He evidently tried to assault her in the car, a Cadillac Escalade she rented from Hertz when she got into town. Victim bailed out of the vehicle and tried to escape. She called for help, but no one was around. The suspect gave chase." He paused, flipping through some papers. "After the suspect caught her, a struggle ensued. The victim found a piece of plywood on the ground and used it to defend herself. When did you last see your husband, Judge Forrester?"

She didn't answer. Her mind was going in a thousand different directions. "I may know the victim, Detective. Does she reside in Ventura?"

"Yep. Is she a friend or something?"

"Anne Bradley is a common name," Lily continued. "Did she say what she did for a living?"

"She's a lawyer, but she's not affiliated with a law firm right now. Said she just moved to California from New York."

Lily said, "My husband claims he met Ms. Bradley at a bar in Thousand Oaks. Is that what she told you?"

"Yep. Says she met the perp at the Indigo Lounge. I'm sorry, Judge Forrester. Guess I shouldn't call your husband a perp yet. Talking to a judge isn't something I do every day, so please excuse me."

"Go on, Detective."

"Victim said she mentioned something to him about a trip she had planned to Vegas. Mr. Donnelly asked if he could meet her for a drink since he was going to be in town at the same time. When she met him in the bar at the Aladdin, he was already intoxicated, even made a scene with the bartender. He insisted they go to MGM because the bars were nicer. Ms. Bradley intended to drive him there and then ditch him, but he forced her to turn into the parking lot of the Sands, where he proceeded to assault her."

Lily swallowed hard. It didn't sound like a concocted story. It sounded like all the other crimes against women she had handled over the years. The only difference was the perpetrator was a man she had loved and trusted. "Has he been arraigned yet?"

"Set for tomorrow morning at nine, Division Thirty-four."

"I see," she said. "Thanks for your time, Detective." She started to hang up when she heard him talking.

"I can understand how something like this could be embarrassing, you being a judge and all. I wouldn't lose any sleep over it. Things like this happen all the time in this city. If we broadcasted all the bad things people do in Las

Vegas, we'd lose a lot of business. You know, we sweep the streets clean every morning."

"Goodbye, Detective Smith." Great, Lily thought. Now my husband is no better than garbage. Someone tapped lightly on her door. "Is that you, Jeannie?"

"May I come in?"

Before Lily could answer, Jeannie opened the door to her office and walked in. "Are you okay, Judge Forrester? I heard you, um, talking loud and I wondered if something was wrong. Can I help you with anything?"

"No one can help me with this problem, Jeannie, but I appreciate your concern." Lily picked up the phone, but her assistant didn't move.

"It's your husband, isn't it? He sounded terrible. You've been asking if he called for several days, so I knew something was going on. I wondered if he'd been in—"

Lily cut her off. "Its not your job to wonder," she told her, a muscle in her eyelid twitching. "I'll call you if I need you, Jeannie."

After Jeannie left, Lily called Tessa on her cell. "Can you talk?"

"Yeah, it's recess."

"Isn't it still raining?"

"When it rains, we let the kids run around in the gym. You didn't come to the club again this morning. I was going to call, but I figured I'd bothered you enough this week."

"I need to ask you about Anne Bradley."

"Oh, yeah," Tessa answered, sounding peeved. "She didn't show up this morning, either. Are you two working out somewhere else? Every time she's absent, you are, too."

"Don't be ridiculous," Lily said. "How long have you known Anne?"

"I don't know. A little over a month, I think. Why?"

"Just bear with me," Lily said, feeling as if her head

were about to explode. "Have you ever been to her apartment?"

"No. Why are you asking me these things?"

"She's claiming Bryce tried to rape her."

"You're shitting me. Bryce doesn't even know her, does he?"

"He does now," Lily said. "He met her at a bar in Thousand Oaks. Then he met up with her in Las Vegas. Bryce is in jail, Tessa. Anne called the police and told them he tried to rape her."

"Jeez," Tessa said, taking time to assimilate what she'd just heard. "Bryce wouldn't do something like that, Lily. He adores you. Besides, he's not some asshole that goes around trying to rape women. Have you talked to him, heard his side of the story?"

Lily kept her voice low so Jeannie couldn't overhear. "He rendezvoused with Anne in Las Vegas, believing they were going to have sex. Do you have her cell phone number?"

"No, I've never had a reason to call her. Are you telling me Bryce was having an affair with her? Think about it, Lily. If Anne was sleeping with your husband, you're the last person she'd want to hang out with. Are you certain it was her? It might be someone else with the same name."

"Someone who just moved here from New York, who just happens to be an attorney? It's her, Tessa." Lily filled her in on what she'd learned from Bryce and the police detective. "Isn't this too big of a coincidence?"

"Not really," Tessa said thoughtfully. "Everyone in California goes to Vegas, Lily. Anne isn't working, and she just moved here from New York, so it seems plausible for her to want to see Vegas. Hell, maybe she's a gambler. There's this teacher who's a gambler, Lorraine Prichard. She lost her house, and her husband filed for divorce last week. The district is threatening to fire her because she disappears for days without notice. We don't have enough teachers as it is. There are forty-five kids in my class. How can I teach that many children? I'm going to apply for a job at a private school."

Lily sighed, wondering if Tessa realized how thoughtless she was being. She'd just told her Bryce was in jail for attempted rape, and she'd already turned the conversation back to herself. But Lily needed her. When you need someone, you have to take the good with the bad. "I thought you were considering going back to college to get your master's."

"Yeah, well, I'm under contract for the rest of the year."

"Did Anne ever say or do anything to make you think she was a gambler?"

"No," Tessa answered, "but neither did Lorraine Prichard. If you were a compulsive gambler, would you run around and tell everyone?"

"Do you remember the name of the law firm in New York Anne was with before she moved?"

"I have no idea," Tessa said, kids yelling in the background. "You were talking to her about that stuff, not me. Anne and I took aerobic and spin classes together. There wasn't a lot of time for chitchat. She was also pretty serious about weight training, so I generally kept my mouth shut. You know me, I'm not good with the weights."

"Let me go, I need to see what I can find out."

"What are you going to do about Bryce?"

"I haven't decided yet."

"I know how you get when you're alone, honey," Tessa told her. "My God, you were crouched in the corner the other morning. If you want, I can sleep over at your house tonight. Fred certainly won't miss me. All he does is watch television."

"I love you," Lily said, tears streaking down her face.

"I know, even though you don't always show it."

"I'm sorry, Tessa."

"Hey, I know I'm a blabbermouth. Most people can't handle me. You get a merit badge for putting up with me for so long. Hold on, Lily." She stopped and shouted, "Riley Foster, come here right this minute. If I ever catch you pulling hair again, I'll send you to the principal's office. Now everyone line up by the door."

Lily tapped her nails on the desk while she waited for Tessa. "You're busy. I'll call you back later."

"Listen, I'll go home, grab some clothes for tomorrow, and be at your place around six. Then we'll go out and get something to eat." She laughed. "You talk about me having an eating disorder. When you're upset or under stress, you turn into a toothpick. And don't give me a bunch of crap about how you can't eat, or I'll have to force-feed you. You're going to need the strength to get through this, sweetheart. I know about these things. My brother's in prison in Alabama."

Lily was shocked. "You never told me your brother was in prison."

"Like I said, some things you just don't talk about."

TWENTY-THREE

❦

THURSDAY, NOVEMBER 30
QUANTICO, VIRGINIA

"How's this sound?" Genna Weir asked, holed up in Mary's office. The room had two desks in it, but no one was assigned to the other workstation. " 'Handsome white male, forty years old, successful business owner, seeking twenty-something female who wants to be spoiled.' "

Mary was preparing her own ad. "Only hookers are going to bite on that. Axe the spoiled line and it's fine. Part of the reason guys want to fool around with a married woman is they think they won't have to spend any money on her."

"But we're not looking for a married woman," Weir pointed out.

"We're not looking for a hooker, either. Check this out." Mary read from her computer screen. " 'Experienced philanderer seeking discreet lady. Professional with family. Dark hair, five-foot-ten, one hundred seventy pounds, excellent lover.' "

"Clever," Weir commented. "You're describing the victims' profile. If I write the same thing, though, they might get suspicious."

"Just change it around a little. It's not like anyone checks these things. It's like eBay, just an interactive database." Mary spun her chair around and kicked off her shoes. It was nine at night, and cartons of half-empty Chinese food were piled up in the trash can. "While you're doing that, I'd like to take a look at Waverly's credit card statements. The police went over them and didn't find anything unusual." She smiled. "We're the FBI, though. And don't forget, the PD didn't know what they were looking for."

All of Belinda's charges had been circled. Boy, Mary thought, she is one hell of a shopper. The former beauty queen charged thousands of dollars per month, mostly at upscale department stores like Neiman Marcus and Saks Fifth Avenue. Stan's charges were for restaurants, hotels, gas, and a health club, basically nothing out of the ordinary. She was about to set aside the statement when something caught her eye, and she turned to Weir. "Stan Waverly's American Express shows a charge three weeks before he disappeared. The company name is Khan's Preston Exxon in Dallas, but the amount is precisely two hundred dollars. The price of gas is high, but not that high. Waverly didn't drive a big rig."

"Interesting," Weir said, working on the computer. "He probably had his oil changed or something. It's worth checking out, though. Is there a phone number to the business?"

"Yeah," Mary said, already punching in the phone number.

"Exxon Mobile," a man with an Indian accent said.

"This is Agent Stevens with the FBI. I need to get in touch with the owner."

The line went silent for a while. "I am the owner."

"Can you tell me your name, sir?"

"Why you want my name? Is there a problem?"

"Before I continue this discussion, I need to know who I'm speaking to."

"My name is Bob Smith?"

"Sure it is," Mary said. "Where are you from?"

"Where I am from is of no consequence. I am an American citizen."

Mary had an excellent ear for accents. "You're from Pakistan, right?"

"Yes, but as I told you, I am an American citizen."

"Fine, you're a citizen. Tell me your real name or I'll send someone from our Dallas Field Office over to talk to you in person."

"Nevin Khan."

"Pleased to meet you, Mr. Khan. We're checking on a charge made by a man named Stan Waverly on his American Express Card. The amount is two hundred dollars. Can you tell me what Mr. Waverly purchased?"

"I do not know," he said. "I will have to speak to my accountant. We sell gasoline. All of our customers buy gasoline."

"Do you do oil changes or offer other services?"

"No, we only sell gasoline."

"When will you be able to speak to your accountant? Two hundred dollars buys a lot of gasoline, Mr. Khan. What's curious about this is Mr. Waverly drives a BMW. The tank doesn't hold that much gasoline. Do you allow customers to get cash back?"

"No, we do not."

"That's what I thought," Mary said. "About your accountant—"

"My accountant is out of town. I have customers. I must go now."

When Mary heard a dial tone, she was almost happy, since Mr. Khan had been so uncooperative. She excused herself and walked out into the hallway, calling Brooks from her cell phone.

"Hi, baby," she cooed when a man answered.

"Are you looking for Agent East?" the person said. "He took his wife and kids to the movie."

Mary started to hang up when he said, "Hey, I'm pulling your leg. You must be the illustrious Agent Stevens from Quantico. Don't worry, Brooks is single. I'll put him on."

"Who was that?" Mary asked when Brooks got on the phone. "My God, he sounds just like you."

"You mean the Texas accent?"

She placed her hand on top of her head. "Forgive me, I'm an idiot. I thought this was your personal number. He's an agent, right? Now everyone is going to know. If it gets back to Adams, he'll eat my ass for breakfast. I was supposed to be working in Dallas. He already jumped on me for not checking my e-mail the night we were together."

East began laughing. It was the kind of laugh that couldn't be faked, a laugh that only a genuinely happy person could make. It was so infectious, she began laughing as well. "It isn't funny," she said, falling serious. "I thought we agreed not to tell anyone we were seeing each other."

"That was my brother," he said. "Do you know what time it is?"

"Oh," Mary said. "I'm sorry, we're working around the clock here. I'm actually calling on Bureau business. Do you have something to write on?"

"Always."

Mary explained about the charges on Waverly's credit card and asked him to see what he could find out. "It can wait until tomorrow. I forgot to ask Khan when he closes the station."

"When are you coming to Dallas again?"

Her voice dropped to a whisper. "The way things are going here, it could be a long time. Are you going to forget me?"

"No, I'm going to buy a plane ticket."

Mary slouched against the wall. Was it really going to happen? Had she finally found the right man? "You shouldn't come until we put this case to bed. That is, if we ever do. You know what Adams told me? I might work this case the rest of my career. I think I'd go mad if that happened." She paused, then added, "I want you to meet my mother, Brooks. If you'd rather not, I understand."

"Of course I want to meet your mother," he told her. "I think I'm in love with you."

Mary's body felt like rubber. "It was only one night, Brooks. A person can't fall in love in one night. We just had good sex. Really, incredible sex is more like it."

"I'm not so sure about that," East told her. "It wasn't just one night. We spent the day together. We woke up beside each other the next morning. I'm serious, Mary. I knew as soon as you got off the plane. Why is that so hard to believe?"

"See if there are any openings in the Washington office," she said, excited. "I wouldn't want you to transfer until we spend more time together, but it wouldn't hurt to see what's available."

"I agree. See how easy that was? I'll call you tomorrow."

"Wait." Mary looked up and down the corridor, making certain no one was around. She turned and pressed her forehead to the wall, sliding her free hand up her dress. "I wish you were here with me."

"I'm there, you just can't see me."

"Brooks?"

"Yeah, baby."

"It's insane how much I want you."

"Me, too."

"Oh, Brooks," Mary panted.

"Yeah, baby."

"I think I'm in love with you, too."

"I know," he said. "Get some sleep."

"That was disgusting," Lily said, opening the door to Tessa's Taurus and sliding into the passenger seat. Most of the rain had passed, but you could still smell it in the air.

"Hey," her friend said, "you're the one who picked this place. I don't eat at Taco Bell. If I knew you were going to make me consume a zillion calories for barf food, I would have cooked dinner for us at your house."

Lily wrapped her arms around her chest. "Jeannie, my assistant, figured out what was going on. She's probably told everyone by now. Judge Forrester's husband is a criminal. Hennessey will drool all over himself when he hears. He's been waiting for me to slip up so he could get rid of me." Her eyes were wild. "I don't want anyone at the courthouse to see me. That's why I wouldn't go to a regular restaurant."

Tessa backed out of their parking slot. "That's going to be hard to do, sweetie. You're in trial, aren't you?"

"The Stucky case was continued until Monday."

"Okay, so you have the weekend to put yourself back together. You've got to calm down, Lily. Shit happens." Tessa reached over and patted her thigh. "When my brother told me he'd shot a man in Mobile, I went nuts. Jess had always been a wild card, but I never thought he'd end up in prison. I spent a fortune on his legal fees. We could have bought a new house with that money. That's why I haven't gone back to get my master's. We ran through all our savings."

"I would have helped you. When did this happen?"

"Five years ago," Tessa told her, turning down Lily's street. "You were living in Santa Barbara, and we didn't see each other on a regular basis. How could I ask you for money? You've spent your life putting people like Jess behind bars."

They pulled in the driveway and parked. Once they were inside, Tessa flopped down on Lily's new sofa in the den. Lily opened the sliding glass door so Gabby could go out, then sat across from her in Bryce's lounge chair. She could smell his cologne. "Something isn't right, Tessa."

"For sure, but things will eventually get better."

"No," Lily said, massaging her temples. "Maybe Bryce is telling the truth and Anne is some kind of psycho. You know how I feel about coincidences. She was almost *too* friendly. And she kept talking about this case in Florida. You know, the preacher's wife who killed her husband and got away with it."

"I read about that," Tessa commented. "She didn't get away with it, though. She went to prison, didn't she?"

Lily's speech was rapid-fire. "They convicted her of voluntary manslaughter. She used a pump-action shotgun, and she'll only have to serve a few years. Anne hates men. I could tell from the way she talked."

Tessa went over and trapped Lily's face in her hands. "You're losing it, understand? You're my best friend. You have an important job. You can't go around blabbering like an imbecile." She released her, then returned to the sofa. "Stop trying to put the blame on Anne. She doesn't hate men, Lily, and she didn't *lure* Bryce to Vegas. Bryce is a grown man. No one forced him to concoct this big story about a business trip, buy a airline ticket, and fly to Las Vegas. He even left you a phony itinerary. I never thought I'd hear something like this come out of your mouth. The victim isn't responsible. Jesus, you, of all people, should know that."

Lily knew she was becoming paranoid. On the other hand, she suspected Tessa might get a certain amount of pleasure seeing her life crumble. What was she thinking? How could she remain friends with a person like that? Tessa was right. She was losing it. "I'm going upstairs to shower, then I'm going to decide what to do about Bryce."

Tessa had picked up a magazine off the coffee table and was thumbing through it. "I thought you already made that decision."

"He's my husband," Lily told her, pausing by the stairway. "I have to do something. Bryce has more than enough money to buy himself a decent defense. The problem is I only know one good attorney who has a license to practice in Nevada."

"Oh, really?" her friend said, responding without listening.

"Richard Fowler."

Tessa dropped the magazine on the floor. "You've got to be shitting me. If anyone has fucked up your life, it's Richard. There's got to be tons of lawyers who can practice in Nevada. Don't they have reciprocity?"

"No."

"Then look in the phone book, for God's sake. Letting that man back in your life is a recipe for disaster. All he's ever done is hurt you."

"Our relationship was too complex," Lily argued, gripping the handrail on the stairs. "You don't understand, Tessa."

"Fine, fine," she said, tossing her hands in the air. "But if you're going to call him, I'm leaving. You're already a basket case."

"Don't leave," Lily pleaded, staring at the shadows in the yard. She rushed downstairs and called Gabby. Once the dog ran inside, she quickly closed the door and locked it. She then scooped Gabby up in her arms, clutching her to her body. Taking a seat beside Tessa on the sofa, she said, "If Richard can get them to plead the case down to misdemeanor, it might go away. I don't even have to see him. I don't want to hire someone I've never met. They're going to arraign Bryce tomorrow morning. I need someone fast."

"It's your life, honey," Tessa said, brushing a curl off her forehead. "Go take your shower and try to put this stuff out of your mind for right now. I'm here for you. I'm not going anywhere."

Just then, Tessa's cell phone rang. When she saw the name on the caller ID, she began waving her hands around, but Lily had already gone upstairs. "Anne, gosh, how are you doing?"

"I'm sorry I haven't been at the club, Tessa. Do you know how I can reach Lily?"

"Yeah, sure," she said. "Hold on a minute." She left her phone on the end table and raced upstairs to get Lily. "She's on the phone."

"Who's on the phone?" Lily had already slipped out of her jeans and was pulling her sweater over her head.

"Anne," Tessa said, her eyes enormous. "She wants to talk to you. What do you want me to tell her?"

"I thought you didn't have her number."

"I didn't, but I gave her mine. This is the first time she's ever called me."

Lily marched downstairs wearing only her bra and panties. Tessa grabbed the phone and handed it to her. "This is Lily."

"I'm so sorry, Lily. I assume Bryce has called you. I had no idea he was your husband. Did he tell you what happened?"

"Yes." Lily dropped down on the edge of the sofa. "But I'd like to hear your side of the story."

"I'm sure you would," Anne said, sounding anxious. "Look, I don't want to discuss this over the phone. There's a Starbucks across the street from the health club. Can you meet me there in thirty minutes?"

Lily rattled off her cell phone number in case something happened, then raced up the stairs again to put her clothes back on. She saw Tessa had followed her.

"What did she say? Aren't you going to tell me?"

"I'm going to meet her."

"Why didn't you have her come here?"

"Think about it, Tessa. I don't want her to know where I live."

"Bryce is the one who did something wrong, not Anne."

"We don't really know that for sure yet." Lily put the same clothes back on and grabbed her keys. "You'll have to move your car."

"Why?" Tessa frowned. "Aren't I going with you?"

God, Lily thought, now I have to deal with this. She walked over and placed her hands on her shoulders. "Anne may not talk if you're there, Tessa. This is something I have to do by myself. You can go home if you want, or you can stay here and watch TV until I get back."

Tessa sat down on the edge of the bed. "I'll stay, I guess. I want to hear what she says. Where are you meeting her?"

"Starbucks, the one near the club."

"Can't I go with you and wait in the car?"

"No," Lily shouted, heading back down the stairs. "You can't go, Tessa. Why can't you understand that? I'm under tremendous pressure right now. If you're my friend, you won't interfere."

Tessa peered down at her from the top of the stairs. "You don't have to yell at me. Since you don't want me around, I'll go home."

Lily ignored her and went through the door leading to the garage. She got inside the Volvo, but when she hit the garage door opener, she saw Tessa's car was blocking her. She took several deep breaths in an attempt to calm herself. She couldn't face another confrontation, so she decided to wait. It had been a mistake to ask Tessa to stay with her. After ten minutes had passed, she became furious, returning to the house. "Move your car, Tessa!"

The woman bumped Lily as she walked past her. "I was in the bathroom. You know, Lily," she said, turning around to face her, "you've been treating me like shit ever since you became a judge. I'm tired of putting up with it. I left Fred alone to stay with you tonight. You never appreciate the things I do for you. I came over to see if you were okay the other morning, and you acted like I was invading your privacy. You were crouched in the corner like a terrified child. You don't need a friend, Lily. You need professional help."

"Move your damn car, Tessa," Lily said, incredulous. Her friend was only a step away from being a stalker. She had entered her home unannounced and scared her out of her wits, then spent an hour talking about herself.

"I don't know why you're so upset about Bryce," Tessa

continued. "You treated him like a doormat. He was just someone to look after you. You were going to toss him aside one day and go back to Richard anyway. Everyone in your life is disposable. All you do is use people."

Lily's face was flushed with outrage. "Get out of my house!"

"So what if you were raped?" Tessa shouted. "It's been over ten years. Isn't it time you got over it?"

"Get out!"

"Fuck you," Tessa said, disappearing out the front door.

Lily arrived at Starbucks fifteen minutes later, still livid over the hateful things Tessa had said to her. Through the glass, she saw a man working on a laptop and another person wearing a red sweatshirt with the hood pulled up. When she entered the coffee shop, she realized the person in the hooded sweatshirt was Anne. She looked up at Lily, causing the hood to slip off. Her chin was scraped, and she looked as if she'd been crying. Lily took a seat in the chair across from her.

"Would you like a coffee?" Anne asked, taking a sip out of a paper cup.

"No," Lily said, craning her neck around when a young woman in jeans and a black leather jacket stepped up to the counter. "Why don't we talk in my car? It'll be more private."

"Sure."

Once they were situated in Lily's Volvo, Anne began speaking. "Bryce swore he wasn't married. Please believe me, Lily."

There was a strange energy inside the car. Lily could almost feel Anne's exhaustion and despair. It had taken courage for her to call her, let alone meet her face to face. Under the circumstances, most women would have run in the opposite direction.

"Let me try to explain," Anne said softly. "Ventura is a

bedroom community, something I didn't give much thought to when I decided to move here. It isn't that easy to meet people. I got lonely and—"

Something didn't make sense. Lily interrupted her. "How did you find out Bryce was my husband? We don't use the same name."

"I guess that's part of the problem," Anne told her, leaning against the passenger window. "You having a different last name. When the police arrested him, Bryce kept telling them they couldn't put him in jail because he was married to a judge. After he said your name, I put it together."

The area around Lily's lips felt numb. Anne moved and Lily noticed that the fabric in her jeans was torn around the knees and her skin was scraped. An odor caught her attention, the distinctive scent of Bryce's aftershave.

Seeing Lily sniffing, Anne pulled her sweatshirt off, exposing a white tank top. "I didn't take the time to shower. I've been beside myself ever since I found out Bryce was your husband. I came here hoping I could clear things up, maybe make you feel better."

"Why? You hardly know me."

"I know," Anne said. "But I like you. We connected the other day in the gym. I thought I'd finally found a friend. Tessa told me about what you went through, how you and your daughter were raped. I'm so sorry you have to deal with this, Lily. You've gone through enough."

Lily was livid. How could Tessa reveal something that personal without her permission? She talked incessantly, and to anyone who would listen. And Tessa had the gall to call her a user. She was the user. The woman was using the nightmare Lily and Shana had suffered as a means to get attention, particularly now that Lily was a public figure. If Shana found out, she would never come to Ventura again. She felt like driving to Tessa's house and slugging her.

Anne leaned over and touched her arm. "Are you okay?"

"Not really," she answered, stifling her anger. "Please don't repeat what Tessa told you."

"I won't, Lily. I shouldn't have said anything. I just thought you should know that she discussed it with people. I heard her talking to someone else about it at the club. I've upset you. I'll go."

"No," Lily said, putting her head down on the steering wheel. When she sat up, she asked, "How long have you known Bryce?"

"Five or six weeks. I got an invitation to join the Thousand Oaks Country Club in the mail. I went over to take a look at it, mainly because I didn't have anything else to do. When I left, I saw this bar outside the back gate and decided to stop for a drink. Are you certain you want to hear this?"

"Probably not, but go ahead."

"I was sitting at the bar. Bryce came in and sat down beside me. We started talking, and he seemed like a nice guy. He told jokes and made me laugh. When he started hitting on me, I told him I wasn't interested, that all I needed was some occasional companionship. That probably sounds naïve, but I enjoy hanging out with guys. I had a number of male friends in Manhattan. We'd go out to eat, maybe take in a show. I should have known Bryce was married when he would never go anywhere but the Indigo."

"Did you invite Bryce to go to Vegas with you?"

"God, no," Anne told her. "I was bored and decided to take a trip. I thought I'd stay at a nice hotel with a spa, maybe take in a few shows. In New York, I went to Broadway shows all the time. When I mentioned it to Bryce, he said he was going to be in Vegas on business at the same time and suggested we get together. It was only supposed to be for a drink, Lily. I never said anything about sleeping with him. I wasn't physically attracted to him."

Anne was a striking and fit woman, so it was understandable that she wouldn't be attracted to Bryce. He was also at least a decade older. What got Lily the most was that Bryce had demanded sex the night before he left. The bastard must have been fantasizing about Anne the entire time. She thought of all the nights he'd come home drunk. Not once had she suspected that he'd been with another woman. All she'd worried about was his drinking. In retrospect, he was always talking about his bachelor days and boasting how he'd had a different girl every night. Lily felt as if she'd been run over by a train without realizing she was anywhere near a railroad track. "How many times did you see Bryce at this bar?"

"I don't remember," Anne told her, fidgeting. "Four, maybe five times. Being alone in a new place isn't easy. In New York, there's something to do almost every hour in the day. I was lonely, so I started hanging out at the Indigo. The food wasn't bad, and I didn't have to eat alone."

Through the windows, Lily saw the woman in the black leather jacket sitting at the table with the man she'd seen earlier. Had he met her over the Internet? She wondered if he had a wife at home. She turned back to Anne. "Tell me what happened in Vegas."

"Bryce called me on my cell phone and asked me to meet him in the bar at the Aladdin. I was running late, and by the time I got there, he was already pretty plastered. I should have left then, but that's what people do in Vegas. You know, they drink."

"What about you?"

Anne tugged on an earlobe. "I have a cocktail or a glass of wine now and then, but I don't have a problem and I certainly wasn't drinking when I met Bryce. It was in the middle of the day, for Christ's sake. If all I wanted to do was get wasted, I could have stayed in Ventura."

"Go on," Lily said. "I shouldn't have interrupted you."

"Bryce wanted to go to the MGM because it's a nicer hotel. I had a rental car, so I decided to drive him there and then take off." Anne raised her shoulders and then let them fall. "I don't know how to sugarcoat this, Lily. Your husband turned into a drunken pig in the car. He ripped my blouse, squeezed my nipples, shoved his finger up my vagina."

"While you were driving?"

"Some of it," Anne said, wrapping her arms around her chest. "I kept trying to fight him off. When I realized he wasn't going to stop, I turned into the first driveway I saw. It wasn't until the police came that I learned it was the Sands, and that the hotel was closed. I thought someone would be there to help me, but they weren't."

Lily remembered how she and Shana had screamed the night of the rape, praying one of the neighbors would hear and call the police. Anne was breathing heavily now, re-living the fear and panic.

Anne began talking faster. "I managed to get out of the car and started running. He came after me . . . jumped right on my back. I tried to get him off me, but he was too heavy. I finally got away and crawled to the trash dumpster, thinking I could hide behind it. Then I saw this board on the ground. I—I swung it at him. I just kept swinging it at him until he stopped." She locked eyes with Lily, tears streaking down her face. "What else could I do? I wasn't going to let him rape me. No man should treat a woman like that."

Lily wanted to comfort her, tell her it would never happen again. The truth was it could, which was one of the reasons she still lived in fear. "It's over," she said, reaching into her purse and handing Anne a tissue. "You're safe now."

Anne wiped her eyes, then blew her nose. "Maybe if I'd known he was your husband, I wouldn't have reported it to the police. I'm sorry, Lily."

She got out of the Volvo and started across the parking lot toward a black Nissan. Lily ran after her. She was so much taller, Anne seemed like a child. "You shouldn't make decisions at a time like this. I'm the one who owes you an apology. My husband attacked you."

"No," Anne shot out, walking around in a circle. "People will find out. You're the one who will get hurt, not Bryce. Think about your career, Lily. Anyone can get a law degree. You're a judge. I can't let something like this tarnish your reputation. I'll go away, maybe move back to New York. Ventura isn't the right place for me."

"Stay here, Anne, don't move away."

She stopped and peered up at Lily. "Do you really mean that?"

"Of course I do. I know a lady who's about to get divorced, and she's going to need a single friend."

"Who?"

"Me," Lily said, impulsively embracing her. "You're one of the kindest people I've ever met. You've been through this horrible ordeal and all you're concerned about is hurting me."

Anne pulled her car keys from her pocket. "I'm going to call the PD in Vegas tomorrow morning and tell them that I changed my mind about pressing charges. Bryce was scared, Lily. I doubt if he's ever done anything like this before. Spending a night in jail should be enough of a deterrent. He needs to go into some kind of alcohol rehab, though. If he hadn't been drunk, this might not have happened."

"If you insist on not pressing charges, I can't stop you. But don't do it right away, Anne. I want Bryce to sweat it out for a few more days. Besides, the state can still prosecute him."

"You know they'll kick him loose if I refuse to testify. I'm an attorney, remember? I know how the system works."

Anne moved closer, until she and Lily were only inches apart. She whispered something, and Lily bent down to hear what she was saying. Anne put her arm around her neck and kissed her on the lips. Lily got lost in the moment, finding the kiss intensely erotic. She tried to pull away, but instead she wrapped her arms around Anne and pulled her closer to her body. She was so soft, so fragile. Her breath was fresh and Lily could smell the scent of her shampoo. A car pulled up beside them and parked, the moment fractured.

Lily dropped her head, embarrassed and yet excited. So this was what it was like? When she pictured a lesbian, she conjured up images of unappealing, masculine-looking women who never wore makeup and dressed like truck drivers. She'd never given thought what it would be like to be with another woman.

Anne waited until the man got out of his car and headed for the coffee shop. "In case you haven't figured it out by now, Lily, I'm gay. I wanted you to know so you'd understand. I didn't seduce Bryce. I thought he knew."

Lily's head was still spinning. She started to say something, then stopped.

"You're an amazing woman," Anne continued. "You don't deserve to be with a man like Bryce." She glanced back at Lily and winked, then got in her car and sped off.

Lily stood there for a long time, the damp night air blowing through her hair. She touched her finger to her lips, savoring the sensation. Almost every man she'd ever known had hurt her. Had the feeling she'd experienced with Anne been caused by the stress she was under, or was she merely making a natural progression, something she'd been headed toward for years? She shook her head as if to clear it, then turned and walked back to her car.

First thing in the morning, she would call a locksmith

and change the locks. It was Bryce's house, however, so she would eventually have to find another place to live. Then she would have to hire an attorney, file a petition for divorce, and decide how to divide their possessions, all while she was sitting two major trails.

As Lily drove home, a question kept reappearing in her mind. Was Anne the only one? Could it be possible that not all of Bryce's former sex partners had been willing? And why had he been able to score with so many different girls to begin with? He wasn't that good-looking, especially now that he'd gained so much weight. Had his father's money bought him out of similar situations? Her outrage turned to hate. God help him if she ever found a reason to seek revenge.

TWENTY-FOUR

FRIDAY, DECEMBER 1
QUANTICO, VIRGINIA

Mary trudged through a foot of snow in the parking lot, bundled up in her red ski parka, her feet encased in fur-lined boots. This was the time of year when she asked herself why she had left California. She missed the beach, the palm trees, her quaint little house a few blocks from Ventura College, paid for from the proceeds of her father's life insurance policy. She'd used part of the money from the sale of her house to buy her mother's condominium, but she worried about her living alone in Washington. What was she eating, had she been out recently, had she made any new friends at church? She had promised to go to lunch with her today, but she'd called last night and told her mother she couldn't make it. The way things were going, she had no idea when she would have time to see her.

Last night they talked again about her getting a place in Quantico. Her mother had used the same argument, that there was nothing here but the FBI and the Marine base. When the weather was decent, she liked to jump on the bus and visit the museums and monuments in Washington. She rarely went out during the winter. Mary had sold her mother's car three months ago. She refused to drive in a strange city, and all the car was doing was sitting in the parking garage.

But her mother had gone downhill since she had stopped driving. Washington and her daughter's decision to join the Bureau were chipping away at her mother's independence. If she'd stayed in Ventura, everything would have been fine. Her mother knew her way around, and there wasn't that much traffic.

When she reached her office, Mary peeled off her gloves and sat down at her desk, keeping her parka on until she warmed up. Right now it felt like a refrigerator. Of course, the fact that the ISU used to be a bomb shelter didn't help.

Adams had instructed them to work in teams of two, and Genna Weir was now her partner. That afternoon, they were having a meeting and everyone in the unit had been ordered to attend. Mary's job was to organize the materials that would be distributed. She made folders for each agent containing the crime scene photos, as well as copies of all the forensic reports and evidence.

Agent East called her from Dallas. "I've got something for you."

"Oh, really," she said, thinking he was playing around. "It wouldn't be between your legs, would it?"

"I've got that, but I was referring to your case. I stopped

by and had a long chat with Mr. Khan last night. To our benefit, he has a morbid fear of anyone carrying a badge. I ran him through Interpol and found out he served time in a Pakistani prison for theft."

"Wow," Mary said. "You work fast."

"Okay, here's what I found out. A Caucasian male who went by the name of Chuck Brown walked into Khan's station approximately a year ago, offering to pay a twenty percent fee for running credit card charges through on his service station account. Brown told him his customers purchased embarrassing things like sex toys and didn't want them to show up on their credit card statements. Each week or so, Brown would fax him a list of charges and credit card numbers. Khan suspected that Brown's business might not be entirely legal, but when no one ever complained, he continued running the charges through."

Mary asked, "How often did he see this person?"

"Once," East told her. "Brown mentioned he was flying back to Los Angeles the same day, then stated that he had numerous partner businesses such as Khan's, which caused him to spend most of his time traveling."

Mary's foot started tapping on the floor. "Chuck Brown must be an alias, don't you think?"

"More than likely," East told her. "People do have common names. I have a college buddy named John Smith. I agree with you, though. It's probably an alias. Hold on a minute."

He came back on the line. "This isn't the only case I'm working, you know. Okay, Khan claims he's had no communication with Brown for over six months. The last time he ran charges through was last July. Khan is coming in this afternoon to work with our sketch artist. Brown's description is five-foot-ten, one hundred eighty pounds, longish dark hair, hazel eyes, olive skin, with a tattoo of a snake on his forearm. Khan's not certain if it's on Brown's right or left arm, but he said the tattoo was located about three inches from his wrist."

Mary jotted down the description, then began drawing snakes on her pad of paper. "Is it vertical or horizontal?"

"Vertical. The head points toward the elbow."

"Damn, Brooks, everyone and their dog has snake tattoos. Why couldn't he have had something unusual? You know, the name of his girlfriend, his cell phone number. His social security and driver's license number would be helpful."

Brooks laughed. "He may have a Tinkerbell tattoo on his ass, for all we know." He immediately fell serious again. "All Khan saw was his forearm. He's not certain as to the guy's age. His best guess is early to mid-thirties. Chuck is probably a nickname, so we went with Charles. I've got our guys running every possible combination based on the description. Without more identifying factors, I doubt if anything will come of it."

"Send a forensic team to Khan's station."

"We don't have a search warrant."

"We'll start working on it," Mary told him. "Won't Khan cooperate without a warrant?"

"Not without immunity. He served time, remember? We can't cut a deal with him until we figure out if a crime was committed."

"It's obviously some type of credit card fraud."

"I'm not so sure about that," East told her. "Khan collected his twenty percent from Brown, so who was he stealing from? That's under the assumption that Brown didn't hike up the bills. Even if he did, Brown's the one perpetrating the fraud, not Khan."

"He's a coconspirator, though."

"Do we really want to charge Khan right now? I'd rather keep him in our pocket. Brown might show up again. We're going to set up surveillance at Khan's station."

Mary was becoming frustrated. "Khan must have a means of contacting this person."

"He swears he doesn't, that Brown just faxed him the list, and he ran through the charges." East paused and cleared his throat. "Brown was only in the station on one occasion. Since then, there's no telling how many people have passed through that place, so pushing for a warrant doesn't make sense. Khan isn't set up for pay-at-the-pump. He makes the customers come inside. He has some of the lowest prices in town, and business is booming. I'm going back tonight to fill up the tank on my Porsche."

"Did you trace the credit card charges?"

"We're working on it. Khan claims he destroyed all the paperwork a few months ago, fearing the authorities would come knocking on his door if Brown had gotten himself arrested. We confirmed the number Khan claims he received the faxes from through ATT. It's been disconnected since September. The name on the account was Mabel Richardson. Her address was listed as 1313 Adams Road in Thousand Oaks, California. Mabel's residence as of June of last year is Holy Cross Cemetery. Thousand Oaks is close to your old stomping ground in Ventura, isn't it?"

"Yeah," Mary said, scribbling notes to herself on a yellow pad. "Do you have a next of kin on Mrs. Richardson?"

"She was ninety-four and died in the Hillsdale Convalescent Home. Medicare picked up the tab. Seems the old girl must have outlived all her relatives. We need to find out what happened to the house."

"You're telling me," Mary tossed out, doodling another snake.

"I managed to get in contact with someone at Hillsdale, and they said Richardson was brought to their facility in an ambulance. As far as they know, no one ever visited her. She had a prepaid burial plan." East put her on hold again.

"Sorry, we have a lead on a bank robbery suspect. Back to Brown. If you ask me, whoever he was working with probably rented the house in Thousand Oaks. Finding that person might not be that easy. It was probably leased through a real estate agent, unless it's just sitting there empty, waiting for the taxes to pile up so the state can seize it."

"Thousand Oaks is an expensive area," Mary said, drawing a casket for some reason. "If you have something of value, you have heirs. When my dad was killed, twenty nephews, nieces, and cousins came out of nowhere, all trying to get a piece of the action."

Mary typed in "Zillow.com" on her browser and found the house there. "The property is worth almost four hundred grand, cheap for California, but I bet Richardson owned it outright. That's unless the relatives who let the poor old girl die alone already got her to sign it over to them. Chuck Brown might be her grandson or something."

"That would explain why the utilities weren't disconnected until three months after Mabel Richardson died. I'll try running variations of Chuck Richardson and see if we come up with anything."

"While you take care of that," Mary told him, "I'll ask the sheriff in Thousand Oaks to roll by the house and see if it's occupied. In situations like this, I'm always afraid the local police are going to blow it and whatever evidence is there will disappear, along with the UNSUB." Mary rolled her neck around to relieve the tension. "You know what this means, don't you?"

"You finally got a break in the case."

"No," she said. "I was certain the killer was a woman."

"Well, look on the bright side. You have more today than you did yesterday." He paused and then added, "How many men has your UNSUB killed so far?"

"Three that we're aware of," Mary told him. "We have

no idea what the real body count is. Since the head and hands are removed, and the remains turn up in places they aren't supposed to be, no one even knows where to start looking. This one is smart, let me tell you. He or she lets the victims do all the work."

"I'm lost."

"Join the crowd," Mary said. "The killer isn't the one concocting the alibis. We believe the victims belong to one of these alibi clubs. That's probably what the credit charges are for, not sex toys or whatever." She explained how the alibi clubs had seemingly gone underground. "They also have philanderers' clubs, where married men and women look for people to have affairs with."

"You've got to be kidding. What will they think of next?" The line fell silent, then East spoke up. "These are gruesome crimes, Mary. We know enough that we might be able to stop future victims from falling into the same trap. Has anyone talked about going public?"

"That's Adams's decision," Mary said, already pondering the same issue. "We're having a team meeting this afternoon, and I'm certain that's one of the things we'll be discussing. The problem with going public is we'll tip our hand and the killer might disappear, then resurface years later. We haven't made a dent in the alibi clubs yet. I'm almost certain this is where the killer is getting the victims. These cases are so complex, Brooks, even I have trouble keeping the facts straight. Can you imagine what a circus the media will make of this? You won't be able to pick up a newspaper or turn on the TV without hearing about it. This is almost as sensational as Britney Spears shaving her head."

East chuckled. "Serial killers generally put a damper on a person's sense of humor. I'm glad you're not letting this overwhelm you."

"Hey, I'd rather laugh than cry."

"Amen to that."

"Are you still going to check out a possible transfer? Maybe I could talk Adams into bringing you on board."

"You know I'm assigned to bank robberies," East told her. "I don't have the stomach for what you do. My mother is another problem I haven't mentioned. Dad passed five years ago. My brother is living with her right now, but he needs to get out on his own. Mom has rheumatoid arthritis and has to use a walker to get around. Dallas is a great town. They always have openings here."

Mary knew it had been too good to be true. Then an idea popped into her head. "How old is your mother?"

"Seventy-three. Why?"

"She's almost the same age as my mother," Mary said, excited. "Mom has a two-bedroom condo in D.C. Maybe they could be roommates. Then if they get to the point where they need full-time help, we'd only have to hire one person."

"Pretty far-fetched, don't you think?"

"Not really. We can introduce them and see what happens. They might get along great. They're both Baptists, which has to account for something. Maybe I'll fly Mom to Dallas once this case is settled. The weather here is killing her. She'll probably like Dallas better than D.C."

"You're something else," Brooks told her, laughing. "Who knows, maybe it could work. We could combine both our assets and our liabilities."

Mary heard footsteps behind her. Genna Weir had come in and was setting up at the desk behind her. The room was small and each desk faced the wall. "I have to go," Mary whispered, then raised her voice again. "Let us know the minute you get the composite. Good work, Agent Brooks."

"Agent Brooks, huh?" Weir said, a grin on her face. "I thought his last name was East."

Mary fiddled with some paperwork on her desk. "I just got his name turned around, that's all."

"Yeah, right," Weir said facetiously. "I saw you last night in the hallway. 'Oh, Brooks,'" she said, moaning. "'Oh, Brooks . . . it feels so good.'"

"I didn't say that," Mary protested. "I could have said, 'Oh, Brooks,' because I forgot to tell him something, but I didn't say . . . well, you know."

Weir removed the wool scarf around her neck. "Looks like you mixed a little business with pleasure. Don't worry. We've all done it at one time or the other. Just don't make it a habit."

Mary nodded. She was about to tell her what Brooks had found out when she decided something this good had to be shared. "Promise not to tell anyone?"

"Scout's honor." Weir hung up her coat on the rack, then sat down and typed her password into the computer. When Mary just sat there with a dreamy look on her face, she said, "So tell me, all right? We have about three minutes for socializing before we dive back into these murders."

Mary scooted her chair back until they were facing each other. "He's outrageously handsome, polite, and a Baptist, just what my mother ordered. Not only that, he's a fantastic lover."

"How fantastic?"

Mary's eyes expanded. "I had five orgasms. Can you believe it? This was a first for me. I've had two, but never five. And they weren't all at the same time, either. I think we're in love, Genna. I mean it. This is the real deal."

"Five orgasms," the agent said, tapping her pen against her teeth. "Jesus, does he have a brother?"

"Actually, he does, but let me tell you what he found out about the case first."

As soon as she updated Weir, Mary's other line rang.

"This is Rollins at the sound lab. I have some findings for you on the tape you submitted."

"Great."

"Your UNSUB must be a fan of NPR. Most of the voices are from a two-hour show called *All Things Considered*. The two women are Michelle Norris and Melissa Block, and the male is Kevin Kling. There's a fourth voice that we couldn't place."

"It could be the killer's."

"That's what I'm trying to tell you," Rollins said sarcastically. "The unidentified voice speaks only three words: hypothermia, entity, and perverted. Since these particular words aren't commonly used on the radio program, the UNSUB may have become impatient and recorded them himself. Then again, the voice could have been pulled from somewhere else."

"Is it a male or female?"

"I personally think it's female, but some of my lab partners believe it's male. There's no matching voice prints on file. Anyway, I'll e-mail you the report."

"Okay," Weir said, standing after Mary told her what Rollins had said. "We're making some progress. The meeting is at three. Let's see if we can't bring something to the table. Get your hands on the credit card statements for the other two victims. See if you can find any oddball charges. Also, call your buddies in Ventura and get them out to that house in Thousand Oaks. Were there any other phone lines leading into that place?"

"Not that we know of," Mary said, uncertain if they'd even checked. "You think this is the headquarters for an alibi club?"

"Possibly, but maybe we're barking up the wrong tree with these alibi clubs. They're morally reprehensible, but we're not here to save souls."

"Let me tell you something," Mary argued. "No one

believed me when I said eBay would turn into a hotbed of criminal activity. Crooks can unload stolen merchandise without ever leaving their home. It's a global pawnshop. The same holds true of thieves and robbers. They steal boats, cars, diamonds, you name it, and they don't even have to expose their real identity. They just take over someone else's eBay account."

"Why are we talking about eBay?" Weir said, perplexed.

"Because the alibi clubs are worse, and I'm certain our victims are using them. Don't you think it's too big of a coincidence that all three victims left their wives neatly typed itineraries?"

"These are professional men. Businessmen use itineraries."

"Itineraries that are flat-out lies?" Mary said, her voice elevating. "These alibi and philanderers' clubs are self-perpetuating leviathans that may have cost a lot more than three men their lives. The people who use them are scum, understand? This is far worse than simply having an affair, or some married guy picking up a chick in the bar and banging her. What they're doing is organized, contrived. What's the difference between second- and first-degree murder?"

"Premeditation."

"Exactly."

"Most affairs are planned," Weir said. "If they weren't, the people having them would get caught."

Mary shook her head in frustration. "You don't understand the point I'm trying to make. The killer has no guilt. How sorry do you feel for a person who slugs down a fifth of bourbon, then decides to go swimming and drowns? How about gangsters who shoot their foot off while they're playing around with their new gun? She's not going to stop. There's no telling how many men she's killed that we don't know about, or how many she'll kill in the future. She's not like Jeffrey Dahmer, who was stark-raving insane and tried to turn his victims into zombies so they could be his sex slaves. This is a female Ted Bundy. Bundy may have confessed to killing thirty people, but you and I both know he probably killed up to a hundred."

"This is good," Weir told her. "Be sure to bring it up at the meeting."

"It's a woman," Mary insisted. "Forget about the tape and what was said about the father having sex with another woman, then abandoning his child on a highway. If it was a man, he might grow up bitter, even turn out to be a violent offender. He'd understand the male sex drive, though, that a penis is like a heat-seeking missile."

"You got a lot of enjoyment out of one of those heat-seeking missiles," Weir said, returning to her desk. "But you're not psychologically impaired. Guess what, I agree with you. Now get in touch with the authorities in Thousand Oaks, and then work on the credit card bills."

Bulldog McIntyre's massive frame filled up the doorway. "You guys making any progress?"

Mary started to answer, but Weir spoke up as she was tapping the keys on her computer. "We'll let you know at the meeting. How about you?"

He had a smug smile on his face. "You girls are nice to have around, but it takes a man to get the job done."

Weir finished what she was doing and leveled a finger at him. "Make another sexist remark like that and you'll no longer be an FBI agent. Now get your ass out of here so we can work."

"You'll be eating crow, Weir. I'm going to catch this maniac."

Weir shot him a look that would drop an elephant. "Oh, yeah? Then you better hurry. You've got some big competition. Stevens is beginning to shine."

McIntyre rubbed his chin. "Is that right?"

"Why are you still here? Didn't I ask you to leave five minutes ago?"

McIntyre threw his palms in the air. "What are you going to do, shoot me? I'm leaving, okay?"

Once McIntyre left, Mary walked over and closed the door so no one else would be tempted to interrupt them. "I thought we worked as a team."

"We do," Weir told her, leaning back in her chair. "A little competition is healthy. In case you didn't get the drift from what I told Bulldog, Adams made the right decision in bringing you on board."

Mary's spirits soared. She was making headway on the case, had a new boyfriend, and her coworkers were beginning to respect her. What more could she ask for? The killer's head on a stick would be nice.

TWENTY-FIVE

FRIDAY, DECEMBER 1
VENTURA, CALIFORNIA

Lily couldn't get Anne out of her mind.

After calling in sick, she'd stayed in bed until ten o'clock that morning, wondering what it would be like to make love to Anne. She might finally be able to have sex without it reminding her of the rapes. No more men hovering over her, no sweaty masculine bodies. People would think she and Anne were just friends. They could go shopping together, see movies, dine out at nice restaurants. Maybe one day they might even open a law practice together. Being a judge didn't pay enough, not for the amount of stress and responsibility it carried.

No, no, no, she kept screaming inside her mind. She had a daughter to consider. Maybe after she got through the divorce, she could put her life back together, even meet a decent man, someone like Chris Rendell. But how could she ever trust him? How could she trust any man again?

Still in her nightgown, Lily went to the closet for her purse and pulled out the piece of paper with Anne's number on it. She walked back to the bedroom and picked up the phone, then realized she had unplugged it so she wouldn't have to talk to Bryce. Her cell phone was in the charger in the bathroom. She unplugged it and punched in the numbers, then quickly hung up.

She decided to take a Jacuzzi, hoping it would relax her and give her time to sort through things. Maybe Anne would call her, she thought, filling the tub with hot water. Then she wouldn't be the one making the first move. Letting her nightgown slide to the floor, she studied her image in the mirror. Anne's body was perfect, and she was young, whereas Lily was a middle-aged woman. Why would Anne want to be with her? Her breasts were beginning to sag, her stomach was lined with stretch marks, her back was a disaster. In a few years, she would probably have to undergo surgery. She got up close and plucked out a gray hair. There were dozens of them. Her once-vibrant red hair was fading. There were lines around her eyes and lips. She could jump on the plastic surgery bandwagon. Why not? Everyone else did it.

Climbing into the tub, she leaned back and stretched out her long legs. A few minutes later, she got out and grabbed her cell phone off the counter, then jumped back in. She'd dialed Anne's number so fast, the message indicator hadn't had time to register. She saw now that she had three messages. Her finger trembled as she depressed the button to call her voice mail, hoping one of the messages was from Anne. The first message was from Tessa. She deleted it without listening. The next was from Bryce.

"Thanks for being there when I needed you," he said angrily. "I paid a fortune for a shit-faced attorney here in Vegas. The judge set bail at twenty thousand dollars because I'm out of state. Maybe if I'd had my wife here, a judge, they would have released me on my own recognizance. I can't get the bank to wire the money until Monday. Because of you, I have to spend another three nights in this miserable hellhole. And just so you know, I'm divorcing you." He stopped speaking and then shouted, "I'm your fucking husband, Lily. I thought, of all people, you would believe me. Instead, you believed a lying little slut who's probably after my money."

Lily deleted his call. Good, she thought. He'd saved her the trouble of getting an attorney. Hearing him talk to her like a dog after he'd tried to rape Anne eliminated any chance she might reconsider ending their marriage.

She would have to move out. The only question was when. The fact that Bryce had been charged with a crime, combined with her position and the fact that she was in trial, would hopefully buy her some time.

Getting out and drying off, she put on a pair of jeans and a T-shirt, then went to the library and plopped down in Bryce's father's lounge chair. Colored beams of light were streaking in through the stained-glass windows. Before she knew it, she was sobbing. She loved this house, and she'd worked so hard decorating it and planning the remodeling. Her husband was a spoiled, perverted, alcoholic bastard. She hoped he rotted in hell, but then, she was convinced that was her final destination and she never wanted to see his stupid face again. Bryce might be a sinner, but he wasn't a murderer and hypocrite like herself.

He would probably go to purgatory, if such a place existed.

Lily's thoughts returned to Anne. The Catholic church believed it was okay to be gay as long as a person didn't act on it, which she thought was ridiculous, particularly in light of the recent scandals involving pedophile priests. She also speculated that many priests were homosexual. Everyone deserved to be loved. What difference did it make if it was a man or a woman? If fewer people procreated, the planet would be better off.

On the other hand, if she started something, it wouldn't be fair to Anne. Their kiss had been a novelty, a new experience at a time when Lily had been desperately in need of a distraction. She was merely trying to grab on to someone so she wouldn't have to face her demons alone.

Lily decided she would rent the smallest apartment she could find, maybe in a family building where it was crowded and noisy. Wandering aimlessly from room to room in the big house, she looked lovingly at the antique furniture she had painstakingly restored. All of it belonged to Bryce. Most of the furniture she'd had in her home in Santa Barbara had either been sold or given away. Bryce didn't deserve these things. If it were up to him, he would have sold them long ago.

In the formal living room, she stared at a framed picture of Bryce's mother and father. Everyone said they were a wonderful couple, deeply in love. How had they produced such a jerk for a son?

Lily ended up in the kitchen. Gabby had slept at her feet the night before, and had been following her around whimpering. She realized she had forgotten to feed her, and poured some food into her bowl. She would have to get a place that accepted pets.

Lily fixed herself a bowl of cereal, eating it standing up at the counter. Her eyes rested on a silver bowl where she kept business cards, coupons she never used, and other stuff she didn't know what to do with. She dropped her spoon and picked up the card with Chris Rendell's number on it. Plugging the main line back in, she called him, expecting to get his answering machine.

"Lily?"

"How did you know it was me?"

"Caller ID," he said. "Where have you been for the last ten years? Forget that, it's great to hear from you. I'm sitting here trying to figure out something to do. Want to go to lunch?"

"Sure," Lily said eagerly. "It'll take me about thirty minutes to get ready."

"Do you like the Biltmore in Santa Barbara?"

"It's one of my favorite places, but don't you have to be back?"

"My calendar is open for the rest of the afternoon. Can I pick you up or do you want to meet somewhere?"

"Come to the house." Lily gave him the address and hung up. Another man was the answer, the quicker the better. She raced upstairs to get dressed and put on her makeup.

Lily and Chris had a delicious lunch on the patio at the Biltmore, which overlooked the ocean. The nicest thing about Santa Barbara was you could dress up. Most places in California were casual, and spending every day in a black robe had gotten old quick. She wore a blue silk pants suit, one of the few new pieces of clothing she'd purchased since her appointment to the bench. The top was strapless, fashioned along the lines of a bustier. She fingered her pearls as they drove back to Ventura in Rendell's Volkswagen. He was happy and enjoying himself.

The wine, the walk on the beach, the glorious day— Lily started talking and almost never stopped. Having a handsome, attentive man with her made her feel like a new woman. She told him about the situation with Bryce because she didn't want the day to end. Letting him come to the house had sent him a signal regarding her marriage, but she wanted it perfectly clear.

"Are you sure you're not going to take him back?"

"Heavens, no," Lily said, adamant. "Some things are unforgivable."

Chris was tactful enough to move on to other topics. They chatted about various cases and people around the courthouse. He told her a funny story, and she burst out laughing. Before she knew it, he was pulling into her driveway. "Is it okay for me to park here? I want to walk you to the door."

"You can park on the lawn, for all I care. This is Bryce's house, not mine. I'm headed for an apartment."

When they reached the front door, an awkward moment occurred. Lily wanted to invite him in, but she didn't want to appear overly eager.

"I really had a good time today," he said, shuffling his feet around. "It's been a long time since I've been able to say that."

"Me, too," she said. "I miss Santa Barbara. My house there wasn't as big as this one because of the price of real estate, but it was nice. I had a beautiful rose garden."

"Would it be all right if I came in to use the bathroom?"

Tactful way to get your foot in the door, Lily thought. "Of course."

When they stepped inside, she directed him to the powder room, then kicked her shoes off and took a seat on the sofa in the den. Gabby jumped into her lap, but she shooed her away.

Formal living rooms were a waste, Lily decided. No one ever used them. She'd eventually buy another house once she got through the divorce and analyzed her finances. Unfortunately, she hadn't made much money on the property in Santa Barbara. Bryce had pushed her to lower the price so she could move in with him. What did he care? He had his father's millions at his disposal.

As astronomical as the real estate prices were in Santa Barbara, a person had to sit on a property for years to make a significant profit. There was another phenomenon at play in one of the country's most desirable cities. All the real estate agents for the area resided in Santa Barbara, and many of them were investors. Either that or they made deals on the side. If you were an outsider, which included anyone who hadn't resided there for at least two decades, you were considered fair game. The realtors would try to keep your property from selling until you became desperate and lowered the price to a ridiculous level. The cottage she had owned had since been torn down and a five-million-dollar home erected. New money moving into town didn't care about rose gardens or the kind of elaborate landscaping that had made Santa Barbara famous. All they were interested in was square footage.

"You look cozy," Chris said, appearing beside her on the sofa. When Gabby jumped in his lap, he picked her up like an infant. "Who's your little friend here? She's a beauty. What kind of dog is this? I don't think I've ever seen anything like it."

"An Italian greyhound." She took Gabby from him, and deposited her outside in the yard. "She's not supposed to jump on people like that."

"I don't mind, Lily. I love dogs."

"Not everyone feels the same. Anyway, I forgot where we left off in the car."

He stared at her, his arms limp at his sides. "Do you

know how beautiful you look with the light behind you? You look like you have a golden halo. Come, sit down beside me. I want to smell your hair."

As soon as Lily sat down, he nuzzled his head in her hair, then kissed her on the mouth. "If I'm going too fast . . ."

"No, I want you."

He pushed her back onto the sofa, but they were both too tall, and their arms and legs got tangled up. Lily said, "Let's go upstairs."

Chris stood and unbuttoned his shirt, taking it off and dropping it on the floor. His chest was tan and muscular, his face flushed with excitement. He kissed her again, pulling her tight against his body. She must have drunk too much wine, as she felt dizzy and almost tripped over her own feet. When she stepped back, she realized he had undone the snaps on the back of her top. It had a built-in bra, so she wasn't wearing anything underneath. She held it together with her hands.

He dropped to his knees in front of her, unzipping her pants and pulling them down to her ankles. He reached for her panties, then his hands moved across her breasts. Reaching behind her, he pulled her hand forward, causing her top to tumble onto the carpet. Gabby was barking and lunging at the window, all four paws striking the glass. Chris didn't seem to notice and pushed Lily back onto the floor, then climbed on top of her.

"My dog thinks I'm being attacked," Lily said, staring up at him. "This might be more fun on a bed, don't you think?" She started to tell him she had a bad back and couldn't roll around on the floor like a teenager, but it would ruin the moment. She certainly wasn't going to tell him that she had a phobia of having a man on top of her. At the moment, she was more concerned with Gabby breaking a leg.

He stood and pulled her to her feet, then swept her up in his arms.

"Put me down, Chris. This isn't a romance novel."

His face fell in disappointment. She gave him a quick peck on the lips, then headed up the stairs. Her back was already throbbing. He wasn't heavy like Bryce, but he was taller and more muscular, and muscle weighs more than fat. She glanced over her shoulder to make certain he was coming. "Hurry up, slowpoke," she tossed out.

Lily halted when she reached the top of the stairs. It was daylight and they didn't have drapes in the master bedroom. She and Bryce never made love during the day. Chris would see everything, and so would she. Maybe she should take him to one of the guest bedrooms. She couldn't drag the poor guy around the house, though. The bottom line was she had made a reckless, stupid decision. He wouldn't understand. She tried to tell herself to calm down, but she was already trembling. What if she panicked when he got on top of her?

She was about to turn around and tell him she couldn't go through with it. But it was too late. He had come up behind her and wrapped his arms around her waist. She felt a bolt of pain hit the center of her back, in the spot where the disk was herniated. It was as if she had a boa constrictor wrapped around her, squeezing the life out of her.

He lifted her hair and began kissing the sensitive spot on the back of her neck. She gave thought to simply bending over and letting him have his way with her. Women weren't the same as men. A woman might find it exciting to make love to someone for the first time, but it wasn't always sexually gratifying. This held true even for women without Lily's history. Women needed time, not just to reach a point of arousal, but to feel comfortable enough to let go. They also had to train a partner to do the things they found pleasurable.

They were standing in the doorway now. In her rush to get ready earlier, Lily had forgotten to make the bed. As soon as Chris saw the tousled covers, he unzipped his pants and pulled down his jockey shorts. His erection was enormous.

He climbed onto the bed, reaching out and pulling her down beside him. "I'm too aggressive, aren't I? My God, you're shaking."

"It's okay," she said. "I'm just nervous."

Chris slapped his forehead with the back of his hand. "What was I thinking? This is the bed you share with your husband. You're getting back at him. Isn't that what this is all about?"

"No, please," Lily said. "I just need you to go a little slower."

"We can go to my place if you want."

"It's all right, I promise. And I might be getting back at Bryce, but that's not all of it. I'm attracted to you, Chris. I was attracted to you the day we went to lunch." She curled up in his arms, and he gently stroked her back with the tips of his fingers.

"I haven't been with a woman since my wife died," he told her, speaking in hushed tones. "It's taken me all these years to find a woman I'm even remotely interested in. I'm not here just to sleep with you, Lily. Obviously, I desire you, but I want a relationship and it's too soon for that. You're not even divorced yet. Jesus, are you even officially separated?"

"Bryce asked me for a divorce," Lily said, becoming more comfortable now that they were talking. "I was going to divorce him anyway. How could I stay married to an attempted rapist? Don't worry about him walking in on us. He's in jail until Monday." She linked eyes with him, then turned away. "We basically had a marriage of convenience. Bryce knew it. He was jealous of my position. He and my daughter despised each other. What can I say? The man's an imbecile. I have no idea why I even married him."

Chris reached down and pulled the sheet over them. "Why was it a marriage of convenience?"

"I've had a problem being alone since the rapes."

"I understand that, Lily. I've had the same problem since Sherry and Emily were killed. Some nights it's as if they're in the room with me. It used to comfort me. Now it freaks me out." He paused and cleared his throat, clasping her hand tightly. "I still have Sherry's clothes in the closet, and Emily's toy chest at the foot of my bed. I've tried, but I just can't let go."

Lily sighed, wishing she could help him. "You will, Chris. Just by being here with me today, you've made your first step."

"I'm sorry about the way I acted downstairs. I assumed that's what was expected of me." He ran his fingers through his hair. "You have no idea what a sheltered life I've led. Most of what I know about sex I learned from books and movies. Your husband might be an idiot, but I'm not much better. I know what you've been through. I should have realized that type of behavior was inappropriate."

Lily found his honesty and innocence touching. They remained locked in each other's arms, each of them holding on for their own reasons. She could love this man, she told herself. He'd been through something far worse than she had. There was even a possibility that together they could become whole again. Maybe if she'd been honest with Bryce, their marriage would have been more meaningful.

Could Chris accept the fact that she had killed Bobby Hernandez? If she provided proof that Hernandez had been a vicious murderer who had taken the lives of five innocent people, she believed he could. He would understand the rage she'd felt when her child was violated.

His body was so warm, Lily wanted to crawl inside of it. They stroked each other, embraced each other until he fell silent. When she saw he had fallen asleep, she turned over on her side and drifted off.

The room was bathed in evening shadows when Lily was gently awakened by his touch. She rolled over into his body, and they finally made love. It was nothing like she'd feared. He was tender, considerate, and emotional. Instead of heaving on top of her, he pulled her onto his lap and slowly moved her up and down on his body. Then he would stop, gaze into her eyes, and gently caress her. When his hands moved over her body, she felt as if her skin had turned into silk. He would cup her face in his hands and kiss her, then slide his finger between her legs where they were joined, causing Lily to moan in pleasure.

After it was over, he experienced such a release that he broke down and wept and Lily found herself crying with him. She had never felt such an intense, intimate connection with another human being.

When Chris got up to go to the bathroom, Lily stared out into the dark room. His clothes were in a pile over by the chair. She didn't see a man crouching there, waiting to jump out and rape her. It was only a few pieces of harmless clothing. Her eyes drifted to the light emanating from the bathroom. The terrifying image of Marco Curazon, as she had seen him just before he'd fled the night of the rapes, was no longer present. She thought Bryce would make her feel safe, but it hadn't turned out that way. With Chris, the demons were finally receding.

All she had needed was a good man to chase them away.

TWENTY-SIX

❦

FRIDAY, DECEMBER 1
QUANTICO, VIRGINIA

Mary called Hank Sawyer, her former partner at the Ventura Police Department. Supervisor over the homicide division, Sawyer was a rugged old-school cop. He'd been hell to work for, but he had taught her everything she knew. "Hank," she said once the switchboard transferred her to his office, "it's Mary."

"Mary who?"

"Come on, Hank, don't play games with me. You know who I am. You could recognize my voice even if it was coming from inside a toilet."

"Oh, that Mary, the one who flat left me for a job with the FBI. How the hell are you, stranger?"

"Up to my asshole in murders. I need your help." She gave him the particulars of the house in Thousand Oaks.

"My God, woman," he said, "has the FBI sucked your brains out? The sheriff's office covers Thousand Oaks, not us. Don't you remember that?"

Thousand Oaks was located in Ventura County, but the PD only covered crimes committed in the city of Ventura. "Of course I do, Hank, but the SO is huge and I doubt if anyone there remembers me. I need a warrant and I need it fast. Do you know a judge who'll sign a half-baked warrant without making a big deal about it? The house is probably empty, but we can't be certain. The killer may be running an alibi club out of it. That's where we think she gets her victims."

"What's an alibi club?"

"I don't have time to explain everything," Mary told him. "It's just what the term implies, a club that furnishes alibis."

Hank fell serious. He knew the unit she was assigned to and the type of crimes they investigated. "How many?"

"Three that we know of," Mary told him. "We only got wind of the case last Monday. We're chasing the clock, Hank. This one isn't going to stop until we catch her."

"You keeping saying 'she.' Are you telling me you've got a female serial killer? That's a strange duck. Shit, we haven't seen one of them since Aileen Wuornos."

"You know how it works, Hank. We're not certain what we have yet, other than three dismembered men and a few promising leads. Whatever you do, keep this under wraps. We haven't gone public with it, and my SAC will have my head on a chopping board if it gets leaked to the press."

He thought a few minutes, then said, "Do you remember Lily Forrester?"

"The DA who was raped? I thought she became a prosecutor in Santa Barbara."

"She's a superior court judge in Ventura now," he told her. "I know her pretty well. Compared to some of the other judges, she's your best bet. Someone's got to write the request for the warrant, though."

"Hold on." Mary put the call on hold and coughed to get Genna Weir's attention. It made her nervous to have someone looking over her shoulder. The meeting was scheduled to start within the hour and she hadn't had time to go over the credit card records yet. "Who should handle the paperwork on this? My old supervisor thinks he knows a judge who'll sign it."

"Go for it," Weir said, spinning her chair around.

Mary punched back into the line, putting Hank on the

speakerphone. "Can you get in touch with Forrester to-day?"

"I think so," he told her. "She might be on the bench, so I can't guarantee when, but I'll get right on it."

"You work for the FBI now," Weir told Mary. "We have jurisdiction everywhere. Have him track down the judge and tell him the warrant's coming. Can you write it in an hour, Stevens?"

"Impossible," Mary exclaimed. "It would take me a week to put all the facts together. Besides, we have the meeting at three. It's already two-thirty."

Weir leaned back in her chair and stretched. "So you'll be late. You don't have to document everything. All you have to do is justify a need for a search warrant. You said the owner of the house was deceased, so it shouldn't be that difficult. The other agency can execute the warrant once a judge signs it."

"Find Judge Forrester," Mary told Hank. "I'll e-mail you the request for a warrant as soon as I finish it. Maybe you should call the SO and advise them they're going to be executing it."

As soon as she disconnected, she turned to Weir again. "Shouldn't the L.A. Field Office be involved in this?"

"They've already been informed," she said, staring at her computer screen and clicking her mouse to open a document. "If anything or anyone in that house looks even remotely suspicious, they'll go out. Otherwise, I'd rather not waste their time. I checked it on a map. Thousand Oaks is a good distance from Los Angeles."

"I haven't had a chance to go through the credit card charges on Madison and Goldstein yet."

The printer started spitting out paper. "Just write the warrant," Weir told her, walking over and picking up the sheets. "I'll go over the credit card charges." She stopped and glanced around the room. "What's that noise? It sounds like a woodpecker. They're not around this time of year."

Mary placed her hand on her knee to keep her foot from tapping. "Must be rats," she tossed out, attempting to organize her thoughts into something cohesive enough to get them the warrant.

Fifteen minutes later, Weir called John Adams. "The cards are falling into place, chief. Now isn't the best time to grind to a stop and worry about profiling. I'm about ninety percent certain Stevens has nailed it for us. I'll fill you in on the details later. We might be zeroing in on our target."

"What's going on?" Mary asked.

Weir's face was flushed with excitement. "What are the chances of a person who lives in Denver and another who lives in San Francisco using an Exxon gas station in Dallas?"

Mary's jaw dropped. "Are you certain it was Khan's?"

Weir dropped the stack of papers on her desk. "Khan's Preston Exxon is listed on both Goldstein's and Madison's credit card records. You can't get any closer than that, Stevens. It's a good thing you twisted Adams's arm and let him send you to Dallas."

"Thank you, Jesus," Mary said, shoving her fist in the air. "We've established a definitive link between all three homicides. I knew the tape wasn't a fake. I just knew it."

"Congratulations," Weir said, smiling. "I'll get in touch with the L.A. Field Office and have them respond to Thousand Oaks. How far along are you on the search warrant?"

Weir had kicked into high gear. The inside of the small room was turning into a whirlwind. "I've got it outlined," Mary said. "Now all I have to do is type it and shoot it to Hank Sawyer. If he can't get Forrester, he'll have to track down another judge."

"I'll take it to the Justice Department if we don't hear from him within thirty minutes," Weir told her, exhaling a long breath. "We need to get inside that house in Thousand Oaks immediately. I'm going to call Agent East and have him book Khan for credit card fraud, then instruct him to get a search warrant so we can rip that gas station apart."

"Don't you want me to do that?" Mary said, eager to talk to Brooks again and update him on their progress. "I mean, I've been working with him."

Weir arched an eyebrow. "Not everything you've been doing with Agent East can be classified as work. You're about to make a name for yourself with the Bureau. Now isn't the time to be playing patty-cake with another agent. Are we clear?"

First she commended her, then she spanked her. Mary cursed herself for telling Weir about what had transpired between her and Brooks. "Perfectly, Agent Weir."

"Take care of the warrant. Leave everything else to me."

Anne's bloodlust had finally stopped.

She spent most of the day cleaning house, and attempting to erase all traces of her former life. She collected all her pay-as-you-go phones and tossed them into a plastic garbage bag. The next to go was her collection of wigs, her sexy clothing, and all shoes with high heels. Her feet hurt like a bitch every time she wore them. She stood back and smiled at the neat rows of tennis shoes. The closet was now filled with sportswear, gym clothes, jeans, classic tops, and skirts and dresses. She started to toss her collection of designer purses, as she had carried many of them when she was courting victims. She had paid too much money for them, though, so she decided to keep them.

The house didn't have air-conditioning and she was sweating. She kept an ice chest in the kitchen, so she grabbed a bottle of water and poured it over her head. She thought of going to a church one day and having herself baptized. Maybe she could become a born-again Christian and her previous sins would be forgiven? Nice idea, but she didn't think for a minute that getting submerged in water would do anything more than get her wet.

Some of her most abusive foster parents had been regular churchgoers, which had soured her on organized religion.

The next place Anne attacked was the bathroom cabinets. She trashed all her diet pills, laxatives, and the majority of her makeup. As long as she didn't have to look like the slut of the month, she could get by fairly well with lipstick and a dab of blush. She hated mascara, as it clumped, and was almost impossible to remove. If you did manage to get the damn stuff off, you lost half your eyelashes.

The house she was in was a dump. Chuck had rented it, and after he was shipped back to prison, she'd kept it more or less as a staging area, as well as a possible hideout if the police put any heat on her. She'd rented an apartment in Ventura, but hadn't gotten around to moving the rest of her things. There was also the problem that someone might see her coming or going in one of her disguises. Her plan was to buy a house, but she decided to stay in the apartment until she found out how things went with Lily.

Moving on to the bedroom, Anne pulled a hatbox from underneath the bed that contained her collection of wigs. What little furniture there was in the house was junk. She made a note to call the Salvation Army on Monday and have them pick it up. She now had three partially full garbage bags, so she dropped a wig in each one.

Deciding it would be the first to go, she called the Realtor who had sold her the house in Seattle and instructed her to put it back on the market. She hadn't used it as a kill site for a number of years, and since she'd already given thought to leasing it, it was ready to go. The weather was lousy in Seattle, and real estate prices were declining.

The cleaning service she had stumbled across on the Internet specialized in cleaning crime scenes, and the irony alone was worth the risk. No one suspected a woman, one of the reasons Anne had slipped under the police's radar. The previous owner had died inside the Seattle place, so she told the cleaning service she had inherited it from her uncle and wanted it decontaminated because he'd recently spent time in the Congo.

Since he had resided in Denver, Seattle had long since forgotten Russell Madison. The Denver police were probably still getting pressure from the family, but the police in Seattle were already classifying it as a cold case. As far as she knew, they didn't have one lead.

Before she'd called in the crime scene cleaners, Anne had scrubbed the Seattle house from floor to ceiling, but evidence was hard to find. She kept a variety of products such as Luminol, used to detect bloodstains, at every kill site. The stuff came from Web sites that allegedly supplied forensic labs, but no one cared who you were as long as you had a credit card. Some of the sites were scams, though, set up to plug online schools for people who watched shows like CSI and thought they could become forensic technicians. Several of them had grabbed people's money and disappeared. The Internet was like a black hole.

The boat she'd dumped Madison's remains on had been described in the newspaper accounts as abandoned, which wasn't true. She had actually purchased the boat under one of her fictitious identities, then never changed the registration. Greed solved a lot of problems. The boat was a 1967 Chris-Craft, and the ad read fifteen hundred or best offer, which meant the owner was basically trying to unload it to anyone who would take it off his hands. When she'd handed the guy three grand in cash, acting as if she'd never seen the ad, he hadn't so much as blinked. He was stooped over with arthritis and didn't look like he could chop off the head of a chicken, let alone a man.

Anne assumed the police had shown up on the owner's doorstep after the body was found, but the old geezer deserved it for trying to take advantage of a woman. She knew the cops wouldn't consider him a viable suspect. Like stealing from her victims, which Anne felt was morally wrong, she did her best to make certain an innocent person didn't take a fall for her.

The plan she'd come up with to cover her tracks with Lily's husband had been brilliant. Since she'd been seen by so many people in Las Vegas, even a police officer, how could she have followed through on her plan to kill him? She'd been elated when the bastard had popped up alive.

Because of the Versed, Bryce didn't know she had drugged him. For all she knew, the idiot believed he had tried to rape her. Snatching a person's memory away left him wide open to any number of false accusations, one of the reasons Anne loved this particular drug.

Still, she had never dreamed her plan would turn out as spectacularly as it had. Bryce had been forever tainted in Lily's mind, and she'd created a direct path into the judge's life. Regardless of the situation, she and Lily were perfect for each other. Both of them were victims of violent and disgusting men. After Anne told Lily what Bryce had done, she probably never want to be with a man again.

The kiss had been an integral part of the plan. The only purpose was to eliminate any chance that Lily would believe Bryce's story. When Lily unexpectedly embraced her and kissed her back, Anne's mind had shifted from black to white. Even now her heart was beating so fast, she felt like she'd just snorted ten lines of cocaine. Becoming Lily's friend and confidante would have been a significant accomplishment, but being her lover was heaven. Doors had flown open that she hadn't even been aware existed. She had driven home and fallen into a blissful sleep, then awoke this morning with a feeling most people took for granted—happiness.

Lily had looked her straight in the eye and told her she was the kindest person she had ever met. She had turned herself into a cold-blooded killer, so why couldn't she become the person Lily thought she already was?

Anne threw two large suitcases on the moth-eaten mattress and headed to the closet. Why had she ever felt the need to kill men? Her father had been a cruel, worthless man, but then his father had been no better. She recalled the scars he had shown her from where his father had beat him.

But her father was the only person she had a justifiable reason to kill. When she'd questioned herself throughout the years as to why she hadn't tracked him down and sought revenge, she'd always tricked herself into believing various excuses, such as he wasn't worth her time, or it was too big of a risk.

The truth was, even after all these years, Anne was still terrified of her father. If you managed to escape the devil, you didn't go back. You ran. And that's exactly what she had done.

But the devil always won in the long run.

Had God finally intervened and decided to give her a life? Probably not, as she had damned herself the day she had put that wire around Blue's neck and ended his life. The man's liver was gone, though, and he would have died within months. In reality, she did the guy a favor. She'd seen people die on the streets and it was far from pleasant.

She shoved the suitcases aside and sat on the edge of the bed to remove the prosthesis that allowed her to walk normally. She sniffed back tears, fearing Lily would be repulsed when she saw her feet. But Lily was a compassionate woman. She would love her even more because of her deformity. And Anne would tell her everything. Not about the murders, of course, but about what her father had done to her, and the life she had been forced to live.

As of today, Anne no longer cared if married men fucked around on their wives. Her new motto was it wasn't her problem. She would be like the people who saw starving children on television and headed to the kitchen to make themselves another bag of microwave popcorn. The suffering of the world was entertainment.

Anne yanked down the blackout drapes covering the windows, letting the light wash over her. She then went outside and jumped into her Nissan, going through the drive-through at KFC down the street. Driving off with a bucket of extra crispy fried chicken, mashed potatoes with gravy, and biscuits, she decided to celebrate.

When she returned to the house, she sat in the backyard on the grass and ate her lunch. For the first time in years she felt full, really full. She didn't need to be rail-thin anymore. All that was over.

There were a few challenges ahead of her, but nothing she couldn't handle. She would contact the district attorney's office in Las Vegas and convince them to drop the charges against Bryce. She might not be able to accomplish that over the phone, though. If the state felt certain a crime had been committed, they could move forward with the case without her consent. On the other hand, it was hard to win a case with a hostile witness.

If the Las Vegas authorities subpoenaed her, she would vow not to show up and and would chastise them for wasting the taxpayers' money. That would create another problem, however, as the court would issue a warrant for failure to appear, which meant she would have to stop using the

Anne Bradley identity. Without the Bradley identity, she would lose Lily. She didn't worry; she was prepared.

The charges weren't as serious as they sounded. In Las Vegas, attempted rape must be a common offense. And not all of the claims were legitimate. A man would have sex with a prostitute and then refuse to pay, and the woman would go to the police and say she was raped. These type of cases didn't fly, but the john ended up giving the prostitute her money.

As a last resort, Anne would tell them this was what happened with Bryce. Under no circumstances could she allow the case to continue, even if she had to tell them she was a prostitute. Bryce had probably already hired a first-rate attorney. When the police had asked her for her driver's license, she had given them a California license in the name of Anne Bradley. Anne Bradley had been reported missing in New York, but it was a common name and she'd used a different date of birth when she'd obtained a California license.

The other thing that could potentially hurt her was the fact that she'd told Bryce her name was Anne Hall, not Anne Bradley. Once she formulated her plan, she'd decided to give the police the Bradley identity, as this was the name Lily knew her by. At the time of Bryce's arrest, he was too out of it to know the difference, but his memory might return once he sobered up, and the discrepancy could become a factor in his defense if the case continued.

Although women frequently gave men false names these days, the fact that she had lied could support Bryce's story. No matter how it went down, she was a murderer. The only time she would appear in a courtroom was if the police apprehended her.

The good thing was that a woman named Anne Bradley

had practiced navigational law in Manhattan, and then
suddenly disappeared without a trace. The law firm Wharton, Cannon, and Byerman had told Stan Waverly that
Bradley had became disgruntled because they'd made her
handle the client who was throwing sex parties on his
yacht. But after Bradley had quit her job, she'd never returned to her apartment, even to claim her clothing and
personal effects. According to what Stan had told her, the
woman's parents suspected foul play, but NYPD had only
conducted a cursory investigation.

Most individuals would be shocked if they knew how
many people simply dropped off the face of the earth. Anne
Bradley was one of the women Stan Waverly had bragged
about sleeping with, and he'd commented that Anne could
be her double. Bradley was twenty-seven, which worked
well. She'd been intrigued by the type of law the woman
had practiced. After she'd killed Waverly, she had spent her
cooling-down time studying navigation law.

Anne wasn't certain of her real birth date, as her parents had never told her, but she was fairly certain she was
between twenty-five and twenty-six. The authorities had
searched for her birth records, but had failed to find them.
She remembered her mother telling her she had given
birth in her grandfather's barn, then taken her baby and
ran away. Her parents must have failed to register her birth,
probably because of her father's warrants or her mother's
drug addiction. She wasn't even certain her mother and father were legally married, or that the man her mother lived
with was her biological father.

Why hadn't her mother just left her at her grandparents'
farm? Anne couldn't fathom why women on heroin, crack,
and other hardcore narcotics thought they could raise a
baby. She remembered Blue telling her a lot of them did it
for the welfare money. Although many people didn't realize it, the only way a woman could qualify for public as-

sistance was if she had children. Adults didn't get welfare unless they were disabled.

She tied up the garbage bag and went to the other room to get the other bags. Stealing Anne Bradley's identity had taken all of six hours. The only problem was she couldn't use Bradley's driver's license or credit cards because the woman had been reported missing. The credit cards didn't matter, as she always paid cash, and she had legitimate credit cards under her other fictional identities. When she needed a credit card for things such as renting a car or a hotel room or purchasing an airline ticket, she paid the bill as soon as she received it. All her fictional identities had excellent credit.

Anne turned her thoughts to the other properties she wanted to liquidate. The alibi clubs were a pain in the ass, primarily because she couldn't find trustworthy employees. In addition to the money she had in various savings accounts, she would have more than enough once all the properties sold. If she ran out of money in the future, she would just get a job. Of course, by then, she fantasized, she would be sharing her life with Lily.

After placing the trash bags by the front door so she could just jump out of her car and grab them to take to the dump, she began packing, neatly folding the clothes and other items she was taking to the apartment and placing them in the open suitcases. She checked the house again to make certain she had everything she wanted. Picking up the suitcases, she lugged them out to the car, then came back to the house to do more cleaning. Although she'd never used this particular place as a kill site, she wanted to wipe down the walls and scrub the floors so it would be nice for the new tenants. During the occasions when she came to the house at night, she used gas lanterns. She would have to return later to pick up the garbage bags, as the Nissan was a sports car and the suitcases were bulky.

When she picked up one of the garbage bags to place at the door, she peered inside and suddenly jumped back, seeing severed limbs and bloody torsos. The chances of her living a normal life were the same as a skeleton climbing out of a coffin and hitching a ride. She had danced with the devil far too long. The devil owned her now, and no matter how fast she ran, or how cleverly she hid, he would find her.

For Katie Collins, though, the little girl whose father had left her to freeze to death on the interstate, it had been a good day. In a life that had been filled with unspeakable misery, one good day could go a long way.

TWENTY-SEVEN

∼

FRIDAY, DECEMBER 1
VENTURA, CALIFORNIA

Christopher Rendell got out of bed, dressed, then bent down to kiss Lily goodbye. "Please don't go," she said, stroking his hair back from his forehead. "Spend the night with me. I can sleep when you're here. I've never felt so rested."

"I'm not sure that's a compliment or a complaint."

Lily propped herself up on her elbows. "It's a compliment, Chris. It's hard for me to fall asleep. I deal with it by working until I collapse. I certainly wasn't referring to your performance in bed. You're a wonderful lover."

"Relationships have to be built over a long period of time, Lily. You and your husband only recently decided you wanted to break up." He saw the disappointment etched on her face. "It isn't that I don't want to stay here with you because I do. We just have to handle this the right way."

"I'll stay at your place, then," Lily told him. "You're just worried that Bryce is going to walk in and find you here. He can't make bail until Monday. He even had the gall to blame me because I wouldn't fly to Vegas and take care of it. He believes I can use my connections to get him off."

Chris bent down and kissed her again, cupping one side of her cheek in his hand. "It isn't right for us to . . . you know . . . make love. Not until you're divorced. I shouldn't have pushed things today. It's my fault, not yours. I got carried away."

"But it will take six months for my divorce to be final." According to his moral principles, he had committed a serious sin. Lily didn't care because she wanted to be with him. When a spouse made a mockery of his marriage vows, the way Bryce had, she believed the other party was morally free to do whatever she wanted. It certainly went against her Catholic upbringing, as the church didn't even recognize her marriage to Bryce due to his former marriage. She was okay since John was dead, but the church still felt she was committing adultery by sleeping with Bryce, regardless of the fact that they were legally married. Mormons must have similar rules, probably more strict than Catholics. The irony was she could marry Chris in the church since his wife was dead. These were the kind of convoluted rules that made people sour on certain religions.

"Why can't we be together now?" Lily hoped she could convince him to let it go. He'd told her he wasn't actively involved in the church anymore. Of course, that didn't mean he didn't still believe. "I'm not going to reconcile with Bryce, if that's what you're thinking. You know about my past. For God's sake, Bryce is a sex offender. I can't live with a man like that. I was going to leave him if he didn't stop drinking, anyway."

"I'm not saying we can't spent time together," Chris told her. "We can see each other as much as you want. It's just that sleeping with you right now is wrong. You're still another man's wife."

"There doesn't have to be sex involved." Lily was willing to accept any terms he offered, and although she'd enjoyed being with him, sex wasn't that important. "I understand your religious beliefs. As long as we can still see each other, it's fine."

Lily got out of bed to get dressed. He reached out and grabbed her hand, then quickly dropped it, turning his head away. "This isn't going to work if you walk around naked. I'm a man, Lily."

She grabbed the sheet off the bed and wrapped it around her. "Can I make a suggestion? I'll get dressed and we'll go to your place. Maybe one night next week, we can drive to the children's hospital in L.A. and distribute Emily's toys to the sick kids. They're not making anyone happy now, even you. What do you think?"

"That's a terrific idea," Chris exclaimed. "I have more than her toy box. There's at least six boxes of her stuffed animals in my garage. I wrapped them all in plastic, so they're like new. The kids at the hospital will love them." He stopped and stared at a spot on the wall. "Emily would like that. Sherry worked at the homeless shelter and Emily used to tag along. She wanted to be a missionary when she grew up."

Lily was as excited as he was. "We can stop off at the grocery store on the way. I'll cook us a nice dinner. Wait for me, I'll go get dressed."

Chris moved to the chair while she darted into the bathroom and pulled on a pair of jeans and a white sweater. She was about to grab her purse on the way out when her phone rang.

"Excuse me," Lily told him. "I'll have to answer that. I

have distinctive rings, and this is the one I use for court emergencies. Why don't you wait downstairs? If you want a snack or a soda, just look in the refrigerator." She picked up the receiver. "Judge Forrester."

"This is Hank Sawyer with the Ventura PD. I'm sorry to disturb you, but we need a search warrant."

No, Lily thought, not now. But these were the kind of responsibilities she couldn't shirk. "Give me a quick rundown, Hank."

"The FBI is working a case that may involve a serial killer. They've asked us to submit a warrant for a residence in Thousand Oaks, and for an individual who goes by the name of Chuck Brown."

"A serial killer in Ventura County!" Lily said. "That's impossible. I would have heard about it."

"The Bureau has no reason to believe any crimes have been committed in Ventura County," the detective continued. "Three men have been murdered, though, all of them dismembered. They found the torso of one victim near San Bernardino. There's a possibility that the suspect or someone linked to the suspect may be either living or working out of the house in Thousand Oaks. The owner is dead and the house is in probate."

"Say no more." Something came to mind and Lily asked, "Why isn't the FBI handling this?"

"Do you remember Mary Stevens?"

"The name sounds familiar." Lily could hear Gabby barking. She'd been in the yard for hours, and she wasn't an outdoor dog. One of the neighbors might hear and be concerned something had happened.

"Stevens used to be a homicide detective here in Ventura," Sawyer explained. "She's an FBI agent now, assigned to the unit that profiles serial killers. I have the warrant in my hands. Can I come over and get you to sign it?"

Lily knew Hank Sawyer. He'd been with Ventura PD

for longer than she could remember. He reminded her of
an Oxnard detective named Bruce Cunningham, the man
who had saved her from going to prison. After Cunningham had let her go, he'd resigned from the Oxnard PD and
moved back to Omaha where he'd grown up. She'd kept in
touch with him throughout the years, then stopped calling
because it stirred up bad memories. Cunningham was up
in years now, so she assumed he'd retired from law enforcement. She wondered if he knew she was a judge.

Lily returned her attention to Detective Sawyer. "Bring
the warrant to my house, Hank. How long do you think it
will take for you to get here?"

"First you need to give me your new address."

"Oh," Lily said, rattling off the information. "You realize I'll have to review this document thoroughly before
I sign it. Are you going to wait here or come back and pick
it up when I'm finished?"

"To expedite things, I think it would be best if I waited.
If you have guests, I can wait in my car. It shouldn't take
me more than ten minutes to get there, if that's okay."

Lily was so drained, she asked him, "What would you
do if I said no?"

"I guess we'd have to find ourselves another judge."

"That won't be necessary," she said, thinking it would
be absurd if the next person he called was Chris Rendell.
"How big is the document?"

"Thirty pages."

"I'll see you when you get here." She hit the disconnect
button and started down the stairway to tell Chris what
had occurred when she heard the front door opening. This
was the first time she'd ever prayed it would be Tessa.

It was Bryce!

Lily felt like locking herself in the bathroom and
screaming.

"What the hell are you doing in my house?" Bryce shouted at Chris. "I'm calling the cops. What have you done to my wife?"

"I'm fine," Lily called out, rushing down the stairs. Chris was standing by the sofa with a horrified look on his face, as if he were certain his picture would be on the front page of tomorrow's paper. "Get out of here, Bryce," she said, her voice booming. "I don't want you here. I demand that you leave at once or—"

"Or what?" he said, furious. "This is my damn house. You get out. First explain to me why there's a strange man in my den. Have you already replaced me?"

Bryce was unshaven, and his clothes were filthy. She could smell the alcohol seeping through his pores, and she was several feet away. "How did you get out of jail? I thought you said the bank couldn't send the money until Monday."

He was wobbling around, so intoxicated he had trouble maintaining his balance. "Caught you, didn't I? I used a fucking bail bond company. Did you think I was going to sit in jail all weekend? I've got enough money to buy my way out of anything."

"Calm down, Bryce," Lily said, lowering her voice. She was mortified this was happening in front of Chris, and hoped she could get Bryce to come to his senses and leave. "This is Chris . . . Judge Rendell. An emergency has come up, and a detective is on his way over here."

Bryce's eyes darted from Chris to Lily. He swiped at his mouth with the back of his hand. "What emergency? Its looks like the emergency is between your legs. Now I know why you never want to have sex. How long have you been fucking this guy? He's not a judge. Nice try, Lily." He shifted his red-rimmed eyes to Chris. "What are you, asshole? An actor or some kind of male prostitute?"

"You're drunk, Bryce," Lily shouted. She pointed at Chris. "He's a superior court judge just like me. How dare you talk to him like that. Get out!"

Bryce just stood there, uncertain what to believe.

"Didn't you hear me?" Lily said, adrenaline pumping through her veins. "A cop will be here any minute. He'll arrest you for being drunk and disorderly, and you'll end up back in jail."

"They can't arrest me in my own house."

Chris's hair was disheveled, and he had missed a few buttons on his shirt. "I should go now," he said, heading for the door. He stopped and turned back around. "That's if you're certain you'll be all right, Lily. I can stay if you need me."

Bryce pulled back his fist. Lily seized his arm, but he managed to connect with Chris's jaw. She slapped Bryce in the face, and he retaliated by slugging her, causing her to fall to the floor on her back.

The minute he saw the blood on her face, Chris wrestled Bryce to the floor, then rolled him onto his stomach like a police officer would do and yanked his hands behind his back. "How bad are you hurt, Lily?"

She looked down and saw blood on her white sweater, then pinched her nose with her fingers. Chris's sedate manner had vanished. He was banging Bryce's head against the floor. "You never hit a woman, understand? Never! Move and I'll break your arm. Move again and I'll break your back."

Lily went to the powder room a few feet away and returned with a handful of tissues, holding them to her nose. "I'm okay. He must have scraped the inside of my nose with a fingernail. I don't think it's broken."

"Let me go, asshole," Bryce shouted, trying to wrench away. "Let me go or I'll kill you. This is my house. You can't treat a man like this in his own home."

"Shut up!" Chris was perspiring and his face was flushed in anger. His knee was in the center of Bryce's back. "You're guilty of assault. That means you're going to jail. I *am* a judge, pal, and I witnessed this crime. You won't make bail this time." He caught his breath and peered up at Lily, looking as if he were only seconds away from tearing Bryce apart. "If you don't get the police over here fast, I'm going to hurt him."

Lily wrapped her arms around her chest, the bloody tissue crushed in her fist. "Detective Sawyer should be pulling up any minute. I can't believe Bryce threatened to kill you. I've never seen him like this before. I'm sorry you had to be a part of this."

Chris was struggling to keep Bryce on the ground. Bryce was a big man and the thought of going to jail had sobered him and made him fight harder. "It's my fucking house, every penny of it. My own wife set me up. She wants me in jail because I'm going to toss her ass out on the street."

"Do you understand what you're doing, Bryce?" Lily asked. "You're already facing attempted rape charges. Now you've assaulted two other people. Judge Rendell is an officer of the court. He's making a citizen's arrest. If you keep fighting him, you could be charged with resisting arrest along with everything else. You'll be lucky to stay out of prison."

"I didn't do it," Bryce said, raising his head a few inches off the ground. "I swear I didn't do anything to that woman. Why won't anyone believe me?"

"I don't think you should wait for that detective," Chris told her. "Call 911 and get a patrol unit out here. We're not going to be able to hold him much longer."

Bryce began blubbering. "You're breaking my arm. Jesus, Lily, don't let them send me to prison. I just wanted to get some clean clothes. I shouldn't have hit you. Is this guy really a judge?"

Lily ignored him and went to the garage. She refused to keep a gun in the house, but she had a baseball bat and she was mad enough to bust Bryce's head open. She couldn't let him go upstairs. He'd see the bed and know she and Chris had been having sex.

She stomped back in with the baseball bat, standing over Bryce and waving it in a circle over her head. "Let him go, Chris. If he gives us any more trouble, I'll clobber him." She was so angry she couldn't contain herself. "You don't need your clothes, Bryce. I packed your bag when you went to Vegas. How can I believe anything you say? You lied and told me you were visiting clients in Lexington and Charleston. You even gave me a phony itinerary."

Chris got up, reaching down to help Bryce to his feet. "I'm sorry I hit you, Lily," Bryce said, breathing heavily. "You know I didn't mean it. I thought something was going on between you and this guy." He started walking toward Lily and Chris grabbed him again from the back. "Can't I even talk to my wife? I'm not going to hurt her, I swear."

Chris stepped backward, opening the front door and dragging Bryce with him, then dumping him onto the grass. Hank Sawyer had just pulled up at the curb. The detective could tell something was wrong and rushed over. When he got up closer, he looked confused. "Aren't you Judge Rendell? I thought this was Judge Forrester's residence. What happened here?"

"Judge Forrester is inside," Chris told him, bending forward at the waist and bracing his upper body with his hands. "Handcuff this man, Detective, and read him his rights, then secure him in the back of your car."

"Is he a burglar? Can you at least tell me what I'm arresting him for? It's obvious he's drunk, but I get the impression something else is going on here." Sawyer patted Bryce down, then dangled the cuffs in the air. "No disrespect, Judge Rendell, but I can't just arrest this man without knowing what he did. Now, if you're making a citizen's arrest, that's a different matter."

Chris just stared into space, refusing to answer.

"I brought a search warrant over for Judge Forrester to sign," the detective went on. "She acted strange when I called her. Was he inside the house at that time? Is she injured?"

Lily walked over and stood beside the detective and Bryce. Her eyes darted up and down the street; she was thankful there were no neighbors outside, although they could be watching from a window. "I'm all right, Hank. This man is my husband, Bryce Donnelly. He assaulted me, as well as Judge Rendell. Have them dispatch a patrol unit to assist you, then come inside so we can discuss this in private."

Chris patted his pocket, making certain he still had his car keys. He stared at his Volkswagen, eager to escape, but Bryce's car was blocking him. Reluctantly, he followed Lily back into the house.

TWENTY-EIGHT

❧

FRIDAY, DECEMBER 1
QUANTICO, VIRGINIA

Pizza boxes were stacked up on a table at the back of the conference room, and a fresh pot of coffee was brewing. Another winter storm had blown in late that morning. The temperature inside the building couldn't be more than forty degrees. Mary and several of the other agents had put on their coats. She decided the heating system must be on a cycle, and some bureaucrat who worked nine to five had decided the temperature could be dropped to its lowest point at eight-thirty on Friday nights. Sheets of ice were forming on the windows.

Each of the agents had their own stack of crime scene photos and forensic reports in front of them at the long oak table. Two hours after Weir spoke to him, Agent East in Dallas had compiled everything he possibly could on Chuck Brown and the link to Khan's service station, sending it out to every law enforcement agency in the country.

Adams had scheduled a press conference at ten o'clock tomorrow morning at FBI headquarters in Washington, but he had already released the information the team had gathered on the homicides and the possibility of a link to alibi clubs as a top-priority bulletin to every agent in the Bureau. Multiple copies were sent to the agents' computers, cell phones, or any other communication devices they had in their possession, FBI or personal. In addition, each agent was required to send back an acknowledgment via e-mail to confirm he had both received and read the bulletin.

Jim Hunt, Bulldog McIntyre, and Mark Conrad were assigned to field any phone calls and handle all inquiries or responses on LEO, the Law Enforcement Online interactive computer system, or intranet, exclusively for law enforcement, which linked all levels of law enforcement in the United States. The bulletin Adams and Weir had prepared was also posted on CJIS, Criminal Justice Information Services, the largest division within the FBI.

The phones began ringing almost as soon as Genna Weir pushed the send button on her computer. According to Hunt, they'd already received over a hundred online responses, and he'd requested that Adams call in more agents to help them.

The long-overdue meeting had finally begun. Everyone

had eaten except Mary. Just as she sank her teeth into a slice of pepperoni pizza, the only thing she'd eaten all day outside of a banana, Bulldog McIntyre came in and whispered something to Adams.

"Listen up, people," Adams barked. "Agent McIntyre, tell them what you've got." When a case started to come together fast, as had occurred today, Adams insisted on formality, knowing it was easy to get confused. By prefacing each name with a title, people had more time to make notes and mentally link whatever was about to be said with the person who was speaking. He had explained this to Mary personally as part of her orientation into the unit. Seeing it in action, she could understand why he had made such a rule.

"I just got off the phone with Special Agent Thomas Thornton from our San Diego Field Office." McIntyre spoke as he walked to the front of the room, where a United States map was posted on the wall. In case they needed it, there was a drop-down screen in the same location. On the opposite side of the room was a projector. "Agent Thornton is fairly certain Chuck Brown's real name is John Joseph Baker. Subject John Baker is presently serving the remainder of a five-year sentence for mail fraud at FCC Lompoc. Baker violated his parole just over six months ago." He coughed several times and then snatched a bottle of water from the table behind him, unscrewing the top and gulping it down.

"Can't you take a break some other time?" Adams snapped, fidgeting in his chair.

"Sorry, chief, I'm hoarse from talking," McIntyre told him, setting the half-empty bottle down. "Six agents actually called me to find out where they could find an alibi club. I should clarify that. It was six *male* agents. I thought they were joking, but they were serious. We're going to need a hell of a lot more people manning the phones to-morrow after your press conference, chief. Trust me, it's going to be a madhouse around here."

"Incredible," Mary said, tossing her pen down. "Don't they know what kind of crimes we're investigating?"

Adams slammed his fist down on the table. "We're not interested in jackasses, Agent McIntyre, not when a serial killer might be out there carving up another victim."

"Certainly, sir," he said. "Special Agent Thornton was asked to speak to John Joseph Baker, aka Chuck Brown, one of sixteen aliases, by his parole agent. He claimed to have information about several underground businesses run by a woman he knew only as Katherine. One of those businesses was called the Alibi Connection. He claimed she made a ton of money, and he was certain she didn't pay her taxes. Guess he was trying to cut a deal. Since Agent Thornton wasn't able to locate a business by that name, and all the phone numbers subject John Baker gave him appeared to be bogus, Thornton passed the information off to the IRS, and told the guy to enjoy the remainder of his prison term. I asked Agent Thornton if he had a physical description of the woman Baker knew as Katherine, but he said it didn't seem relevant at the time."

Mary leaped to her feet. "Sir, I could fly to Lompoc and interview this prisoner. Lompoc is only a few minutes from Vandenberg, and Vandenberg is maybe a hundred miles from Thousand Oaks. If you can get me on a flight to Vandenberg right away, I might be able to catch a heli-copter to either Santa Barbara or Ventura. Thousand Oaks is midway between those two cities. There's also the naval base at Port Hueneme in Oxnard."

"What's holding up that search warrant, Agent Stevens?"

"There's been a minor glitch," Mary said, pacing be-hind her chair. "Detective Sawyer called me from Judge Forrester's residence in Ventura about ten minutes ago.

He said he would have it signed within the hour. Agent Weir has been in contact with two of our agents from—"

Adams cut her off. "What kind of glitch?"

"The judge had a personal problem, but she's reading the document now. It's long, sir. I wanted to make—"

"I'm not finished," Bulldog shouted over the flurry of noises in the room. "The last known address for John Joseph Baker is 1313 Adams Road in Thousand Oaks. That's the residence where the faxes came from, correct?"

"Correct," Mary said, her eyes flashing with excitement. She was holding her breath, hoping that Adams would let her go. She'd been right all along. The killer was a woman. "We need to get a composite of the UNSUB right away, chief. Then you could release it at the press conference tomorrow."

Adams glowered at her. "I'm aware of that, Agent Stevens. And please sit down. I thought I made it clear that I like my people to remain in their seats during meetings. This isn't an airport."

Mary dropped down in the chair, her left foot instantly tapping, one of the reasons she preferred to stand. She held her knee down with her hand. When Hank Sawyer had been her supervisor, it had driven him nuts. He even made her go to the doctor to see if she had some type of muscular disorder. There was nothing whatsoever wrong with her. She was a runner. People used the term "going for a run" all the time, when to Mary, they had gone for a moderately paced walk. She had broken the record in the four-forty in college, and had what was referred to as fast-twitch muscles.

Adams became quiet, assimilating the information he had heard before deciding how they should proceed. "Have Agent Hunt and Agent Conrad check on flight availability ASAP." The agents were quickly jotting down notes to themselves, either on paper or on their laptops. "Special

Agent Weir, get in touch with the Lompoc police authorities and have them get a sketch artist to go out to the prison to work with John Baker. I don't care if they have to send a car over and drag the guy out of bed. I want that composite tonight. Agent Stevens, find out what's holding up that warrant."

"Right away, sir," Mary said. "Two of our agents are responding from the Los Angeles Field Office, but they're not even en route yet. I think it's important that someone who has worked the case be there when they execute the search warrant."

Jim Hunt walked out. He must have run into Mark Conrad in the hallway, as they both reentered the room at the same time. Conrad walked over to Adams and bent down on one knee. The color drained out of Adams's face by the time Conrad stopped speaking.

"We have another possible victim," Adams said, causing a flurry of excitement. "A Portland physician went missing two years ago. The authorities saw no evidence of foul play, so they decided he disappeared intentionally. According to the wife, Dr. Samuel Blakemore was supposed to be attending a medical conference in L.A. As it turned out, there was no medical conference in L.A. that week." He was already half out of his chair. "Agent Conrad will fill you in on the rest of the details. I'm going to order us a jet."

TWENTY-NINE

∿

Lily was upstairs in the library, reading through the search warrant. Chris had left, and Bryce was in jail. Hank Sawyer was downstairs in the den, playing with Gabby and watching TV.

Agent Stevens was extremely thorough, she thought, and her writing skills were excellent. Now that the fiasco with Bryce was over, Lily did recall meeting her on one or two occasions. As a judge and a former prosecutor, she was accustomed to reading this type of document from various law enforcement agencies. Some officers were barely literate, while others used stilted language that almost obliterated the only thing necessary: the facts.

A search warrant was one of the most invasive tools allowed by law, and could never be taken lightly. Once Lily affixed her signature to the document, unless specific exclusions were listed, anywhere from one to a hundred police officers had the right to enter the home without the owner's knowledge or presence and search every item inside. After a warrant like this had been executed, a person's home looked as if it had been struck by a tornado. Furniture was ripped and tilted on its side, drawers were open, the contents spilled out onto the floor; pictures and cherished mementos were broken or carted off in evidence bags. Even an innocent person, who had somehow become a suspect in a crime, could have his life and reputation destroyed by a few pieces of paper. And Lily would be the one who was ultimately responsible. All the law enforcement agency did was request the warrant. If she found the requesting agency had not established sufficient grounds, which sometimes occurred, she would refuse to sign it and the officers would walk away empty-handed.

Hank Sawyer had informed her the legal owner of the property was deceased, and that the estate was in probate. The fact that the owner, Mabel Richardson, had lived and died alone in a nursing home was sad. Lily prayed that didn't happen to her. Fortunately, she had Shana. Wait until she told her about Bryce. Shana would want to fly home so they could celebrate.

Chris had decided not to press charges against Bryce, which Lily understood. She was thankful Hank had shown up when he did. At least she felt confident the detective would do whatever he could to keep what had transpired today away from the media. The press had access to arrest records, but since she and Bryce used different names, it might go unnoticed. She'd had no choice but to tell Hank about the attempted rape Bryce had been charged with in Vegas, because a new crime would violate the terms of his release. Once he was arraigned on the new assault charge against Lily, which she refused to let slide, they would ship him back to Las Vegas. That is, unless Anne had already contacted the authorities there and told them she no longer wanted to press charges.

Lily appreciated Anne's magnanimous gesture, but she would prefer she didn't refuse to press charges. Bryce was like any other man and should be held to answer for his actions. She hated to make Hank and the FBI wait for the arrest warrant, but she needed to discuss the situation with Anne and find out if she'd already talked to the Las Vegas authorities.

She went to get her cell phone out of her purse, finding Anne's number and depressing the send button. As soon as she answered, Lily began speaking. "I'm sorry I didn't check on you today, Anne. Something came up at my work. How are you?"

"I'm okay," Anne said cheerfully. "Want to get together for a drink? It would be nice to have some company for a change. I don't think I'll be hanging out at the Indigo anymore."

"I'm not sure when I'll be finished," Lily told her. "Could we make it in an hour? If I'm running late, I'll call you."

"Do you want me to pick you up, or would you rather meet me somewhere?"

"Come to the house. Do you have a pen?"

"No, but I have an excellent memory."

Lily gave her directions and then disconnected, picking up where she left off in the warrant. This killer, if it turned out to be the person who had sent the FBI the tape, had certainly gone through a horrendous childhood. The mere thought of a young child being abandoned at night on a highway in the dead of winter was heartbreaking. Heaven help us all, she thought, wondering how anyone could be so cruel to their own flesh and blood. She glanced at a few of the crime scene and autopsy pictures, her compassion for the killer quickly dissipating. How could a person commit such unspeakable acts?

Lily turned the gruesome images upside down so she wouldn't have to look at them. Her eyes became glued to the text as she read about the alibi clubs and the various services they provided their customers. She reminded herself that a good percentage of what she was reading was speculation. The FBI wasn't even certain the residence in question had anything to do with the series of murders. Right now all they could link the house to was credit card fraud.

Flipping the page, Lily braced her head on her fist as

she read the particulars on the victims. She thought it interesting that the men were all in the same age range as Bryce, and all three were professionals with wives and families. When she read the part about each victim leaving his wife a detailed itinerary, she dropped her coffee cup and it shattered on top of Bryce's father's antique desk. My God, she thought, ignoring the coffee dripping off the edge of the desk onto the new carpet. Her heart was pounding against her rib cage. None of these men had been at the hotels listed on their itineraries, the same exact situation she'd experienced with Bryce. And their wives had called the hotels they were supposed to be at just as she had. The FBI had come to the conclusion that the people who'd answered the phones at the numbers listed as hotels on the victims' itineraries had been employees of an alibi club. She remembered how the voices had sounded the same in both Charleston and Lexington. These people, whoever they were, had also confirmed the victims were guests in the hotels, when it was later verified that the hotels had never heard of them.

Lily's fingers trembled on the papers. Had Bryce used an alibi club? She tried to convince herself it was a coincidence, but the circumstances were identical, except Bryce was alive and the other men were dead. If he'd crossed paths with this serial killer, she reasoned, he would be buried somewhere without his head and hands. She rubbed her palms back and forth on her jeans as she continued whipping through the pages. There weren't enough expletives to express how she felt about the ordeal Bryce had subjected her to. Knowing he'd gone to such great lengths to cover his tracks made her feel physically ill. His deception was almost worse than finding out he'd been arrested for attempted rape.

Lily was sorry now that Chris had declined to press charges against Bryce, but she understood he didn't want anyone to find out he had been at her house. They could have explained it by saying she'd asked him to assist her with the search warrant. Chris knew that it would still look suspicious. The bottom line was he refused to lie, commendable yet slightly childish under the circumstances. Bryce deserved a lengthy jail term, if nothing else, to deal with his alcohol problem. At most, he would probably get a fine and a week or two in jail.

Poor Anne, Lily thought. Her dick-for-brains husband had tried to seduce Anne into a three-day Vegas lust fest, not realizing his would-be love bunny was a lesbian.

At least he wasn't involved in the FBI's case. According to the FBI, there were probably dozens of these underground alibi clubs. Anyway, their only named suspect was Chuck Brown, and Bryce would never fly to Las Vegas to meet a man unless the person was blackmailing him.

The authorities were pressed for time. Sign the warrant, she told herself. The people were waiting. She was certain a lot of judges didn't read every single page. The FBI had already established the legal grounds to substantiate a search. So much had happened, though, it was almost impossible to concentrate. Her mind was splintered in too many different directions. Hadn't Bryce realized that Anne was gay?

Ah, she thought. If Bryce had known Anne was gay, it could be used as an aggravating circumstance in the attempted rape. The courts used circumstances in aggravation and mitigation to determine which term of imprisonment to impose. California had determinate sentencing. The crime of rape, for example, carried a term of three, six, or eight years in prison. If the crime was determined to be aggravated, the term of eight years could be imposed, or if the court determined mitigating circumstances existed, the lower term of three years. When circumstances in aggravation and mitigation appeared to be equal, the median term of six years would be appropriate. Although Bryce had only been charged with attempted rape, the above factors would still be considered in determining his sentence should he be convicted.

Lily stared at the warrant, but she hadn't finished reading it. The FBI was asking for access to everything in the residence. She couldn't sign it until she decided what, if anything, should be excluded.

How could she think until she sorted through this thing with Anne? Lily recalled how crazy Tessa had been acting lately. She doubted if such a pretty young woman as Anne would be attracted to Tessa, but how did Lily know what type of woman she liked? Lily was almost old enough to be her mother and she'd appeared interested in her. She had kissed her, hadn't she? Then there was that flirtatious wink she'd given her just before she had driven off. Maybe Tessa had been having an affair with Anne, and that's why she was so jealous, thinking Lily was going to steal her away.

Lily thought of how Anne had gone into the Jacuzzi naked, although it wasn't unusual, as the majority of the women at health clubs went in without bathing suits. But Anne had flaunted her body, Lily now realized, sitting on the ledge exposed like that. The other truth that she'd failed to acknowledge was she *had* felt mesmerized by Anne from almost the first time she saw her.

Lily felt a sudden wave of nausea and raced to the bathroom, the paperwork clutched in her hand. She dropped to her knees in front of the commode, certain she was going to vomit. Her skin was cold and clammy. Her back always ached, but the pain was now excruciating. She decided it was from a combination of rolling around in the bed with Chris, Bryce knocking her down, and the tremendous stress she was under with the Stucky trial.

She finally straightened up and tried to get to her feet when another dagger of pain struck her. What bothered her was it wasn't where her herniated disk was located, but higher up her spine. Had Bryce caused her to sustain a new injury? In the heat of the moment, the fall hadn't seemed to bother her.

Lily kept seeing the dreadful images of the three dead men. Where were their heads and limbs? Had the killer eaten them like Jeffrey Dahmer?

As a child, she had toyed with the belief that pain might be God's way of getting your attention, perhaps to keep you from going down the wrong path. She'd been ditching school when she'd broken her arm. After that, she started paying attention to her studies and regularly attending classes.

What was she doing wrong now?

She had slept with Chris before her marriage was legally terminated, and for some reason she was obsessed with Anne. Maybe she never should have accepted the judicial appointment. What right did she have to sit in judgment of anyone?

Once her stomach settled, she went to the sink, washed her hands, then splashed cold water on her face. The search warrant had ended up on the bathroom floor. When she picked it up, she realized she hadn't dried her hands and the papers had water spots on them. She got out her hair dryer and pointed it at the papers, holding them tight so they didn't blow away.

The pain was getting worse by the second. She hated taking drugs for pain. It was too easy to develop a dependence, but even holding the hair dryer was agony. Glancing over at the glass-paned medicine cabinet, she saw a bottle of Vicodin. She reached over to retrieve it, then stopped herself. She couldn't take a drug like that on an empty stomach.

Lily decided that she couldn't worry about Bryce tonight. People were being murdered, and he'd already taken his pound of flesh. She walked down the stairs, signed the search warrant on the kitchen counter, and handed it to Hank Sawyer. Gabby had found a friend, and followed the detective to the door.

"Good luck," Lily said, wincing in pain as she picked up the dog so she wouldn't run after the detective. "I hope they catch this one."

"I really appreciate you taking care of the warrant. It's a shame about your husband. Are you sure you'll be okay here by yourself?"

"As long as he stays in jail." Lily sighed, eager for him to leave.

"Sorry we had to bother you." Sawyer took off down the sidewalk, looking back and giving her a quick wave.

The cool night air refreshed Lily somewhat and eased the queasy sensation in the pit of her stomach. She would call Anne and tell her she couldn't make it, then take a few Motrin and go to bed. Even lifting the seven-pound dog was painful.

Returning to the house, she walked over to the sofa and set Gabby down. Maybe, if she was lucky, a good night's sleep would work wonders. Tomorrow was Saturday, thank God, and if she had to, she could stay in bed all day.

Lily tried to make it up the stairs, then gave up. She had to find a way to break the spasm. She went to the downstairs guest bathroom, removed her clothes, and jumped in the shower, letting the hot water pound against her back. When she got out, she put on the same clothes and stretched out on the sofa with Gabby. All she wanted to do was rest her eyes for a few minutes, then she would call Anne and tell her she couldn't get together with her tonight.

THIRTY

Mary Stevens, Genna Weir, and SAC John Adams were hurtling through the sky on a military jet en route to Vandenberg, where a chopper was waiting to take them to Ventura.

"The warrant's signed, sir," Mary said, having just got off the phone with Detective Sawyer. "The sheriff's office has units standing by at a Ralph's Supermarket about five blocks away from the residence. They'll be assisting us in executing the search warrant."

"Do we know yet if the residence is occupied, Stevens?" Adams asked, leaning around in his seat.

"They had a unmarked car do a drive-by earlier today. My instructions were to make no contact, only observe and report."

"You didn't answer my question. Is the residence occupied or not?"

"We're not certain," Mary said, anxious. "Deputy Covington reported that he saw a black Nissan 350Z at three-fifteen, bearing Florida license XIU555, backing out of the driveway of the residence. The vehicle is registered to Anne Hall, 1435 Palm Lane, in Fort Lauderdale. Deputy Covington checked Florida DMV, and Ms. Hall is a twenty-three-year-old Caucasian female, five-foot-five, a hundred and nine pounds, with red hair and hazel eyes. Deputy Covington ran wants and warrants on her. She came up clean, sir."

"They set up surveillance on her, right?"

"No, sir," Mary said, holding her breath until she was forced to exhale. "Covington said he was afraid she would spot him, and he'd been instructed not to make contact." Adams's head disappeared. Genna Weir gave her a disapproving look from the seat across from her. Mary gripped the arms on her chair as if the jet were about to go into a nosedive.

"Damn it, Stevens!" Adams roared. "Why would you give orders not to tail the subject? You know how many strings I had to pull to get this jet in the air on such short notice? Aren't we trying to arrest a serial killer? A serial killer you've convinced everyone is a woman?"

"Sir, sir, be reasonable," Mary pleaded, unsnapping her safety belt and moving to the seat across from him. "I didn't know a female subject would be at the house. The only person linked to this residence is Chuck Brown, or the man we believe is John Joseph Baker. Baker's not going to be there because he's in prison at Lompoc. I was afraid some rookie cop would start prowling around and contaminate any evidence that might lead us to the killer. Someone totally unrelated to the crimes may have been driving that vehicle. Maybe it was a cleaning lady, or one of Mabel Richardson's relatives. Just because they didn't visit her in the nursing home doesn't mean they don't exist."

Weir interjected, "Twenty-three is a little young, chief, considering how long ago some of the victims disappeared. To be fair to Agent Stevens, I've been working her ass off all day. She was only trying to protect the integrity of the crime scene."

Mary reminded herself to thank Genna Weir later. She leaned across the narrow aisle, hoping Weir and McIntyre wouldn't be able to overhear. "Can't you cut me some slack, Uncle John? You're making me look like an idiot."

"Don't call me that when we're handling official business."

Mary got in touch with the sheriff's office and requested that they use all resources available to find the Nissan. As soon as she disconnected, she told Adams, "They've already got their chopper in the air, sir. We'll find the girl, I promise. The sheriff's office is comprised of approximately two thousand deputies, so we have ample manpower at our disposal."

"Call Lompoc and find out what's happening with the composite."

"I'm already on it, chief," Weir told him. "We should be getting it within the hour."

"Good," Adams said, reclining his seat. "Now, unless something else comes up, I'm going to take a nap. It's going to be a long night, people. I'd advise you to do the same."

When Lily called earlier, Anne had been en route to the house in Thousand Oaks. Instead of taking the trash to the dump as she'd intended, she'd rushed back to the apartment and jumped in the shower. She dressed in a red cowl-neck sweater and a pair of black jeans. She could dispose of the trash later, after she saw Lily.

Anne walked to Lily's door and rang the bell. When no one answered, she tried calling Lily on her cell phone. She became annoyed when her call went to voice mail, and disconnected without leaving a message. Lily had promised to call her if something came up. She pounded on the door with her fists, then called out Lily's name several times.

As she turned around to head back to her car, a Volkswagen pulled into the driveway and a man stepped out. She squinted, trying to get a look at his face to make certain it wasn't Bryce. As he moved closer, she decided it couldn't be Bryce, as this man was at least four inches taller and fifty pounds thinner. She waited for him on the porch, afraid now that something had happened to Lily.

When they were only a few feet apart, they both stopped and stared at each other. Rendell said, "Have we met before?"

Anne dropped her eyes. "Not that I know of. I'm a friend of Lily's. Who are you?"

"Chris Rendell," he said, extending his hand. When her arm remained at her side, he added, "Lily and I work together. Is she home? I tried to call her several times and didn't get an answer."

Anne turned around and jiggled the door handle, surprised when it opened. She started to go inside, but Rendell stepped in front of her. "Wait, let me make certain everything's okay first. You can't just barge into someone's home."

"That's what you're going to do, isn't it?" So this was her competition, Anne thought. He was certainly good-looking. Lily couldn't possibly be having an affair with him, though. Only a few days had passed since she'd found out about Bryce.

"You don't understand," he argued. "There was a problem here today."

"You mean with her husband? I thought Bryce was in jail in Vegas."

"Oh, you know about that?"

Anne saw him staring at her again, as if all the pieces somehow didn't fit together. "We were supposed to have a drink tonight. What did Bryce do this time?"

Rendell ignored her, quietly stepping into the entryway. Gabby started barking and ran up to him, pawing at his leg. A short time later, Lily appeared, looking disheveled. "Anne, I'm so sorry. I fell asleep. Please, come in."

Lily's hair was still wet from the shower. She reached behind and twisted it into a knot. She'd also washed her makeup off. Without makeup, her skin was so pale, she resembled a ghost. Anne had probably been shocked as well.

Lily gestured for Rendell to follow her outside. When he did, she pulled the door closed behind her. "I was supposed to have dinner with Anne. I guess this afternoon drained me. I fell asleep and forgot to call her and tell her not to come."

"I left my watch here," he told her. "Sherry gave it to me. I probably left it on the nightstand in your bedroom."

"Is it okay if I bring it to work with me Monday? As you can see, I've got company right now. To be honest, my back is acting up. The fall this afternoon must have aggravated it. If you don't mind, I'd rather not climb the stairs."

"I could go get it."

"Chris, please," Lily said sharply. "I thought we didn't want to broadcast what's going on between us until my divorce is final. If I let you go into my bedroom, Anne will figure it out."

His brows furrowed. "That watch means a lot to me, Lily. It was the last thing Sherry ever gave me. Can I come over tomorrow and pick it up?"

"Sure," she told him. "I'll make sure nothing happens to it. Now, if you don't mind . . ."

After he left, Lily made certain to lock the door this time. Anne was squatting down on the floor petting Gabby. She watched as Lily staggered over and collapsed on the sofa. "What was that guy carrying on about?"

"Nothing," Lily said, then decided to tell her what had transpired with Bryce.

"He hit you! The bastard hit you! Jesus, I'm so sorry, Lily. If I'd been here, I would have beaten the crap out of him."

"My back was already a problem, Anne. Falling down might not have caused this pain. I have it from time to time. Anyway—"

"You want me to go out and get you something? Have you eaten?"

"No," Lily told her. "But you don't have to go out. There's tons of food in the refrigerator. All I need is something in my stomach so I can take my pain meds." She paused and then added, "Are you hungry? You can make yourself a sandwich. I've got stuff for a salad, too."

Anne walked over and tenderly brushed Lily's hair off her forehead. "I'm sorry you're in pain. Where's your medicine? I'll go get it. Then you can take it as soon as you eat."

"In the upstairs bathroom," Lily said, grimacing. "It's really sweet of you to do this, Anne. The master is on the right. When you walk into the bathroom, you'll see a cabinet on the left-hand side. I don't have any other prescriptions, so you can't miss it. It's Vicodin. Just bring the whole bottle down in case I need to take another pill during the night."

Anne abruptly halted when she walked into the bedroom, staring at the rumpled sheets in the unmade bed. Then she walked closer and saw a man's gold watch on the end table. She felt an instant burst of rage. Lily wasn't the perfect person after all, not if she would sleep around behind her husband's back. She picked up the watch and carried it with her to the bathroom, placing it on the marble countertop. Returning to the bedroom, she couldn't find what she needed, so she headed down the hall until she saw the door to the library. On top of the desk was a crystal paperweight. She brought it back to the bathroom and kicked the door shut behind her to muffle the sound, then smashed the face of the watch.

Sweeping the broken glass into her hand, Anne dumped it in the trash, then placed the watch back where she'd found it on the end table. She yanked the top sheet back and leaned close, sniffing the bed. She would recognize that odor anywhere. Almost leaving without the pills, she went back and retrieved them from the cabinet.

Spoiled bitch, she thought. Lily wasn't any better than the men Anne murdered. She wasn't satisfied with a beautiful home, an important job, and a fat bank account. She and Bryce deserved each other.

When she came downstairs, she glared at Lily, marching past the sofa with the bottle of pills clutched in her fist. "You're bleeding," Lily exclaimed. "What did you do to your hand?"

"I accidentally broke a bottle of perfume looking for your pills. I guess I cut myself cleaning up the glass. It's nothing. I'll make your sandwich now."

"That's a nasty cut. You should cover it to prevent infection. There's some medicated Band-Aids in the drawer by the sink." Funny, Lily thought, Anne didn't reek of cologne. She also didn't seem bothered that she'd destroyed her property. Regardless if it was an accident, a normal person would apologize. A bottle of cologne today was costly.

"Don't worry," Anne shot out, "I'm not going to bleed on your carpet."

"I'm worried about you, not the carpet."

"I doubt that," Anne said, opening the refrigerator and staring at the contents. "No one gives a shit about me. They never have and they never will."

Lily propped a pillow behind her head. "Are you mad at me about something? You seem so hostile." When Anne didn't answer, she said, "Forget the sandwiches. I need to talk to you."

"Oh, yeah. About your affair with the blond stud? Does Bryce know you're cheating on him? How long has this been going on?"

"I don't have to answer your questions," Lily said, her temper flaring. "Chris Rendell is a judge. We work together. Even if there was something going on between us, it's none of your business."

Anne leaned back against the counter, the refrigerator door standing open. The look on her face suddenly changed and she walked over and stared at Lily's face. "Fuck, it was you! I can see it now. You killed that man. You blew him away in broad daylight. No one ever found out, did they? The cops never figured out it was a woman. You had something over your head, some kind of cap. But your skin was too pale and your features were too delicate. The neighborhood thugs called you a spook. They knew something wasn't right."

"I have no idea what you're talking about," Lily said, her heart pounding against her rib cage. "Maybe you should leave."

"I'm not going anywhere," Anne said, laughing. "I was a kid then. The foster home I was living in was in Oxnard, right next door to where the shooting occurred. It was early in the morning, dawn, I believe. You were driving a little red car. You used a big gun, a shotgun or a rifle. Ever since that day, I've hated loud noises. You know how often I've thought about you, fantasized about you? I didn't tell anyone I was hiding behind the fence that day. I was afraid they'd arrest you."

Lily struggled to her feet. "What you're saying is absurd, Anne. Please go home and leave me alone. I'm not feeling well."

"I know I'm not mistaken," Anne continued. "That mole on your right cheek."

"Millions of people have moles. Don't you realize how foolish you sound? Even if the shooter had a mole, it's doubtful you could have seen it from that distance. Hearing you talk like this makes me question exactly what happened between you and Bryce in Vegas. Filing a false accusation is a serious crime, Anne."

"Not as serious as murder." Anne shook her head as if

to clear it. "It all makes sense now. You killed the man who raped you and your daughter. I think I even remember his last name . . . Hernandez. They were all gangsters over there. I was beginning to develop breasts and the two brothers were always saying nasty things to me. I ran away because I knew they would eventually catch me alone and attack me."

Since Tessa had told Anne about the rapes, Anne had wrongfully come to the conclusion that her neighbor, Bobby Hernandez, had been the rapist. What other reason would Lily have to shoot him? "Didn't you hear me before?" Lily shouted, unable to tolerate her inside her house a moment longer. "I want you to leave! If you don't, I'm going to call the police." She headed to the kitchen to get the portable phone, but Anne grabbed it and shoved it down the back of her jeans. How could she call the police, anyway? Anne could expose her. Granted her story might sound far-fetched, but there were people like Hennessey who would jump at the chance to take her down.

"You can't make me leave, Lily," Anne said, smiling. "I witnessed you kill a man, and now you're a damn judge. I could call the Oxnard police right now and they'd reopen the case. Murder has no statute of limitations. Your life would be ruined, even if they weren't able to convict you."

Lily felt trapped and desperate. She couldn't just dismiss her. She had to find a way to deal with her, convince her she was mistaken. "The man who raped my daughter and me is on death row. His name is Marco Curazon, not Hernandez. Everything about this case has been documented. If you don't believe me, you can call the DA's office tomorrow and confirm it. Now will you please go home and let me rest? I'm in pain."

"You're were my hero," Anne said, a dreamy look in her eyes. "You had the guts to stand up for yourself. I hated my life. Everyone had hurt me. My father abandoned me on the side of the road in the dead of winter. I almost froze to death."

She walked around Lily and sat down on the edge of the sofa, removing her shoes, socks, and then the prostheses. "This is what my father did to me. Do you have any idea what it's like to be a deformed orphan? After I saw you blow Hernandez away, I wanted to be just like you. I wanted to kill every rotten man in the world."

Jesus Christ, Lily thought, I've invited a serial killer into my home! Anne was the person the FBI was after. She didn't appear to be armed, but Lily couldn't be certain. Regardless, now was the time to make a run for it. The woman couldn't chase after her without the prostheses on her feet.

Lily sprinted toward the door, ignoring the pain in her back. Anne lunged at her, knocking her face first onto the floor. Lily kicked out and connected with Anne's forehead, then pulled herself up by the doorknob. Before she could get the bolt unlatched, Anne slammed into her back, pinning her to the door.

"You're not going anywhere," Anne said, her hot breath in Lily's ear. "I want to hear the truth, understand? Every last detail. I want to know how you got away with it, how you tricked everyone into believing another man raped you and your kid."

"I'm telling the truth," Lily shouted. "Bobby Hernandez wasn't the rapist. I—I killed the wrong man."

"You blew away an innocent person?"

"Hernandez wasn't innocent. You said it yourself. He was head of one of the most violent street gangs in the county. They killed for fun. He and four of his buddies raped and murdered a young couple. They shoved a tree limb up the girl's vagina. They played target practice on her breasts. I was certain he was the man who raped us. It wasn't until my daughter picked Marco Curazon out of the lineup that I realized I was wrong." Lily stopped and sucked in a breath. "Are you satisfied now?"

"I'm never satisfied," Anne told her, releasing Lily.

Lily placed her palm on her forehead. "If you want to call the police, be my guest. All I want is my medicine. Where did you put the Vicodin?"

"I'll get it," Anne said, limping to the kitchen and removing a glass from the cabinet. She turned her back to Lily, then shoved her hand into her pocket and brought forth a small vial of Versed. Pouring several drops of the liquid into the glass, she filled it up with tap water.

The doorbell rang and Lily saw Hank Sawyer through the peephole.

"Don't answer it," Anne said, grabbing the glass of water and the bottle of Vicodin.

Lily flung open the door and shoved her hand inside Hank's jacket, snatching his service revolver and spinning around to face Anne. Before the detective could stop her, she pulled the trigger and fired. The explosion was deafening.

When Lily turned around, expecting to see Hank, Anne rushed toward her, coming from behind and placing her in a choke hold.

They both heard a loud crash and jerked their heads around. The sliding glass door was shattered. Mary Stevens had her arm extended, her gun trained on Anne. "FBI. Release Judge Forrester or we'll blow your head off."

Hank had circled around to the back of the house. He reached through the broken glass and unlocked the door. Two officers quickly stepped through.

Mary yelled, "Put your hands over your head where I can see them. If you have a weapon, put it on the floor, then kick it towards me."

Anne had a strange look on her face, surprised but

accepting. Knowing the officers could open fire at any moment, Lily dropped to the ground. She grabbed Anne by the ankle, trying to pull her off her feet. Anne turned to the side, flailing her arms around as she struggled to maintain her balance.

A barrage of gunshots reverberated throughout the room. Anne was blown off her feet, landing on her back with her arms stretched out at her sides. Blood squirted out of a gaping hole in her chest. There was another gunshot wound in her upper thigh in the location of her femoral artery. Anne only made one sound, a barely audible whimper.

Mary Stevens holstered her weapons. A slew of county sheriffs, FBI agents, and Ventura police officers swarmed the room. Lily heard the police dispatcher's voice squawking from one officer's portable radio. People were barking orders, and feet shuffled on the hardwood floors. A moment later, police sirens pierced the night air.

Lily crawled over to Anne, thinking of the unspeakable acts she'd committed, the untold number of lives she had destroyed. Anne's face had drained of all color, and something was gurgling in her throat. Although Anne's eyes were slowly closing, Lily had heard the last thing to go was a person's hearing. "They're waiting for you in hell, Anne. Did you wait until your victims were dead, or did you start butchering them while they were still alive?"

Someone was speaking. Lily looked up at the tall woman who had arrived on the scene with Hank Sawyer. She must be the FBI agent Mary Stevens. "Let us take care of this, Judge Forrester," Mary told her. "The paramedics will be here any minute. Are you injured?" She knelt down and placed her hand underneath Anne's body, pulling out the silver portable phone Anne had stuffed in her jeans. "Damn, it's a phone. I was certain she was reaching for a gun."

Lily linked eyes with her. "Have you ever killed anyone before?"

"No," Mary said, swallowing hard. "I should have aimed for her arms or legs like Sawyer did. I felt certain she was armed. You may not know it, but this woman is our serial killer. Her real name is Katherine Collins. She's killed at least four men, maybe more."

"I figured it out from the search warrant," Lily told her, horrified at the thoughts she'd had about Anne. She'd kissed her, for God's sake, even fantasized about what it would be like to make love to her. "I just didn't figure it out soon enough. How did you know she'd be here?"

"A deputy from the sheriff's office spotted her at the Thousand Oaks house earlier today. Once we executed the warrant, we found three bags full of evidence linking her to the homicides. We broadcast a description of the car, and a helicopter spotted it parked in front of your house. She must have intended to use you as a hostage."

Lily knew that wasn't true, but there was no reason to reveal the truth. The paramedics were working furiously over Anne. Now she had something else to feel guilty over. If the things Anne had said were true, which appeared to be the case, Lily had inspired a young girl to become a murderer. She saw Mary staring at Anne's feet, and watched as a line of perspiration appeared on her forehead. "She told me the injuries were caused by frostbite. You know the rest of the story."

"Can you imagine a father abandoning his child like that? He's the one who deserves to be shot. Shit, how did she even walk?"

"Don't feel sorry for her," Lily cautioned, a wise look on her face. "You'll have enough trouble sleeping as it is. She was her father's daughter, remember? In cruelty her actions even surpassed his. She was also attractive, intelligent, and resourceful. Regardless of what happened to her as a child, she didn't have to become a killer. If she killed four men, she deserved to die. She was a brutal, unremorseful murderer. And regardless of how much evidence you found, there's no guarantee she would have been convicted. Keep reminding yourself of these facts and you'll be okay. Oh, I must have shot her in the leg. I stole Hank's gun and fired it at her."

"You were acting in self-defense," Mary told her. "There won't be a problem. What I'd like is for you to go to the hospital. It's obvious you're in pain, Judge Forrester. Hank said you got into a physical confrontation with your husband this afternoon as well."

"All I need is my pain meds."

"Go to the hospital. We'll all feel better if you do. You're very fortunate, you know," Mary continued. "Many people who cross paths with a sociopath like Katherine Collins don't come out of it alive."

Lily refused Mary's offer to help her to her feet. She stood on her own, watching while the paramedics continued their fight to save Anne's life. When they stopped CPR, it was obvious the battle was over.

She went outside into the yard. Her emotions ran the gauntlet. She was glad it was over, but shaken by the things Anne had told her. Had anyone else witnessed her shoot Bobby Hernandez? She would live the rest of her life looking over her shoulder and wondering.

"Fine, I'll go to the hospital," Lily said, seeing Mary standing beside her.

Another team of paramedics arrived with a gurney. When Mary directed them to Lily, they came over and began checking her vital signs. Her legs were trembling, so she climbed onto the gurney and lay down. Once she was loaded into the ambulance, her thoughts turned to Bryce. He had told her the truth all along, but she had believed a stranger rather than her own husband. Sure, he'd acted awful when he'd come to the house today. If she'd been falsely accused, she probably would have acted the same way. The bottom line was still the bottom line, however. Bryce may have been enticed by Anne, but he had been more than eager to jump on a plane and fly to Las Vegas to have sex with her.

The afternoon with Chris Rendell passed through her mind. Would she have slept with him if she hadn't believed Anne's story about Bryce? Certainly not, she told herself, feeling a sense of self-righteousness. Was she being perfectly honest with herself? Of course not. No one ever admitted their shortcomings, and it was impossible to know how she would react until the situation presented itself. She had cheated on John with Richard Fowler, something she deeply regretted. Chris Rendell was another notch on her sin belt. All this talk about adultery, and she appeared to be the only guilty party. Now she would never get out of purgatory.

"What's the best narcotic for pain?" Lily asked the fresh-faced paramedic as the ambulance hit a bump in the roadway. "I want to be numb, understand? I want to go to sleep and not wake up until the pain is nothing more than a memory."

"Dilaudid should do the trick."

"Dilaudid it will be, then."

"The patient doesn't decide which drug they will receive."

"I'm a judge," Lily told him, deciding she could use her position to her advantage. "Oh, and be sure to have the hospital call Shana Forrester, my next of kin. Her number is in my wallet. A mother should have her daughter by her side at a time like this, don't you think? Have them tell her I was involved in a situation where someone was killed, and I've asked her to come right away."

"No problem."

At least one good thing would come of all this, Lily thought, adjusting her position on the gurney. She knew Shana wasn't too busy with her studies to come and see her.

Safely inside the ambulance, Lily experienced an overwhelming sense of relief. She had faced a killer and survived. How could she complain about a little pain?

Then she remembered Gabby.

With the officers coming and going, the dog could have run away. "I've changed my mind," she told the paramedic. "Just take me back to my house. I have to take care of my dog. I have a bottle of Vicodin. That's all I need."

"Are you sure? Your house is a crime scene. I doubt if the police will let you stay there tonight."

"Then I'll drive myself to a hotel."

"What about notifying your daughter?"

Lily smiled. "It wouldn't be right to frighten her. Once she hears her stepfather is out of the house, she'll jump on the next plane."

Turn the page for a preview of

MY LOST DAUGHTER

NANCY TAYLOR ROSENBERG

*Available in September 2010
from Tom Doherty Associates*

A FORGE HARDCOVER   ISBN 978-0-7653-1903-6

ONE

∾

Once the jury was seated and the defendant was led in and placed at the counsel table beside the defense attorney, the bailiff stepped to the front of the courtroom. "All rise," Leonard Davis announced, "Division Forty-seven of the Superior Court of Ventura County is now in session, the Honorable Lillian Forrester presiding."

A tall, slender redhead entered through the backdoor of the courtroom, ascending the three steps to the bench in a swirl of black robes. Lily's hair was one of her most distinctive features, and she wore it long, an inch or so past her shoulders. Today, however, she'd swept it into a ponytail at the base of her neck. Wispy tendrils had already escaped onto her forehead and neck. Her skin was pale with a scattering of freckles across her nose and cheeks. She was a striking woman, with a natural, fresh look and delicate features.

Lily knew the prosecution of criminals was a cat-and-mouse game. The majority of cases never made their way to trial. If every case required the time and resources of a jury trial, the criminal justice system would collapse. Even in the most gruesome homicides, a plea agreement was the preferable way to put a case to rest. But plea agreements in cases of this magnitude weren't normally offered right away. The system was similar to a boa constrictor. The longer it squeezed a criminal, the more information would pop out and the more willing a defendant would be to accept whatever sentence was offered. This was particularly true when the alternative was death.

The courtroom was packed and noisy. Lily had forbidden the proceedings to be televised, so members of the media filled most of the seats. Reporters were scribbling on notepads or creeping down the aisles with their cameras in hand to snap photos. The case was sensational, the kind that turned murderers into celebrities. The defendant, Noelle Lynn Reynolds, had been a popular local girl, a former cheerleader and prom queen at Ventura High. The petite blonde with the round face and dove grey eyes didn't look much older than her high school yearbook photos, although she was only a few months shy of her twenty-third birthday. The last thing she looked like was a cold-blooded murderer, a woman so callous she would kill her own child in order to enjoy a carefree existence.

Gone were the plunging necklines and bare midriff Reynolds had so proudly displayed in the various nightclubs, bars, and beaches she'd frequented in the weeks following her two-year-old son's disappearance. She was dressed in a dowdy polyester suit, her large breast implants squashed inside the beige fabric of her jacket. Her hair was slicked back from her face and she wore no makeup. The flamboyant party girl had been intentionally disguised for the benefit of the jury.

Lily's eyes came to rest on Clinton Silverstein, a district attorney she had known and worked with since the beginning of her career. One of the judges was retiring and Clinton was hoping to get his slot. This case could be a deciding factor, and in Lily's opinion, the prosecutor had already made a poor decision. The state was asking for the death penalty. Lily felt it was highly unlikely that a middle class Ventura jury would send a young woman like Noelle Reynolds to her death, regardless of the unspeakable crime she'd committed. Lily had called Silverstein into her chambers on several occasions, attempting to get him to reconsider. In a case of this magnitude, prosecutors generally filed numerous counts such as second-degree murder, or even manslaughter, along with other crimes that were considered lesser or included, meaning if the jury decided guilt in one count, they couldn't find the defendant guilty of the others. The benefit of this type of filing is that it gave the jury an alternative other than acquittal. Pleading special circumstances, which justified the death penalty, was also used to pressure the defendant into accepting a plea agreement.

Silverstein wanted justice, though, and had given little thought to offering Reynolds a deal. An adorable little boy had died terrified and alone at the hands of the one person in the world who should have loved and protected him. The prosecutor argued that an attractive, young, and manipulative woman such as Noelle Reynolds would do well in prison, even if she had killed a child. If she'd been a man, another inmate might have sought revenge, as even criminals looked down on people who victimized children. Women weren't as violent as male offenders, though, nor were they as willing to throw their future away to make certain a fellow inmate received the ultimate punishment.

Tragically, Noelle Reynolds wouldn't be the only woman in prison for murdering her child. When women killed, they generally murdered individuals they had once loved—husbands, boyfriends, parents, or children.

In most instances, in exchange for their guilty plea and the millions of dollars they would save the state by not taking the case to trial, the defendant would be offered life without the possibility of parole, or twenty-five years to life in the state prison. In an indeterminate term, such as twenty-five to life, the defendant would be eligible for parole in approximately twelve years.

After spending months studying autopsy photos of a lifeless toddler whose decomposing body had been stuffed in garbage bags and tossed into the ocean, Silverstein had turned the case into a personal vendetta. What Noelle Reynolds hadn't realized was that bodies that ended up in the ocean in Ventura always washed ashore at the sewage plant in Oxnard, adding another disgusting element to an already heinous crime.

Lily let her eyes slowly drift over to the defense attorney. Richard Fowler was a former lover, and she'd given thought to asking Judge Hennessey, the presiding judge, to assign someone else when she learned Fowler was representing Noelle Reynolds. But the case was important and she didn't believe there was a conflict of interest. The Ventura justice community was tight and everyone knew each other. They not only knew each other, they had sex, married, and divorced each other.

Lily hadn't seen Fowler in years and was shocked at how much he had aged. Of course, the fact that she was engaged to Christopher Rendell, a brilliant, handsome judge who was several years younger than Fowler, played a prominent role in purging any lingering attraction she might have for the attorney.

Her eyes narrowed, however, as she checked out the young blonde serving as Fowler's co-counsel, wondering if she was the woman he'd married several years ago. Good lord, she thought, the girl didn't look older than twenty-five. Talk about robbing the cradle. But regardless of the grey hairs and the lines around his mouth and eyes, Richard Fowler was still a good looking and desirable man.

Accepting the court file from the hands of her clerk, Susan Martin, Lily's penetrating gaze swept over the room. "People versus Noelle Lynn Reynolds, Case number

A367428912–a violation of Section 187 of the California
Penal Code, Murder in the First Degree." Special circumstances had also been pled, but would be decided in a
separate penalty stage of the trial once the defendant was
convicted. And she would be convicted. The evidence was
overwhelming.

Lily repositioned the skinny black microphone closer to
her mouth and then looked over at the prosecutor. "Mr.
Silverstein, are you ready to present your opening statement?"

"Yes, Your Honor," he answered, pushing himself to his
feet. A short, overweight man in his late forties, he ran his
hands through his bushy brown hair. "Ladies and gentleman, the people will prove to you that Noelle Reynolds
willfully and intentionally, with malice aforethought, murdered her two-year-old son, Brandon Lewis Reynolds."
He paused, letting the weight of his words sink in. "What
kind of mother could do this to her own child? What led
up to such a depraved act? Let me paint you a picture of
such an individual.

"Noelle Reynolds lived a life of privilege. Her father was
a doctor and earned enough money to give his only daughter whatever she desired. At sixteen, he bought her a Porsche
and gave her an American Express card with no spending
limit. And as we all know, privilege can lead to popularity.
Noelle was captain of her cheerleading team, as well as prom
queen at Ventura High. Her grades were exemplary, enough
so that she gained admittance to UCLA."

He walked over to the jury rail. "But something went
wrong, and it went wrong fast. Noelle failed almost every
class. Noelle's roommate at UCLA will testify during the
course of this trial that Noelle paid her to do her work as-
signments. Having others do her work was a lifelong habit
for the defendant. Another witness will testify how she
bleached her hair to look more like Noelle, and took the

SATs for her, the only reason Noelle was accepted to UCLA. Earlier classmates will testify as to how they were consistently paid by Noelle to do her work and steal answers to exams." He spun around and faced the defendant, pointing an accusing finger at her. "Noelle Reynolds, the woman sitting comfortably before you in an air-conditioned courtroom after leaving her precious toddler to suffocate in the trunk of her car, has lied her way through life and lived off the backs of others. But the one thing she wanted, she couldn't have. She wanted Mark Stringer, a fellow student at UCLA. She wanted him so desperately that she set out to get pregnant with his child with the belief that he would marry her. When she didn't immediately get pregnant by Stringer, the defendant went on a promiscuous binge, sleeping with an untold number of men until she accomplished her goal. What Noelle didn't know, and even Mark Stringer himself wasn't aware of at that time, was that he was physically unable to father a child. Mr. Stringer was sterile.

"For the first time in her life, Noelle tasted failure and rejection. And she now had a baby to care for when she had never cared for anyone or anything other than herself. As her lies began to unravel and her gravy train came to a screeching halt, the defendant began to plot ways she could rid herself of what she saw as a liability—her own flesh and blood, her son, little Brandon Reynolds."

As Silverstein walked back to the counsel table, his face frozen into hard lines, he stopped and stood beside a large poster-size photograph of Brandon, propped up on an easel. The boy had white blond hair and enormous blue eyes, and there was a happy smile on his young face. "Does this look like a liability to you, something to be shoved in a garbage bag and left to float in the frigid waters of the ocean until his tiny ravaged body ended up in a place his murderous mother believed he belonged—floating among human waste at the Oxnard sewage plant? I don't think so."

Several of the female jurors had tears streaming down their faces and even a few of the men found it hard to remain dry-eyed in the face of such depravity. At the counsel table, Silverstein leaned down to quickly confer with his co-counsel, Beth Sanders, a fortyish woman with brown hair and a masculine jawline. "When the defendant ran home to her father, believing he would take care of her problems as he'd always done in the past, Dr. Reynolds became furious and refused to let his daughter and her new baby live in his home. He also cut the defendant off financially, forcing her to get a job to support herself and little Brandon. Ms. Reynolds begged her friends in Ventura to help her, but by now, they all had responsibilities of their own."

Many judges actually went to sleep on the bench, especially during this stage of the proceedings. Prior to a case reaching her courtroom, a preliminary hearing was held in the municipal court. A preliminary hearing was similar to a mini-trial without a jury. At the conclusion, the municipal court judge decided if the defendant should be held to answer in superior court. Of course, Lily had already read through the court reporter's transcript on the preliminary hearing, so she was all too familiar with the facts of the case. She had never fallen asleep but her thoughts occasionally wandered, and having Richard Fowler only a few feet away was hugely distracting. She tried not to look at him, but she was only human and as hard as she fought, she couldn't stop herself from remembering the first time they had made love.

The district attorney's office had been having a party. She generally didn't go to these affairs, but it had been her birthday and no one had remembered except her mother. Her husband hadn't remembered. Her daughter hadn't remembered. If her mother hadn't sent her a card, even Lily would have forgotten. But she would never forget that night.

She had experienced pleasure she never knew existed, went on to end her marriage to Shana's father, and had set a chain of events in motion that had possibly led a rapist to her doorstep and turned her into a killer.